P9-AGK-385

DATE DUE

Air Glow Red

Also by Ian Slater

FIRESPILL

SEA GOLD

Air Glow Red

BY
IAN SLATER

DOUBLEDAY & COMPANY, INC.
GARDEN CITY, NEW YORK 1981

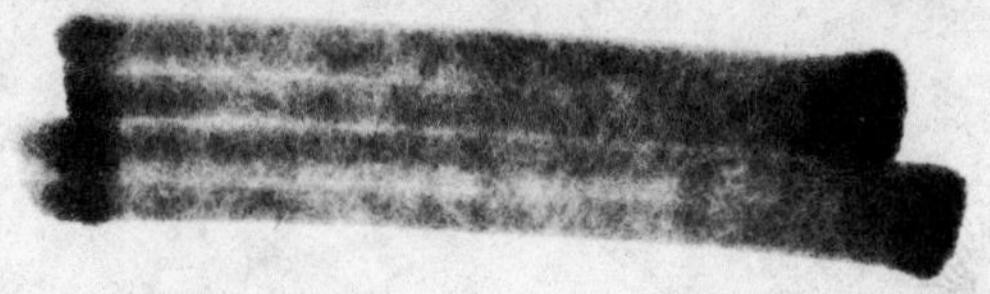

All characters in this book are fictitious, and any resemblance to persons living or dead is entirely coincidental.

ISBN: 0-385-17186-2
Library of Congress Catalog Card Number 80–1820

PRINTED IN THE UNITED STATES OF AMERICA
FIRST EDITION

For MARIAN

ACKNOWLEDGMENTS

I would like to acknowledge Paul Brodeur, whose articles and book *The Zapping of America*, have thrown so much light on various aspects of electromagnetic radiation; Peter E. Glaser, whose articles and pioneering work on the SPS concept put him at the forefront of the search for alternative energy sources; Messrs. J. Richard Williams and Gordon R. Woodcock, who have had articles on the SPS in *Astronautics and Aeronautics*, and Messrs. Jerry F. Kerrisk, Robert J. Yaes, and John Zinn, whose responses in *Physics Today* (July 1977) to the SPS concept were also helpful in the writing of this book.

In Vancouver, special thanks must go to Dr. Noel Boston of Beak Consultants. His expertise and willingness to aid were of great assistance, as were those of members of the Vancouver Police Department, especially Corporal John Flaten of the police indoor revolver range.

Most of all I am indebted, once again, to my wife, Marian, whose grammatical and typing skills along with her patience continue to give me invaluable support in my work.

Air Glow Red

CHAPTER 1

The White House—March 23

"But, Norman," I said patiently, "it's not even built." I waved at the piles of suggestions on my desk—they looked more like an avalanche. "It's just one proposal in a hundred. It's not even approved, so who's got time to study it?"

"Well I think *you* should," he said agitatedly. "*Now*. If it is approved, God help the world if something goes wrong. And I mean the world, Harry—every man, woman and child—not just here in the United States."

"Norm, it's a *proposal*. Okay? Look, I've been here less than two weeks and already I'm submerged by files. Everything's coming apart at the seams." I tapped the "Most Urgent" stack. "Gas rationing, home fuel shortages, transit cutbacks. And now the airlines are grounding half their fleets. I don't know what it's like over at National Security Agency, but it's a madhouse here. The shortages we had in the seventies look like orgies compared to this. Plus I'm still trying to find my way through White House politics." I pointed again at the hills of files. "I'm an evaluator, Norman. That's what my promotion from Seattle EPA really amounts to. An evaluator—not an investigator. I pull a file, read it, and rate it on a scale of one to ten regardless of creed, race, or color. I know the promotion notice says, 'Harry Sturgess—Adviser,' but they've got me anchored to a desk. So why come to me?"

"Because you told them what could go wrong with the nuclear plants. You were the one who warned EPA about those nuclear construction sites. No one listened—until it happened. Well, I'm saying that if something goes wrong with this scheme it'll be . . . it'll be catastrophic. We're not talking here about some dinky solar panels on the sides of houses."

He still hadn't sat down. At six feet tall, six inches taller than I, Norman Tier stood, or rather hovered, above the files like an aging Damocles—the sword about to drop. His arms rose in wings of exasperation. "Harry, I know the White House is snowed under with the energy crisis. So's Congress. So's everyone in the country. It's damned near panic out there. But, Harry, that's just when mistakes are made. Consumers are screaming and politicians react. For the short term. That's a fool's road to the kind of situation I'm talking about." He walked quickly over to the window that looked out onto the Washington Monument.

I tried to calm him. "The danger to the world, as you see it, Norman, does sound"—I hesitated—"a bit farfetched . . . with all due respect."

He stood there—silently. Not a word.

"Well"—I smiled in the interest of compromise—"just a little exaggerated. Don't you think?"

"No," he said. "I don't."

I looked at my desk. There must be at least thirty reports, I thought. "Norman, I know you're concerned and I don't want to be rude, but I do know more about this area than you do. I'm trained in environmental physics, remember."

"I know you are, that's why I'm . . ."

I held up my hand. He'd go on till midnight if I let him. "You're all worked up about this solar-power thing when all our efforts are being directed toward nuclear power stations." Before he could object further, I dragged over a pristine manila folder. "Now here is something I'm really worried about. This joker has a plan to market a do-it-yourself gasohol scheme all over New York. If I don't study this, and very soon, Manhat-

tan could be gone by Friday." I tried a smile. It didn't work. Norman's sigh was like a tire going flat. Wings collapsed, he turned toward the coat rack for his hat. He never went anywhere without it. We used to tease him about it in Seattle, where he'd been stationed with the National Security Agency and I'd been working for Environmental Protection Agency. He used to come in of a morning and casually toss it onto a peg. He wasn't casual any more and clearly this wasn't a joking morning. He fingered the rim of the hat thoughtfully and thanked me for seeing him without an appointment.

"Any time," I said.

"Harry, I've a gut feeling there's something cooking on this."

"You *feel* or you *know*?"

"Well—nothing specific."

I tried to be polite. "Norm, it's being discussed like everything else. These days every possible energy source is on the back burner, but as I've said, it's just one of the proposals, and as long as the nuclear plants look like the best bet, I can't see . . ."

He wasn't listening. "Just can't put my finger on it yet," he cut in. "I know I've got nothing definite but . . . I'll work on it at my end—see if I can't get more information."

"You do that," I said.

He sensed the patronizing tone. I hadn't meant to be insulting, but those files looked as if they'd grown in the last ten minutes.

"All right." He headed out the door, jabbing the hat like a pointer. "I'll do some digging, but you think about it."

Right now I was thinking about Norman. You see, he did have part of it right. The Satellite Solar Power Station, or SPS, had been on the books since 1968. Certainly it was by far and away the most daring plan to help reduce the energy crisis. But as I'd told him, I hadn't studied it in any great detail because it was still only a proposal. Still, I'd heard enough about it to give it a plus 6 rating for sheer ingenuity alone.

That much Norman had straight. As for his vague fears about the future—perhaps they resulted from the anxiety of someone no longer willing or able to assimilate change. As I dragged another file toward me, a scheme for reactivating a long disused high-sulfur coal mine in South Carolina, I made a mental note to have a few quiet beers with Norman and try to help him get things into perspective. If that didn't work, I mean if I thought he was really cracking up and not just overworked, I'd have a chat with one of the White House medical staff and see what I could do.

I owed Norman a lot, ever since I'd met him on an interdepartmental undercover orientation course for various federal branches stationed in Seattle. Hailing from the National Security Agency at Fort Meade, he'd given me backup when I sorely needed it during the investigation on kickbacks and irregularity in the nuclear power plant construction business. One of the "irregularities" was air pockets I'd discovered in the outer protection walls of some nuclear plants—not the sort of thing you want if there's a leak. Some of the people involved whom I referred to in my EPA report as having "criminal connections" hadn't taken kindly to my quasi-investigative jaunt, and Norman had fished me out from a near-fatal dunking in Puget Sound. But that isn't why I should have given his visit more thought. I should have remembered that despite the urgent tone of his present pronouncements there had once been a calm, reflective mind. In Seattle, whatever he did—whether arranging backup, taking me skiing with an ex-colleague of his in British Columbia, or camping in the green wilderness of the Olympic Peninsula—had always been well thought out. In short, Norman Tier never used to cry wolf unless he could hear howling in the distance.

I never rang him for a few beers. I was keen to do a good job at the White House and the manila folders just kept on coming. Besides, I was working overtime trying to convince the ardent nuclear advocates on the White House staff that it wasn't nuclear energy I was against because of my EPA study so much as further construction of nuclear plants by companies who were still, incredibly enough, allowed to use their own investigators. And it wasn't just the White House staff I'd been trying to make this point to. Even my old outfit, EPA, had thought I was making too much of the air-pocket business. In fact, they were quite glad that the President liked my report and had promoted me to the White House. In the words of one EPA superior they were getting a little weary of "Sturgess and his nitpicking." I told them I'd rather pick nits than go on letting nits build nuclear reactors with air pockets in them where there should be cement.

Two months later, after I'd joined the White House and six weeks to the day since I'd talked with Norman Tier, there was another big nuclear accident at the Macphearson plant in California. It was similar to the problem at Three Mile Island in April of '78, only much worse—a steady radiation leak right through an air pocket and a thin crust of outer wall. Thirty-three killed, forty-seven lingering radiation deaths, and who knew how many other long-range cancer effects, birth abnormalities, etc. The subsequent shutdown of more than a dozen plants built by the same consortium halted the current drive for nuclear power dead in its tracks and forced a lot more people to think about alternative energy sources. The specter of an ever-worsening energy crisis, attendant riots, crime waves, and deepening recession hung about the White House corridors like a pall.

Now I knew that the pressure to come up with some alternative system to relieve the energy crisis would be enormous. The system would have to be something so big, and of necessity so far-reaching, that it would affect everyone on this earth. Consequently there would be no middle ground. You'd either be for it or against it.

That's when the trouble began.

CHAPTER 2

The White House—June 25

"Mr. Sturgess!" It was a command, not a request, and even before I straightened up from tinkering with the air conditioner I knew it was Mrs. Gort. The voice was always the same, imperious with age and annoyance. The Panzers took five days to overrun Holland—old Gort could have done it in three.

"Yes," I said. "What can I do for you?"

"*You* can't do anything for me, Mr. Sturgess. The President wants to see you."

"Right." I gave the conditioner's panel a thump. They put Armstrong on the moon but they can't cool my office.

"The President would like to see you, Mr. Sturgess—at once."

I could tell the "at once" was hers. She'd never liked me and I wasn't thinking of proposing either. She was looking at me so disapprovingly that I thought there must be a law against having brown eyes and wearing blue suits. Our private war had started the day I arrived at the White House. One of the younger secretaries told me that it had a lot to do with my being what Mrs. Gort called a "recent American."

That is, with my having had the effrontery to be born and educated in another country—England in my case—and having taken out citizenship only ten years before while doing a postgrad science degree at Cal Tech. I couldn't help wondering what she'd thought of Kissinger's arrival. He must have driven her to Rolaids.

On the way down from the second floor of the West Wing, Mrs. Gort and I stood in silence. Despite my cavalier attitude toward her, I was really on edge. I'd been itching for something concrete to do, but a Junior Adviser being summoned downstairs? That didn't happen every day and I couldn't help wondering what report I'd goofed on. I saw my reflection in the elevator mirror and decided that at thirty-seven and 157 pounds, I looked my age. I'd been so busy I hadn't noticed my normally short dark brown hair was edging over the white collar. And the blue suit was due for a press. Problem was, no suit suited me. I never was an off-the-rack type. Gort was looking at me looking at her looking at me. I could smell her perfume—Je Reviens—reminding me that someone probably loved her and that perhaps a little civility on my part wouldn't go astray. "Wonder what's up?" I asked, with my best "let's be friends" smile. She gave me one of her specials—condescension Mark I. It was directed at my slightly battered tie.

"Oh, not very much, I expect."

She'd put me into the peasants' pigeonhole, and very adroitly too, I'll give her that. I was scrambling for a cutting rejoinder when the elevator door slid open and she stepped out. I watched her walk away—I always liked watching her walk away. I straightened the thinly striped tie that someone said made me look forty-seven instead of thirty-seven, walked briskly to the southeast corner, and tapped lightly on the partially open door.

"Morning, Sturgess."

"Morning, Mr. President," I replied, and stood a little awkwardly, halfway between attention and confident ease.

The Oval Office is impressive. Oh, I know it's very fashionable among some of the White House staffers to talk breezily about the "O" Room, the Chief's Room, or the Boss's Room, as if it were just any old room—it gives them an aura of sophisticated nonchalance and professionalism calculated to awe the newcomer and the visitors. And it does. But the office of the President of the United States will always be impressive. I told a friend once that just being inside it sent a shiver down my spine the way Pavarotti does when I hear him hit those high C's. I've watched the coolest of the cool, including the harder-bitten Press Corps types, enter that room, and their whole deportment changes. The back nearly always straightens slightly, the step moves from a shuffle to a respectfully measured pace. It's not just the luxurious decor, the turquoise rosettes set in the plush gold oval rug, the long bow windows, Greuze's eighteenth-century portrait of Benjamin Franklin or Remington's Bronco-Buster in bronze, which are all so richly impressive—it's the overwhelming calm of assured and undeniable power. Walk in there and you walk above the silly pettiness of the Gorts versus the Sturgesses.

The President was sitting thoughtfully behind the dark-stained oak desk that had been carved from the timbers of H.M.S. *Resolute* over a hundred years ago. He looked worried. I soon understood why. Like Truman and Kennedy before him, President Walter Sutherland had developed a calcified mistrust of highly specialized "experts." The experts had told Truman that the Marshall Plan would break the country, Kennedy that he could win at the Bay of Pigs, and Sutherland that the firespill—the result of a two-supertanker collision—couldn't happen on the Alaska-California tanker run. Crude oil wasn't supposed to burn. Well, normally it won't, unless one of the supertankers is carrying high octane. That burns like lighter fluid, raises the crude from the other ship to flashpoint, and then all you can do is watch.

Sutherland showed me the satellite closeups of the sea burning off the Alexander Archipelago, the carpets of red-black flame belching skyward over a hundred square miles in area, fanned by wind and pushed by tide around the islands into the surfless, tinder-dry inlets of the Alaskan panhandle. The last helicopters out of Sitka had brought back movies of fishboats making a frantic run for it seaward, trying to outflank the multi-tentacled fire. There was no sound track—only the pictures of exploding boats and tiny black figures aflame. Once ashore, the fire was racing through the vast timberlands. The U.S. panhandle and northwestern Canada became obliterated by huge blankets of smoke that rivaled the great ash fallouts of Mount St. Helens and trapped a hundred times as many people—mostly the result of old wooden bridges burning out and timber clogging ferry escape routes. Finally the helicopters were helpless in the dense, tear-gas-like smoke, and over two thousand died—not including the entire crew of a destroyer, U.S.S. *Tyler Maine*, steaming toward the collision site. Enveloped in low, invisible, high-octane clouds, it had disappeared in a napalmlike flash.

After that, Sutherland wanted more generalists, with my kind of background, whom he could send out anywhere to appraise problems—"to separate the froth from the beer" as he put it, and report back. Right now he wanted me to read another "expert's" report on Bill 457, the SPS plan, and tell him what I thought of it after I'd attended the meeting about it that was scheduled for Friday—three days away. I was flattered. It was an updated summary of the solar-satellite idea. Based on the fact that the sun provides five thousand times as much energy as all earth sources, it was a plan to launch a Satellite Solar Power Station, an SPS, to collect the sun's energy twenty-four hours a day (except for seventy-two minutes a day during the equinoxes) and to send the energy as a microwave beam to an earth station for reconversion to electric power through the existing grid systems. The House of Representatives was split 206 For, 197 Against, with 32 floaters. It was the same kind of seesaw as the Panama Canal Treaty debate in '78, and, in the light, or rather the dark, of the firespill disaster, and the Macphearson nuclear leak, the lobbying by both sides for those 32 Undecideds was becoming fast and furious. I could see that Doug Hoskins, the President's Senior Domestic Affairs Adviser, wasn't exactly enthusiastic about my being given the report. Like Mrs. Gort, he didn't approve of a new breed of subspecies upsetting the old familiar status system by having special access to the President. Quite correctly, he saw it as an erosion of his power. Handing over the report, he instructed me curtly to "read it as soon as possible and return it"—as if I might take it home and put it in the freezer.

The President was ticking off the possible "yes" and "no" House votes like an anxious punter at the track having lost on the first nine races and wondering whether he should bet all he had left on the last mile and sixteenth. Preoccupied as he was with the voting lineup, he was talking at me but not to me.

"I want you to drop everything else. This is top priority."

"Are you for it, Mr. President?" I asked.

He looked up from the House list, then at Hoskins, surprised, I think, by my directness.

"Possibly," he said. "But there are objections as usual. That's why I've had to schedule the Friday meeting. It's your job to help me weigh the pros and cons."

"I'll do my best, sir."

"You'd better." He opened the firespill folder and showed me a color "satshot" of what used to be the verdant forest of the Alaska-Canada border area. It looked as if it had the mange.

"A living thing a year ago," he said. "Now it's ruined for twenty years at least."

The shot next to it showed lines of corpses on the ice hockey rink in Juneau, the only place big enough apparently to hold the 637 bodies they'd found burned in the area. The President ran his fingers through his gray-streaked hair. "And now this damned nuclear leak—this Macphearson thing. What is it?—forty-three killed?"

"Forty-seven, Mr. President," corrected Hoskins.

Sutherland tapped the SPS folder. "Well," he began slowly, "maybe this is our answer out of the energy mess. You like it, Doug?" It was more an assertion than a question.

"Yes, sir," said Hoskins. "It looks safe to me."

The phone blinked.

"Yes?" said the President.

After a few seconds his brow lowered ominously. "That sonofabitch told me he'd stand firm."

I could hear the faint voice on the other end. It seemed the safest place to be.

"Yes, all right," concluded Sutherland. "I'll get back to you."

When he put the phone down you could feel the electricity in the air.

"Amish from State," he said disgustedly, "has informed me that OPEC has just raised the price of crude by another five-seventy a barrel."

"But our Intelligence . . ." began Hoskins.

"Never mind our Intelligence," snapped Sutherland. "The fact is we're desperately short of oil, all grades, our nuclear program is dead in the water until this damned air pocket situation is fixed—if it can be fixed—and—" He knew he didn't have to explain to us. It was just the steam roaring out of the superheated Administration.

"Gentlemen," he said, leaning back and trying to cool off, "this has been the worst week of my presidency. And, damn it! I want a turnaround." He leaned forward over the solid timber of the *Resolute*. "Hell, we're not even treading water. We're sinking. And I don't mean politically—this Administration. I mean the country, goddamn it!"

The President simmered down for a second, pointing to the SPS report I was holding. "Well, maybe this scheme'll help. See what you think."

"I'll get right to it," I assured him.

"Of course," Hoskins interjected, "you'll want to hear what Erica Sarn says before you make up your mind." From his tone I could tell that Erica Sarn, whoever she was, must be a fellow supporter of the SPS.

For all his problems, or probably because of them, President Sutherland could still manage a smile. "You mean he'll want to *see* her."

"Beautiful?" I proffered, in the same spirit.

"More than beautiful," said Sutherland.

"White House staff?" I inquired, trying to strike the right balance between sexual curiosity and professional interest.

Sutherland's eyes smiled again. "We only won the election," he quipped. "We're not that lucky."

"She's a solar specialist," Hoskins added rather stiffly. "Would have thought you'd met her in your nuclear travels."

"No, can't say I have, but the name rings a bell." A memory slid into place—a report. "One of the scientists at the Macphearson plant. Whiz kid?"

"Yes. She's fast becoming a solar specialist. She works for Professor Roth . . . Cornelius Roth on the Solar Energy Commission."

I had no trouble placing Roth. He was on half-a-dozen energy commissions. If he wasn't in every edition of *Time*, it was a bad week.

"Both of them will be at the meeting on Friday," Hoskins concluded, gathering his papers.

"Fine," I said, turning to leave.

The President held up his hand wearily. "One more thing, Harry."

"Yes, sir."

"I hear you're not very keen on having to go to the practice range?"

"No, Mr. President. I mean, I'd rather . . ."

"I understand. Don't like guns myself. God knows I've tried to push through enough firearm legislation—but I want everyone around me, especially newcomers, able to defend himself. No mad terrorist bastard is going to get any of my people killed if I can help it and that's final. So you keep in practice—once a week."

"Yes, sir."

"How're you handling the courses at Langley?"

"Fine," I said. "I'll end up a first-rate spook."

It was a joke. Hoskins didn't think so.

"We prefer the word 'Intelligence,'" he said soberly.

"I'll remember."

The President smiled. "We've begun integrated Agency practice sessions. You'll get a chance to meet some of the other Security people assigned to White House duty. Take advantage of it."

"Yes, sir." I nodded and left, wondering how the CIA and other Intelligence types in Washington would enjoy sharing a common range with an outsider—especially from such an unglamorous organization as EPA. At least I'd know Norman. Not being able to put a face to the name, I didn't think much more about Erica Sarn that day—though "more than beautiful" intrigued me no end.

When I got back to my office, the air conditioner had packed it in. I was still having words with it when I noted that ISO* had declassified the SPS report from "Secret" to "Confidential." Maybe "Happy" Gort was right—perhaps I hadn't been called downstairs for very much after all. With the relatively wide distribution that "Confidential" would give the SPS file, my opinion probably wasn't going to excite anyone. As it turned out, she was wrong. If I had any doubts on that score they evaporated that evening when I got home to my house in Rockville.

* ISO is short for Information Security Oversight Office established by President Carter's administration to act as watchdog over the bureaucratic tendency to overclassify government documents. Under Carter's sixteen-page Executive Order of July 1978, limits were set on the use of classifications above "Top Secret," and government officials when challenged must give reasons to ISO or to a court as to why a document would harm national security if declassified.

CHAPTER 3

It was late and so I walked quietly upstairs to Jenny's room. As I entered I nearly tripped over her little yellow dollhouse. I cursed softly—I'd told Mrs. Reardon a hundred times not to let her put it there.

Mrs. Reardon had been live-in housekeeper for my daughter, Jenny, and myself for seven years, ever since my wife, Linda, died. She was more than a housekeeper, she was extraordinary. Cooking, cleaning, mending, yes, but she was one of those people who understand the nuances of a situation and who know instinctively what to do without detailed instructions. I paid her twice the going rate, and she was worth every cent. She'd been a great help after I lost Linda, because her husband had been killed unexpectedly and she'd been through the trauma. She was used to my occasional black depressions and flareups and rode the storm serenely. But she was at her best protecting Jenny—a surrogate grandmother with fierce dedication. One night in Seattle, some young kid, completely unrelated to my EPA investigation, tried to burglarize our house in Bellevue. He managed to get one leg in Jenny's bedroom before Mrs. R. got him with a carved African head. They let him go, of course—someone had read his rights improperly—but he was never seen in our street again.

Well, I thought, picking up the dollhouse, if she can scare away burglars why couldn't she teach Jenny Sturgess to put away her toys? But one look at Jenny and my annoyance fled. In the past I must have looked down at my daughter a thousand times—she was eight—but it was always new and always good. She could be a pain in the neck, like all kids, up and around and trying on a tantrum occasionally to test the limits. But watching her sleep, the light blond hair on the down-soft cheeks, I felt that full, warm feeling that wells up inside you sometimes and almost wants to make you cry. I stroked her gently and waited, watching anxiously to make sure she was breathing. I looked up at the old photo of Linda, remembering our first and last holiday.

It was in Venice, two years after we'd been married. Everything had been good for us. In the snapshot, taken on the Lido, she was dressed in an emerald green one piece swimsuit done up in the front with four small gold cord toggles that stood out sharply against the cobalt blue of the Adriatic. At her feet, oblivious to the world, Jenny, then only a year old, sat with her knees wide apart, studying a red plastic ball as if it were the most lovable mystery in the universe. The photo which I'd placed so it would always catch the morning sun was fading badly and I wished again that I'd taken more of her, but there was no way that I could have known she would be gone three months later.

It was pneumonia, something which I thought had virtually disappeared with the nineteenth century. I could still see her in the hospital—so pale that the few freckles, normally lost in the light tan of her face, now stood out like brown measles. And I could still hear the coughing. She never stopped, every time it was like someone was punching the life out of her and every time I felt it with her and there wasn't a thing I could do. I touched the photo and all the silly but powerful recriminations flooded over me. If only I hadn't taken her on the fog-shrouded gondola ride. The doctors told me that it was a viral pneumonia and I couldn't have prevented it. Anyway it was no good wishing about what might have been. I had to live with what was. So I was lonely—who isn't, underneath? I should get married—for Jenny's sake. No, for my sake. I closed the door gently and went down to the kitchen to make a sandwich, more for diversion than from hunger. Mrs. Reardon, with her usual efficiency, had separated the mail into personal and bills. The envelope caught my eye straight off because it wasn't the usual size. It was one of those little square bridal-shower kind.

The note read:

"Support the SPS."

No signature. Two other things bothered me. The first was the timing—I'd talked to the President just that morning about the SPS. The second thing was the old photo of me—cut in half. It wasn't cut straight across but jaggedly—in a sawtooth pattern. I told myself it was just a sick joke. I ripped the card up and threw it into the toilet. The trouble was, the pieces kept floating back.

I tried to take my mind off it and Linda, and began reading the one-hundred-page SPS report. My job was to keep an open mind, to make any critical notes, any suggestions right across the cost-benefit analysis. Naturally the proponents had presented it in the best possible light—the opponents in the worst. Harry the Just must stand in the middle.

The first diagram, a five-and-a-half-inch-long band showing the electromagnetic spectrum going from sound waves and radio waves at one end to X rays and gamma rays at the other, with microwaves in between, held my interest because I was reminded again that less than 2 percent, the thickness of a fingernail, of the whole spectrum accounted for visible light. The rest was invisible. The possibilities of what we didn't yet know about our world were staggering, to say the least.

Around page 33, I started to nod off now and then, but the same dream kept jolting me awake. It always began with me floating in an endless calm turquoise sea; then suddenly pieces of white paper from the note I had just ripped up would float back to the surface, shiny and thick with cherry-red blood.

CHAPTER 4

June 29

"Another one, Mr. Sturgess."

That made it file number 68.

The clerk dropped the manila folder on my desk and was gone, whistling a tune about love fulfilled. I'd seen the morning headlines: "Fuel Rationing Spreads—President Considers Solar Energy Bill." No one should have been whistling—fulfilled love or not. It looked like a cold winter ahead. I made a mental note not to become a grouch before my time and flipped open the folder. It was some kind of medical transcript. I was puzzled. As the new Environmental Adviser, physics was more my field than medicine. All the report had by way of an introduction was that this was a copy of taped conversations between several patients and their M.D.—the kind you have with your family doctor—except that the following was underlined in red:

"Chest pain?"

"Sometimes."

"Any pain in the arms?"

"No—don't think so. Just the chest. Feels tight."

"How about your breathing?"

"Kind of shallow. Feels as if—"

"As if you're not getting enough air?"
"Yes."

Then I came to the part where one of the patients—a farmer, aged thirty-four—had suddenly said, "I can't do it anymore." I had the uncomfortable feeling that I was about to intrude on something very personal. Reminding myself that I had no business dabbling in medical reports I looked at the folder's cover again.

Attention: Mr. Harry Sturgess,
Energy Adviser,
The White House (West Wing).

Well, it *was* addressed to me all right. The transit slip was blank—sender unknown, no return address. What struck me about the report, apart from the fact that it covered a diverse selection of occupations—a farmer, secretary, student, retired city worker, and businessman—was how moving it was. It wasn't meant to be moving, of course. For the most part it looked like any other dull government report. But there was something very different about it, and I don't just mean the farmer's story. It had none of that stilted formality that makes most bureaucratic transcripts unreadable, as if some big machine is interviewing a lesser machine. That was the first indication I had that it hadn't come from a large metropolitan area where a government secretary would have been well schooled in expunging all hint of emotion—everything but the cold, hard facts. Either that or the secretary who'd transcribed from what was obviously a tape was new to the job because as well as having reported exactly what the five people had told the M.D. on the tape, she had the annoying habit of consistently typing what should have been capital letters in the lower case.

Naturally the report of doctor-patient interviews was supposed to be strictly confidential. No one but medical staff was supposed to have access to it. Some concession to privacy had been effected by whiting out all the real names and replacing them with pseudonyms: Smith, Brown, Hall, Wilmot, and

Jones. Essentially all the patients told the same story. Smith's, the farmer, was typical:

"I can't do it anymore, Doc."

"Make love?"

"Yeah. Me and the missus. I mean, I can't—"

"We'll do some tests."

"I can't do it no more, Doc. I—"

"We'll do some tests."

All of them complained of headaches, general fatigue, nervous tension, insomnia, and shallow breathing. The tests on Smith turned up an alarming list of symptoms for a man aged thirty-four—testicle pain, occasional memory blackouts, bradycardia (slowing of the heartbeat), breathlessness, reduced vision, pain and bleeding in the right eye. In the left eye there was pain and the formation of a cataract on the "posterior capsular" surface, which the doctor reported as being rare in an eye that seemed to be free of any other abnormalities. Diabetes, chronic uveitis, cortisone steroids, and advanced senility were discarded as possible causes for the unusual cataract. As for impotency, this could be due, wrote the doctor, to a plethora of psychological problems and not to any physical cause. The interesting thing, however, was that he ruled out psychological causes as "definitely not" fitting Smith's personality profile. The farmer came from a "small, quiet community" and stress both within and without the home was ruled out. Smith and his wife had also become sterile—despite the fact that they'd parented three children, including one in the past year. This, said the doctor, was the second case in—the name of the place had been whited out but I could still see the word "port" which, I assumed, given the typist's penchant for typing capitals in small letters, should have been capitalized—as in Port Arthur.

What also perplexed the doctor was that in addition to Smith's complaint, Brown, Hall, Wilmot, Jones, and two of the wives had also become sterile. The M.D. had requested a federal investigation but added pointedly that no one had come. Was this phenomenon, he asked, occurring elsewhere in the country? The odds against its happening in his own community, he made clear, were "astronomical." This too was underlined in red.

I asked a few discreet questions, trying not to sound too new around the second floor of the West Wing. Maybe I was *supposed* to get medical files for some reason? I even read my job description again. But there was nothing in it about evaluating medical reports—I was merely to act in the general capacity of adviser to the President "when requested" on environmental-energy related matters. How was this related—why had the report been sent to me?

If I'd known the answer then, I'd have done two things immediately. First I would have doubled my insurance premium, and second, I'd have hightailed it back to EPA. I would have given up everything a White House appointment brings, and it brings a lot. But I didn't know the answer then. As it turned out, I didn't really know the question, so I stayed on. All I was sure of that morning was that red underlining meant that someone considered the report important. I looked at my watch, locked away the file, grabbed a quick coffee, and dutifully raced for the practice range. If I hadn't been in such a hurry to have done with my practice I might have thought more about it. I might have remembered that red underlining doesn't only indicate importance—it also stands for danger.

CHAPTER 5

Even amid the muffled thumps of police specials and the squeak of an unoiled target cable, I could hear the range sergeant very clearly.

"Eyes open, Mr. Sturgess. Eyes open. We can't hit the target if we can't see it now, can we?"

"No," I said, "we can't," and instinctively closed my eyes the next time I pulled the trigger. Despite the regulation double grip, the .38 jumped as if I'd done something indecent to it. I heard the thump through my earmuffs then a faint rattle as the errant .38 hit the pocked lemon-colored louvers of the baffling plate twenty yards away. The acrid smell of cordite hit my nostrils as I reloaded, this time with Remington street load instead of wadcutters.

The lights dimmed for "night shoot" practice. A blue flash, then a thump, erupted from farther down the range. I lifted the .38 toward the target, breathed in, exhaled slightly, held it —saw sunspots before my eyes, and pulled instead of squeezing. "Damn it!" I found it hard to remember everything at once, probably because I resented spending time in the subterranean chamber with its heavy stench of sweat and gunpowder. The air ventilators were from the Ark, and it was summer. I had another reason to curse my botching the shot because no matter what the President says, the bureaucrats rule in the lower regions, and if you don't get 65 percent on your scheduled practice day you have to suffer more than one practice a week which means fifteen minutes a day "at your leisure" until you get your percentage.

I could see the sergeant shaking his head at my last shot. His expression was somewhere between exasperation and fatigue. Beneath the D.C. police badge he was still the dapper little ex-Marine drill sergeant. Unlike most noncoms he was unusually articulate and something of an ascetic. You know the type—jogs at five in the morning and has an ongoing affair with whole wheat.

"Maybe," he went on, "we should give you a shotgun, Mr. Sturgess. Then, if your quarry is heading toward the West Coast, all you'll have to do is aim in the general direction of Australia—bound to hit something."

Except for Norman Tier, there was long, echoing laughter from the other eight agents on the practice range, all standing in the pale green stalls, facing the targets, their bobbing earmuffs making them look like a line of rabbits waiting for morning lettuce. I pressed the "Recall" button and waited until the target came close enough for me to see my last attempt in detail. It was the cleanly pierced hole of street load rather than the jagged tear of a wadcutter. I'd hit the silhouette in the shin. Mind you, with the hydraulic shock of the .38, really an elongated .357 Magnum, he'd be ill enough. But so would anyone in a crowd nearby. I had to admit it wasn't CIA or FBI standard. In England I hadn't grown up with sidearms, and although I'd packed them occasionally in Seattle and in the crash courses I'd had to do at CIA since my arrival, I still wasn't used to them. "Dapper" was right, a scatter-gun was more my style.

"My mother taught me it wasn't nice to point," I said feebly, and returned the target with the punctured shin bone.

"Well, Mr. Sturgess," advised Dapper. "Think of it as someone you don't like—someone you really hate—that'll help your aim."

"I thought the manual said, 'Be cool and dispassionate.'"

"The manual wasn't written for people who close their eyes." Dapper smiled patronizingly.

"You know," I said, "that Edward G. Robinson shut his eyes when he fired in *Little Caesar*."

"Well," retorted Dapper cheerfully, "we're not making pictures, Mr. Sturgess. Just think of someone you want to get even with."

The next shot actually hit about an inch above the heart.

"Very good—very good," said Dapper, ticking his scoresheet like a happy cubmaster. "Who did you blast?"

"I'm not sure," I said, putting the Smith & Wesson down. "It was either you or the IRS."

The rabbits laughed again. Even the dour Tier smiled or maybe he winced. Dapper took it well. Tier finished his cylinder quickly and joined me as I painted the gun with Hoppe's solvent, then signed out. He watched me wearily writing out my score—64 percent.

"Bad night?" he inquired.

"Bad week. You'll be glad to hear I've spent every spare hour boning up on the SPS—your favorite subject."

"Well, what do you think now?"

Every question sounded as if he was opening a new dossier on me. "I don't know," I said. "Haven't made up my mind. I'm neutral."

"You mean safe?"

"I'm paid to be safe," I said casually, as we headed for the stairs that led up from the cave of darkness. "Strictly non-political."

"Wish I had your job."

"I'm a message boy," I said, with so much false modesty that even Norman grinned. "No," I continued, "you wouldn't want it. The experts resent you because they argue that everything's so specialized no layman can possibly grasp the 'full implications' and the laymen don't like you because they think you're not expert enough to advise."

"Yes I would," he said. "I'd like your expense account."

"Isn't enough. Besides, I forget to ask for receipts."

"That's your fault."

Well, at least he wasn't as morbid as he had been in my office. Still, there was a telling silence as we climbed the stairs. Norman, I thought, is one of those people who are very good at stroking and talking to cats but have as much sense of subtlety with human beings as a hippopotamus—which said something about the state of the spy market.

"So you're neutral, eh?" he pressed.

We were out on Pennsylvania Avenue and the sunlight hit us like a Very flare. He whipped the hat on for protection. "Norm," I said irritably, "let's cut the crap. You can tell Fort Meade that I'm no one's bum boy. I'll evaluate the environmental impact of the SPS on the basis of the facts I've been given and what's said at the big meeting this afternoon. Anyway I don't understand why you guys are so against it. It'd be low-dose microwaves and it would mean expansion for National Security Agency. More energy for you. You people use more microwaves than anyone else."

His hand was on my shoulder. "Christ, no! You've got it all wrong, Harry. Officially we want the bill. I've just been talking to you unofficially."

I was stunned. "You mean National Security Agency supports the SPS bill officially, but not really."

"That's right, and it's got nothing to do with my personal fears that I've discussed with you." He paused. "Maybe I was a bit too pessimistic."

"Glad to hear it, Norman. For a while there I thought you'd been putting in a bit too much overtime."

"Oh, I'm still not convinced," he said, "on the environmental front but quite apart from that if they put those things up above the earth it could interfere with all our big harmonics."

"What the hell's that, Norman?"

"ELINT—Electronic Intelligence."

"Listening in on the Ruskies?"

"Yes. Besides, we've got enough to do. We don't want to expand."

"But publicly you guys are on the 'For' side?"

He shrugged. "Well, you know how it is."

"Yeah, I know. You don't want to upset all the electronic and space contractors that lobby for you, so publicly you advocate Satellite Power Stations but privately you try to stop them. And it helps because personally you're against it."

"It's in the interest of national security. The best transmission frequency for the SPS is around three point three gigahertz. But even using static filters, it's likely it would create widespread interference with other transmissions—CB radio, shipping communications—armed forces radar. Not to mention long-range control of our nukes."

"With you guys even your brand of aftershave is in the interest of national security." I couldn't help but shake my head at this latest game in the capital. "This is a crazy town."

Norman offered to buy me a hamburger and a tea at a new cafe off Pennsylvania Avenue near Lafayette Park. The humidity was so high the red geraniums were limp and even the squirrels were shuffling. I was glad the air conditioning was working, but the decor was early *1984*. There was chipped formica everywhere, mirrors that lied, making my brown hair and eyes look black, and those high little security cameras jerking quietly around in the corners to catch anyone stealing a side of fries.

Norman pulled his hat closer beside him. "You ever heard of Erica Sarn?" he asked as I had it out with the ketchup bottle.

"Yes."

He was looking around nervously for something.

"What are you after?" I asked.

"There's no sugar." He borrowed some from the next table.

All he had was a hamburger and Coke. "You put sugar in your *Coke*?"

"No," he said, "for your tea."

"Thanks. So what about Erica Sarn?"

He pushed the cream across. "She'll be at the White House meeting after lunch."

"I know. So?"

"She's one of the 'For' people."

I decided to corroborate the President's opinion. "Good-looking?"

He looked puzzled. He'd never really thought about it. "I guess so."

"You spend too much time listening to Ivan, Norman."

"Ivan?"

"The Terrible. Ruskies. You know, Bolshoi Ballet—"

"And the S-18 missile."

Norman wasn't too hot on attack but he was great on defense—it came with the territory, I suppose—eavesdropping.

"She's a little hysterical."

That was very good coming from Tier.

"Look, Norman, knock it off. You're not going to push me. I told you I'm neutral. Okay?"

"You have access. I know you're not top banana over there," he said, "but why do you think you were transferred from EPA in just the last few months?"

"Because I'm very good at my job. You said yourself I forecast construction problems in the nuclear plants. I've cracked more environmental puzzles than anyone in EPA. Pardon the modesty, but I'm hot."

"Okay, you're one of the best. So why aren't you out in the country tracing another possible nuclear leak or something? Why suddenly the White House? And why the courses at Langley? You think every adviser has to take CIA courses?"

Before I could give an answer, he was spouting forth with his. "You were picked because you're the best. Your science background. That's true—and because you'd fit in with the Brits and Canadians."

"What the—" I began, but Tier kept on. "If the SPS goes, if you jokers over there endorse it, the Brits and Canadians'll be involved. They've done a lot of work on receiving and converting solar energy. I peg you for liaison—your British background, education, and all. Stands to reason that's why you were seconded. LSE* before you switched to environmental studies at Cal Tech. I mean you don't . . ."

* LSE—London School of Economics and Political Science.

"Go on," I said tartly. "Don't let me stop you."

"I mean that's why the crash intelligence. Apart from your time in Seattle you don't exactly have a lot of experience in our area do you—in Security?"

"So?"

"So you were chosen because you get on with the Limeys. Security liaison probably. If the SPS goes through, that could be important. You know their lingo."

"You speak English too, Norman."

"You know what I mean."

I did, but now I was playing humble Harry. In some strange way most of my native-born American friends—especially those few working in the security agencies—thought more highly of me because I understood the British better than they did. They just never had the opportunity to work out the class system. It wasn't a great loss but they thought it was, as if being able to tell cockney rhyming slang from a Yorkshireman's dialect somehow gave you the code key to British secrets. Tier was right in a way, though. I did know their lingo from my time in the United Kingdom and could pick up a British or Canadian nuance a lot quicker than most of my colleagues. Still, I tried to change the subject. The practice range always made me hungry.

"Can we eat?"

"Okay, okay," he said, glancing unhappily at the menu. "You want the dessert special?"

"What is it?"

"Chocolate sundae."

"I'll have two."

He grinned disbelievingly. "Come on," he said moodily.

"I'll have *two*. Ask for a receipt. Fort Meade'll reimburse you." I was beginning to enjoy the dessert, when he started up again.

"I just don't think you're as concerned as you should be, Harry."

"Oh? I'll tell you what I'm concerned about, Norman. I'm concerned about the double shuffling in this town. You can't even relax and be honest. You even corrupt lunch. You spooks can't say good morning without meaning good night. That's what concerns me."

"You've only been on the job two months. You'll learn."

As it turned out, he was right. And so was Dapper at the firing range—you couldn't hit the target if you couldn't see it. And that morning I didn't have a solid clue as to who, or what, the target was. But the first inkling I did have, apart from the nasty note I'd received, that something was wrong didn't come from any training I'd had in the last two months of crash courses in coding or decoding and whatnot at the CIA "farm" or its headquarters in Langley but from good old gut caution.

What bothered Harry Sturgess, what started me anxiously scratching the palm of my left hand, was something Tier did in the *1984* coffee shop. I mean, how many people do you know—even close friends—who can remember what you take in your tea or coffee? Norman knew. I tried to recall when he'd last seen me drinking tea. I couldn't recall that he ever had. Perhaps I was worrying too much, but if he wanted an ally that badly, if he'd studied my habits to that extent, I was convinced something must be cooking. Another thing: he'd been arguing strenuously against the SPS bill because its passage would unquestionably mean NSA expansion. Now if you know anything about bureaucrats at all you'll know that they're more likely to kill their mothers than argue against departmental expansion.

When I left him and got back to the White House before the big afternoon meeting, I made a call to NSA headquarters at Fort Meade to the deputy director, Art Lane, one of the first people I'd met in D.C. I didn't mention Tier by name and played around for a few minutes—wife—kids—"Baby walking already?" I couldn't believe it. "Tennis—sure." I'd thrash him any week he liked—but not this week. Too hot and muggy. How did he feel about the SPS bill?

"All for it."

I asked again. "*Unofficially*, Art?"

"All for it. And you?"

"I'm neutral."

He laughed easily. "Guess you have to be."

"I'm just a messenger."

"Sure."

"Thanks, Art."

"Any time."

I put the phone down and started to worry in earnest. Was Arthur lying to cover up any covert attempt by NSA, through Tier, to influence the President through me, or whomever else they were working on? Or was Norman Tier lying? And if he was lying, why was he lying? Surely he knew I'd check it out—or maybe he thought I was too green to check. But then he'd said I'd learn, as if encouraging me, or was that just an off-the-cuff comment? My head felt like a baby's rattle. And that was *before* the meeting.

On the way over to the White House my beeper started. I hated the thing. It wasn't worth all the expense accounts in town. The message was to ring Mr. Art Lane—via scrambler—at Fort Meade. Urgently.

"Yeah, Art?"

"Harry, you should have used the scrambler, you dumb bastard. That's basic trade craft. Didn't they teach you anything at Langley?"

I don't like being called dumb—especially not on Fridays. "Pardon me. I'll kill myself. I only wanted to know what your position was. It should be a matter of public record. I mean the SPS is hardly classified information, is it?"

"If you ring here on open line, Harry, all you'll get is official support of SPS. I want to assure you, however, that NSA is in fact unalterably opposed. The reality is that we can hardly appear to go against the defense hand that feeds us."

"The contractors?"

"Right. And they want to develop big satellite capability."

I knew the script. It was the same story his man Tier had given me. "Okay," I said, feeling a little sheepish at checking up on Norman's story only to find out that what he'd told me about NSA policy was absolutely true. "But what makes you and Tier so agin it?" I asked. "Interference with your radar?"

"No."

"What then?"

"Listen carefully at the meeting. We'll talk after. All right?"

"All right."

CHAPTER 6

The President hadn't arrived in the cabinet room yet, but already they were ranged either side of the long oval table like two opposing armies: the pro-SPSers on the left of the President and the "antis" on his right. The second rankers, supporting staff, etc., were seated behind in the slightly smaller, darker leather chairs which, unlike the others, didn't have brass name plates, and were lined up along the edge of the turquoise carpet that runs the length of the pale cream walls. I was in between, on the President's right, just in front of the fireplace, so that I could look out into the Rose Garden if I got bored but was close enough to Slavin's portrait of Harry Truman to feel the no-nonsense gaze daring me to doze off. Little chance of that. The noise in the room promised a lively meeting. As it turned out, it came close to a verbal brawl. I'd heard that the President encouraged people to let off steam, preferring to get opposing views right out in the open, "to give them a full airing." They were about to be aired, all right—any more open and it would have looked like spring cleaning.

We were all watching the big map that almost covered the entire south wall of the room—a blowup of a satellite picture of the earth, the dark blue and green of sea and land magically suspended beneath the frozen white spirals of cloud. It looked beautiful.

Pinned at a point high above the earth in the black void was a silver cross, representing the collecting and transmitting end of the proposed 30.8882-square-mile Satellite Solar Power Station that, depending on the outcome on the Hill, the President's decision, and so on, might or might not be placed in geosynchronous orbit 22,300 miles above the earth. Pinned nearby was an explanatory note:

> Though a large number of orbiting bands are available for space vehicles, the ideal is the orbit which is 22,300 miles above the equator. When a satellite is launched into this geosynchronous orbit at a speed which has it traveling once around the earth every twenty-four hours, then it will, practically speaking, remain fixed above any given point on earth.

From the cross, a thin white tape ran to earth—to Washington at a spot representing the receiving antenna or "rectenna." I had to give the SPS people their due—they had done it with brio, leading the tape directly to Washington. In reality, everyone knew that if the bill passed, the rectenna, whose chicken-wire-like grids would cover a hundred square miles, was certain to be far from the capital's cosmically priced real estate, most probably in some desert. Some people I'd spoken to outside the cabinet room would have preferred the tape to end up in the middle of the Pacific. The beam, which the pro-SPSers envisaged being received by the rectenna, would be 1.2 kilometers across as it left the satellite, spreading to 11.5 kilometers, or 10 miles, in diameter by the time it had traveled over 22,000 miles to earth.

A larger and more detailed replica of the cross at the end of the cabinet table revealed an elaborate model of four square panels, similar to the arms of a giant Dutch windmill. The massive 2.4856-mile-long, 660-foot-thick panels would be largely metal ribbed and joined together in the form of a cross with steel rods. The panels represented millions of tiny cadmium sulfide solar cells, lying flat like long, shallow ditches in some vast irrigated field. These solar cell ditches were designed to receive the sun's light, reflected into them by the rows of angled mirrors raised between them. Were it not for the 3,937-foot-diameter transmitting disk, or antenna, planned for the center of the cross, the whole array would have looked like two great tin washboards superimposed on each other.

With gravity up there ranging from only one ten thousandth to an infinitesimal one millionth of earth's field, the entire SPS would encounter no gravitational problems once in space. It could be moved with relatively tiny motors. It was getting the SPS's prefabricated parts into GEO (geosynchronous orbit) that had taxed the engineers. At one time they had thought it would take more than a decade, taxiing back and forth, to haul the various parts of the massive array into place. But that was before the latest development in the space shuttles and the giant bell-shaped reusable liquid oxygen/hydrogen powered HLLVs (heavy lift launch vehicles). Now they had it beaten.

First the prefabricated parts and CONLOC (construction on location) machines would be hauled out of the earth's heavy gravitational pull into LEO (lower earth orbit) then taxied by the lighter, faster space shuttle into the higher GEO to be slotted into position.

The HLLVs had a solid reputation. Thirty stories high, twenty engines for stage one, the lift into LEO, and ten engines for re-entry and landing, they had a base girth of 150 feet, waist girth of 130 feet and a payload nose 120 feet in diameter. They hardly looked graceful, but, if called upon, there was no doubt they'd do the job. I'd commented idly about the squat shape to someone before the meeting. Whoever it was clearly hailed from NASA. "It's a cargo carrier," he'd replied tartly and accurately, "not a goddamn missile!"

I glimpsed the distorted image of myself in one of the long mirrored panels. I'd worn my best jacket, a tan Dutch corduroy. The tie, a chestnut brown, even matched, and I'd run the lint picker over my smartly pressed navy slacks. And all because I'd heard that a pretty girl would be here.

When the President entered, the eager rumbling fell to a

faint buzz. It was then that I first saw her. A little shorter than I'd expected. She moved gracefully but purposefully, the sheen of shoulder-length brown hair catching the light as she turned and stood by the SPS display, ready to field questions. The most striking thing about her beauty was the equanimity of the eyes, in marked contrast to the flushed, almost excited color of the cheeks. I opened my briefcase, pulled out the profiles Mrs. Gort routinely issued, and by way of comparison, glanced at the Xerox of Erica Sarn's personnel file. If there was one thing I had, it was lots of files. The description of her belonged to her days with the Atomic Energy Commission when she'd still been working in nuclear rather than solar energy:

Erica Sarn: Caucasian
Height: 5′4″
Eyes: hazel
Hair: brown
Distinguishing marks: small birthmark below left breast
Degrees: B.Sc. (U. Cal.), M.Sc. (Princeton), Ph.D. (Princeton)—nuclear physics.

The physical details matched all right. But the personality profile from her earlier days didn't exactly fit Tier's description of her as "a bit hysterical":

> . . . A competent and highly efficient researcher. Since she joined us a year ago she has demonstrated a willingness not only to address herself wholeheartedly to the task of alleviating the energy crisis through the advanced application of nuclear power but also demonstrates a readiness to go beyond the paradigms of accepted research. Quite apart from her academic qualifications she is an especially congenial colleague and in an area too often populated by the overzealous she is refreshingly calm while both giving and receiving criticism of the projects involved. I would not fail to recommend her for any position requiring . . .

The President was talking. "I want this to be a candid, freewheeling discussion, ladies and gentlemen," said Sutherland. "Bill 457 demands it." His blue eyes, tired by the White House but highlighted by the California sunburn, swept the room. "First question."

I raised my hand, remembering the note I'd received in the little square envelope, and telling myself as forcefully as I could that neither anonymous scribblers of threats, nor NSA speculation, nor brunettes were going to intimidate Harry Sturgess. Whether the scientific arguments against the program would sway me was another matter. I remembered Tier. "Dr. Sarn," I began. "What if something goes wrong with the SPS? What if there's a sudden shift in position? How would you focus the beam?"

Murmurs of approval from the environmentalists.

"Nothing can go wrong," she shot back with a defensiveness that belied the "refreshingly calm" of the AEC file.

"With all due respect, Dr. Sarn, that's what they said about the Titanic—and Three Mile Island." More murmurs of approval from the environmental bench. A stabbing glance from Sarn.

I'd hit a sensitive nerve all right. I couldn't blame her; after all, from what Hoskins had said, she'd only recently made the switch from being an advocate of nuclear energy to one of solar energy following the screwup at the Macphearson plant. The last thing she needed after going through with such a major shift was a question that resurrected the kind of doubts that had driven her out of her once chosen field.

"*If* there was a malfunction we'd have it under control very quickly, Mr.—ah, I don't know your name."

"Sturgess."

An elderly representative of Northwest Aerospace Industries bent toward the cabinet table from one of the wall seats and whispered to her.

"*If* there was a malfunction, Mr. Sturgess, we'd just press the DT button," she said confidently.

"What's that, Dr. Sarn?" asked the President. "Delirium tremens?"

Mild laughter from the Aerospace-Military people, loud guffaws from the environmentalist lobby. One of the antipollutionists, a large, barrel-shaped man, was so tickled I thought he'd have a coronary. Erica Sarn's quick eyes tried to force a smile but the residual anger at my question still burned her cheeks. I noticed her breathing had suddenly quickened. Sutherland held up his hand to silence the court.

"Just a joke, Dr. Sarn. The air's getting a little heavy in here."

"The DT button initiates the Deactivating Transmission mechanism, Mr. President," she said, her eyes friendlier now and her bosom rising and falling more slowly in the maroon sweater but just as rhythmically. Thirty-six and one of the top physicists in the United States. She was something to see.

But there are legions of beautiful women in Washington; the money and political power attract them like bees to the hive. What made Erica Sarn so different and so immediately attractive was her integrity. True, the Macphearson leak no doubt helped her decision to switch from nuclear to solar but there must have been more to it than that. After all, in terms of the difficulties of readjustment, her change of field in mid-career was analogous to a baseball pro's switching to pro football. It took guts for a start—and for her to do it because she believed that solar energy would benefit mankind added up to an old-fashioned virtue called caring. Together with her good looks, it put her on top of my list. Also, that flash of anger, of vulnerability, was, for me, the sexiest thing about her that afternoon. I hoped there would be many more afternoons, and, if I was just lucky enough, some very long evenings. It could only be a hope. After all, my question had hardly served as the most auspicious introduction. But the tone of her response also told me something decidedly unromantic—namely, that she couldn't guarantee that something wouldn't go wrong with the SPS if it went up.

"But let us say," continued the President, "as Mr. Sturgess suggests, that something does snag. For example, could the DT fail?"

Vigorous shaking of heads from all the aerospace boys. No

wonder—they stood to get 300 million at least in federal funds to build the SPS. The environmentalist who'd nearly had a heart attack was waving his hand urgently as if he wanted to go to the bathroom.

"Yes, Mr.—?"

"Davidson, Mr. President. CAS. Clean Air Society."

Another acronym. The meeting had only started and already we were being invaded by the initials. If the Russians had as many hunter-killer satellites as we had acronyms, we didn't stand a chance in hell. The President nodded and Davidson clambered to his feet. "Mr. President, this is the very point we've repeatedly put to the advocates of the SPS. We know the advantage of the shorter microwaves over radio waves is that they can be beamed with much greater accuracy and that space is a perfect medium for their transmission—an efficiency of plus or minus ninety-nine point two percent, I believe." Davidson paused. Everyone was suitably impressed—he'd done his homework. "But if"—he continued, walking surprisingly quickly for his weight to the white tape that ran from the small, silver SPS cross to earth—"*if* the microwave beam at its satellite source shifts, say, a mere five degrees in its synchronous orbit . . ." He held up his two fingers in the V for Victory sign to remind us just how little five degrees was.

"Same to you, fella," someone whispered.

"If it moves just five degrees," continued Davidson, "then using the SPS as the apex of the triangle, the resulting arc, or shift, on earth would be three and a half thousand miles long. A swath of microwave radiation ten miles wide stretching from New York to Los Angeles, from Florida to Alaska, from London to Istanbul, right across Europe. It would expose millions to—"

Great murmuring from the National Aeronautics delegation. "Rubbish . . . science fiction . . . comic books!"

There was a flash of gold cufflinks and immaculately starched white cuffs. It was Roth, the Churchillian godfather of the SPS. The President reached for iced tea as if suddenly needing sustenance. "Yes, Dr. Roth?"

Resplendent in a dark pinstriped suit, Roth rose imperially, the blue eyes against the white face large and generous-looking, while the mouth, arching slightly above the well-fed jowls, was thick and predatory, as if it could devour opponents together with their arguments. Roth didn't explain why he did things. He just did them. His impatience now at having to explain his championship of the SPS to what he clearly regarded as the assembled morons was evident in the exasperated way he pushed his six-foot bulk away from the shining mahogany. A long, thin green-leaf cigar was held captive between baby-pink fingers. He was the only man in the room to even toy with the idea of violating the no-smoking rule. I was sure he did it just to drive up the blood pressure of the environmentalists, several of whom he'd baited into staring at the cigar as if it were Satan incognito. That took their minds off his outflanking strategy. He didn't even consider a possible arc.

"Mr. President." The voice was heavy with feigned tolerance for the non-learned opposition. "Mr. President. We have no substantial evidence that electromagnetic radiation emitted between the radio and infra-red wavelengths—microwaves—used in the concentration we propose will produce any adverse biological results."

"That's what you told us about X-ray shoe machines," snapped Davidson of Clean Air. "Before you recalled them!"

A colleague, a Southerner, touched Davidson on the sleeve and rose half in defense, half to cool him down. With a slow, friendly movement, all the time looking benignly over bifocals, the southern gentleman put out his hands as if welcoming us all to long, cool drinks beneath shady magnolia trees. The drawl was just as slow. "Mr. President. Dr. Roth here knows full well that we have no proof either to categorically state that low-level micrahwaves do not harm. Ah expect he's heard of the micrahwave oven? We now have six million of 'em in American homes and restaurants." With a broad, engaging smile he added, "In case Dr. Roth hadn't noticed, they use 'em to cook roasts"—looking at everyone—"in seconds."

More murmurs and shuffling of chairs from Aerospace Industries. Roth was on his feet. "In high doses, yes." The cigar darted forward. "But my learned colleague knows damn well—

excuse me, Mr. President—but my learned colleague knows very well that it's no one's intention—"

A boyish, bearded scientist, Clean Air Society, name tag Dermit, jumped up. "Exactly! Microwaves cook meat. Now is anyone here going to tell me that the human brain is tougher than rib roast?"

"Depends on whose head it is, young man," retorted Roth, and that's when President Sutherland's hand slapped the table. For the first time that meeting I could hear the Louis XIV clock ticking.

"All right. Let's cool it, ladies and gentlemen."

Dermit's profile listed him as a government-funded researcher on microwaves—some part-time teaching at Georgetown—and an environmental activist. I'd seen him on the PBS channels a few times.

Roth was still standing, his red polka-dot bow tie drooping against the blue suit sitting stylishly on his heavy, six-foot frame with the cultivated nonchalance of authority. "You have the floor, Dr. Roth," said the President. "This is tougher than dealing with the Russians." Easy laughter. "Or Congress." Residual grunts.

Roth grinned, putting down a small pearl-handled knife that he'd just used to taunt the cigar. "Mr. President, if the argument against our launching the SPS is *allowed* to be reduced to the simplistic level of microwaves cooking people, then we might as well go home. One could use the same meat-headed argument . . ."

Sutherland took another sip of iced tea. Young Dermit flushed. Roth sailed on. "We could use the same argument against alcohol. A drink or two before lunch and dinner is fine —too many and you're an alcoholic." His arms went up like a prophet. "We're not talking about absolutes here, but matters of *degree* surely? Low doses of microwaves from a wide range of appliances, from TVs to CB radios and radar, to name a few, haven't been shown to have any particularly adverse effects."

There was a visible tremor of agitation among the opposition. "Particularly adverse" was the phrase that had done it and I knew there'd be a fight now.

Roth's voice rode serenely over the rumbling like a balloon high above the earth. "Large, uncontrolled doses are injurious to health, granted. But I must emphasize, we would not be using such levels. In any event, it boils down to a matter of *control* and we're confident that we have that control—to provide, via safe, *low-level* microwaves, millions of kilowatt hours of electricity not only for ourselves but for an energy-hungry world. We feel sure that if Congress gives us the go-ahead we will have at least ten seventy-five-hundred-megawatt stations within the next ten to fifteen years. Enough power by the year 2000 to run London, Paris, Toronto, Tokyo, and New York or a city five times the size of New York." He paused while reaching for the water. It was for effect rather than from thirst. Dermit, the Clean Air kid, was biting at the bit, but Roth gulped quickly and continued, "Above all, Mr. President, as our brief to you and the Congress indicates—and this cannot be stressed too strongly—when the solar heat is converted to electrical power through the photovoltaic method . . ."

The mention of "photo . . ." jolted me. Was my anonymous note sender someone in this room? I looked at the environmentalists.

Roth's voice rose and fell with practiced ease. "The maximum MPD*—power density—17.2 kilometers from the beam's focus point would more than meet the U.S. safety standard."

Dermit rose in utter astonishment, the skin flushed beneath the baby beard. Across the room a tall, immaculate figure from Texas Space Instruments glared malevolently at him as if a lynch rope were coming, but Dermit was nervously undeterred. "What about the *center* of the beam?"

"It might be appropriate," sneered Roth, "if I finish first."

Sage nodding of heads, mostly silver-gray. I was fantasizing about Erica Sarn. She'd come floating out of the peach-colored light in a translucent black nightdress. "I'm yours," she'd say playfully, and I'd say, "After I've finished shaving, dear."

Dermit was on the edge of his seat.

"However," continued Roth, unruffled, "I realize that the

* MPD—Microwave Power Density is the measurement of microwave radiation referring to the number of milliwatts per square centimeter.

environmentalist lobby which, I might suggest, includes all of us"—muffled approval—"the environmentalist lobby here has been preoccupied, *and rightly so,* about the hundred square miles that would be required for each of the ground receiving and conversion stations. But our studies show that approximately seventy-five percent of this area could be made transparent. And so while the heat given off by the microwave beam at the focus point of the rectenna would be admittedly high, relatively speaking, the transparent material would be impervious to microwave radiation. This would allow sunlight to filter through to the land beneath and turn it to prime agricultural use. A veritable greenhouse."

Dermit was ready to explode. "Dandy!" he said, threatening to snap the back of the chair he was gripping. He was smart all right. He'd seen Roth's adroit shift from the question of microwave radiation to the less volatile land-use question, but he wasn't buying it. "I suppose you'd like us to live in plastic bubbles. We could even go jogging in plastic bubbles. We could all grow vegetables. But if we go outside we get zapped by your 'admittedly high, relatively speaking' *radiation*—which is two to nine times the U.S. safety standard!"

Roth's hand brushed out as if he were chasing a fly. "High only at beam center. Not seventeen point two kilometers beyond, where, as I've already stated, the MPD—"

"Yes, yes, I know," said Dermit. "The MPD is lower than the U.S. standard of ten milliwatts per square centimeter. Now I'm not even going to talk about the thermal pollution problem around the station due to wastage heat from the beam or how vulnerable the SPSes would be to hunter-killer satellites. Or . . ."

"Then," interjected Roth dryly, "what, pray, *are* you going to talk about, Dr. Dermit?"

Guffaws—from both sides, including me, but the only way you can shut up Dermits is to lock them up. The young scientist was back into the foray before the last chuckle had died.

"What I particularly wanted to mention, Mr. President, is that no one has said anything about the fact that the Russians have done much more research into low-level, that is, nonthermal, microwave damage than we have. If a laboratory rat doesn't start to broil we don't see any danger. But the Russians do and they've carried out extensive investigations on *low-level* nonthermal microwave radiation. And they've been doing it for a long time."

The second I saw Roth looking impatiently at his watch as if the meeting had gone on far too long, which it had, I knew young Dermit was coming up with a killer satellite of his own.

"Yes, yes, we know that," said Roth, altogether too hastily. "So?"

"So why is it that the Russian safety standard is a *thousand* times more stringent than our own? Point zero one milliwatts and not ten!"

"Traditionally conservative," snapped Roth.

"Exactly," came the reinforcement from Texas Space Instruments. "That's why they're so far behind us. Haven't got a fighter now that can touch ours. Ask the A-rabs where they buy from."

Roth could have done without that and his eyes told Texas Space to keep quiet. The man looked puzzled. Unlike Roth, he couldn't see Dermit's trap closing.

"Conservative?" Dermit asked, feigning puzzlement. "The Russians? Politically perhaps, but technologically they'll try anything if they think it works. Seems to me the Russians put the first man in space. A bit of a gamble—wouldn't you say? Hardly what you'd call 'traditionally conservative'?"

Silence.

Dermit was in top gear now. "No, ladies and gentlemen. The reason they've made the microwave safety standard a thousand times tougher is they know something our scientists don't or something that we know but don't *publicly* acknowledge." I thought of what Art Lane had said. I was listening carefully. Dermit's finger stabbed the air and there wasn't an eye that wasn't watching it. "The Russians know that the cumulative effects of continued exposure to microwaves, even to low doses of fewer than ten milliwatts per square centimeter, are plain dangerous; that such waves attack the entire central nervous system and affect the brain. But apparently we don't, or won't, acknowledge this. In just the same way as Western medicine bypassed acupuncture we have arrogantly bypassed the Soviet standard. After all, American must be better! With everything from military radar to CB radios on every highway, microwave ovens in millions of homes, we live in a sea of microwaves." Dermit paused. No one moved or spoke. He pointed beyond the rose garden. "So far we've managed to keep our roast-sized heads above that sea. However, if you go ahead with your plans we risk a tidal wave and—"

"Rubbish! I've never heard . . ." The speaker stopped at the sight of the President's raised hand.

"Let Mr.—Dr. Dermit finish please."

"Mr. President," continued Dermit, "we knew as early as 1962 that the Russians were bombarding the American Embassy in Moscow with low-level microwaves. Results of a subsequent secret U.S. medical study in 1966 on the effects of low-level microwave radiation, under the code name 'Project Pandora,' were not made available to the public. Why? Because the results were 'inconclusive.' If so, why are they still classified? Why, in November 1968, did the U. S. State Department designate Moscow as an 'unhealthful post'? And why was it that in the late 1970s twenty-nine employees at the American Embassy in Moscow were found to be ill with abnormally high levels of white blood cells? Despite a mountain of such evidence, ranging from cataracts, pancreatic cancer, sterility, chromosomal abnormalities, brain dysfunction and brain tumor, and a suspected connection between those exposed to microwaves and their Mongoloid children, we persist in the proliferation of microwaves in this country. The so-called 'safety standard' for microwave-oven leakage is millions of times greater than the whole microwave spectrum emitted by the sun." Dermit's voice was taking on that cracked, throaty fatigue that comes with emotional pleas, but he wouldn't risk a water break. Roth was doodling—parallelograms and squares—all very neatly shaded. "I will conclude . . ." said Dermit.

"Thank God," from somewhere behind me.

"I conclude by quoting Vladimir Vernadskii, who, as early as 1922, knew that even from the sun and stars we are 'surrounded and penetrated, at all times and in all places, by eternally changing, combining, and opposing radiations of different wavelengths.' We ask, Mr. President, the Clean Air Society asks, that you place a limit on this *new* bombardment of the population. A bombardment over three million times that of the natural biospheric radiation. If the public knew the dangers, they would take to the streets. Apart from government unwillingness to alert them to such dangers, the only reason that they have not risen up in anger—have not cried out against this massive form of pollution, against this *oven* which surrounds them and makes any other kind of pollution look innocuous—is due to the simple fact that microwave pollution is 'invisible.' They can't see it, and a plate can remain cold even as the meat on it is cooked. If they could see the amount of radiation, Mr. President, we would have revolution." I could hear someone on my right trying to clear his throat. It was the only sound in the room.

Roth started to rise laboriously, but Dermit flicked over a page. I knew it would be important, but just as you sometimes can't help dozing off during a sermon, I was seeing Erica Sarn naked in a far-off motel. Flushed now with passion, gliding voluptuously through the flickering glow of the open fire—and then Dermit's voice wrecked it all like a croaky talk show invading the golden dream.

"Mr. President, if I may, I would like to end with one more quote." Someone moaned, but before Roth could object, Dermit was delivering it, without benefit of notes, the intense eyes directly challenging the line of opposition. " 'Unless adequate monitoring and control based on a fundamental understanding of biological effects are instituted in the near future, in the decades ahead, man may enter an era of energy pollution of the environment comparable to the chemical pollution of today.' "

"From Vladimir also?" interjected Roth dryly. "Another up-to-date analysis from 1922?" Someone clapped. The President turned around, registering mild surprise and distinct disapproval.

"No," said Dermit. "It's from a report entitled 'Program for

Control of Electromagnetic Pollution of the Environment'—prepared for President Richard Nixon in 1968."

That K.O.'d Roth very nicely. Silence. I couldn't help hoping that whoever had written the threatening note to me was in the room—that they would see me smiling a mite condescendingly at Dermit's latest anti-SPS stab. It wasn't my most heroic thought, but it was prudential for my safety—until I'd made up my mind which way I'd advise the President.

Roth looked supremely dignified as he rose from his corner, every inch the heavyweight. Erica was watching him and I was watching her. She suddenly looked straight at me. I was as embarrassed as a teenage valentine. For a moment I felt sure she'd seen what I was thinking. It was a bad fault of mine, even a dangerous one, letting sex raise its head so often in completely unrelated matters, but there was little I could do to prevent it.

Roth glanced at Dermit. "I'm sure," he countered with a sigh that bordered on disgust, "that when someone discovered fire, someone else immediately said it wouldn't work. Mr. President, I don't deny the possibility of some risk, but it's a moderate risk, an acceptable risk in light of our rapidly worsening energy crisis."

The pink fingers spread over all in a gesture of paternal understanding. "In the wake of the Macphearson tragedy it is precisely because I am unhappy—that the Energy Commission at large is so unhappy—with the risk of recurring leaks in nuclear plants that the President has advised us, and I think wisely, to effect wider diversification of our energy dependence. And that is exactly what we would be doing with the SPS—turning to an abundant energy source, using a process which we believe, which we are *convinced*, will pose no serious threat to man and his environment."

"How about the animals?" asked Dermit. "How about birdlife? If they—"

"Even if a bird strayed directly over the rectenna its body temperature would only be slightly affected. If you want the reference, Mr.—Dr. Dermit, I'll be happy to acquaint you with the research."

Roth's steel-gray eyes swept over the cabinet room, gathering in the disciples and anyone who'd strayed. For a second I thought he was the President. He wanted everyone to hear what he was about to say, and everyone, especially Erica Sarn, was attentive. "Surely, Mr. President, we'll perish much sooner from loss of heat in our basements than from an abundance of microwaves."

More sage nodding and knowing glances among the aerospace crew.

"When," Roth continued, "when our Russian friend, in 1926, *not* 1922, I might add, told us that we are bombarded with 'radiation of different wavelengths,' he was quite right. But he didn't die because he was bombarded to death by microwave angels of death." The forced benevolent gaze swept the room. "I have it direct from Heaven that that's not the way it works."

Even a few of the aerospace boys didn't like the "Heaven" and "angels" bit. That was getting a little too close to apple pie and God Bless America. I didn't like it myself. But now Roth, with his ace energy-crisis card, had delivered his karate blow to Dermit. It was one-all. I couldn't help feeling a bit sorry for Dermit. For a moment he'd obviously thought he'd won. Last of the Dr. Spock generation, intelligent and pacifist, he wasn't worldly enough to know that what the playwrights call "presence," like Roth's, as much as scientific fact, is what carries the day in the political arena. Still, I couldn't really warm to him. He had that apostolic, health-food look that always reminds me of the sandaled, bearded youths who love mankind but don't give a damn about their neighbors.

As the President called the meeting to an end, I studied Dermit forlornly gathering his papers. His was the type you can empathize with intellectually but never emotionally. It's not their fault, of course, but they just don't have any sense of humor. Hoskins bent down by my ear. "Don't worry about him, Sturgess. A granola bar and he'll be fit as a guru."

I grunted. I didn't like Hoskins either; he was the other end of the spectrum. If Dermit was radiowaves, Hoskins was gamma—sharp, efficient, played squash four times a week, and rising fast. I was envious of the rapid rise. Surely Walter Sutherland could see that such loyalty was motivated by pure self-interest, nothing else. Power, I thought to myself, not principle. If only they were all like me.

"You hear about Art Lane?" said Hoskins. I glimpsed Erica Sarn through the departing crowd. I'd get her phone number. An apology for my questions should get me a hearing at least, and maybe dinner as well.

Maybe. But right now she was going out with Roth and I was torn between watching the rhythmic tightness of her skirt and having dark thoughts of the old SPS champion in his sordid sixties taking her off to some elegant hideaway in Georgetown—discussing exploding nebulae under the sheets, no doubt. "What about Art Lane?" I asked Hoskins grumpily.

"Dead. Car accident coming back from lunch."

He said it as if he was merely announcing a change in the weather.

I swung around. "What do you mean, accident?" I didn't know Art well enough to be shocked into silence and to tell the truth I was only interested in the details, but now Hoskins decided to play woeful countenance, mistaking my agitation for grief.

"I'm sorry," he said. "I didn't realize . . ."

"Had he been home or downtown?"

"Downtown, I think. Probably the Sans Souci. A lot of those guys meet there every . . ."

"Was he driving?" Hoskins was puzzled, but I didn't have time to explain. "Was he driving?"

"I—I don't know."

"Find out!"

Sutherland was waving me over toward a group of anti-SPSers. I lowered my voice. "Find out if he was driving, will you?" I said, adding, "Please." Junior advisers do not get away with broadsiding the President's chief adviser.

Young Dermit was still looking dejectedly at his manila folder while the President assured an elderly congressman from

Maine that he'd give both briefs on the SPS equal time before he decided to throw the power of the White House behind or against the bill.

After they'd filed out of the cabinet room, I followed the President as he swung right, past the Roosevelt Room and the entrance to the Oval Office, and into his study, where most of his work was done. He sat down behind the desk, swiveled, and put his feet up, his shoes almost touching the globe's equatorial rim. He was gazing out at the climbing Blaze roses. The room, barely eighteen by seventeen, and carpeted warmly in a soft, autumnal gold, encouraged an informality not possible in the larger Oval Room. It was just as well, for I was certain that the next few minutes could change the course of the country. The wrong decision on this bill could mean a full-scale war between power companies and consumers in votes, and the loss of the presidency. And someone called Harry Sturgess would be looking at the want ads.

CHAPTER 7

"Well, Sturgess, now you've heard Roth and Dermit and read the file. What do you think?"

I blocked out Art Lane, Norman Tier, everything and everyone but the facts. I thought of the note and mutilated photo I'd received and hoped the office wasn't bugged.

"I wouldn't sign it, Mr. President."

"Why?" The President waved the silver letter opener toward the camel-hair recliner. As I sat down, I could see the digital time box and the seven buttons that allow an instant readout of time and weather conditions in Moscow, Paris, London, Peking, Cairo, Berlin, and Tokyo. The constant flickering put me on edge.

"Well," I confessed, "to begin with, I'm for much wider use of the conventional solar receptors we already have on earth."

"The kind we put on roofs—that kind of receptor?"

"Yes."

"But we lose two thirds of the energy in the dark hours."

I heard a dull thump. I started. It was the pool's diving board. I guess I'd been thinking about the note. "True," I said. "But we can move earth receptors a heck of a lot easier than a satellite."

Sutherland looked surprised. "To move a satellite? All they

have to do at Houston is push a button," he said, tapping the letter knife on his left hand.

I was going to mention Skylab's unscheduled descent of July '79; its eighty-five tons bursting in a white-hot rain of fragments. Houston called it "random re-entry." The buttons hadn't kept it from falling.

"It's a massive expenditure," he said, getting up and walking thoughtfully toward the window.

"It is."

He glanced out at the roses for a moment and then, half turning, picked up a list of objections I'd noted. Running the letter opener over them he read them out quickly—too quickly for the number of hours it had taken me. Norman Tier would have loved that list:

(1) *Scattering* of the microwave beam due to rain, hail, and ionospheric irregularities.
(2) *Accidental Re-entry* of SPS due to unforeseen circumstances (e. g., failure of ion-propelled thrusters to maintain antidrift attitude of plus or minus two or three degrees).
(3) *Potential Noise and Atmospheric Pollution* caused by exhausts of reusable HLLVs (Heavy Lift Launch Vehicles).
(4) *RFI* (Radio Frequency Interference) between SPS and present communication systems.
(5) *Land Use* of seventy to one hundred square miles for every rectenna.
(6) *Air Glow Red* signaling imbalance in ionosphere due to heating effects of concentrated microwave beams.

The letter opener was tapping again. "This land use objection for the rectenna. Wouldn't matter if we leave it in the desert."

The President's use of "leave it" struck me as if in his mind he'd already seen way beyond the troubled passage of the SPS bill.

There was a series of rapid thumps from the pool board. They sounded like .38s. I thought of Norman Tier and Art Lane. Hoskins should know by now. The note . . . Tier . . . Lane . . . the meeting . . . I was trying to get some sort of picture but it kept blurring. Maybe there wasn't any. Maybe I was trying to make a pattern where there were only random particles.

He sat down, poking irreverently at objection number six—the last. "Air Glow—possible adverse biological effects?"

"Yes, sir. Clean Air Society predicts that if the atmosphere, especially the ionosphere, is overheated due to concentrated microwave beams, it will produce a red glow."

"And—?"

"Signaling that hot electrons are playing hell with the ozone layer. And ozone, or concentrated oxygen, is our vital screen against the sun's ultraviolet radiation. If we destroy the atmosphere, we destroy ourselves."

He let the list of objections slide to the desk.

"Formidable," I proffered by way of consolation.

"Sure as hell is," he grunted, dropping the letter knife carelessly on the inlaid glass and loosening his tie. And then I knew . . . I'd known him long enough for that. I could see a long line of presidential cruises on the Potomac with selected congressmen and just as many presidential breakfasts.

"I'm going to push for it," he said. "Goddamn it, Sturgess, we can control it! That's the point. You heard what Roth said. We won't be using high doses. Besides, one switch and it's off." The set of his jaw was determined, unrelenting. He looked at the roses again. "We're desperate for energy. God knows we're desperate." He paused, swung around, and slapped the desk. "I'm going for it. I'm going to call in some congressional IOUs—kick some ass on the Hill and get that bill approved." He pointed the knife right at me. "If the Senate balks and screws around with any amendments I'll veto every goddamn thing they send over here." He spun the globe again, watching it whirl into a blue-brown blur. "We farted around with the SST—let the Frenchies and Brits get the edge. We're not going to fart around with this." Hands in his pockets he strode over to the other window, tapping one of the twelve lower panes as if testing for resilience, and gazed out at the wilting petunias. "You know why I'm going to push? Apart from getting more energy of course?"

"No, sir."

"Prestige." He paused. "What value did the moon landing give us? I mean in dollar return? Oh yes, some, admittedly, like this inertial navigational system they're always telling me about. But not nearly enough to warrant the cost. Even the geologists were disappointed, and they got a hell of a lot more from it than most. But that doesn't matter—all that mattered was that we got there. First! It was a symbol of national expertise and pride. J.F.K. understood that before anyone else. He ignored all the economists and advisers who were against it. That was part of his greatness."

I squirmed in my seat, but he was too excited to notice. He smacked the globe again.

"An SPS would be an orbiting flag." He turned abruptly back toward the desk. "You know about President Harrison?" he asked. "Benjamin Harrison—about him and the electric light?"

"No."

"Well, Harrison—Republican—served from 1889 to 1893. He was here when they first installed electric light. He was so terrified of that electric light he wouldn't touch the switches. Servants had to do it for him and his wife. He'd 'served with distinction,' as they say, in the Civil War. Did some first-rate work settling a big Bering Sea dispute with Great Britain. Inter-American Conference took place under him too. No one knows that, but they all write about those damn electric lights—how he wouldn't go near them. What a thing to be remembered for. The point is—"

The President's phone winked red. "Yes—all right. Twenty minutes. Yes. Good-bye."

He turned back to me. "The point is, I'm not going down in history as another Harrison but as a Teddy Roosevelt of space."

I had trouble envisaging him riding up San Juan galaxy on a beam of microwaves but decided my earthbound imagination wouldn't be well received. He pulled on the herringbone seersucker jacket that Mrs. Gort thought too "unpresidential." "You know, F.D.R. in 1939 took time to read a note from a funny little man with frizzled hair and we got the A-bomb ahead of anyone else. And J.F.K. overruled all the doomsayers of the moon project—'a dice game,' they told him, a multibillion-dollar dice game. And then Armstrong planted the flag. No, Sturgess! Great nations have to take great risks. Besides, for Mr. and Mrs. Joe Average—all over the world, not just in America—they're not going to lose sleep over the possible risks you've outlined. They'll take one look at their monthly power bills, shiver and say, 'Let the S.O.B. put those satellites up as fast as he can.' That's the beauty of this, you see. It isn't *just* keeping our nose ahead in the space race. It isn't *just* a matter of boosting our pride, though it sure as hell needs boosting, but it could end the energy crisis too. SPS could *end* it!" He picked some errant balls of Kleenex from his pocket, tossing them expertly into the waste basket. "Anyway, do you *really* think there'll be any trouble? We've got the technology. The shuttle."

I thought of Art Lane. "I think there's trouble already," I said hesitantly. Beyond Lane's death and the fact he'd warned me about SPS, I couldn't give any distinct shape to my uneasiness, but if I didn't air it now, I never would. I told him briefly what had happened.

"Coincidence?" he proffered in the way people do when they don't want to think of alternative explanations.

"Yes," I nodded. "Could be. If he was downtown for a martini lunch and was driving that would easily push him into the coincidence bracket along with all the other drinking/driving statistics. But if he wasn't driving, he was government chauffeured. And those boys know how to drive—in any situation. Especially since the terrorism. But I don't know—it's only a hunch."

Then Walter Sutherland showed me why he was President.

"Check it out," he ordered, even though it was clear he thought it was nothing. As it turned out, he was wrong, and I know now that right then and there I started earning my pension.

CHAPTER 8

The President pushed the phone toward me and I dialed NSA at Fort Meade. No, they said, I couldn't speak to Norman Tier, but I could leave a message. No, I didn't want to leave a message. I inserted my blue-and-white-striped phone card in the slot, waited for the green light on the scrambler, and announced, "Code bleach"—the day's security clearance. No, I still couldn't talk to him. He was on assignment. Would I leave a message?

"No," I snapped. Good reason or not, I get angry when I can't reach people on the phone. I rang the head of the Washington Division; at least he should be able to tell me something about Art Lane. "Yes, it was an accident," he said. "Let me see—"

Sutherland was reading a memo. "Squash. Three-thirty, General Oster. Try yellow dot ball." I was glad one of us was worried.

"Nope—" came the Tennessee drawl on the phone. "He wasn't drivin'. Chauffeured by William Potter, age forty-three. Caucasian. Address . . ."

"Never mind," I said. "Who hit him?"

"Well now—lemme see—" That took another minute.

"Three witnesses. One says it was a green LTD, the second says it was a gray T-bird . . ."

"No. I mean *who* hit him?"

"Oh, hell, I dunno. We're still workin' on it. You wouldn't believe the number of . . ."

"Hit-and-runs?"

"You got it."

"Thanks."

Sutherland shrugged, and I couldn't blame him. With over twelve hundred and seventy hit-and-runs a day in the United States, maybe there'd been no connection at all between Art Lane's death and the SPS debate.

"If you want to pursue it," said Sutherland, "I'll give you carte blanche. I don't think there's any connection, but Art Lane was a high official and if I'm to sign that bill I don't want anything screwing up on me."

I got the message quickly. In the event anything did go wrong, he didn't want to have to explain in front of a packed press conference why such and such a possibility wasn't followed up by the Environmental Protection Agency—a representative of which (me) he'd seconded only months before. This way he'd be covered, particularly by the offer of carte blanche, and I'd have to do all the explaining to the phalanx of reporters. I didn't blame him. I would have done the same thing. We all like to be covered. "All right, Mr. President. I'd like to know where Norman Tier, an NSA man, is. He might be able to throw some light on this but he's on assignment and Fort Meade won't say where."

Sutherland pressed Hoskins' button. The orange square spluttered nervously. "Doug. Get Fort Meade—P.P." (Presidential Priority)

Two minutes later Sutherland gave me the information. "En route to Vancouver, Canada." He pushed the piece of paper across to me. "Bayshore Inn. Want him recalled?"

"No," I said. "I'll leave immediately."

"I envy you." The President smiled. "I hear the sailing is unbelievable."

It sounded odd, too forced somehow to be a joke, as if he'd just come up with something to smother embarrassment.

"I don't plan to have the time for sailing," I said, trying to make it all sound strictly business, but he wasn't listening. He'd put his hands into the prayer position, the thumbs darting anxiously back and forth. "Hold on." He pressed another button, and I could hear Hoskins' secretary. Sutherland mentioned a CANUS* file number and a CIA file. A few seconds later Hoskins appeared. As he passed the material to the President, the icy eyes told me, "If I had my way, fella, you wouldn't be in on this." Of course, Hoskins wouldn't have had me in on anything. On that, Mother Gort and he were of one accord. It wasn't that he didn't trust me—just that junior advisers should remain junior. How else could you remain senior? Sutherland had caught the hostile glance. "It's all right, Doug," he said. "I think Sturgess needs to know. Something's come up with one of the NSA people and I want him to check it out."

"Yes, sir," said Hoskins, but he still meant "no, sir." I smiled.

Sutherland glanced at his watch. It was almost time for squash. "You know that part of Canada well? British Columbia?"

"Fairly well," I said. "I used to go up skiing sometimes from Seattle."

He nodded thoughtfully, the way people do when they want to tell you something very personal but are hesitating—maybe they'll have a falling out with you and you'll take out an ad in *Time*. His hands were praying again. "You know what Harry Truman said?"

Everyone knows the logo on the Oval Office desk: "The buck stops here."

"Truman said that the most difficult thing to achieve in this office is to give an order and have it executed in its original form—before it gets mangled to hell by all the bureaucracy. The problem is that the Civil Service is so big, so vast, it's like a goddamn octopus. One tentacle reaches out to do what you tell it, and another, from who knows where, comes out and

* CANUS—Canadian-U.S.

strangles it. I sincerely hope that hasn't happened here with NSA poking its nose in."

I caught a glimpse of the digital clock face—the President had a squash game and I had a plane to catch at National Airport—if I wanted to see the Rockies by daylight. I really didn't want to hold a seminar on the evils of bureaucracy. Then he hit me with it—what was in both the CANUS and the CIA's presidential daily brief, which went only to Sutherland, his immediate aide—Hoskins, the Vice President, Secretary of Defense, and the National Security adviser. I'd seen the *National Intelligence Daily*, for which I was on the distribution list, but it hadn't said anything about solar energy and so I wasn't at all prepared for the President's bombshell. He was speaking quickly.

"The proposed SPS receiving antenna, or rectenna, will be situated in the Okanagan border area between British Columbia and Washington State—to start with—and later in northeastern Washington, in the open country near Grand Coulee. Headquarters for the operation will be out of Vancouver, temporarily. I wanted to wait until Congress approved. They will, of course. But meantime, Doug has persuaded me, and I think wisely, that we ought to think positively on this and develop the administrative machinery beforehand so that if, or rather when, it's approved, we won't waste time." He grinned, a little too self-consciously for my liking. "The winters aren't getting any shorter and our energy needs aren't getting any smaller. Not with the Mid-East in a constant state of flux."

"Why?" I'd meant it to come out a little more nonchalantly than that but it sprang out unchecked. "I mean, why British Columbia?"

"The Canadians and British are highly advanced in microwave reception and 'plug-in' techniques—the technology of hooking up the energy to our existing grid system—just as they were ahead with the Concorde. We're not far behind, the reports tell me, two years at the most, they say."

"Roth?" I proffered, knowing the President hadn't picked up that kind of information by himself.

"Well, yes," he conceded. "Naturally, Professor Roth is enthusiastic about an early start."

Hoskins gave me a withering stare. He was clearly pro-SPS and I'd advised against it. I thought of Erica Sarn's advocacy too—the calm yet spirited gaze.

"The point is," cut in Hoskins, "that any delay on the SPS could cost us a Soviet lead."

"Exactly!" endorsed Sutherland. He was definitely going to be late for his squash game. He glanced at his watch impatiently. "I'm not having another Yuri whatever . . ."

"Gagarin," I said.

"I'm not having another Soviet coup. Not in my presidency. The deal is, we supply the satellite technology. The Canadians don't even have a good slingshot. They supply the rectenna. We launch and transmit. We share the electric power all along the forty-ninth parallel."

"If Congress approves?" I said insubordinately.

"Yes." Sutherland frowned. "Of course."

"And the British?" I asked.

Sutherland stared at me. "Well, they're mixed up with the Canadians, of course." He might just as well have said that drizzle is rain, the connection was so obvious to him, but I thought of a street in Montreal where you'd get your head bashed in if you ordered tea instead of *thé*. "Of course," I said.

"Naturally we're only officially *investigating* the possibility of an Anglo-American cooperation should Congress approve."

I nodded. And if it isn't approved, I thought, then everything would suddenly be a Canadian and British venture on the other side of the line and Sutherland wouldn't be left holding the bag. Very neat.

"I'm late," he said. "The general'll be warming up. See what this Tier is up to, will you? My guess is, he's just checking security. NSA are bound to be watching this one closely. They're a bit miffed already at my not taking all their advice. I don't want to interfere with them unnecessarily. They've got their job to do. But I want everything kept cool. Doug will answer any more of your questions."

"Yes, sir."

"You agree this hunch of yours about Art Lane could be nothing."

"Right."

"So I don't want our British friends getting their backs up at you poking your nose over the forty-ninth parallel. Doug can arrange a cover for you. We'll say you're working for someone other than the White House . . . let's say . . . something bland. How about Environmental Protection Agency? Sound innocuous enough?"

"Sounds good," I said, not bothering to remind him that it was the "bland" department he'd seconded me from. It was more comforting than disconcerting to know that, like common mortals, presidents sometimes forget. On the other hand I didn't want him to forget too much—like democratic process.

After the President had left, Hoskins showed me a Vancouver address. "This is the proposed office of the U.S.-Canadian SPS headquarters."

"Great," I said with a facetiousness I could never have managed in front of the President, who, I was starting to think, took Hoskins and Roth and all the others too much at their word. "When I get to this *proposed* office will there be real people there or just *proposed* people? And what if Congress doesn't come through?"

"We'll worry about Congress, Sturgess. You check out Tier. I don't know what the hell National Security Agency is doing, but the old man's right. If our advance planning gets out, it'll delay SPS three years—could kill it, not just temporarily but for all time. Besides, we're only talking about a *proposed* site. We're just getting the administrative machinery ready to roll." He could see I didn't like it. "Look, Sturgess," he said. "I've come down a bit hard on you. Nothing personal. But we're in one hell of an energy crunch."

"Really?"

"All right, you of all people know how far back that nuclear screwup has put us. We've *got* to find new sources of energy and be damned quick about it."

My nod was conciliatory.

"So all we're trying to do is to keep a lot of people warm in winter. And not only Americans. It's strictly an energy problem. It's that simple and it's that serious. And we have to solve it. Nothing devious about it, believe me."

"Okay," I sighed. I didn't bother pressing him on his avidly stated desire to beat the Russians. It had been a long day and I didn't want any complications. But walking out past the Oval Office under the elegant white-pillared colonnade, past the stark profusion of climbing rose thorns, I had the distinct feeling that I should have called in sick. When I saw Dermit—the Clean Air disciple—following me outside the east gate, I knew I should have.

CHAPTER 9

"Excuse me, Mr. Sturgess, could I talk to you for a moment?"

I wanted to say no, but above the beard he had that Hound of Heaven look and I knew he'd talk my ear off anyway. Besides, there was something fervently unselfish about him. I didn't like him, but I couldn't help admiring such persistence.

"You want a coffee?" I asked. I wasn't thirsty but I could see one of the White House security cars driving slowly down Pennyslvania Avenue. It would be the dummy. The real one would probably be a cab with its flag up or more likely a wildly painted van with a pair of swingers in the front. Whichever it was, I didn't want to be on view talking to Dermit now that I knew the President was definitely behind the SPS bill. It was a bit gutless, I suppose, but I was just paranoid enough to think it might go down on my file. There were enough hurdles in the bureaucracy without making your own. As it happened, it went down on my file anyway.

Despite the sticky heat, Dermit looked cold. He wore a light green cotton jacket, but it hung on him loosely, a size too big. He'd obviously bought it just for the White House meeting. Sackcloth would have looked better on him. He was one of a whole generation of kids who had grown weary and skeptical of government after Watergate and Vietnam but who hadn't yet learned that their skepticism wasn't unique to this century or any other. Still, he impressed me—at least he kept me listening because, unlike most of his breed, he was in government. He was trying to play it up front, from inside, and that's more than the placard battalions did. I also liked Ph.D.s calling me "sir."

"Sir, if this goes through, a lot of people are going to suffer."

I glanced at my trusty Timex, which had raised some eyebrows at 1600 Pennsylvania Avenue. It was three-thirty already. At this rate, Dermit was going to cause me to suffer a two-hour layover at O'Hare before the Vancouver connection. "You made that clear at the White House," I said. "About everybody being in danger."

"No I didn't. Otherwise they wouldn't have laughed."

"Don't get pouty, Dermit. Roth is a sharp customer, that's all."

"Like a car salesman. He glides over the problems so smoothly you think only of the benefits. He'd sell you an Edsel."

"So what's your point?"

It was then that Dermit did the 1930 spy bit. You know, looking nervously around the coffee shop, except that he really was nervous. He pulled out a red pocket diary. From the "S" section, which I saw contained my name and address, he extracted a black and white three-by-four matte-finish photograph and pushed it across at me. What should have been the black pupils of the man's eyeballs were completely white. If there hadn't been the dark stain by the ears I'd have thought he looked funny, like a startled Peter Lorre.

"Dead?" I asked.

"What—oh yes," said Dermit. "No question."

"What is this?"

"It's the photograph of a dead man."

"Don't be a smartass, Dermit."

"He's a Finn. Or *was* a Finn."

"So?"

"He came from a small hamlet called Koitsanlahti."

"Where's that? Don't tell me it's in Finland—I've guessed that."

"It's a small hamlet facing the Russian border across Lake Lagoda."

I studied the photo again. Apart from the piercing whiteness of the eyes, the thing that stood out most prominently was the man's wristwatch and a lunch pail opened by his corpse. They were sharper than anything else in the photograph. I pushed the photo back to Dermit. "Go on."

"In 1974 a Russian scientist named Sadcikova studied a hundred cases of what the Russians call MW, or microwave, sickness. Sadcikova discovered that seventy-one of the patients with cardiovascular problems had been exposed to microwaves anywhere from five to fifteen years. Some of them had been exposed for much shorter periods. Anyway, following this the World Health Organization from the UN carried out a study of the population of Koitsanlahti which borders the Soviet Union and where an unusually high incidence of fatal heart attacks and increase in cancer had occurred. Strange thing about the heart attacks was that the victims were a lot younger than normal."

"So?"

Dermit was shifting nervously again, looking out at the street. "Koitsanlahti lies on the axis for Moscow's air defense against the ICBMs that would be launched from the U.S. midwestern silos. Across the lake from Koitsanlahti there's a huge Russian early warning station."

"So?"

I saw Dermit's hand start to tremble. "It uses massive scatter units which have to operate over large areas of water so that their microwaves won't be prematurely deflected." He tapped the photograph. "This Finn got in the way."

"What the hell's this got to do with the SPS? It's still in debate."

"I know."

He picked up the photograph and gave it to me. The blind eyes stared out at us. "You keep it," he said. "Maybe it's nothing but I can't help wondering if it's some kind of warning." He delved into the battered briefcase and pulled out an HEW report headed:

> *Carcinogenic Properties of Ionizing and Non-Ionizing Radiation—Volume II—Microwave and Radio-Frequency Radiation*, Department of Health, Education and Welfare (National Institute for Occupational Safety and Health) Publication No. 78–134.

He'd made a mark in the margin by the passage that read, "Between 1,000 and 10,000 megahertz, the organs most readily damaged by RF/MW [radio frequency/microwaves range] are the testicles and the eyes." He pointed at the print. His voice was cracking with fatigue. "Look at the pupils. They're white. They should be dark. They've been cooked. The protein has been literally fried—like two eggs. That's not low density. That's high. Very high."

"Where'd you get this photo?"

"I don't know."

"What the hell do you mean, you don't know? You telling me a ghost dropped it off?"

"Sort of," he said. "As Clean Air Rep I get all kinds of mail." He glanced around again. "I've been on TV."

"Congratulations." I was getting weary of his jittery surveillance of the other tables. "Who gave it to you, Dermit?"

"It was in the mail. Postmarked Kelowna."

"Where's that?" I asked, looking anxiously about. Now he had me doing it. "Kelowna? Doesn't sound Finnish," I said ingenuously.

"No. It's in southern British Columbia—in an area called Oka . . . Okanagan, or something like that."

I tried not to show any surprise. "No letter?"

"An anonymous note, saying the same thing is happening in this country as happened around Lake Lagoda."

"Why didn't you bring this up at the meeting?"

"I'm concerned, Mr. Sturgess. I'm not stupid. I think it's genuine, but it could be a photo of any old corpse. And I'm showing it to you because you're close to the President. You're the only one in this business without a vested interest. I *think.*"

"Except my job," I said. "You should have taken this to—"

"To who?" he cut in, almost hoarse. "Who would listen to me? A junior scientist from an antipollution group with a photo that anyone in creative film could've fixed in ten minutes."

"What makes you so sure it isn't a fake?"

"I'm not. But I thought I'd pass it on."

I didn't believe it—not the photo, I mean, but Dermit's story. I believed he believed it—that he'd been singled out at random by some concerned northern citizen. That was hardly unusual. Congressmen, public officials in all departments got that kind of mail all the time, from all parts of the country, like the little crackpot note that had been sent to me.

And if you started acting on every crackpot note you got as a public official you'd end up bananas yourself. But the mention of the Okanagan border area twice in one morning from two different sources, once from the President and once from Dermit, was the kind of coincidence that makes you go out and buy lottery tickets—or more life insurance.

I said nothing to him about the President's mention of the same area. Instead, I muttered "I'll check it out," as noncommittally as I could.

"Thanks. I must emphasize," he said, "if that—if that's right"—his hands were shaking slightly—"if that photo's for real—if the same thing *is* happening here, it means very high levels of microwave radiation somewhere. Even old Roth agrees about the dangers of that." He was tapping the photo again. "Here we're talking about very high density levels." He gestured urgently. "You see, it's like turning a stereo up. Doesn't matter what the wavelength is, it's the amplitude—the volume if you like—that's what counts. That's what does the damage. Even the pro-SPS scientists who disagree with us on the effects of low level or low power densities agree that if the power density is high enough then you're in trouble."

A cold, sick wave passed through me. I was remembering the medical report that had been addressed to me: the testicular pain, the bleeding from the eyes. "What would it be caused by?" I pressed quietly. His right hand had stopped shaking. Now it was trembling. He saw me watching it.

"It's the coffee," he said. "Caffeine and I don't get along."

"What could it be caused by?"

He dumped in half a cup of cream. "I don't know," he replied, looking skittishly at an old lady who had just entered the shop. "The SPS frequency could do it with enough power."

"Have you looked in the sky recently?"

He frowned. "I don't know what you . . ."

"The SPS would be so big you could see it at night with the naked eye—like a star. You can't sneak one up."

"Exactly." He almost spat his coffee out. "All this SPS stuff is still up for discussion—still in the proposal stage. But—but when I see photos like this!" He was almost stammering. "What the hell's going on?"

I didn't have an answer.

Then Dermit shocked me as much as if he'd flashed in the restaurant. He pulled out a cigarette and lit it. It didn't fit the environmentalist stance, the beard, or the wild, evangelical eyes. "You're right," he said.

I was thinking. "What?" I asked.

"You're right. You would see the SPS."

"Yes. Besides, the House still has to vote on it." I hesitated for thirty seconds or so. I knew there must be a much more sophisticated term, but I couldn't think of one and I didn't want to sound like something out of Buck Rogers. But at least there would be no confusion. The dead eyes were looking up at me. They *were* like fried eggs. I put the photo in my pocket. "Dermit, the thing that caused this"—I said it very quickly—"you think it's a—a kind of *death* ray?"

He drew heavily on the dying cigarette. "Yes."

"Christ! But surely . . . surely it was unintentional? An accident?"

Dermit shrugged.

"Do *you* believe the same thing's happening here, in North America?"

"Someone does, whoever sent me this photo."

"Do you?"

"I don't know. I just don't know."

That made two of us. I thought of old Davidson, the Clean Air man who had explained what would happen if an SPS moved a bare five degrees. But, dammit, the SPS didn't exist—I *knew* that much. You simply cannot hide an array over seven miles wide even if it is 22,300 miles from earth. In any event, Roth had just been arguing about how safe such an SPS beam would be. Through the greasy window I could see a group of children laughing and playing in the park beneath the statue of Lafayette and I thought of the medical report again. I thought of Jenny. I thought of all of us.

"Right!" I said angrily. Dermit looked up, surprised. It was my way of saying that I'd had a bellyful of questions—that it was high time I got some answers.

When I left the coffee shop, Dermit didn't wave good-bye but just scurried off, his smoke wafting behind him in the thick, humid air like the breath trail of a frantic beaver scrambling for cover. I hailed a cab and told the driver to hurry to National Airport. He started mumbling something about bigshots always in a hurry. He saw a break in the traffic and pulled out, mumbling now about tourists.

As we drove away, I saw Dermit being escorted to a waiting car on the other side of Fourteenth Street. One of the men was slapping him on the back and laughing at the other gently mussing Dermit's hair like an old buddy guiding him into the back seat. I glanced at the number. I'd been trained to remember such things at first sight but it's like anything else—if you don't do it all the time you get rusty so I wrote the number down and turned to the driver. "Take me across the river instead. To Langley."

"Cookie Factory?"

"Yes." He was mumbling again. The lawn stretching down from the Washington obelisk was pockmarked with garbage, and a gentle breeze sent small pieces of paper fluttering downhill.

CHAPTER 10

Even if the process is familiar to you—the "restricted" areas with their black punch combination locks, the green-lettered EYES ONLY files and the spooky little electric trolleys that roll silently, orange-eyed, past you through the dim inner corridors delivering and collecting the files—getting information at the Agency is still very much like getting a job. You can walk miles, fill out a hundred requests, and write yourself silly, giving your credentials and what your favorite dessert is, but in the end, quick service depends on whom you know.

I'm not trying to pretend that my White House status didn't help, although I had to go through the thumbprint and ID card computer checkouts behind the thick glass walls, but in the end it was Ralph Stein who saved me from much of the time-wasting requisitioning.

We had a private code from my EPA days. Whenever we wanted each other's help and needed to keep it quiet we'd always chat about tennis and work in the phrase, "It was forty–love. Match point." It cut right through the red tape.

Ralph was one of the best analysts in the CIA. The Agency has never been very good on its long-range or what they call "over-the-horizon" political predictions. They know as much about who'll win the elections in Italy as I know about what horse'll win the million at Ruidoso Downs. But if you want to know the ratio of Soviet land-based ICBMs to those of the United States (1,477:1,054) or when the Soviet ASAT (Anti-Satellite-Satellite) Cosmos 970 was shifted from a 588- to a 712-mile-high orbit, their Directorate of Intelligence people can tell you (December '79 by ground control). And on the basis of a Social Security number they can shock you in less than 3.71 minutes by knowing more about yourself than you can remember.

When I was escorted to Ralph's office by the guard, his secretary told me he was cleaning up after giving a slide presentation in the "Bubble"—the 2001-style auditorium adjacent to the main building.

As I walked down the center aisle of the massive dome, I could see Ralph picking up some papers on the polished walnut lectern to the far left of the podium. Only half the lights were on, shining from the smaller beige-colored saucers that cling to the walls like huge plastic growths, each of their six lights sunken so as not to break the smooth contours. The bank of high-intensity lights behind me on top of the projector room shone brightly against the towering sky-blue backdrop as if someone were expecting a basketball game to start any minute below. Even so, only part of the red seats showed up, the others swallowed in deep shadow. The result was the same eerie feeling you experience in most empty auditoriums, and I couldn't help thinking how a man might lose touch with reality if he spent too much time inside bubbles.

Ralph's hand came quickly up over his eyes as he heard my footsteps muffled by the carpet. His was the movement of someone who is perennially suspicious but whose human instinct is alien to secretiveness, who has let secretiveness overtake him because in it there is at least some protection. There are men like that not only in the CIA but right through the web of security agencies. For the most part they are leftover experts from old, forgotten wars who joined the game in the early days out of a thirst for adventure and a patriotism that is now unfashionable. Some of them had gotten out in time, before the rot set in, but others had been in too long to try anything else. Ralph's job wasn't on the covert operations' side anymore. We shook hands, chatted about the weather, his eleven-year-old boy who suffered from diabetes, and his wife who'd been mugged right outside on the George Washington Memorial parkway. "Can you believe it?" he said, anxiously wiping his bifocals. "Right outside the Agency?"

It didn't seem that strange to me. I'd just seen Dermit picked up right outside the White House. "It's credible," I said.

"If they catch the mugger, they'll probably give him a warning."

"No," I said. "They're really getting tough now. They'll make him write a hundred times on the blackboard: 'I mustn't kill people.'"

Ralph's worried, weathered face shifted into what could pass for a grin.

"How is Madge?" I asked.

"Oh, all right. Still shook up. Doc's given her some tranquilizers."

"Nothing physical? Wounds?"

"No, thank God. So what do you want?"

His abrupt shift irked me, but it was warranted. I'd only been passing time of day and Ralph knew it. He glanced at the drugstore receipt I'd scribbled the number of the Virginia plates on. In his office, a twelve-by-eight cubicle on the fourth floor, overlooking a green thicket of alder, he punched the number out on the computer console and asked for a K-3 readout. It took five seconds, just long enough for me to look at the cover of the latest issue of the Soviet *Ekonomicheskaya Gazeta* that topped a pile of foreign journals, secret charts of underground Chinese oil installations, and various colored plastic covers that designated the different security classifications of the documents within.

The information was so abbreviated, computer style, that I was still trying to figure it out when Ralph said casually, "It's a company car."

"You mean—it belongs to you? A CIA car?"

"No, I mean it's a company car. A regular company. Belongs to S.S.—Sudley Steel."

"Who are they?"

Ralph tapped the keys again and the green letters vanished from the screen just as others began to pop up silently in a line of tiny luminescent ghosts. "Sudley Steel," said Ralph. "It's a popcorn manufacturer."

It was the closest Ralph could get to a joke. I smiled weakly. "Cut the crap."

"Big contractor out of Birmingham, England—American plant in California. Prime supplier of high-tensile steel and titanium."

"What's that for—jets?"

Ralph cleared the machine and nodded. "Yes, and satellites, disk antennas, nuclear plants, that sort of thing."

I thought for a moment, then I asked, "Anything to do with the Canadians?"

Ralph was patient but a little annoyed that I hadn't told him what the information was for. He played on the machine again, the hollow, rhythmic clinking of the keys reminding me of an old Sinatra tune.

"There's the breakdown," he said. "Four percent Japan, three, Australia, fifty-one percent English. Canada is forty percent."

"That only adds up to ninety-eight percent," I said.

"Two percent is so small a split-up we don't register it."

"Sloppy," I joked. "Who's its biggest customer?" I knew I was getting into sensitive country.

"Sorry about that before," he said.

"About what?"

"Cutting you short. I'm a little teed-off these days."

So I was to play psychiatrist. This was the price for finding out the name of the biggest customer. "What's wrong?" I said.

"Something's going on," he said. "I had to take an LD this morning."

"What the hell for?"

"Oh, it's not just me. It's everybody. Apparently there's been a leak. A lie-detector test—after seventeen years with the Agency."

"Yeah," I said sympathetically. "Still, you're all right."

"It's the principle," he said. "It's the goddamn principle."

I found this a bit ironic coming from an old snoop, but he had a point. Captured in Korea, he'd been a prisoner of the Chinese for four years. He'd paid his dues.

"There'll be a record of that print-out we just did," he said. "What do I say it was for?"

"Who's Sudley Steel's biggest customer, Ralph?"

He didn't have to press any buttons. "It's the U. S. Government. All kinds of contracts—mostly under subsidiary names—tax loopholes you see."

"Okay," I said. "Say the info was for the President. He'll clear it."

That appealed to Ralph. He brightened noticeably. Besides, if I didn't tell him what I was looking for, he couldn't lie. He'd have to tell them what I told him, and who was going to question the President? It made Ralph very happy but not me. What was a steel company doing with Dermit?

I called my old secretary in Seattle's EPA office. After appropriate pleasantries, the question I asked was very simple. I rattled off a few companies—names which I remembered were mixed up in the nuclear "air pocket" business. Were any of them, I inquired, connected with a parent operative called Sudley Steel?

"Would you hold, Mr. Sturgess?"

"Yes."

Ten minutes. I tried to relax—after all, I wasn't paying for the call.

"Sorry for the delay, Mr. Sturgess, but to trace through the maze . . ."

"Yes, that's fine," I assured her. "Any connection with Sudley Steel?"

"Only one, Mr. Sturgess—but not under that name. A subsidiary."

"Yes, but what plant?"

"The Macphearson plant I believe."

"You believe or you know? It's very important."

"It was the Macphearson plant."

"Building of the outer wall?"

"Yes." She sounded surprised.

"Any more contracts with Sudley Steel, or its subsidiary, for nuclear plants?"

"No."

"You're positive?"

"Absolutely, Mr. Sturgess. We've very strict control over . . ."

"Yes, all right. Thank you."

Sudley Steel and Macphearson? Coincidence? Maybe, but what about Sudley Steel and Dermit?

As I lifted the phone I hoped he would be home. He was. I mentioned the big shiny car and asked him if he was all right.

"Oh, that," he laughed, making me feel like fool of the week. "They're old college friends."

"What are their names?"

"Ah, Frank . . . ah, Frank Ryan and, ah—ah—James—"

"Bullshit!" I added. "James Bullshit, right?"

"Leave me alone," he said. There was a click and a sound like a bee in my ear.

I hoped there'd be a very funny movie on the flight to Vancouver, because Harry Sturgess was not amused.

CHAPTER 11

"Love me . . . forever and forever," said the heroine, and the hero groped madly as if he were trying to unload a sack of cucumbers from the back of a truck. It had been a terrible movie and I was glad it was nearly over. But now the kid behind me was indulging in Spock-inspired free expression by kicking my kidney through the seat. I gave him a Sidney Greenstreet stare. Mother gave me a protective-lioness rejoinder, so I decided to move. The problem was, where? There were vacant seats in the jumbo but kids everywhere—all in uniform—Boy Scouts, Cubs, Girl Scouts. Some kind of West Coast jamboree, I guess. They were moving about the big aircraft like ants erupting from a hive—changing seats every fifteen seconds, playing havoc with the harried stewardesses—all except Genghis Khan behind me. He was staying put under Mom's orders, and working out his frustrations on my back.

Funny the small things that change your destiny. The stewardess told me that there were spare seats in the rear section if I was prepared to walk about the aircraft and make sure one wasn't simply temporarily vacant before I claimed it. There were a couple of rows all but vacant. I was sizing up the best seat—one by a window—only a short distance from the rear galley when I saw her. She looked dazzlingly beautiful, the cool, glistening wet salmon-pink lips and low-cut maroon dress by contrast made the white-marble roundness of her breasts seem doubly alluring. There were two Cubs beside her practicing their knots on one another's throats.

"Hi, fellas." I said it quietly so she wouldn't hear. I needn't have worried, as she had earphones plugged into the console arm, and her eyes were closed. "Do me a favor?" I asked the boys. "A good deed?" I saw their belt buckles—"Be Prepared."

"What?" asked one of them sullenly.

"Would you like to move into the middle row over there?" She was looking out the window at the mountainous white cumulus.

They eyed me suspiciously—warned about strangers in jumbos no doubt. It cost me two dollars to move them. Well, at least they were prepared for inflation—demanding U.S. rather than Canadian dollars. They'd lose on the exchange, they said.

The movie was a few minutes behind in this section so that as I sat down the heroine was still mouthing silently, "Love me . . . forever . . ." Erica saw me, smiled fleetingly, sociably, but didn't recognize me. She moved her soft Gucci handbag to give me more leg room. Of course I didn't believe for a second that her being on the same plane was coincidence. Or was it? Was I just being too smart, or cynical? She was watching the clouds again. "Miss Sarn?" She couldn't hear me through the earphones. I spoke more loudly and tapped her arm. "Miss Sarn?"

She turned, nodded, and in her uncertainty, just for a moment, there was a childlike vulnerability in the velvety brown eyes, a natural flash of friendliness quickly curtailed by a well-practiced caution. But it had been there for a second, a willingness to trust smothered more by necessity than intent. She took out the earphones.

"Harry Sturgess," I said. "Yesterday. The White House."

"Oh—" The warm-water faucet was off and now she was running cold. "Yes. I remember. Mr. Titanic."

"You heading for the West Coast?" I asked ingenuously.

"I hope so. That's where the plane's going."

"Holidays?"

"Yes." There was no hesitation. Either she was very good—had been well trained—or she was telling the truth. Right now I didn't care. The point was, should I? The azure sky, the clarity of white clouds against it, reminded me of the skies over the Aegean and of my old tutor talking about the all-too-forgotten importance of Greece's clear air to their clear vision of the world. "The Greek ideal," he'd scrawled on one of my essays, "was harmony—the danger, the dominance of passion over reason." Looking at Erica, I could see the problem, but understanding it doesn't mean you can solve it. We'd been trying for five thousand years. And when the stewardess brought her a Fresca and Erica leaned across to take it I wanted to love her "forever and forever."

"You quite finished?" she asked icily.

"I—I—" But I went deep red. I couldn't handle that kind of directness. From old Gort maybe, but not from Erica Forever. "I'm sorry I upset you yesterday," I said, adding with cool reason, "just doing my job."

"Of course," she said condescendingly.

I felt like a Nazi war criminal. "It's my job to probe," I said defensively.

"So I've noticed!"

"I mean, I—"

"You were just doing your job."

"Yes."

She smiled—genuinely warm and friendly. The white-coated physicist had gone. Here was a woman.

"It's all right," she said. "I was doing mine too."

I smiled graciously in return. Here was a lady.

"Your ideas are quite stupid of course."

My mouth opened, but nothing came out.

"You kind of people are so self-righteous it makes me ill. Any new idea, any notion of progress, and you retreat to the cave. I'll bet you loved *Gulliver's Travels*."

Now I got the picture. We were playing oneuppersonship. She obviously thought that old, dumb Sturgess from EPA wouldn't get the analogy.

"Swift wasn't against science, *Ms.* Sarn. He was against *silly* science. Just because you wear a white coat doesn't mean everything you do is for the betterment of mankind. The A-bomb has limited medicinal benefits."

She smiled sweetly. "Why don't you suck on the oxygen mask? Clear your head."

"Don't worry about me."

"Oh, I won't."

"I'm sorry, Miss Sarn," I said with stiff dignity. "I really didn't mean to offend you."

The silence was electric and I read a *Time* ad for Chevrolet eight times before I was anywhere near cooling point. What the hell was all this about? Two grown people—and all I'd said —all I'd asked, was what would happen if something went astray with her dumb pet project. Of course—that was it. Anyone who works long and hard enough on a project—it becomes theirs, and to question it is to question them.

There is a critical limit to childish silences, and I have a theory that it's about eleven seconds. After that you're locked into the pride game—if you speak first you've lost on a technical knockout. If you talk before that there's just a possibility of rapprochement. "I won't call you names if you won't call me names," I proffered. If she smartassed me now, I'd throw her out the exit door.

I needn't have worried. Her expression softened, and, when she smiled, my heart actually sped up. It's true. I hadn't felt like this since I first kissed my wife.

"I'll buy you a drink," she said. "I'm sorry."

"Make it a whiskey sour." I was as relieved as if an aching tooth had finally been pulled.

"A whiskey sour it is."

"And not one word about—" I nearly said SPS.

She gave me a quiet, engaging look and I was ready to mount chargers and fight dragons. Linda used to tell me that a man seldom, if ever, noticed whether a woman was wearing a wedding ring. I discovered she was right and it was only now, as Erica reached into her purse with long, finely tanned fingers, that I saw the pale mark where a wedding band had been.

"Divorced?" I've no idea why I said it—it was about as rude as you can get. But I guess I was so momentarily depressed by the possibility that she might still be married that disappointment beat out manners. Whatever it was I suddenly felt I'd killed any chance I'd have to sink into that beautiful, scented warmth. Slim yet full-figured, she moved voluptuously even in the simple act of reaching for a change purse.

"Yes," she answered, "I am," but everything was cold again. Sleet cold. Oh, she bought me the drink all right and nodded assent when I commented on how disappointing it was to miss seeing the Rockies because of the thick, gray stratus that swirled about us like mad ghosts. But it was all semipolite, the way you might answer a stranger in a train when all you wanted to do was to sit back and be alone with your thoughts. Big Mouth Sturgess had blurted out "Divorced?" like a hungry vulture waiting in the hot sun for the dust to settle so that he could pick up the best of what was left after the final marital scuffle.

Now she had me pegged as a scavenger preying on the lonely and beautiful. I could imagine what must be going through her head. She'd be sure she knew my strategy, buying her dinner, a few drinks, a show, the mouthwash breath, the frantic thrusting, and the plethora of lies. And the morning—"That was terrific. Let's do it again sometime. *Ciao!*"

I leaned over just as we were coming in through the soupy gray air above the wide, winding gold ribbon that was the Fraser River. "Listen," I said. "Erica, I know what it's like. I lost my wife . . . I'm not trying to—"

"Would you pass the glasses please, sir? We're landing."

Some moments are gone forever and some you can get back again. I tried to convince myself that maybe I'd get a second chance.

"Where are you staying?" I asked, with a note of urgent desperation.

"Downtown." It was as emotionless as "Fasten Your Safety Belts."

"Maybe I'll see you around, Erica?"

Silence.

She must have divorced recently, I thought, to be this suspicious and uptight. Perhaps it was all the pressure too. The SPS —perhaps she was just coming out to visit the possible rectenna site—escaping the physical and psychological humidity of Washington for a few days.

"I'm sorry," I said.

"So am I." I felt really done for.

The long white tunnel went on and on from the International Arrival Gate to Customs and Immigration. I took the regular passport out, not wanting to use the special diplomatic passport here and unnecessarily worry the Canadian SPS rep who met me by the opaque sliding doors.

It was 10:30 A.M. and piddling rain as only Vancouver skies can piddle. I saw Erica Sarn heading for a taxi. A man, rushing by, bumped into me, almost knocking me to the ground, obscuring my view of her.

"Sorry," he said, his breath a cloud of incredibly strong garlic, and rushed on.

"So am I," I grumbled. "Everyone's sorry today."

I slipped the passport back into my vest pocket and strained to see her in the crowd. A flash of maroon dress, firm, tanned legs, white high heels. And she was gone. "Damn!"

As the passport slipped into my pocket I felt something else. A firm envelope. It was a photo of Jenny. She would have been grinning but for the razor slash across the photo. I turned it over. "Lovely child," it said. For a moment I thought I was going to throw up. I could taste the plane food overpowering me.

"You all right, sir?" asked the Canadian rep.

"No," I said. "I want to make a call—to Washington. In private."

"This way, sir. Not bad news I hope?"

I ran ahead, plunging into the crowd, looking left and right, forward and back, but he was long gone.

CHAPTER 12

As I dialed area code 301, I was in a panic. I could see my house in Rockville, Maryland, about twenty minutes' drive from the White House. I could feel the hot, oppressive stickiness outdoors, see the rope swing between the two maples, and the specks of tiny gnats that always terrified her—the closed upstairs—unused since Linda had died five years ago. And I could see some bastard watching her from a parked car nearby making his notes: when she played, when Mrs. Reardon would call her in for dinner, etc. I didn't know who it was and if I knew I couldn't do anything right now. All I could do was to make sure she was safe. When Mrs. Reardon answered, pleasantly surprised, I nearly shouted her off the other end. All my White House cool, all my crash courses—"crisis management," "fear control"—left me. The Canadian tried to make out he was reading the paper. I appreciated the gesture, it made it easier to talk. I'd now stopped yelling at Mrs. Reardon as if she'd been doing nothing and not looking after Jenny.

"Where is she, Mrs. Reardon?"

True to form her voice was quietly unruffled. "I think she's out back, Mr. Sturgess."

"Christ! You should be watching her. Bring her in. Bring her in. Right now!"

"One moment."

"Daddy?"

I could feel the sweat trickling down my neck even though it was a cold day in Vancouver.

"Hi, sweetheart." I took a deep breath and slowed my speech. "How's my favorite girl?"

"Fine. Guess what? I got A-plus for spelling. Miss Jordan says I—"

"That's terrific, honey. Now listen, sweetheart . . ."

"But, Daddy, Miss Jordan says I might win a spelling bee."

"That's terrific, honey."

Giggles. "Daddy—?"

"Yes?"

"I thought . . . you'll think I'm silly."

"No, I don't think you're silly. What, honey?"

"I thought Miss Jordan said I'd win a bee. You know, a honeybee. Isn't that silly?"

I felt weak with relief. "That's the silliest thing I ever heard. A honeybee. You nit."

Giggles.

" 'Bye, angel." The Canadian was smiling.

" 'Bye, Daddy."

I apologized to Mrs. Reardon. Jenny was even sleeping in her room. That was fine, I said. That was fine, but right now I didn't want Jenny going outside. I waited until Mrs. R. had told me she'd checked all the doors and locked them, including the basement.

I rang Hoskins at the White House. He answered the phone curtly, listened to what I said, and was the most helpful I'd known him to be. He'd look after it, he promised. A twenty-four-hour guard—seven days a week. Yes, within the hour.

"Well, you can come back if you like but right now that won't add to the security. Anyway, better not scare the child, don't you think? Might as well get a lead on who these jokers are. See what you can find out."

"Don't worry," I said.

As I walked out from the airport toward the waiting limousine with the Canadian, I silently cursed every hijacker. They've made it damn difficult, if not impossible, to carry arms through airports. I'm not a gun man, but right now I very much wanted a Smith & Wesson .38—street load. But if I asked for that, the Canadian would have been alerted to the fact that I just wasn't visiting the possible site of the SPS rectenna as a visiting EPA official. Still, I wanted some protection and I wanted it now.

As I climbed into the back of the government car, the Canadians went out of their way to be polite, to make me feel welcome. But I felt alone and, without the bulge under my arm, very naked. It was time, I decided, to remember my skiing days in the Northwest, to renew old acquaintances this side of the border.

I didn't know what to do with the slashed photograph of Jenny. I wanted to throw it away, never to see it again, but I couldn't. In a way it would've been like throwing Jenny away. I had to carry it with me, and every now and then my fear for her surged up and grabbed my chest like a vise.

CHAPTER 13

Jonas, Norman Tier's ex-colleague, looked like a clockmaker—wearing a soft, crumpled gray suit and glasses that made him appear as if his world didn't extend beyond the small circle of his work light. He'd run a ski shop for a while after he'd retired from the game and before the arthritis took hold was one of the best cross-country people I knew. He'd guided Norman and me through the magnificent Cypress Bowl country more than once. After the ski shop had fallen victim to the big European manufacturers, he'd diversified, as they say, and what had begun with archery and air pistols in a general sports shop now included a wide range of weapons, the sale of which kept him out of the red. I thought it an unusual combination, skier turned gunsmith, but as he bent awkwardly down to retrieve a box from beneath the aged counter I caught a glimpse of myself in the old "Remington" gold embossed mirror that stood behind him. Nonviolent Harry Sturgess, quiet civil servant from the Environmental Protection Agency, looking for a gun. That was an even more unusual combination. Everything was changing. Jonas hadn't wanted to carry firearms at first, having had enough of that in the game, and he'd only gone into the business out of financial necessity. But gradually, like a doctor who hates diseases he's forced to deal with, he had come to know all about firearms, and his language now betrayed a peculiar fascination with them.

I didn't mention Norman, no use enlarging the quarrel, if that's what it was going to be. Still I felt duty bound to tell Jonas I was up on business and that there could be someone tailing me and that they might try to approach him. He grinned—it was almost an expression of hope. He waved at the arsenal that doubled as his shop and at the photoelectric gun alarms he'd set up, and which were almost certainly illegal.

"Installed them myself," he said proudly. "That way no one has the circuit plans. Any sonofabitch tries to 'approach' me uninvited, he'll end up like Swiss cheese."

His wife, Ida, came out from the stock-jammed back room and gave me the old hug and smile and it was nice. Nice and genuine. I'd always liked them. I could talk to Jonas straight—one of those rare friends you could go up to and say, "Joe, I've done a damn stupid thing and I need a thousand dollars." He'd only have three hundred at most, but whatever he had, it was yours. But I couldn't tell him just yet what I'd come for—not after the warm, soft-bosomed embrace of Ida.

"And how's Norman?" Ida asked, pouring more tea. "You ever see him in Washington?"

"Oh," I said. "Yes. He seems okay. Working too hard. Don't run into him that often."

"He always worked too hard. Always pushing himself. Hasn't written to us in years, you know?"

"That's Norman." I forced a smile. If he was in Vancouver, why hadn't he visited them?

"Reminds me of some other people," she said, pushing the chocolate cake happily toward me.

"Yes," I replied absently. Why hadn't he given them a call?

"Reminds me of you, Harry Sturgess!" Ida chided good-humoredly. "Not a word—not even a Christmas card."

"Oh—"

"Oh, nothing! You write in future."

"Yes, ma'am."

Ida had aged much more than Jonas. He still looked in his mid-forties. She looked closer to sixty. The worry of three kids and the battle to keep financially afloat had driven her to the continual snack and now she was huge, barrel-shaped. Still, each to his own, I thought condescendingly, thinking more of Erica Sarn now that the Darjeeling tea was sitting well and hot and I knew that the FBI would be watching over Jenny twenty-four hours a day. But after, when we got down to business and I began talking with Jonas, I knew he and Ida didn't share the same bed. I wanted to feel sorry for him, but there was something disquieting about the way he handled the gun business when I brought it up. At first he simply said, "You don't want a .38."

"I don't?"

"No. Too much damn noise. Too heavy besides. All right in winter—overcoats and things to cover it up—but not now. Where would you put it?"

"Well, I . . ."

"No," he said, "what you need is something small and very accurate at close range."

"All right."

"Yes, well," he murmured, "this is a nice little job. Beretta—relatively quiet, small holster, nine shots. Smooth little erection."

"Erection" pulled me up. But before I could answer he went on, moving the gun in and out of the oiled holster with a fascination that I found distinctly unpleasant. He looked up at me knowingly.

"Lots of it in Washington is there?"

Before I could say anything, he rammed the Beretta hard into the holster. "Three hundred dollars," he said. "For an old friend. They'll never trace it."

"I'm not worried about that."

"Listen!" he said as I left. "Could you do me a favor?"

"Sure." I mustn't have sounded convincing. Either that or he needed to justify himself.

"Harry, you say you're up on business," he said eagerly. "Well, I can always help you up here. I've still got connections, Harry. If it's on the quiet, give Lionel a call next door—the dry cleaner's. Leave a message with him. I can always ring you back on a public phone or wherever—in case mine's tapped." He hesitated. He was embarrassed. "Look, stolen car plates, whatever you . . ."

I nodded as graciously as I could. "So what can I do for you, Jonas?"

"Send me *Penthouse*. They stop it coming up here sometimes. I'd get a subscription but they can tell from the wrapper that the address is in Canada and they can stop it at the post office. If you could buy it and wrap it up so that they couldn't tell what was inside . . . I mean the post office . . ."

I didn't answer for a second.

"Don't look at me like that. It's all right for you, you lucky bastard. You're single. Good-looking. You've got it made."

"Sorry," I said. "I'll send it, Joe."

"I love her, you know."

"I—I know," I stammered.

"No you don't. But I *do*. Swear to God I do. But sometimes I . . . You don't know what it's like."

"I'll send it," I said. "Don't worry."

I did know what it's like, of course. Everyone knows what it's like sometime in their life, but they don't think anyone else does. The magic of the tea was fading. I felt very sad for a moment, for Ida and Jonas, and worried for myself. At least he had Ida to make his tea.

"All right," I said angrily to myself. "All right, Tier. You'd better be here. And you'd better have a pretty good reason for snooping around the President's pet project and for dragging me away from Jenny." I felt the Beretta hugging my chest. Jonas, playing with it like he did, disgusted me no end—and reminded me of Erica. God damn Tier!

CHAPTER 14

"Harry!"

It was Tier—hatless—grinning like a schoolboy and looking like a tourist, waiting at the entrance to the Bayshore Inn. I flushed with anger and embarrassment. I should have been grateful, I suppose, being spared the trouble of tracking him down and finding out the reasons for his sudden flight from Washington. But now I felt cheated. I also felt a damn fool. How did he know I'd be coming? From the un-Tier-like gregariousness I was sure I was in for a good roasting: "Well, if it isn't Dick Tracy!" or some such thing. But no, Norman was better-mannered than I thought, better than I would have been, given the same advantage. But it wasn't just that he was well-mannered. He was acting—in fact he was overdoing it a bit like someone who's had a manhattan too many.

"What are you doing here, Harry?" His voice was loud enough for the doorman to hear.

"On holiday," I said churlishly.

As soon as he was close enough to shake hands he smiled right at me, so full of joy that he looked downright evangelical. This time, I thought, he *has* flipped. "Just check in," he said. "Don't go to your room." It was said quietly, in direct contrast to the booming, loudmouth Yankee greeting he'd just given me. "Smile," he commanded quietly, still grinning. I smiled.

"We're in deep shit."

"Fine," I said, going along. "I'm thirsty as a hog. I'll check in first."

"See you in Trader Vic's, it's straight ahead of the elevators. Hard right."

"Got it."

I waited half an hour, swirling the ice to the last drop. Finally, at three o'clock, I bit the maraschino cherry and went to the desk. "Is there any message for Mr. Sturgess?"

"Ye-s, sir. I believe there was." She checked the mail slots. "No—I must have been mistaken." She eyed me suspiciously. "Mr. Sturgess has already picked up the message."

"When?" I asked.

She was still suspicious, so I gave her my ID.

"Someone picked it up about twenty minutes ago," she said.

I scribbled on a piece of paper. "Would you leave this for Mr. Norman Tier, please?"

I watched the cubbyhole she put the message in—310. I went to the washroom, checked the Beretta, then grabbed an elevator to the third floor. There was a Mountie outside 310; the long gold stripe down the pantleg was ramrod straight. I only got a glimpse as I walked past, but it was enough. Norman Tier was being photographed from every possible angle, the flash bulbs popping off like little bombs.

My hands were shaking. At three-seventeen I rang Washington. They already knew about Tier. They would.

"It was a great shock," Hoskins said.

"Yes," I said. "It *was*." I couldn't get the laughing Tier at the hotel entrance out of my mind. Now I knew what was so strange about it all. He'd been terrified.

"Now I guess we'll never know why the opposition sent him up there," continued Hoskins.

I hadn't really been listening. "What? What are you talking about? Who sent him up here?"

"He was a spy."

"*What?*"

"You mean you didn't . . ." began Hoskins. "He was KGB, Sturgess."

"What the hell are you talking about, Hoskins? He tried to tip me that someone . . ."

"All part of his cover. Our men tried to be civilized with him about it, but—well, that's what happens when you want to play rough. We can play that game too."

"Who told you he was KGB?"

"Dr. Roth. Why?"

"Listen, Hoskins," I said, barely controlling my temper, "what in hell would a KGB man want with a solar power station setup?"

"What would a KGB man want with anything, Sturgess?" he replied ingenuously. "They're so suspicious, they'd investigate the United Appeal. They'll check anything out. You might as well come home now. Anyway, you've heard the good news, I expect? About the program?"

Before I could answer, "No," he went on.

"Latest poll shows support for SPS is growing. Everything looks smooth."

Oh, it was smooth all right. I watched them take Tier out.

"American Tourist Suicides." It was a two-inch column in the evening edition of the Vancouver *Sun*—page 8. That was smooth too. Those bastards can smooth anything, I told myself. Trouble was, I didn't know who those bastards were. Besides, if Tier was KGB, they weren't bastards. Were they?

I called home to make sure Jenny was okay, and reserved a seat on the flight out to Washington next morning. Then I tried to sleep. The early morning flight from Chicago had zonked me. But it was hopeless of course. You can't sleep after you've been shaken up like that. Seeing him sprawled out on the bloodied green carpet like a castaway desperately clawing toward some safe, warm shore, I got to thinking about his family. He hadn't said much about them. It made me feel ashamed and selfish, as you do when people you've worked with die unexpectedly and you realize just how little you really knew about them. I think he'd said something about his mother still living in Springfield or somewhere like that. But I wasn't awake so much because I felt guilty about not paying attention to what he'd said or hadn't said in the past. What bothered me was that I couldn't put the pieces together. I guess nothing in life ever really adds up to a neat mosaic—there's always the odd piece of ceramic chipped and missing here and there from neglect, wear and tear, and from plain accident. But you do crave a minimal sense of order, some kind of discernible pattern. But here I couldn't find it, not a damn thing seemed to mesh.

If Tier was KGB, why would he tip me off about anything? It didn't make sense. No, he couldn't be KGB—"absolutely not, old son," as my LSE tutor used to say. But then, if he wasn't KGB, who was he in trouble with? "We're in deep shit," Tier had said. "*We're*"? That brought me up with a start and unconsciously I reached for cigarettes though I'd given up smoking long ago. If he wasn't KGB who was he in trouble with? The killing, as the newspaper's report showed, was obviously covered up. Did that mean the killing was official? But why would the U. S. Government shoot one of its own—unless he was on to something that someone else didn't want the U. S. Government to know about? What could it—

I snapped my fingers. I'd forgotten Dermit being whisked off in the big, black, shiny car. Ralph Stein's computer printout at the CIA had told me it was a car belonging to Sudley Steel. Just the kind of outfit that stood to make millions—billions—on the SPS contracts that would be awarded if the program was approved. And Hoskins had just finished telling me the SPS looked a sure thing. The contractors would be close to a windfall, but if Tier, whoever he was, had uncovered some kind of kickback scheme, or some substandard supplying operation, those same contractors wouldn't only miss out on the windfall profits. They'd lose their shirts and a few of them would be watching the SPS launch through prison bars. I remembered the massive contract kickback-fraud scheme that had spread through the General Accounting Office during the Carter administration. My time in Seattle came flooding back.

And the torn photo of Jenny that had scared me into getting FBI protection for her. It all smelled of mob tactics, of mob influence or control in some of the big companies that would be supplying the million and one parts required for such a huge operation as the SPS. The pieces looked as if they were coming together. I recalled that Sudley Steel was one of the biggest manufacturers of aerospace metals in the country. So, I thought, it wasn't just the U. S. Government involved in Tier's death, it was someone mixed up with the industries that stood to gain from the whole solar power station enterprise. I didn't know it then but I was only half right, and half right isn't right enough—not when you've seen one half of "*We're* in deep shit" dead on the floor.

The knock on my door almost sent my heart crashing through my chest. "Yes?" The chain was on.

"Bellboy. I've got a confidential message for you, sir. From a"—there was a pause—"a Miss Sorn—Sarn."

I opened the door, holding the Beretta in my bathrobe pocket, but relaxed when I saw it actually was a bellboy. The name of course—Erica Sarn—was what made me so stupidly careless. I was already imagining the message . . . she would be sorry she'd overreacted in the plane and would like to see me—if I still wanted to see her. Certainly I wanted . . .

It all happened as I reached behind me toward the ashtray where I habitually kept change for tips. And it all happened at once. I smelled the overpowering garlic from the doorway, saw the message indicator light on the phone was off. There was *no* message waiting for me. I'd been had. I swung around, glimpsed the silver flash of knife, and fired from my pocket. The Beretta's crack echoed like a stock whip. I heard a tinkle of glass somewhere and smelled cordite. He was gone—fleeing down the hallway. Still inside my room I slammed the door shut, staring down dimwittedly at the great black singed hole in my bathrobe, then up at the splintered glass twinkling like frost in the semidarkened bathroom. Some marksman. My hand was trembling like an aspen leaf. Oh, I know I should have dashed out after him. I might have got him with the second shot, but I didn't go. I was thinking of Jenny. I'd retire.

I'd get a second mortgage on the house and take out a pizza franchise, a chicken franchise, anything but this!

When I calmed down I knew I'd just had an attack of funk. And the reason I wouldn't get out, wouldn't give up my job, was very simple. I couldn't. I'd have to see it through, whatever *it* was, because someone thought I knew more than I did and they weren't going to rest until I was out of the game. Besides, I don't like people who try to kill me. Right then, a crowd spilling in the hallway and police being summoned and my thinking how in New York or Washington everyone would have stayed inside their rooms, I could see my old LSE tutor again, stuffing his pipe and looking out on the pneumonic gray London overcast, proclaiming that we had a choice between two worlds. We could live either in Rousseau's country and believe that man was basically good, or in Hobbes's, where the life of man was "solitary, poor, nasty, brutish, and short." I know I was thinking about this because around five, when the police arrived and asked my name, I replied, "Harry Hobbes."

"Says Sturgess here." The cop was holding up my ID. "You'd better come downtown with us."

"We don't like people carrying around shooters up here do we, Constable?"

"No, sir."

They could have been Americans interrogating me but for "shooters" and "constable." The "constable" bit would have been enough to identify him as a Canuck, but "shooters" told me that the plainclothes gent was an import from Whitehall 1212, which is a quaint way of saying New Scotland Yard, the glass and steel monolith on Victoria Street in Merry Olde. All of which told me in turn that I was being questioned by a Brit, Special Branch, posing as a Canadian. Which meant that somebody besides the Canadians was concerned over my one-shot gunfight in the hotel. What had Sutherland said—the British and Canadians are highly advanced in microwave reception and "plug-in" techniques. Well someone in London was plugged in, watching over British interests. After all, you don't lend expertise to people who can't protect it from snoopy investigators, whether they be called Tier or Sturgess.

I'd moved from shock to anger. I should have followed that creep in the hotel and emptied the whole magazine into him. If only I hadn't missed. Dapper would have been disgusted, but then you don't practice on the range in bathrobes. Still, it was rotten aiming. I've cursed myself ever since, because if I'd hit him I could have saved a lot of people a lot of trouble. Some of them might still be alive.

"What about this shooter then, Hobbes?"

"Sturgess," mumbled the constable.

"Well," I said, confidently and cheekily, "I understand you don't like shooters in Victoria Street, Inspector, but you're on different turf here and if I hadn't had one by now I'd be bloody mince. 'Ground round' to you," I smiled at the Canadian. Inspector West, or whoever he was, grunted, not bothering to contradict me.

"Point is, you should have got a permit. Just as tough here on that you know. Not in the O.K. Corral up here."

I didn't respond. Let him do the work. He asked the constable to get us tea. "Look, Hobbes—er, Sturgess. Problem is we have the press nosing around. Managed to squash that nasty little bit last night but some reporter for the *Daily Sun* . . ."

"Vancouver *Sun*," I interrupted.

"Yes—well, he's got on to this business of yours last night. Now it's all getting a bit sticky, I'm afraid. Get my drift?"

"No." I had enough questions of my own, and being almost carved up by bellboys entitles you to a few answers.

"Your consulate man's been in contact with us."

Hoskins is quick, I thought, I'll give him that.

"In fact he should be here any minute."

"That's nice."

"Point is, Washington doesn't want you exposed to any more danger."

"That's nice." He knew that I knew he didn't believe a word of what he was telling me. I was tired of being front-row pawn on the chessboard. It was time I was promoted to bishop.

"How should I put it?" continued Inspector West.

"Honestly," I said.

He looked at me for what seemed a long time but was only really seconds. He was obviously weighing the official line against his policeman's intuition—what Whitehall had told his boss to tell him to tell the Canadians. He nodded his head, and I knew that intuition had won on a technicality. Maybe my placing him helped, gave him the impression that I couldn't be fooled or rather that I was tired of being fooled and that a suspicious fool was more dangerous than someone who knew the truth.

"All right, Hobbes . . ."

"Sturgess."

"All right, Sturgess. I'll level with you."

"Level? Now we really have breached the Atlantic."

"Fact of the matter is we've got some rather awkward business going on this side of the border. It's something to do with the SPS thing. It's why that chap tried to knife you."

"And killed Tier?"

"Afraid I can't say what it is."

"You mean," I said, "that Norman Tier got onto a massive kickback scheme and if it gets out there'll be a taxpayers' revolt from here to Florida?"

"Don't know. *Honestly* don't know what it is." I looked at him and believed him. We were both just players on northern ice and the managers were rugged up elsewhere. "But you would tell me if you knew?"

"No. But there's something you can tell me, Hobbes."

"Go on."

The tea and the American consul arrived together—both looking pallid. I surveyed the tall, thin consul but was listening to the inspector as he continued, asking, "You can tell me how your knife-happy friend knew to use the name of"—he looked down at the Constable's report—"the name of Miss Sarn."

The consul drew the inspector aside and began whispering. It made me feel like a criminal. "Listen, sonny," I snapped, "let's all hear the good news."

He was so startled he could hardly speak. "You're in a lot of trouble, Sturgess. You've embarrassed the United States Government."

"Jesus Christ! What the—"

"You came up here to find Mr. Tier. After that you should have returned immediately . . .. instead of this . . . stupid cowboy routine you tried to pull."

I was out of the chair. Inspector West was between the two of us. "Gentlemen! Gentlemen! We're all working for the same thing."

"What's that?" I shouted.

Tall and Thin was looking decidedly pale but maintained a stiff dignity. "To make sure Anglo-Canadian-U.S. relations are smooth for the launching of the SPS program. A sensationalist press could sour it before it got off the ground."

I gulped at the tea so that it burned my tongue, which I suspected delighted him. I knew his type, Princeton, Yale—used to mow Dean Acheson's lawn and had about as much tact as a Sherman tank. And him going on about smoothing relations!

"We'd like you to go home," he said curtly. "You and your friend."

I must have looked as mystified as I felt.

"Miss Sarn," added the Inspector. "The name you so willingly opened the door for."

I sipped the tea. Another little piece of the puzzle suddenly seemed to drop into place.

"She is your friend?" asked the consul.

"Yes," I said, almost absentmindedly, not really thinking about his question but about the puzzle. The constable opened the door and Erica Sarn entered as unexpected and as beautiful as ever. But the voice was deep freeze. "We are not friends," she said calmly. "We are—"

"Acquaintances?" I proffered.

"If you like."

"I like," I said. "But I sure as hell don't like these silly goddamn testing games." I was talking directly to Tall and Thin.

"You've been misleading us," he said, obviously referring to my calling Erica a friend.

"You've been annoying me," I snarled. "Instead of helping

me with this mess you've done nothing but get in my way. You're the U.S. consul, man, not the district attorney. Furthermore I have diplomatic-passport status, and if you don't get your ass into gear and start answering a few questions of mine, I'm personally going to nail your hide to the State Department door."

He smiled so maliciously that he would have beaten old Gort by a length. "My instructions come directly from the White House. Mr. Hoskins requests your return immediately before you draw any more attention to yourself. Here are your tickets. Change at Toronto."

I turned on him. "Listen, pretzel, I've nudged onto something up here that someone doesn't want out. Now I've been ordered home. So I'll go. But I'm not going to toe the line until I get an explanation."

"You'll get one," he said.

"When?"

"In Washington. I appreciate how you feel, Sturgess. If I had my way . . ."

"*Your* way? You'd eat shit if you were told. You haven't got a way. You're a machine. A State Department machine."

"No, I wouldn't eat shit if I was told. And neither would you. And I respect you for that. But you'll return to Washington the same as I would. There's a little of the machine in both of us, Sturgess."

Damn him! He'd taken the wind clear out of my sails. He was being very fair at the wrong time. I wanted to punch him right in the eye.

"I still don't know where I fit into all of this," said Erica, undeterred by the flash of tempers. "I'm dragged out of my hotel for no apparent reason—"

"You were dragged out because someone tried to knife me and used your name to get me to open the door."

"Why did you open it?" she asked, looking like something out of *Vogue*—only live.

"Because I'm a fool," I said. It had just the right amount of self-pity and hidden flattery to make her blush. "He said he had a message from you."

"Yes," said Scotland Yard. "But how did he know you knew one another?"

I lifted the cup again. Tea can get me through just about anything.

"Who *is* he?" continued the inspector.

I took another sip. "I don't know. But he must have been on the same flight as we were coming up."

"Why?"

"Because that's the only place outside the White House that we've been together." Erica shifted uneasily at "been together."

"And," I said, "he has a passion for garlic."

"How do you know that?" Scotland Yard was actually getting quite excited.

"Just after we landed someone bumped into me. Slipped this to me." I showed them the photo of Jenny. "My daughter."

Tall and Thin made a face at whoever had done it. I was starting to like him. "Whoever it was," I said, "reeked of garlic. And the knife-man reeked of garlic. Could be sheer coincidence, of course, but I'd say the odds were even."

Scotland Yard nodded in agreement. "It's not much, but it's something. We've nicked them on less."

"Who's them?" I asked quickly.

"Ah—them? Just an expression."

"KGB?"

He recovered very well. "KGB, ABC . . . whoever. All the nasties."

Tall and Thin cut in, looking at his watch. "It's already six. You and Miss Sarn have only forty minutes to catch that plane."

"I don't see why . . ." she began.

Tall and Thin smiled. He could be gracious if he tried, and now he was trying. "You weren't up here on holidays, Miss Sarn. We know that. I think even Mr. Sturgess knew that. You were sent up by Dr. Roth—to make sure there were no hitches in the administrative setup for the Canadian rectenna. We've told Dr. Roth that the consulate is handling all liaison. And from now on all visitors must have clearance through us.

This knife business is a case in point. The consulate will keep everything under control."

"So I see," she said. "One man's dead and now"—she looked at me—"and now a near knifing. I'd hardly say it's under control."

"If Mr. Sturgess had not come there would not have been any 'near knifing.' No offense, Sturgess."

"In any case," added Scotland Yard, "it's really an internal matter for the Canadians."

I was about to ask him what he was doing here then, but I was too tired. I'd had enough for one day and so had Erica. She looked around at all of us and dropped her shoulders in exasperation. We left shortly after in a long, shiny government limousine. "No," said the consul, the Beretta would have to stay behind. I'd already shot one shaving mirror to death.

We took off in a gray soup. Not even the tops of the North Shore mountains were visible. I felt like someone who'd been given the strap and sent home. So did Erica Sarn. That, at least, was something we could share.

"What's going on?" she asked.

I told her what I thought—that while we'd both come up to make sure everything was going smoothly—she for Roth, me for the White House—we'd unwittingly walked into something messy which I thought had something to do with one of the largest contractors. Tier's discovery of kickbacks, or whatever, had got him killed and I'd almost been killed for the same reason.

"Jesus!" Suddenly I was cold and clammy all over.

"What? What is it?"

I'd startled her and the old lady across the aisle who peered over at us.

"It's all right," I answered quickly. "It's all right." But it wasn't. It was so obvious I cursed myself for not having seen it earlier. "They," as Inspector West had called them, had sent a man to kill me. He'd missed. Why wouldn't he try again? He didn't know that I didn't know what exactly was going on. As far as "they" knew, whoever "they" were, it was enough that

I'd talked to Tier. Ten seconds, ten minutes, ten hours—no matter how long I'd talked to him, I was marked.

The lights were going down for the movie. If Bellboy wasn't still on my tail—on this plane—I was Idi Amin. I turned to Erica. "I'm sorry I've involved you." She was about to answer but I was too wound up to stop. "If that creep hadn't seen us together on the way up he'd never have known to use your name. I should have thought," I raced on, "before I opened the door. Then there wouldn't have been any police and you'd be out of it. Still safe in Vancouver. But," I was looking anxiously around the aircraft, "I had to open the door. I thought you might be in some kind of trouble."

I hadn't said it to make points. It was the truth, but often when you're not trying, you strike. She touched my arm softly and said very quietly, "Thank you, Harry." It was the best and sexiest thing anyone had done to me in years. In *years*. I could smell her sweet breath. The eye contact sealed it. It's hard to explain, but at that second I was almost certain we'd make love together. It was as quick and unexpected as it seemed destined. But then, I'd been just as certain I'd win a lottery. I was still buying tickets.

"I'm glad you weren't hurt," she added, her hand still squeezing my arm.

"So am I." I felt sixteen and tongue-tied.

"Relax," she said. "It's over now."

Everything was in darkness for the movie. I whispered, "My God . . . They saw me with you *after* Norman Tier was killed, not only on our way to Vancouver."

She didn't understand. "They're watching us now," I explained. "They'll think that whatever Norman Tier told me I'll tell you."

"Why would they . . ."

"Because these people don't take chances."

The first scene of the movie was a jungle dusk—parrots shrilly screeching and things sliding into river ooze. "Look," I tried to reassure her. "I don't think they'll try anything on the plane. If anything happened on board the police could hold everyone at Toronto Airport. When we change flights, at Toronto, or after we land at National in Washington, that's when they . . ." In the movie, dusk had passed into night. "Erica," I said softly.

"Yes?"

"Have you got anything sharp? Very sharp?"

"A hatpin," she answered. "It's my antimugger device. Happily I've never had to . . ."

"Can I borrow it?"

"As long as you give it back." She laughed uneasily. I couldn't quite muster a witty response. All I could think of was the old ad, the one about the freshest mouth in town. There was nothing fresh about the mouth I was thinking of. It stank of garlic.

CHAPTER 15

At Toronto I was so agitated as we caught the shuttle bus between terminals that Erica asked me if I was feeling all right.

"Yes," I said, not wanting to alarm her further. Then I added, "No, I'm not all right," deciding to share my fright. Besides, it was better for her to be on guard. We would both stand a better chance. In the international building, or rather the great, long concrete barn that passes for a building, we seemed to walk miles. I was passing the W. H. Smith bookshop and caught a glimpse of the title *Modern Russia.* Visions of Ivan the Terrible popped into my mind and I thought of earlier conversations with Norman Tier. Was he KGB?

As we threaded our way through a long train of Japanese tourists, I saw the black-blue blur coming toward us on the blue carpet. I grabbed Erica's arm, shoved her behind me, and reached for the long pin in my pocket. Nothing. Just someone dashing for Customs. Some Japanese women were giggling. Erica took a few seconds to collect herself. "Why—why don't we just ask for a police escort?"

"Sure," I said. "I'll go up to a Mountie—'Excuse me, sir, but I think there's a man after us with a knife. I'm a U.S. official and I'd like protection. What does he look like? Oh, I don't know, about medium height, about medium width . . . oh, yes, and he's very big on garlic.' "

Flight 108 to Washington was rough and all they served were boxed snacks armed with those mysterious sandwiches that are a kind of hybrid between chicken and tuna. As we bumped through a flock of puffy white cumulus at ten thousand feet, my nerves were shot. I was personally holding the pilot responsible for every bounce. I gave up on the sandwich and thought of writing to the Coca-Cola Company that when you order Coke you get some tacky black stuff with no guts in it. Is it sick Coke or another brand masquerading? I didn't even like the way Erica had done her hair up for the trip, into a kind of bun that kept fraying at the edges. "I like your hair down," I said. "You should wear it down."

"What's wrong with it up?"

"Those fluffy pieces. I don't like them."

"I'll jump out of the plane."

"Sorry. I'm uptight."

"Oh, really?" She touched my arm again. "So am I . . ."

The stewardess bent down. I recoiled as my left hand went for the pin. She stepped back smartly into the aisle. "Every . . . everything satisfactory?" she asked.

"Great," I said. "Everything's marvelous. Just great."

"You're right, Harry." It was Erica.

"What?" I snapped.

"You're right. I just haven't had as long as you to think about it. But I see now . . . If he's seen us and—"

"Exactly," I said. "God, I wish I had that Beretta. I'm a knee-jerk liberal—civil rights—busing—'I have a dream'—nonviolence—the Peace Corps—but God, I wish I had a Beretta. A very big Beretta! The biggest Beretta in the world!" The joking helped, as it always does when you're in trouble, for about five minutes, and then I was wondering if my will was properly made out. I'd always meant to add a codicil about leaving something for Mrs. Reardon.

Once we were on the ground at National, walking through the Allegheny Airlines section, it suddenly occurred to me that for some reason, "*they*" might have decided not to bother about me after all. Maybe they knew Tier hadn't really told me anything? "Sure," I heard a little voice in the back room say, "and maybe birds don't fly." Right then I smelled the garlic. I pushed Erica away from me, whirled, and tore out the dagger-long hatpin. An old Italian lady screamed, and two sailors had me—one by the pin arm and the other driving his fist into my stomach. I crumpled like a paper bag, silent, winded, unable even to murmur. The next second there was a lot of running and then I was looking into a shiny black tunnel, the finely oiled barrel of a Smith & Wesson .38. If Airport Security had heard about the Miranda decision they didn't care. They didn't read any little card out to me telling me my rights. All I heard was a sweet southern voice, "Now you just move, ole buddy, and I'll blow your head off."

"I won't move," I gasped. "But can I tell my fiancée to contact the White House?"

"You just sit still," said the guard. But Erica had gotten the message and was already quickly walking toward the exit. When the police arrived they took me into the tiny interrogation room.

"What's your name?" the officer repeated.

"Hobbes," I said. "Harry Hobbes."

"It says your name's Sturgess in your wallet."

"Yes, but I'm thinking of changing my name."

"He's nuts."

"You're allowed one phone call."

"Don't bother," I said confidently. "My friends'll be here soon."

"Who are your friends?"

It struck me that that was a very good question.

July. Hot weather, cold feelings. That's what Washington was like when I returned to work a few days later. The temperature was high, in the eighties, so was the humidity, and they hung about like unwanted relatives. Your clothes stuck to you like Saran Wrap. Jenny loved the weather, spending half her time under the hose. She'd been born in Maryland, during one of my training stints in Washington, and liked the Rockville summer. I didn't. I'd never become used to people who thought 80 percent humidity and ninety degrees could be pleasant. Another thing I hadn't got used to and still haven't is people giving me the cold shoulder as if somehow I'd disgraced the corps. A few of them thought it funny, farfetched—people often do when they're not involved. After several uneventful weeks, the FBI watch over Jenny was ended. Meanwhile no one except the President and Hoskins seemed very worried about my almost getting killed. Old Mother Gort appeared downright disappointed. What they objected to, you see, was the close shave I could have had with the press. They weren't concerned that the press could verbally have cut my throat if they'd sniffed out the story, but they were angry because I'd almost embarrassed the President and, by extension, the whole White House staff. "Want to watch that Sturgess," I heard in the cafeteria. "He's a regular Cyrano de Bergerac."

"Yeah. Hatpin Harry!"

It was no good telling them that it's never as they imagine it in the field when you're on your own without all the little conveniences and security you have at the White House. A hatpin was the only weapon I had available. It's like a football player trying to explain a foolish-looking move to the armchair expert who knows all the right passes except that he wasn't there. "But why didn't you . . ." or "You should have . . ." After a few days of that I was ready to give them a hatpin where hatpins don't belong. Anyway, the truth is I was feeling pretty down. I felt as if I'd been unceremoniously drawn out of some weird carnival tent and told to forget all about someone having tried to murder me.

I hadn't forgotten, and the day after I'd returned I bought myself a little convenience, a Beretta, 9mm, a twin to the one I had to leave behind with Tall and Thin. It would do nicely until they condescended to reissue me with the regulation .38.

Within two days the ribbing stopped and things suddenly got worse. No one, except the President and occasionally Hoskins, would talk to me. Being "sent to Coventry," as we called it in England, or as the West Pointers call it, being given "the silence," by the most gregarious people on earth isn't pleasant. It seemed that a bit of the kidding had almost spilled over the edge of the White House into the public pool, and Hoskins, paranoid that the press would get onto it and upset the final push for the SPS bill, let it be known to the White House staff that I was on the diseased species list. They kept me busy collating and checking the possible evironmental impact of emissions from Japanese motorcycles. Great stuff—I just about had to eat coffee grounds to keep me awake, and on top of it all, Jenny was having trouble with her teeth—fixed retainer—crying about looking ugly—me telling her she wasn't and how it would pay off in the long run and wondering how I'd pay the orthodontist bill. He must have been building a B-52 in his back yard to charge those prices.

Apart from the dentist bills, and the growing conviction that I wouldn't get high enough security clearance to work anywhere else, the thing that made me stay on and got me through the cold-shoulder treatment was the President. Despite the urging from others not to see me, he wouldn't abandon me and send me back to EPA in disgrace. After I'd returned from Vancouver he'd spoken to me for ten minutes, that's all, but he'd told Hoskins that I'd simply been caught up in the mess—which I had—and that it wasn't my fault. In fact, he said, it was because I was bright enough to smell a rat that he'd O.K.'d the trip in the first place. I was to stay on. No more SPS stuff, "wasn't necessary" now, but I was to stay on. I appreciated that and realized, ungrateful though it may sound, that Sutherland was a consummate politician as well as compassionate. He understood that by standing by me through rough weather he'd have my loyalty for life. In any case I was grateful, and to be truthful I was relieved to be off the SPS business. I looked forward to not having to bother with it again. The trouble was, would it bother me? And, underneath it all, was the President really keeping me around because it was still bothering him?

CHAPTER 16

Three days before the House vote on the SPS the leak at Macphearson nuclear plant in California increased in intensity. Another two hundred miles had to be evacuated and another six deaths were reported. Meanwhile Roth and his crew were touting the SPS as being infinitely safer and more promising than nuclear energy. What was to have been a close vote, or a marginal win at best, suddenly became a landslide victory for Bill 457: 242 to 193. The U.S.–Anglo-Canadian venture was jointly announced with Roth, not surprisingly, named SPS director, headquartered in Vancouver.

I had to admit that even though I hadn't supported the program originally, when I saw the orange-red roar of the initial launching of the giant space freighter on TV from the Cape on August 24 and watched the silent, dreamlike quality of its entry into lower earth orbit, I was in awe of all the scientific imagination and technical skill that had made it possible. From LEO they showed the prefabricated parts of the satellite which were already being projected, via shuttle, into the higher geosynchronous orbit. The awe became sheer excitement when, a week later, on re-entry for yet another load, the crimson river of sparks streaming from the heat shield of the

HLLV was visible in the early night sky over the eastern United States. Soon, Sutherland would have his orbiting flag.

Impressive too were the square black acres of capacitor banks—skyscrapers gliding through space—which would store up the solar energy before transmission. The smaller blocks, which together made up the huge banks, were interlocked by multilimbed, canister-shaped SYNCOMPs* with childlike ease, the variously colored identification lights contrasting dramatically against the frost-starred heavens of the Milky Way. Then shots from a dozen or so of the orbiting Fotsats delivered glorious color closeups of the five virginal white CONLOC† cylinders, each two hundred feet long and fifty feet wide. Silently, looking for all the world like enormous tubes of toothpaste squeezing their contents through a multinozzled head, they extruded six parallel rows of six-inch-diameter high-tensile metal rods at the rate of twenty feet per minute. A SYNCOMP then halted the extrusion from one tube even as another continued pushing out the building rods. From this continuous production line, the rods, looking, on the screen, like refills for mechanical pencils, were quickly formed into a plane, as bars in a giant grill, and in so doing formed the rib scaffolding for the whole array of SPS mirrors. It was a mechanic's dream watching the arrays unfold, reminding me of my schooldays, of neatly folding a sheet of paper into accordionlike layers so that, compressed, the sheet made up a rectangle a tenth of its original length and width. In this case the mirrored layers, rather than paper, were concertinaed by plastic hinges so that when the robots—darting about like luminescent fireflies—hovered, lowered their magnetic probosces onto the lids of the array boxes, and lifted them off, the compressed layers of mirrors, together with the microthin wafers of foam insulation between them, magically unfolded, thus forming the great sheets of solar cells, forever turned to the sun, flashing with the brilliance of a newborn star.

Then the antenna materialized—one moment a crescent of metal in space, the next, opened like a fan by the robots into a

* SYNCOMPs—Synchronized Computer Robots.
† CONLOC—Construction on Location.

huge concave dish 1.2 kilometers in diameter, ready to beam the long-awaited energy to earth. Floating off into the blue-black infinity of space, the wafers of insulation were gathered in by a busy SYNCOMP like a sheepdog working a straying flock.

I got quite a kick out of hearing Roger Mudd of NBC describing the SPS, as I had the studio model, as looking like a great "silver cross made out of two washboards." There was a followup of Roth and others telling everyone of the huge increases in power that we would now have. In the euphoria of the initial launch, including completely unexpected congratulations to the United States from the Russian Premier for having "developed an alternate energy source for all mankind," no one said much about any possible problems with the SPS. The public loved it, and after seeing the launch and assembly, who could blame them? Hoskins was the happiest I'd ever seen him. He was convinced we'd turned the corner in the energy crisis, and the President announced we could finally see the end of the oil crisis; it was not disaster but "truly a silver lining." Corny, but they loved it. What's more, they believed it. There *was* a new star above and in the White House. Oh, there were a few killjoys—desperate flags of discontent in the crowd and one dire warning by a sandaled Ph.D. about depletion of the crucial ozone layer that protects us from the dangers of unabsorbed ultraviolet rays, etc., etc. The Clean Air Society had voiced the same worry and the President and I had discussed it before his squash game so many months before. NBC picked it up, but one of Roth's cronies immediately argued that recently published measurements had shown that the ozone layer had in fact been *increasing* over the last ten years. He was right. I'd seen the results myself. Trust the only objection to be a wrong one—a recurrent irony of the energy crisis. Then Erica came on the tube.

She was stunning. The immaculate starched lab coat and clipboard made her look twice as brilliant and just as beautiful as ever. She was standing next to Roth. He was wearing a stupid polka dot bow tie again—at his age!

I studied Erica. I wanted to freeze the picture, because I'd been thinking a lot about her lately, so much that I had trouble sometimes remembering exactly what she looked like. I still didn't have the courage to face her after the airport fiasco. I mean, it wasn't exactly the picture of Harry, cool, calm and collected. I was still getting air-pollution files addressed to "Hatpin Harry." Very amusing to the morons in Dispatch, no doubt, but a little wearing on the old ego. Before I'd been sent to Coventry I even stayed away from the practice range for fear of more ribbing, until a curt memo arrived, informing me that my presence would be appreciated, "starting yesterday." In the end I was grateful because over the next month the range allowed me to work off some of the frustration. Not all of it, mind—there was too much for the range alone.

During practices I used the Beretta and the Smith & Wesson. Sergeant "Dapper" had to tell me repeatedly to relax with the breathing, but never once did he urge me to imagine that the target was someone I hated. In fact, he rather hesitantly suggested one morning—I'd been going in every day except Sundays—that I should try to be a little more "cool and dispassionate."

"Why?" I snapped. I'd had a flat tire on my way to the White House that morning and was even grumpier than usual. "I'm averaging over eighty percent," I said challengingly. "So what's the problem?"

"Oh, it's not the score," he answered politely. "Eighty percent, that's sharpshooter status. There's nothing wrong with your aim. Top class."

"Well then?" I snapped again.

"The eyes. If you don't mind me saying. They're a bit 'too quick' if you know what I mean?"

"No I don't."

"I . . ."

"Go on."

"Well, Mr. Sturgess, you know we used to have a saying in the Marines: 'Don't let the bastards get you down.'"

"Everyone has that saying."

"Guess we all need it at times."

I exhaled slowly. He patted my shoulder paternally. "First

time in the field I shit myself. Sergeant Crapper they called me. I like Dapper much better." He smiled.

"So you've heard too?"

"People talk. Even agents."

"So I've noticed," I said. "Maybe I should take up jogging. Work some of it off."

"Or a woman." He winked.

"Or both," I joined in, immediately beginning to think of Erica.

"You look a bit run down," he said. "You eat a good breakfast?"

"Whatever's defrosted," I said.

He shook his head like a missionary just arriving among cannibals. "You should start with oats," he said. "Rolled oats."

"I'm not a horse."

"Whole wheat then?"

"Can't stand it."

He stood there as if I'd just shot him between the eyes. I couldn't tell if it was mock shock or genuine disbelief. Whatever it was, I left feeling better than I had when I'd come. The shooting and the chat had been therapeutic. I bought a jogging suit, North Star runners, the lot, then rang Erica. She'd love to go out for dinner, but unfortunately she had a previous engagement. Perhaps another time?

"Yeah, sure," I said petulantly. "Okay," and then went jogging. I hated it. Halfway home I sat down feeling like a hot, wet sack. I watched morosely as the others jogged past me—the huffing, puffing beginners and the disciples with the secular Jesuit look. I felt nasty and wanted to call out that we were all going to die anyway, so what was the point? To top it off, Jenny had left the dollhouse in the doorway and I shinned myself in the dark when I went to see her. Mrs. Reardon could sense the black mood as I limped toward the shower.

"There's a message for you," she said.

"Who from?" I growled. If Jenny had spoken to her like that I would have smacked her backside, but Mrs. Reardon had seen this Sturgess mood before and odd calls had been the norm in Seattle. Her tone was polite, even kind, as she handed me the message pad.

"A man rang. No name. Said he was the man from Kodak. He wants you to call this number between midnight and one. He asked you to ring twice, hang up then dial again as he'll be working in the developing lab and he'll need a few seconds to reach the phone."

What a day, I thought to myself. What an absolutely, positively lousy day. You start off with a flat tire and end up with "the man from Kodak" playing idiot games between midnight and one. As I slumped against the wall of the shower and started to sing the love theme from Zeffirelli's version of *Romeo and Juliet* which I always sing as "What's the Bloody Use?" I reminded myself emphatically that I'd been officially taken off the SPS project. Under no circumstances would I ring Dermit back about his bloody photographs whether it was between "midnight and one" or any other time. "The man from Kodak!" I shook my head. It had to be Dermit.

He must have been standing quite close to the public telephone because he answered after the third ring.

"Mr. Sturgess?"

"Yes," I said curtly, going along by not calling him by name and trying to keep my curiosity submerged. His voice took on the forced friendliness of a salesman but underneath there was more than a hint of barely controlled panic.

"I've got your enlargements ready, Mr. Sturgess."

I was about to interject, but he was racing on, probably scared silly that I'd call him by name.

"Sorry we've taken so long. You've probably forgotten the photographs by now, but we've been busy with the summer tourist rush and we're in the new shop now. I've blown up the one of your grandmother to eight inches by ten. Really looks nice."

I hesitated for a split second. "Fine—" and added a touch of my own. "How about the birthday cake? Did it turn out?"

"Sorry—overexposed."

"I set it on automatic."

"Well, sometimes the adjustment's off."

"All right. When's your shop open?"

"Nine sharp. Don't forget we're at the new place on Fourth."

"I know. Which is the best route, straight down Constitution?"

"If you like. I usually go down the mall past the Air and Space building. Works out about the same, I guess."

"I'll pop by."

"Right. Good night."

"Good night."

He hadn't used the mail, so obviously he thought someone was intercepting it. The only other ways were to contact me in person or by phone. If he was afraid of the mail then he'd clearly be afraid to come in person. That had only left the phone. I tossed all night, trying to force myself to sleep. Instead I only dozed fitfully. The realities battling with the dreams, entwining, uncoupling, entwining, finally exhausted me; I slept for a while but woke at six in a sweat.

By eight I was on the freeway and by 8:40 A.M. I had parked in the underground lot. By 8:45 A.M. I'd walked up from the lot and was waiting discreetly a half block from the entrance to the Smithsonian Air and Space Museum. I've many faults, as we all say when we're about to proclaim a single virtue, but I am rarely, if ever, late. I like punctuality—it doesn't make for relaxed holidays, but it does keep the world running.

Dermit obviously wasn't the punctual type, and after half an hour I gave up. Already it was sweltering. I rang his apartment. No answer. I scribbled a note: "Missed you at breakfast," signed it "The Man from Agfa," drove around to the apartment, and slipped it under his door. But the door opened.

Among my favorite pieces is Pachelbel's Canon. It's one of the most beautifully soothing compositions I know and it was coming from Dermit's radio. He surveyed me from the deep, soft recliner like an old wino without a care in the world. I was surprised that beneath the superficial layer of brown he was going bald. On top of his head was an errant piece of down from a pillow. "I've come for Grandma's picture," I growled.

I know the door should have told me the whole story, but the music from the radio had created the illusion of normality and helped make Dermit seem asleep. Under a fallen lock of dark hair, so wet that it looked black not brown, there was a very small, very neat hole—as if a quarter inch drill had been pushed through—and a few more feathers from the ruptured pillow nearby that had been used as the silencer. The mess, the dark red pulp and matted hair with splintered bone was spilling out behind him, running down the neck, catching in his collar. Two things were beyond me: why he looked so well, but I guessed it had been too quick, perhaps by someone he'd known and not even suspected. The second thing that puzzled me was why Dermit, who was clearly frightened, hadn't been prepared to spend a few extra dollars to get an auxiliary cylinder dead-bolt lock on the door. It wouldn't have been breakproof or even much help without a reinforced channel, but it would have stood up longer, perhaps long enough to save his life.

I looked behind the door. The broken chain told me that it was very probably someone he hadn't known and that the radio had been used to calm the neighbors after they'd heard the chain bursting off the door; the music convincing them that everything was all right—that they needn't intervene.

There must have been at least two—he'd have stood a chance with one.

I closed the door softly and sat down opposite Dermit. I wasn't going to panic this time. As I pondered what to do I noticed that a thin trickle of liquid was oozing from the neat bullet hole, running down the side of his nose, disappearing into the bush of beard and re-emerging from the jungle to drip slowly onto his shirt front. I got up laboriously, feeling very tired and picking up my smart-guy note. Tearing it up, I walked into the toilet to flush it away. The bathroom tap was dripping and in the silence it sounded like a drum. I turned to go but suddenly swiveled and remained, vomiting and dry-retching for the next few minutes. The crash courses at Langley hadn't made me immune to the sight, and particularly the *smell*, of corpses. Dermit, just as they warned us at the "farm's" boot camp, had defecated.

It took some doing, but I made myself stay. You can't protect yourself if you don't know who the enemy is. I donned a pair of rubber gloves that Dermit had kept by the toilet plunger and looked for the photos, first diligently searching the bedroom drawers, then the other two rooms down the hallway, one a kind of storage room and the other a spare, apparently unused, bedroom. Whoever had done it before me had been very good. Nothing was strewn about for obvious fear of covering up something else that might be important. It had all been very systematic and the only telltale sign was a couple of tiny feathers that had obviously floated in from the exploded pillow onto the open drawers after Dermit had been shot and they'd searched the big six-room apartment. A small family photo album was resting on some magazines on top of the coffee table by the recliner. Cunning, I thought, very cunning, Dermit. The most obvious and so the least obvious to the deviously trained mind. I scrutinized all the photos. Dermit as a baby, a bewildered but happy grin, ten years old with the inscription "The budding knight" over the photo. Dermit was dressed up as a knight of King Arthur's court—the battle helmet made out of a shoe box, the shield a garbage-can lid with a chalked eagle drawn on it and the lance an old mop handle. Swimming-club photos, holidays in Vermont with the forest behind burning with the colors of autumn, one photo of him standing very stiffly and very much a proud college graduate between proud working-class parents. How little the world knows about us till we are dead. I said a prayer.

There was a bump. I whirled, my hand darting for the .38. But it was only Dermit's right foot, which had slid off the recliner's foot rest. My heart was still bolting, there were beads of perspiration on my forehead from the fright, but one thing interested me. The Smith & Wesson was very still in my hand. Not a shake and I was aware that I'd only half exhaled, holding the remainder of my breath to steady the diaphragm. I was ready.

Instantly I felt better. I closed the album and examined the few remaining framed photos scattered about the apartment, opened them up, but there was nothing hidden as I'd first suspected.

The cramped study had a coziness unlike the rest of the apartment. Here was where the real Dermit had lived. It was more casual and more intriguing than any other room. I glanced at the books, Solzhenitsyn to a Playboy calendar. I lingered over Miss July for a few seconds then moved on to the desk. A few reports from his department but nothing about SPS or carcinogenic properties of microwaves or anything like it—just dull, routine bureaucratic files and a few of Dermit's amateurish attempts at poetry, and a letter:

> Dear Mom,
>
> Sorry I haven't written earlier but as usual have been very busy lately. Glad to hear Lisa's getting better. I know everyone says, "It's going around," but something always is.

There was no more to the letter. I looked at the date, August 20, a week ago. You don't write home when you're down or uptight. And that suggested to me that Dermit had found out within the last week whatever had gotten him killed. Either they'd found it or were still looking. The latter possibility alarmed me the most. If they'd been shadowing him then they would know about the phone booth he'd used and while it was unlikely that they could have recorded his initial message to Mrs. Reardon they could have bugged it in a couple of seconds with a small harmonica and been ready when he used the booth again on my return call. My apprehension became a low groan when I remembered he had my name in his red address book. The book was gone. In any case, even if they hadn't tapped the public phone, my recent, albeit short-lived, official connection with the SPS program would put me at the top of the list. Still using the gloves I rang Mrs. Reardon to make sure Jenny was safe.

"She's at her swimming class, Mr. Sturgess."

"Pick her up. Tell them she's wanted at home urgently."

"But I . . ." It was the one thing she didn't like doing—pulling Jenny out of classes.

"Please, Mrs. Reardon."

On the wall of the study was the Desiderata: "Go placidly . . ."

I flicked through several copies of handwritten, rather amateurish attempts at poetry that were lying scattered around the desk. "Ode to Nantucket," not very good I thought, clumsy rhyme and far too sentimental, the kind of stuff they sell in little gift stores and cover with pictures of lovers strolling hand in hand, walking through endless sunsets. The last poem was "S. S. Egruts."

It's no wonder they'd missed it. Of course everyone who can read or write in this world knows what his or her name looks like when it's spelled backward, but it's a thing you don't think about as far as other people's names are concerned. Dermit had thought about it. It had been his insurance. I sat down and read:

S. S. Egruts

Roaring seas
Invade
Venting rage
Each straining coolie down below
Races, stoking—while up above
Pretty ladies gather,
Organizing games en route
Running for the capital of liberty, where sphinx-like
The lions of Union lie. Waiting.

Unlike some poems I'd studied in English 100, I knew that this one definitely *had* a message. It was addressed to me, and it wouldn't have been written had Dermit not known he was in danger. Whatever else, young Dermit had had guts. He obviously hadn't known who his pursuers were, otherwise I suspected he would have told the police. But in the century of the paranoid he no doubt believed, correctly, that his story, without an identifiable face to put with it, would have been regarded as just another crazy invention by a freaky environmentalist with a beard.

The second bump made me start and straightaway I walked out and looked at Dermit's other foot. It was still on the recliner. Probably from the room above. In any case the noise hurried me up. I stuck the poem into my vest pocket, checked for his wallet—it was gone—and walked toward the door.

You know that feeling, it can hit when you're in a crowded restaurant or in open parkland: you're sure someone's watching you. You don't see them, you just feel them. I looked slowly around the apartment, down its hallway and back into the study. I pulled out the .38 and walked softly toward the bedroom. I'd checked it earlier, the drawers and underneath the bed but maybe—. I stood braced, my back flat against the wall, gun high, exhaled half my breath and went in wide. In a quarter second the .38 arced to cover the area behind the door, then swept to the closet. Nobody! I checked the bathroom again, the storage room and the spare room. Nothing.

Maybe it was just my nerves. Again the adrenalin was pumping, but again the gun was steady, ready, in my hand. I slapped it back into the Menning waist holster and touch-opened the front door. I'd gone about three feet outside the apartment when I noticed the feathers—three or four of them were stuck to the hall rug. They could have been there when I arrived but they hadn't been and one was still falling! I stood rigid, my ears straining for the slightest sound. The elevator doors closed. I ran like crazy downstairs. The doors slid open. No one!

"Excuse me," I said to the doorman, rudely covering my face with a Kleenex. "Did you see anyone coming out of here—" I'd started so I figured I might as well finish. "Did you see anyone come out of here covered . . . I mean, with feathers on them?"

In New York he wouldn't have batted an eyelid, but Washingtonians can still be nonplussed.

"Feathers?"

"Yes." I blew into the Kleenex.

"*Feathers?*"

"Yes."

"Well," he began, rubbing his chin thoughtfully with a growing smirk on his face, "we've got a couple of turkeys living here."

I rang the police from the phone near the Smithsonian, told them about Dermit, didn't give my name—not after the Vancouver debacle—and then went into the Air and Space Museum. Maybe the poem referred to something in there, by the phone booth. It was while I was trying to work out the poem, and concentrating on the sharp, rapierlike needles of one of the early Russian Sputniks, that I was reminded of the neat hole in Dermit's head. My stomach went into a slow, chilly turn as I realized that "they" or "he" or "she" had been in the apartment all the time I was there. That's probably why the door had opened so easily and had not been properly closed—"they" hadn't left when I arrived. The vision of them moving silently from room to room as they watched me searching each room gave me a bad attack of post facto nerves. It wasn't just the hide and seek that put ice in my bladder or the knowledge that they had clearly seen me and could have killed me, though that was bad enough. What really worried me now was that they had left me alone so I might find what they couldn't. Now I had three problems to figure out: what I had found in the poem but hadn't yet deciphered, how to keep them from finding out, and third—a minor consideration to some, I expect—how to keep myself alive and well after I'd found out what I didn't yet know. I was sure of only one thing: I'd have to run this show myself. Tier was dead and now so was Dermit. Until I had a better idea as to who was who, I wasn't saying anything to anyone. The only person I could absolutely trust was Hatpin Harry.

Dermit didn't even make the six o'clock news. Instead, the story was tucked away on page 6 of the following morning's *Post*. The motive, the police spokesman said, was clearly robbery. Several burglaries had been reported in the district recently. I waited for the White House reaction. There was none. Dermit had not exactly endeared himself to the collective memory at Pennsylvania Avenue. The Ralph Nader of Clean Air, he'd had his few moments of glory on TV and in a few national dailies, vigorously, nervously opposing those he viewed as polluters, but beyond that he'd been sentenced to oblivion. I was irritated that no one at the White House had noticed his passing or had thought it important enough to comment on.

Initially I was convinced the police story was a coverup, but what else could they know? Then in a flash it occurred to me that maybe it had been a robbery after all. His wallet *was* gone. A kid, scared stiff once I'd entered, knowing he couldn't silence a shot easily with me walking about and deciding instead to play hide and seek? And the police were right, there had been several robberies in the area lately. The drawers could have been just as easily and carefully searched for money, travelers' checks, and so on, as for photos. After all, it was only that I'd gone to meet Dermit that morning that had led me to assume his death was directly connected to what he'd said on the phone about photos.

But I was still on edge. So much so that I took to wearing a gun all the time. The Beretta was perfect for my jogging suit. That night as I dutifully but resentfully laced up my trusty North Stars, I convinced myself that the connection I'd been making between whoever killed Dermit and his mention of the photos was pure speculation.

The edges of a cold front, sweeping in north of Atlanta, had pushed the temperature down from eighty-nine to seventy and it was raining solidly with lightning flashes rending the sky like great white ribbons thrown across the night.

Afterward I thanked God that I'd been by the river, because had I been in any of the "safer" streets of Rockville with their adequate lighting I don't think I would have noticed the Mustang's lights go out. But down by the river when the lights died fifty yards behind me and I could still hear the faint purr of the beautifully conditioned V-8, I suspected lovers or muggers. I moved away from the river and crossed the old dirt road, stopping beneath a large oak tree that had been silhouetted moments before in lightning. I was breathing quickly from the jogging and was sure they could hear me. One of them had shuffled into a pile of leaves down by the river and the other, closer, was still in the car, rolling slowly toward me. Now muggers seldom bother joggers because runners aren't known for carrying much cash—if any. And they weren't lovers, unless one of them liked to work out first in leaves.

I heard the faint squeak as the Mustang braked, braked again, and the ever closer sound of the engine. There was no way they could find me and they knew it. My crossing the road had blown what was to have been a surprise snatch. But suddenly tactics changed—a spotlight pierced the night. I moved quickly behind the oak. The beam penciled through the trees, stopped, darted back, momentarily froze on some strange configuration of root and brush, then moved on, slowly sweeping as the Mustang rolled forward. My right hand was sticky from running and so I transferred the Beretta to my left, wiping the perspiration off against the tracksuit. The gun felt warm and reassuring. I went down quietly on one knee, taking care that there were no twigs underfoot. In the crouch position I'd scored 91 percent the day before. My line of fire was just left of the trunk. C'mon, Pepperoni, I thought, it's time for lunch. I really wanted them to come at me.

"Over here!" a voice shouted.

The Mustang roared into life, reversed with screeching rubber, the spotlight jumping crazily like a fast bobbing mast light.

"Farther left. No—farther!"

The beam zeroed in on a stump about six feet high—two dead branches that could have been mistaken for a man's limbs. I saw another shape, a man dimly visible at the edge of the beam. I moved the Beretta in his direction, using the tree trunk as a lean.

"Sturgess!"

I felt my heart thumping. The voice came from the edge of the beam—by the river. The car was now between us. The spotlight went off.

"We've got your kid, Sturgess!"

The voice was loud but not boisterous. A clear, cheeky cockney voice.

"Where?" It's the only thing I could think of—the only thing besides moving away from the oak, crouching again, turning the Beretta toward his voice. Thank God this was something straight from the "farm" manual. For once I knew exactly what to do but I had to struggle to keep calm. "Let me see her. In front of the headlights."

I moved again. There were still no headlights. I heard the car roll forward—toward the direction of my voice. A pause. Then the voice from the darkness. "She's all right. She's in the car."

"Let me see her," and I moved again.

A rustle of leaves closer now—coming from the river side. "Tell your fat-footed friend to stay where he is," I called. The rustling stopped. "Let me see her!"

Now the beam struck out, not twenty feet to my left—where I'd spoken moments before. I could shoot out the light, but what if they had her? I couldn't risk it—not until I knew . . .

After a second the spotlight went out—defeated. A long pause. Running feet—up from the river—toward the Mustang. "All right, Sturgess. You win—this time. But you get this straight, Mate. You keep your mouf shut or we'll get her."

I exhaled slowly, held half my breath and ran forward.

"We'll get her, Sturgess. Got it? Keep your mouf shut . . ."

A flash of lightning. The car silhouetted. I pulled the trigger and kept firing, emptying the magazine toward the spot where I'd seen it. Three sounds came almost simultaneously—the crackle of windshield glass, the roar of the V-8, and screaming tires. I heard the last few shots hit the Mustang's body like hammer blows. Damp leaves swirled about my ankles as they roared past. Then they were gone and so was I—running—using every shortcut I knew.

Mrs. Reardon was watching the Muppets, nursing a big mug of tea.

"Where's Jenny?" I gasped. "Jenny! Where is she?"

"In the kitchen, Daddy. I'm drawing. You want to help?"

I collapsed into the nearest chair.

Mrs. Reardon started to pack immediately, then made a call to a close friend in Richmond from the corner phone. I had to assume my line was bugged. I wasn't going to ring Hoskins for FBI protection, or anyone else. There'd be too much explaining, and what could I tell them? Who could I identify? No one.

All I told Mrs. Reardon was that someone had tried to kill me, and that was enough for her. It wasn't true, of course. They could have simply run me over out on that lonely road. Or one shot from the car is all it would have taken. No, they'd wanted to have a chat with me, the kind you have with broken teeth and baseball bats. They'd wanted me alive. They'd figured I'd found something in Dermit's apartment. And although I wasn't taking any chances with Jenny, I knew now that if they'd really wanted Jenny, she'd been here all the time.

At the same time I didn't believe the two thugs for a second when they'd said they'd leave me alone if I kept my "mouf" shut. I knew my only chance in hell was to find out exactly what I was supposed to know already. One thing was indisputable: I could work easier knowing that Jenny and Mrs. R. were out of the line of fire.

As we readied to leave, Jenny started into me with the "why?" game. I know what the child educators say—I'd had to do an intensive course when my wife died—but right now I was too tired, too anxious to patiently explain anything like the truth. We'd be back soon. It would be a kind of holiday, I lied. I kept on lying while packing up all her drawing utensils. She had enough crayons to start a department store. I made a mental note not to spoil her, to teach her the value of things—like not *lying*. Then I had the flash.

It happened when I noticed that one of the drawings Jenny had been working on was a scribble against which she'd printed the explanatory word "TREE." But instead of printing it horizontally she'd printed the word vertically: T
R
E
E.

I took the stairs two at a time and the next second was holding the poem beneath the study light. I put my hand over it, hiding all but the vertical line formed by the first letter of each line. Reading down rather than from left to right they spelled a word: RIVERPORT.

S. S. Egruts
Roaring seas
Invade
Venting rage
Each straining coolie down below
Races, stoking—while up above
Pretty ladies gather,
Organizing games en route
Running for the capital of liberty, where sphinx-like
The lions of Union lie. Waiting.

Excitedly I grabbed the atlas, a fine layer of dust puffing up as I quickly thumbed through the index. There were sixteen Riverports in the United States from Alabama to California to Oregon and one, population 642, in Washington State. Next I went to the maps. Riverport was in the far northeast of the state, out of the dark green of the Rockies and heavy forest country, set in the irrigated desert region around Grand Coulee Dam. It was approximately ninety-six miles from the Canadian border and if you drew a straight line into Canada north across the forty-ninth parallel that separates the two countries you ended up smack in the middle of the area called the Okanagan. As I flicked off the light I had to apologize in absentia to the amateurish typist of the mystery medical report that had been sent to me. Whatever else her faults may have been I now knew she hadn't put the word "Port" into lower case after all. The letters "port" had formed the suffix of another word, River*port!*

Was this the only thing that Dermit had tried to tell me?

With Jenny asleep and the heroic Mrs. Reardon yawning, I had to work hard at concentrating on the road. I recalled the poem time and again. The two lines that radically departed from the meter structure were the last two:

Running for the capital of liberty, where sphinx-like
The lions of Union lie. Waiting.

Was this part of the message about the town? But maybe Riverport was all I needed? "Sphinx-like?" "The capital of liberty" must be Washington, but that . . . A trucker brought me out of my daze with a horn that sounded as though the *Queen Mary* were on top of me. He swore so violently I was glad Jenny was asleep. Maybe I was too protective of her. "Mrs. R.?"

"Yes?"

"You think I spoil Jenny? Come on now, no holds barred."

"No, I don't. But—"

"Yes?"

"She's a lonely little dear."

"She plays with her friends. She has a lot of friends."

"Yes."

". . . But I haven't spent enough time with her lately."

"Well . . ."

"You're right."

"You do your best, Mr. Sturgess."

"No I don't."

We didn't speak for a few moments, and then I said quietly, "I should get married again." Mrs. Reardon didn't reply, but the silence was affirmation. We changed the subject and talked about the hideaway we were heading for in Richmond, an apartment block run by a Mrs. Leern, an old friend. Mrs. R. would check in as Mrs. Dawson. No, she assured me, Mrs.

Leern wouldn't ask questions, why did I think she chose Mrs. Leern? I was suitably rebuked. I arranged a security check—similar to one we'd used once or twice in Seattle. I'd ring her and ask to speak to Sylvia. If everything was okay with Jenny the answer would be, "Sylvia's on vacation." If anything had gone wrong the answer would be, "Sylvia is ill." We drove in subdued silence for a while. "Mrs. R.," I said, "you're a gem."

I also realized she was getting too old for such terrible responsibility. "Mrs. R., you know this is far and beyond the call of duty. If you'd like to . . ."

"I'd like to be with Jenny."

It was said with the firmness of an English nanny—a tone that does not invite further discussion. So instead I started making up an excuse to give to Jenny's teacher in the event Jenny was still away at the beginning of the fall classes, barely a month away. I could do that all right, and Mrs. R. could oversee her in the interim, but I was thinking of how it would affect Jenny; the trauma of the sudden bewildering shift from her home, her school, her friends. I also realized that her being kidnapped would be a far worse trauma. And with mad cockneys running loose, I had no choice but to get her out of Rockville until I got to the bottom of things.

I stopped several times on the way to Richmond to make sure that we weren't being followed. I took side roads, backtracked on Interstate 95, and waited again. I was sure.

I looked back at Jenny asleep on the back seat. I felt so sorry for her. She *was* a lonely little dear. I'd make it up to her.

But I couldn't concentrate on it any longer. The poem kept returning. Damn Dermit! From the day I'd met him I'd been drawn like a fly into a spider's web, but who was the spider? I didn't like having to worry about my child, I didn't like being laughed at or ignored, and most of all I didn't like the thought of being killed. Instinctively I patted the Smith & Wesson to make sure it was still there.

Erica rang me during coffee. Pleasant and to the point. The result was drinks and sunset on the roof garden of the Hotel Washington. From the bright green of the Ellipse and the

Maryland marble of the obelisk to the White House, everything was bathed in salmon pink, the exhaust pollution and natural heat haze combining to mask the late summer sun. As the cold jet stream hit the warmer atmosphere, the cumulonimbus were climbing well above sixteen thousand and flattening out into a line of white anvils that began to bruise in a long line from north to south; soon thunder rolled out of Virginia and the air became as oppressive as wet sheets.

The brewing storm made Erica seem closer, like warm comfort on a rainy winter's night. She was dressed in a long, loose, silky magenta skirt and a white blouse. Her hair was a golden brown sheen and I wondered if she'd worked on it just for the occasion or if she was one of those lucky women who just stands under the shower and it dries perfectly. I remembered that for Linda it used to be like getting ready for D-Day. Erica caught me watching her and smiled. "You approve?"

"Very much."

She touched me. "You sounded offended?"

"Offended?"

"The other night. I really did have another engagement."

"Fine."

She shook her head at my feigned belief. "I've been spending a lot of time with the English engineers on their beam-reception techniques."

"I'll bet."

"Seriously."

"Picking their brains?" I grinned.

"Yes, believe it or not. Some of them are very bright. They're way ahead of the Russians."

"And us?" I asked pointedly.

"A few months." She laughed easily, her head going back and the hair catching the last light of the sun.

"You look good on television," I said.

"Thank you, kind sir."

"My pleasure."

I was starting to get bored, not with Erica but with the nothing talk that is obligatory before the big moves begin. After having been married, I found it a strain to jump through all the hoops again when inside I was simply saying, "I like you and I want to sleep with you." On the other hand I would have been quite put off if she'd offered straight off. The tug of war between impulse and upbringing went on as the sun finally disappeared and the obelisk was bathed in a flush of crimson that gave the lie to the creamy marble.

"You still having a rough time of it?" she asked. "At the White House?" It was as if she'd waited till nightfall to ask the question.

"Yes," I said.

"Did you ever find out what that was all about?"

"Up North?"

"Yes."

"No, I didn't. Did Roth say anything to you?"

"No. Should he?"

"I don't know," I answered, watching the gentle rise of her blouse.

She took a studied sip from the manhattan. "You don't like him, do you?"

"I'm jealous of him."

"Why?"

"Three guesses."

She touched me again, on the thigh. Upbringing had just taken a body blow. Her lips had a wet red look—the kind the advertisers bombard women with on the tube. They were right—it did look seductive. I was watching her so intently that when she spoke I had a hard time really hearing what she said. "Pardon?" I interjected.

"I said I'm sorry that I can't make it for dinner, but I did want to see you."

She had her legs straight out in front on the lounge and for a moment the position reminded me of young Dermit—relaxed and dead in his recliner.

"That's okay," I said. "I'm glad you could make it for drinks."

The lips parted and smiled. "All right. I'll give you a ring. I'd give you a time now, but I never know when we have to work late."

"Fine."

"You sure?"

"Yes."

"Really?"

"Yes. Why?"

"I don't know . . . You . . . you seem preoccupied. Worried."

I could see the feathers floating down toward Dermit's hallway carpet and still feel the eerie shock at the realization that someone had been watching me in the big apartment, moving from room to room. "Well—"

"Tell me," she urged. Her hand was on my thigh again—higher.

"I was thinking of a holiday I once had. In Venice."

"Your wife?"

I was surprised. "How did you know . . . ?"

"I still think of Frank sometimes too."

"Forgive me," I said, "here I am so wrapped up in myself it never even occurred to me that you . . ."

"No, it's all right," she said. "I forget most of the time. He's in California now."

"Married?"

"Yes."

"Want to talk about it?" I offered.

She shrugged. "It's very dull really. He was a Ph.D. in geology. We met in graduate school. And, well, we got married. Outside it was a buyer's market for Ph.D.s. You couldn't pick and choose, even with good marks. He got a job with Shell Oil in Houston. I got a postdoctorate in California. Separation means temptation."

"You or him?"

"Does it matter?"

"Yes."

She was amused, and flattered. "Him if you must know. It could have been me."

"That's sporting."

"Realistic." She pushed the maraschino cherry aside. "We tried to make a go of it for a while—after. But it never worked out, as they say." She glanced over at the obelisk. "It was all very messy and mundane . . . and sad." She glanced down at her watch as if she'd just remembered it was there. "I'm sorry, Harry, I have to run."

"You'll call?"

"I will."

"Good. Excellent. Magnificent!"

She smiled back from the elevator. Was she crying?

CHAPTER 17

She called me—to tell me that the pace of ironing out all the bugs in the SPS grid network was eating up everyone's night and day. It only fueled my determination to use my time more usefully—to find some excuse to go to Riverport. The problem was, what could I do there? Whom would I see? No, I needed more than a name to go on. I looked over my shoulder a lot during the next week and took different routes home at different times, though I was pretty sure that "they" wouldn't try anything, remembering how they could have shot me easily that night and a dozen times since. The safer I felt, the more reasonable it seemed to assume they were convinced that either I'd been scared into silence or that I knew nothing, that they'd got to Dermit before he could say anything and that I'd found nothing.

When you look back on some of the silly things you've done, some obvious clue or nuance you didn't read properly, you often wonder how you could have been so thick-headed, but when you look back you're nearly always seeing a thing out of context—isolated, devoid of the cluster of circumstances that hid it from view at the time. It's like all those stories you hear of how so many people in Intelligence knew that Pearl Harbor was to be bombed, the exact date and time, etc., etc., and how the big brass failed to do anything about it. Well, some of those stories are true but what everyone outside the game forgets is that along with those few Intelligence reports that are dead accurate there are a thousand other reports, many from equally reliable sources, just as convincing and all crying urgently for action. We remember Pearl Harbor because it happened, that's all.

The point is that had I been on the top of a mountain, meditating, the last two lines of the poem might have popped out at me as simply as ABC or Jenny's "TREE." But I'd had my problems that summer, and those two lines of the poem remained a mystery until the afternoon of September 23. Around three o'clock, I was driving, as I had a thousand times, on my way to the Library of Congress, past Union Station, and there they were. Beautifully white and solid, staring "sphinx-like." The two great lions that guard Washington's ("the capital of liberty") Union Station. The lions of Union—waiting for Harry Sturgess to wake up and get off his bum—to realize that Dermit, who now lay cold in the warm summer earth, had used the lions as a hiding place, a "dead drop" as we call it, for photos taken in or around Riverport. I jerked the car to a stop and sat there transfixed by them. I didn't think I was being followed but I was too close to risk a mistake. I got out of the car, pretending to check the tires.

I would return after dark.

CHAPTER 18

I knew I couldn't get the Smith & Wesson through airport security, so I packed it in a Sears auto-parts box in the middle of two dozen 2 by 4-inch nuts and bolts and posted it, surface mail, to myself, care of the Riverport Motel, Washington State. Even if they used an X-ray for surface mail, which I doubted, the nuts and bolts would confuse the shape. I did it with moxie, giving the correct return address, phone number, etc. Then I waited until Hoskins was as busy as a lizard drinking and told him, as if I resented going, that I was leaving for a few days to check out a Near Accident Report at the site of a nuclear energy plant in Nebraska. He was pushing hard, trying to gather support on the Hill for a new energy tax and didn't question my going.

I'd retrieved a microfilm cassette tucked neatly beneath one of the lion's tails. Blown up to five by sevens, the photos showed five corpses. Two were women, two men, and one was a puppy. All the eyes had turned white. The photos were in color so that you could see the big splotchy burn marks that had disfigured the faces. In the corner of each photo was a date: August 20, about a month ago—four days before the SPS launch. Accompanying the five photographs had been a strip of paper with the line:

AACCCFROOOTRNUREITNORVATNRACYERLTYR.

It wasn't so much the naïveté of Dermit that struck me but the terrible urgency he must have felt. Untrained in the more sophisticated coding devices, he had glommed onto an old World War II system. Of course he must have known that he was taking a chance—if "they" were spies. A simple code like that wouldn't have stopped a professional for more than a few seconds but I guess that Dermit, like me, wasn't sure whether they were spies or simply guerrillas hired by someone from Sudley Steel or one of the other contractors connected with the SPS program—people who stood to make billions of dollars now that the program had been given the green light for full development. But the fact that someone had been following him, that he had been so terrified, meant that someone was afraid of something big getting out. And if they had been guerrillas on his trail, then the simple code would have stopped them. At first I tried ten as the basic key, adding five for the photos to five for the corpses. But it came out a mess:

ATRR
ARVL
CNAT
CUTY
CRNR
FER
RIA
OTC
ONY
OOE

And so I tried five as the basic key, and it worked:

AFTERRR
ARRIVAL
CONTACT
COUNTYY
CORONER.

While I sat on the plane imagining what the county coroner was like—was he the one who'd sent the report to me in the first place?—I smelled garlic. I glanced around the plane, telling myself in no uncertain manner that I'd better settle down and not start getting paranoid about sausage meat five minutes after takeoff. But if you've ever been pushed close to the edge, you remember the little details, particularly the smells, and the garlic had brought it all back. No one had bothered me the night before when I'd picked up the microfilm and note, but neither would I, had the tables been turned. If you learn anything in this game it's that it's better to let your mark lead you as far as possible after the pickup. Let him pick it up and follow. "A piece of cake—a gift," as my instructor at the farm was so fond of saying. Then again, perhaps no one had seen me at all. "Of course not," said the little voice inside me. "You just overreact, Sturgess." And that's when the other little voice cut in. "Yes," it said. "And maybe birds don't fly."

CHAPTER 19

September 25

From a satellite photograph the Columbia River basin looks like a big brown pork chop with the wide end, 219,000 square miles, sitting in the United States and the narrow end, containing the remaining 40,000 square miles, poking up into British Columbia where the river is perpetually being born out of the vast Columbia Icefield stretching back into the Rocky Mountains in a quiet white raft of ice 2,000 feet thick and over 100 miles long.

The Columbia's basin covers most of Washington, eastern and northern Oregon, western Montana, much of Idaho, and great slabs of Utah, Wyoming, and Nevada. But like the Nile, much of its course is through desert, in this case a desert created by the great and ancient push of ice that gouged its way south from the Columbia field. But all the dry orange-brown earth needs to bloom is fresh water and that is what Grand Coulee Dam provides. Trapping half of the river's yearly run behind it, the dam feeds millions of irrigation pipes, sparkling in the sun and twinkling on through the nights, dotting this once enormously barren place with dark green oases—islands in a brown sea of sandy loam. From the green islands comes a plethora of crops, from stone fruits and wheat to hops and sugar beet.

For all this development it remains a lonely place. The countless miles of computer-supervised irrigation don't need people for the most part; except for picking time the oases seem merely tolerated by the vast, gorge-scarred land. The quivering heat waves of summer and the white wilderness of winter proclaim that you can pass through but only under sufferance. One careless mistake could be your last.

Farther to the west, away from the desert and the dry stretches of western pine, stands the Cascade Range. This wilderness mountain area is peaked with eternal icecaps, replacing the solitude of desert with the solitude of deep forests of fir, pine, and cedar. This late evening the sun was an orange ball over the rolling purple sagebrush, pierced here and there by the giant black stakes of a huge hop farm that ran on and on, stopping barely twelve miles south of my destination. Washington could be on another planet, and approaching Riverport, I felt that it was.

Suddenly, by way of confirmation, a dust devil racing from nowhere enveloped the Datsun 310 rented car. My eyes burning with the hot sand, I braked hard for fear of shooting off the road and plunging into a wizened creek bed 150 feet below. For thirty seconds I could see nothing but a grayish-red cloud all about me. The gray dust was really ash—the latest burp from Mount St. Helens 150 miles to the south. As in a snow storm, my sense of distance, of perspective, was completely gone. Then gradually the black road emerged before me, surrounded by unutterable silence. At least I had seen the dust devil coming. What I was concerned about was something that could burn your eyes out and wouldn't give any warning at all.

Just over forty miles west of Grand Coulee Dam, as the river straightens out after the big bend around Fort Okanogan and Brewster, lies Riverport, with a population, the sign said, of 647—an increase of five from the atlas—and a rail depot. I drove down the main street, which led directly to the river. It was lined by a handful of cedar-shingled buildings: a hardware store-cum-post office, supermarket, liquor store, police station, three churches, the Riverport Motel, a department store, and a few miscellaneous unnamed buildings, some of which I imagined by their proximity to have some connection with the big corrugated sheds of the rail depot. I was impressed by the neatness of it all. The supporting population of about a hundred houses was scattered. With few exceptions the lawns seemed meticulously kept, bristling with irrigated gardens whose colors, particularly the blues and whites, contrasted vividly with the predominantly brown flatlands and hills that stood silently to the east. Twenty miles westward you could see the bottle green apron of the Cascade Mountains. Here in Riverport the average yearly rainfall was ten inches; in the Cascades it was more than a hundred. The contrast in those twenty miles never left me—it was as dramatic and sudden as the crossing of a foreign border.

There were three surprises. The first was that the motel was almost full, a fact which the old proprietress told me with obvious pride, in order to dispel any notions I might have had about this being a one-tractor town. The second surprise was that in the center of one of the biggest fruit-growing areas in the world I was served tinned fruit salad in the motel coffee shop, and the third was waiting for me in the morning.

I'd got up early and, to fill in time till breakfast, walked down by the river. The Columbia was a long stretch of sapphire blue and struck me as remarkably clear for a river that had passed through the heavily silted country of southeastern British Columbia far to the north.

The squad car came up behind me so quietly that it was almost on me when I turned. The ample-bellied sheriff was friendly enough, walking over, smoking a pipe, as western as you could get, from the suntanned arms to the nonregulation riding boots, but his eyes swept over me for a quiet call to Spokane and an FBI computer checkout if need be. "You say you're with the packing people, Mr.—?"

"No," I said, "I'm not with the packing people."

There was a very pregnant pause.

"Uhuh—"

I could have told him who I was but Dermit had pointed me straight for Riverport and Dermit was dead. Someone was running a secret show and I wasn't taking any chances. Besides, I wanted to save my White House status for a tight corner which appeared sooner and tighter than I'd expected.

Easy access to the alcohol essential to the coroner's grim trade makes it all too often the last refuge of the alcoholic M.D. Conversing with Chas. E. Milt, King Butte County Coroner, was like talking to a distillery. Even through the dense smoke that came from the droopy, homemade cigarettes, and the sweet, antiseptic odor that rose from the refrigerated corpses, the smell of booze wafted over you, particularly on the "h" sounds. But he was one of those competent, hard, conditioned alcoholics and except for the smell, his yo-yo-like moods, and the harsh metallic ring to his voice, he could have fooled a casual observer. I made up a name of a fake relative to test his willingness to talk. He wiped his bony hands on the tattered lab coat. "You'll have to go to the sheriff's office, Mr. Sturgess. I don't give out any information on autopsies on Officially Unidentifieds except through the sheriff's office or in open public enquiry. Sorry."

I had to throw dice now or give up the chase altogether. It helped a little to know that Dermit had trusted him. So I decided to throw dice. I said nothing about the medical report I had but pulled out the photo of the dead Finn and the other photos Dermit had left for me.

It was as though I'd hit him.

The coughing was explosive, wracking his small, sinewy frame, the creased, tanned face turning beet red. He gulped from the bottle marked "Distilled Water."

Six cigarettes and two "water" breaks later I just about had the story.

"Why Dermit?" I asked.

"Wenatchee *Daily News* ran a series of articles on him—anti-radiation pieces. I followed the stories so I sent the photos to him. Anonymously as you know."

"But wait a minute. If it was anonymous how did he know how to contact you? You must have—"

"Rang him. No way I'd send my name through the mails with the photos. No way."

"But why all the secrecy? I mean, this is the biggest . . ."

"You trust the mail, son?"

"More or less."

"Then you're a damn fool." He took another sip, gesturing toward a framed diploma hanging on the wall. Everything else in the office was in chaotic disarray, with a fine Columbia basin dust and old Mount St. Helens ash covering the polished wood of the desk and some files that were "pending." But the diploma was spotless. University of Washington, 1962, but it could have been yesterday, it looked so new. Now Milt's eyes were covering over with the dust of nostalgia. "Did an autopsy on a young lad in Port Townsend, on the coast."

"I know where it is." Like so many drunks, he automatically assumed I wanted to hear his life story.

"Yes—well I was a young M.D.—did an autopsy on this lad one night. Mongoloid he was. Mongoloid and Indian—that's a hell of a start for you! Sonofabitch, you should have seen the house." He shook his head and his arm reached out as if by remote control, dragging the "water" over toward him. "Well, I did this autopsy. Lad was seven . . . maybe eight. Doesn't matter—bit hard to tell with Mongoloids. Anyway took me no more than ten minutes to find out he'd been smothered. Piece of down in the right nostril. Should have seen his old man when I confronted him with it. Only time I've seen an Indian cry. Only time . . . Well, I hushed it up."

He looked up at the diploma. "That was that. Struck from the register. They found out because I put it in a letter, you see." The tired cigarette jabbed toward me. "That's why I don't trust the mail. Antiabortionist group opened it up—thought I was covering up Indian deaths caused by whites or some such foolery. Backfired on them, of course, opening my mail and all, but I was caught in the backlash." He took a hefty swallow from the bottle. "You're wondering how I got this job then?"

I said nothing. I was wondering why he'd risked what little he had by sending Dermit the photos.

"Assisted in disaster areas," he continued. "South America—got reinstated. But the story stays with you, you know. Tried to start a practice for a while down near San Diego. The living wouldn't trust me so they gave me the dead." The laugh collapsed in a grunt. His arm, so thin it looked wizened, swung toward the row of refrigerated slabs. The smile was bitter.

"So you don't trust the mails?" I said.

"No, and I don't care to be pilloried again."

"For what?"

"For breaking the rules."

"Whose rules?"

"*Their* rules." The cigarette swept east to west and the ash joined the company of stains on the splotchy lab coat.

"Who are *they?*"

He looked at me for at least fifteen seconds and I knew intuitively that if I averted his stare I wouldn't get any more out of him. Anger and suspicion passed through the bloodshot eyes, but in the end there was only a steady gaze of resignation. He went to take another swig, hesitated and instead plugged the bottle, punching the cork in with his palm as if to seal the temporary victory. "I thought you'd know," he said. "That Dermit would have told you who they might be."

Puzzled, I asked him, "How would he know? I mean unless you told him?"

Milt shrugged. "Thought he might have picked up something else—from some other source."

I found his probing of what I knew and didn't know irritating. "Look, you can trust me," I said, rather too sharply. "Do you know who they are or not?"

"I don't know who they are."

I was thinking, very hard. I was quickly trying to recall the details of the White House meeting but I had trouble because I kept seeing Erica—the firm, full breasts, and thighs that in a split skirt would . . . There were other aspects to her, of course; her intelligence, her dedication in what she believed, and so on, but when you've been as long as I "without woman," as one of my fellow sufferers had none too subtly put it, the more cerebral attractions of the opposite sex get shoved aside.

"Reason over passion," I reminded myself, forcing my attention back to the details. I was instantly rewarded. Suddenly, I felt my pulse racing. I couldn't be sure but it was just . . . just possible . . . "The hop farm?" I exploded. "The one I saw driving in here, about twelve miles south. How big is it?"

Milt shrugged disinterestedly. "Don't know. About eighty thousand acres, I guess."

I did a quick calculation. "That's about—one hundred and thirty square miles?"

"If you say so. Why?"

"I want to go out and see it. We mightn't know *who* they are but I think we might know *where* they are."

His forehead creased and he nodded slowly as if he was making some vague connection. He scrutinized my light blue and white striped seersucker suit. "You bring any work clothes?"

"That's what you're looking at."

"Huh—any worker'd pick you out a mile off as a city slicker."

He disappeared for a few minutes, then came back with an old gray pair of coveralls. The sleeves drooped on me as if I were the smallest of the Seven Dwarfs. It was the first time I had seen the coroner smile.

"You should eat your Wheaties, Mr. Sturgess."

Then the mood abruptly changed and for no apparent reason. His tone was clear and challenging. "The medical report I sent you? Tell me the names."

I don't know why I was so surprised. After all, he'd sent the photos to Dermit telling him in code to contact him. No reason why it shouldn't have been him who'd sent the report to me. But why hadn't he told *me* to contact him? That's what rubbed. I told him the names: Smith, Brown, Hall, Wilmot, and Jones. "Satisfied?" I didn't like being treated as an imposter after coming all this way.

He must have been reading my thoughts.

"I didn't know how far to trust you—being an official in Washington an' all."

"Thanks."

"Nothing personal. But, well, Dermit was in the news. A bona fide environmentalist. You were in the White House. Unknown quantity. That place has a way of corrupting unknown quantities."

"Thanks!"

"I knew Dermit would know who to trust. Left it up to him."

"You can trust me," I said pointedly. "If you couldn't, there'd be cops all over this place by now. Don't you realize that?"

"All right, all right. I wanted to be sure, that's all. When you . . ."

"How about the hop farm?" I interrupted.

"What about it?"

"The farmers, the ones in the report. Did they live anywhere near the hop estate?"

He drew heavily on a new cigarette. "In the general area. Why?"

"I have a hunch. I think—"

"Look, son!" He extinguished the cigarette he'd just begun. "I don't want you to go risking your neck because of the likes of me. Well, what I mean is . . . maybe I've become a bit . . . you know, a bit paranoid about getting back at . . ." He wasn't simply extinguishing the cigarette, he was killing it, the tobacco bursting out like innards. "Well, I know the booze can make you a little paranoid." He looked up at me sharply, almost accusingly, almost paranoid. "'Course, I guess you wouldn't know anything about that?" he snapped.

"I worry without the booze," I said as gently as I could. "I'd still like to have a word with one of those farmers on the perimeter. You know any of them?"

"If you'd like to, but I don't see . . ."

"I'd like to."

He stood absolutely still—for a whole minute. He was trembling. I thought he was going through some kind of fit, delirium tremens or something. "Are you okay?"

He was staring at the morgue's refrigeration compartment.

"No matter what happens," he said, "I want you to know I want to help, deep down."

"I know that."

"No," he said vigorously. "No you don't."

He looked around at the door, biting his lip so hard I thought he'd drawn blood. Then he swung back at me and without a word beckoned me over to one of the refrigeration units. He pulled out a concave aluminum slab from its bay. Now the smell of gin was temporarily gone, taken over by the sweet, antiseptic odor that wafted from the shroud-covered corpse. He rolled the sheet down to the mouth. The face had been that of an old man, about seventy. The once sunburned, cherry-red cheeks were now a sickly yellow. The eyes were white blobs.

"From around here?" I asked, quickly averting my gaze from the thick, gelatinous lumps toward the forlorn-looking toe tag—T.O.D. Time of death was four days before. God knew what the rest of the body looked like. I didn't want to know. Milt shoved the tray back in, its clang echoing around the morgue.

"From around here?" I repeated.

Milt was nervously biting his bottom lip again. "Laborer. Thompson. Worked for one of the orchards thirty miles south of here. Near the hop farm."

"Near the others? The guys in the report?"

He seemed to stare beyond me. "No. Funny, it's about thirty miles in the other direction."

"But the eyes looked the same—as in the photos you sent Dermit."

"Yeah."

"Where did they come from? The bodies in the photos?"

"Let's see—a couple near the hop farm, a couple twenty, forty miles away."

"The farmers in the report you sent me. How many near the hop farm? Any of them really close?"

"Yes . . . Will . . ." He seemed caught halfway between uncertainty and unwillingness to commit himself. He was staring at the refrigerator again. Something was eating away at him.

"Will who?"

"Huh?"

"You started to say a name. Will somebody?" I was almost in need of a drink myself.

"Will Orlet," he said. "He was Smith in the report."

"What about him?"

He took out another cigarette. "Sterile. Things have gotten much worse for him lately," he said softly. "In the last month especially."

"He tell you?"

"Yes." He let a new cigarette hang unlit. "People often see me. Saves them a trip to the doctor up in Coulee."

I couldn't stand the cigarette drooping any longer and lit it for him.

"They—" he began but stopped for a second, staring at the damned refrigerator again. "They've been good friends, the Orlets . . . really . . . you know. When I first arrived and didn't know anyone and—"

There were tears in Milt's eyes. You never know with alcoholics. One minute up, the next minute in the depths.

"What's this Thompson doing here?" I asked by way of drawing him out of his lightning depression over Orlet.

"For identification. That's been done. They'll bury him tomorrow in Lincoln County South." He snatched up a pair of mirrored sunglasses. "Come on then! If we leave now we can fit in both the hop farm and Orlet's place if you must see . . ."

"Fine, if it's okay with—"

Suddenly he turned, snapping, "I don't like the dark. All right?"

"Sure." I started wondering just how much of all this *was* the booze talking?

"Right. Let's go." Already he was needing another belt, his hands working anxiously in the pockets of the lab coat.

A dust devil, about twenty feet high, scurried abreast of the battered red pickup as if challenging us to a race, then showed its undoubted superiority by roaring ahead out of sight into the sere brown hills.

"Where did you get the report?" I asked. "You don't get people until . . . I mean . . ."

"Until they're dead."

"Sorry . . ."

"I stole it."

"From who?"

He mashed the gears of the dusty pickup. "Friend of mine. Another doctor in Grand Coulee. Found it during a routine autopsy."

"You mean he was too frightened to do anything himself?"

"He asked for an investigation." Milt turned to me. "It's in the report."

"I know. No one came, right?"

"They came." Milt crashed into another gear.

"But not to investigate what he'd reported?"

"Right. He's got a wife and kids to look after."

"So they leaned on him and you decided to go Lone Ranger?"

Milt rose to the other doctor's defense. "Don't be too hard on him, Harry. He took a risk in telling me. They told him to shut up, period."

"Did he say who *they* were? What department?"

"No. Who knows what department? Who ever knows what department? Just government."

"Didn't he try to find out?" I looked out at the long stretch of blacktop that was buckling ahead in the glaring heat.

For a few seconds Milt said nothing. There was only a gin-creased face hidden beneath the purple-mirrored sunglasses. When he spoke it was like someone about to explode. "It's all right for you to judge. You don't know the kind of pressure they can . . . you don't know, Sturgess."

There was no point in pursuing it any further right now. He was worked up enough, having left the distilled water behind. Turning my attention to the scenery, I pushed my feet forward to stretch the tired muscles and felt them pulled up short. It was the barrel of a twelve-gauge shotgun, five-shot pump action, clipped to the floorboards in front of the gearshift. A little white cloth like a tiny nightcap was tied to the end of the barrel to keep the dust out. In the open glove compartment lay a packet that normally held twelve rifle slug cartridges. There were only seven left in the box, which meant the shotgun was loaded, including one in the breech. Now you don't use rifle slug to shoot birds. If you did, you'd have no bird left. Dapper came to mind as I remembered asking him once what exactly you'd use a slug cartridge for. He'd given me his old soldier's smile. "For stopping locomotives," he'd said. "Very large locomotives."

CHAPTER 20

The bang came from behind my left ear and the pickup immediately began to slide into the ochre-red shoulder of the road. Milt calmly accelerated out of the powdered dust, then pumped the brake until we came to a slow stop next to a clump of invading sage. "Damn!" he said, in another mercurial change of mood, jumping out to change the tire. It took us ten minutes, after which I felt like a broiled lobster in the high midafternoon sun.

The entrance to the hop farm didn't look like anything out of the ordinary till you saw the eight-foot barbed-wire fence and the Rottweilers roaming around. German shepherds are tough and some handlers will argue that Dobermans are better but give me a jet black Rottweiler; heavier than the Doberman and wider than the shepherd. Like most dogs, they're friendly as Christmas if you treat them fairly, but when they're angry the Rottweilers' jaws are something to behold, a kind of walking bear trap.

"I thought most orchards were unfenced," I said.

"They are."

I saw the dogs, immediately alert at our approach, sprinting out from the heavily green-vined trellises a hundred yards in and heading toward the fence. Something came to mind from the Langley course: "Attack dogs—trained to react to movement rather than scent." The locks on the gate, three of them, were as big as fists. Slowing down, Milt gunned the engine.

We never got to the gate. Two men in khaki security guard uniforms sauntered over toward our pickup, their faces lost for a second in the shadow cast by the huge sign: GOVERNMENT AGRICULTURAL STATION—TRESPASSERS WILL BE PROSECUTED. They'd put two of the Rottweilers on a sit-stay and brought only one of them out, which was plenty.

"Hi." It was the little one talking and he was friendly as your uncle and his "Hi" was as British as big boots, despite his attempt to be genuine American.

"Hi," said Milt, equally friendly. The smaller man, six foot three, patted the Rottweiler affectionately. "What can we do for y'all?"

"Y'all?" was about as native to Washington State as Peking duck.

Milt had a fake coroner's inquiry all planned, but inspiration struck me and before he could speak I said, "We're looking for Spring Coulee. By the map it looks about six or seven miles south from here. That about right?"

"Yup," said the other, taller man. "Seven miles, more or less."

"Good. Then we're on the right road."

"Sure are."

"Thanks." I held up my hand against the glare but used it as a blind to peer ahead at the base of the tall wired trellises of lush green hops. I could see a line of disks poking up a foot or so from the ground.

As we moved off, the Rottweilers were still visible in the side-view mirror. Milt was nonplussed. "Where the hell's Spring Coulee? Never heard of it."

"Neither have I." I held the lighter steady as he sucked in on his home-rolled Durham.

"Crazy sonofabitch." He smacked the wheel good-humoredly. "What would've happened if he'd said he didn't know it?"

"Then we would have been on the wrong road, wouldn't we? Besides, he wouldn't have said he didn't know. First thing I learned in EPA is, when people don't want you looking around —factory effluent, blocked chimneys, whatever—they bust their ass to get rid of you. Say anything. Anyway if they said they hadn't known Spring Coulee then they would've been admitting they're new around here and they don't want to do that."

"You see the disks?"

"Yes, about a foot across, I guess."

"What you think?"

"Heat sensors."

"*Heat?* In this country? In summer?"

"It's all relative. Point is, any change in heat emission other than what's ordinary for the surroundings will show up on the screen. Use them sometimes to monitor furnace leaks in factories."

"Well?"

"Well what?"

"Expensive hops."

"Very."

We took a sharp right turn three miles from the hop farm and headed over a rocky, dry creek bed, up a tortuous switchback, and onto a plain where all you could see was a huge golden circle of wheat, its big irrigation arms rotating slowly and winking happily in the slanting light.

"Orlet's place?"

"Yes."

"He's the one who was impotent wasn't he?—as well as sterile."

"One of them." I saw Milt glance at me suspiciously, as if I should have known there was more than only one impotent case. It was just a momentary lapse on my part, but I could tell he wasn't 100 percent sure.

"What can we say we're out here for?" I asked. "Can't claim we're lost again."

"You've spent too long in Washington, D.C., my friend.

Don't need a damn cover story for *everyone* you visit. I know these people. I care about them. Hell's bells, I don't need an excuse to pop in for coffee. Not in God's country—or what used to be God's country. Anyway I'll just say you're a health inspector. It isn't really a lie."

The thump of big rocks bouncing off the chassis almost drowned the sound of the engine as we veered crazily down a hidden gulch and up the other side of the bed, screaming in overdrive.

"You going to spell it out?" shouted Milt.

"What you mean?"

"Whatever you think it is?" he said, wrestling with the wheel which had momentarily gone berserk.

"I think it's something to do with the solar satellite project," I shouted. "Thing I can't figure out is that the first SPS was only launched a month ago. The report you . . . borrowed was *six* months ago."

"The hop farm was there six months ago."

"And its tenants?" We were yelling above the pickup's rattle.

"Don't remember. Wasn't interested who was there until after Will Orlet's trouble. I noticed them then."

"You want to go back?" I asked.

"To Hopsville?"

"Yes."

"No."

"I do."

The wheel spun wildly again. "You're crazy!"

"Must be the heat." I smiled. "Come on, Doctor, you never brought rifle slugs for quail. Don't tell me you didn't wonder about a new government research station popping up."

He pushed up the sunglasses as we slowed down near the big golden circle that was now bending gently with the wind like an inland sea. "The fact is, I've been scared to go it alone. Dogs scare me shitless."

"I'm very good with dogs."

"What's your secret?"

"I run," I said. "Very fast."

Milt shook his head.

Will Orlet walked out of the open-verandahed bungalow that was off-white against the saffron wheat and was straight out of a Wyeth painting despite the high TV aerial in the back yard. He was tall, his face polished brown by the sun, eyes alive with the blue of a western sky and a nod which said, "Sit yourself and rest awhile." His wife, small, with short-cropped blond hair and a complexion as sunburned as her husband's, came after him, busily wiping her floured hands on her apron. The two little girls stood shyly by a rust-brown Massey-Ferguson tractor while a small black cocker spaniel, Taffy, one ear lolling and the other upright, was gruffing at us, walking in wide circles, wanting desperately to be patted.

They all belonged in a Norman Rockwell poster, and once again I had the feeling that Washington, D.C., was on another planet. These people were what my parents used to call the salt of the earth, but the openness of their greeting belied any self-knowledge of it. For them, friendliness was godliness, as natural as hard work and having children. The cynic in me looked for guile in the sunbrowned smiles but there was none, no forced hospitality. It was all genuine. It wasn't meant to highlight your own deficiencies, but it did.

"Glad to meet you, Mr. Sturgess."

The handshake was firm and direct. I remembered I used to shake hands like that, but the city makes you too hurried to bother. Mrs. Orlet had a tiny wooden crucifix around her neck.

It was going to be tricky because Milt had told me that Will Orlet didn't know about the confidential medical report being forwarded, and he would naturally be hurt and angry if he thought that his private conversations with his physician had found their way to me, no matter what the intent. Milt lied that I was a government health inspector and that I was doing a general water-quality test by interviewing people who lived along the Columbia. Will Orlet didn't suspect a thing. If he'd been living in Washington, D.C., he would have been called naïve. Out here he was just plain honest.

"No, the drinking water's fine, Mr. Sturgess."

I shifted uneasily in my charade. "You've had no diarrhea," I asked Orlet, "or anything like that?"

"No."

It must have been the first time Will Orlet had lied in years. His wife asked us inside. In the twenty seconds or so it took us to walk past the back yard garden of dark green broccoli, cauliflower, and giant orange beefsteak tomatoes, Rona Orlet had spoken quietly to her husband. I suspected it wasn't so much unwillingness that was holding him back as pride. She made it easier by excusing herself and going into the kitchen to make coffee. Also sensing it would be easier one on one, Milt volunteered to see the kids' pet goat. I could hear a baby gurgling from one of the rooms—the baby they'd had before their trouble.

Will Orlet and I sat facing each other across an old-fashioned but very comfortable living room. He was pushing one of his hands along the overstuffed lounge chair as if he were drying it by sheer friction. "Mr. Sturgess, there is one thing. I . . . we don't know if it's got anything to do with the water or . . . well it's kind of personal sort of. I don't know whether it will help, but Rona thinks . . . this is all—uh—this is all kind of private. Isn't it?" He was sweating as if he'd just plowed the back forty.

"Absolutely confidential, Mr. Orlet."

His left thigh was now getting the friction rub and the perspiration was coming out in beads above his eyes. I didn't move. He studied his boots, bent down and flicked a grain of wheat from the sun-scorched laces. "Well . . ."

"Mr. Orlet, some people up river, beyond the dam, along the Roosevelt Reservoir . . . they've had medical problems."

"Yes?" He leaned forward eagerly. It was a plea.

"There've been a few cases of impotency in the last year."

He exhaled loudly and sank back into his seat from sheer relief. "I'll be . . ."

I toyed with the slightly frayed arm rest. "Is that any kind of problem for you, Mr. Orlet?"

His head dropped but then it lifted and looked right at me.

"Yes, sir, it is. I don't know what's wrong. Huh," he attempted a laugh but it collapsed. "I even wondered if it *was* the water or something?"

There was some rapid beating coming from the kitchen. The whipping cream was getting hell.

"It's not anything to do with the water, Mr. Orlet. So you can forget about that."

"Thank the Lord. What is it then, Doctor? Insecticide?"

I was in my old territory now. "What are you using?"

"Four C Eleven."

"You wear masks?"

"Yes." He was alarmed.

"No, it's not that," I said. "If you wear masks, there should be no problem."

"What then?" His hands were locked so tightly they were speckled with the arrested circulation.

"We don't know, Mr. Orlet. We just don't know. That's what we're trying to find out."

"Then how do you know it's not the insecticide? Or the water? Or Mount St. Helens dust?"

"The government's done a lot of testing on it," I lied. "EPA's done most of the experimenting, and neither the water nor insecticide is the cause of impotency. And it's not volcanic dust. Have you been depressed?"

"Sure. I mean we can't have any more kids. I—"

Suddenly Mrs. Orlet appeared like a brave little Bantam standing gamely, her eggbeater in hand and apron embroidered in wild roses. She moved next to her husband and put her hand gently on his neck.

"Mr. Sturgess. We're . . . we've . . . there's no problem between us."

I smiled. There was a few seconds silence. "Of course, Mrs. Orlet. That's obvious."

Her tiny hand was rubbing him lovingly on the neck. I doubt she was even aware of it. "Then what can it be?"

"Have you noticed anything at all out of the ordinary since you've had this?" They looked at one another.

"Anything at all?"

"We told everything to Dr. Jensen in Coulee. Dr. Milt knows him."

"Yes, but I mean anything beyond the personal medical things. Anything on the farm for instance?"

Mrs. Orlet was trying to think so hard she didn't even see the drop of cream that had formed and had fallen from the eggbeater. The dog saw it. It vanished.

Will shrugged. "Only the static."

"What static?"

"Well," said Will, "I'm a ham radio operator. You must have seen the rig when you came in?"

"I thought it was for TV."

"It's a short-wave antenna. Well, last . . . when was it, Rone? Three months?"

"More like six."

"Yeah. Well, I was having a lot of trouble. Static so bad that I just had to shut her down."

"High sunspot activity?" I proffered.

"No. I checked with some of the other operators. They didn't have any trouble."

"They in the same area?"

"No. I'm the only one for a couple of hundred miles. The nearest is in Kelowna, British Columbia. Whatever it was, I was blanked out—and I mean *blanked out* by static. Nothing but noise."

I sat, pensive, while Rona Orlet disappeared back into the kitchen. I started scratching the palms of my hands on the sofa's tattered edge. "You sure the other operators never had the same trouble?" I pressed.

"Yes. I remember because I thought there must be something wrong with my equipment. I had it checked out. There was nothing."

I did a quick mental recall of the objection list I'd given the President—especially the one about Radio Frequency Interference. I remembered that beam attenuation, or beam dispersal, could occur with heavy moisture content in the atmosphere. The scattering might only be 5 percent, but it was all relative, and 5 percent could be more than enough. And so the next question was very important. It could mean staying around or going back to Washington, D.C., empty-handed and every bit as perplexed as before.

"Mr. Orlet," I said, mussing Taffy's ear and looking as casual as I could, "did it happen to be raining at all? When you had the static?"

He thought hard for a second. "I don't know." He went out and asked Rona. She couldn't remember. He'd check his ham operator's diary if I liked. I'd like very much. He put on bifocals which made him look completely out of place, like a professor in coveralls. Thirty seconds later he returned, studiously surveying the hide-bound log. "Yep, raining," he said, "cats and dogs. Just as well," he smiled. "Cuts down my irrigation cost."

"But did it rain each time? Each time you had the heavy static?"

He flicked the pages again. I was so anxious I could have snatched the diary from him.

"Let's see . . . static five times. Rained . . . let me see. Rained three times. Why?"

"Mr. Orlet, do you keep a record of just how intense the rain is? Other than just being heavy?"

"No, sir."

Three nights out of five was by no means conclusive, but the odds were mounting. Will Orlet's bright eyes looked as if a cloud had just passed over them. "What has static got to do with my—my problem?"

It wasn't for me to alarm him unnecessarily without any proof. I paused. "Mr. Orlet, I can't tell you if there's anything environmentally involved that caused the trouble. But as soon as I know I'll tell you. I promise you that."

He nodded resignedly as we ambled outside. "I know you will, Mr. Sturgess. Milt trusts you. That's enough for me. Besides . . ." He tried not to sound like a whiner, but the hurt came through. "Besides, Doc Jensen said it's irreversible."

"I'm sorry, Mr. Orlet. Must . . . it must be a hell of a thing."

He kicked a stone as we walked toward the truck. Taffy ran ahead looking up at him, ready for a game.

"Heck," he said. "Could be worse. I've got three great kids."

"And a ferocious hound," I joked.

He forced a smile. "Yeah."

I studied his eyes for any signs of cataract. There were none. He stopped suddenly on the gravel.

"There is one thing," he said, "that's a bit funny but . . ." He grinned self-consciously. "I don't go with all this UFO nonsense, y'know."

"UFO?"

"Yes, well I mean I don't believe in it. But—funny thing—during one of these storms we were just talking about I went out to check the antenna."

"When? Six months ago or recently?"

"Three weeks ago. The last lot of static. It was blowing like Hades."

I saw Taffy rushing a mole whose head had popped up and disappeared just as quickly. The barking was so loud I had difficulty hearing Orlet.

"The clouds were black as tar, y'know, and in the middle of them, just for, oh, I dunno, maybe five, six seconds, I saw this light. Well, not a light exactly but a kind of glow."

My pulse shot to ninety a minute. "Yes?"

He kicked another pebble. "Sounds kind of dumb, I guess."

"No. Go on," I said evenly.

"Well, it was sort of glowing."

I picked up a small stick and threw it for Taffy. He took off as though it were dessert. "What color was it?"

"Red."

"Uhuh. Might've been the sunlight reflected. You know, a ray passing through. Before it started to rain."

"No. Whole sky was really black. It was already raining."

"Could've been an aircraft's light. The wing-tip indicator."

His face screwed up. "No." It was the most certain he'd been. "It was about a quarter-mile across."

Taffy brought back the stick and I tossed it again. "You tell anyone else about this?"

"Not likely." He laughed easily. "They'd think I was a UFO freak."

"Guess they would," I added, trying to sound jovial, my heart now doing about 120 thumps per minute. "Could have been a meteorological balloon. They're responsible for half the UFO sightings. There's a candle right underneath them you see. Casts quite a light. Even in a storm it won't blow out. It travels at the same speed as the storm wind."

"But they're not red—are they?"

"No."

"'Course, I guess it could be something strange with the heat rising up. We have two or three mirages a day in the flat country. Could have been reflected off a cloud."

"That's probably it. Three weeks ago. You sure?"

"Positive."

Things were clearing a little in my brain. At first I'd thought that the problem was that the SPS wasn't even launched when Orlet was mentioned in the report. But now there was a connection between what happened six months ago and just three weeks ago. The answer was that Will Orlet had been hit twice—once before the launch and once after. I asked him about the hop farm. He knew nothing—only that he'd never seen any crop sprayers flying over. Unusual, he said, for such a big hop farm. "No wonder the bugs are getting at the leaves."

"What bugs?" I asked.

"Don't know what kind exactly. Like I said, I've never been over there but in a high wind around here wheat husks and leaves get scattered all over. The hop leaves are sort of pockmarked."

As we drove off, I sat in silence for a while, making a few last waves at the kids and the dog. I was excited and afraid, and full of admiration for the ability of people like Rona and Will, who had learned to accept things, good and bad; to be patient with the world, not to press and poke at things. But sometimes you have to press and poke. I turned to Milt. "Can you hold out?" There was a slight edge to my voice which told him that I expected the answer to be yes.

He nodded sharply, his neck tendons stretched taut as nylon rope.

"Then," I said, "I think we should visit Hopsville. You have wire cutters at your morgue?"

He nodded tensely again, then stopped the truck. "You want to drive?" he asked.

"Not particularly."

"I'd appreciate it."

I shrugged, got out of the truck and I'd no sooner got in the other side than a fifth of rye had materialized out of nowhere. He'd already guzzled about three ounces. I shoved the gearshift into first. "Don't you get pissed on me."

He shot an angry glance at me, his fingers drumming frantically on the bottle.

I knew it wasn't impossible to get into Hopsville, but it wasn't going to be easy. In Washington, D.C., I could have arranged with Ralph Stein for the proper equipment, but here I was three thousand miles away and had to improvise as best I could. I discussed my plan with Milt. He was either skeptical or grumpy from the shakes or both. The speedometer hit seventy miles per hour as I raced back to his office. "How much dry ice do you use when you go out to bring in a corpse in this heat?"

"About twenty, thirty pounds. Depends on distance, amount of putrefaction."

"Have you got that much at the lab?"

"Yes."

"A raincoat?"

"I keep one in the back of the truck."

"Is it plastic?"

"Yes."

"No good. Have to be double lining."

"I've got an old army coat. It's lined."

"That'll do."

Reaching into the glove compartment, he took another swig and offered it to me to ease his conscience. I shook my head.

He flipped the glove-compartment lid up, hoping that if the bottle was out of sight it was out of mind. "If those dogs come for you you won't be able to move fast."

An oncoming car already had his lights on. I blinked at his high beam and pressed the dimmer switch. "If those dogs find me, I won't need the coat. I can ditch it."

"I'll cover you with the shotgun."

"What?" I could see Riverport coming up, its few street lights white pin-pricks against the darkening desert hues. "If you fire that gun you might as well send up a flare. No. Thanks all the same. I'll take care of the dogs."

"With what?"

"Aniseed. I'll get a package from the drugstore. I'll need a bottle of your chloroform too. Five hundred milliliters should do."

"It'll be pitch black by the time we get back there," he complained. "The hop trellises don't come right up to the barbed wire, remember. They're about a hundred yards in."

"I'll only need ten, fifteen minutes at the very most. Just enough to get through the wire, past the sensors, and to the trellises and back. It's better than trying in broad daylight."

He rolled a cigarette. The booze had calmed him. "Well, I did say I wanted to find out what was going on."

"You did."

Ten minutes at Milt's place and I had all I needed. The dying sun threw such beautiful shifting and variegated shadows over the land that I would have stopped the truck to sightsee if I hadn't been so keen to get to the hop farm. The shadows played back and forth over the rolling sere brown hills and long stretches of plains like great inland seas at once ominous, tranquil, all interspersing, separating, and finally coming together in the awesome purple twilight. As soon as the sun had dipped behind the high Cascades a deep blueness descended and the country was so still, so quiet, that it seemed blasphemous to be invading it with the barbarous whine of the pickup. Milt blew out a long gray-white trail of smoke and studied it as it disappeared piece by piece into the slipstream. "You know," he said, "I've never seen them spray the hop farm." The hills were now dark bumps on the horizon.

"I know," I said. "Will Orlet noticed the same thing."

"Maybe . . . maybe we're all wet." He turned to me with a questioning glance. "Maybe the experimental farm *is* an experimental farm. That's why they're not spraying. They've found a way to grow hops without chemicals. Insecticide free?"

"Dammit! You know, you could be right. It's usual for government research stations to forbid trespassers on the property. And Will Orlet said there were diseased-looking leaves being blown about his place. No spraying means they're probably experimenting with injecting nontoxic chemicals. That could be it!"

Every sage bush stood out sharply in the sapphire twilight, and a fingernail moon sat in a cloudless sky. We turned eastward just south of the long silver sliver that was the southern end of Lake Chelan. We'd taped the lights so that only narrow slits remained, and I was straining to see the road, but it was safer than having the lights full on and recognizable from miles away. About five miles along the western border of the hop farm we came into a gulch. It was as good a hiding place as any we'd find.

While Milt opened the two coolers he used to carry dry ice for packing the corpses and began to chip away amid an eerie white cloud of rising carbon dioxide, I slit open the linings of the old army coat. The aniseed was in oil form, but I knew that it wouldn't freeze on me for ten minutes or so, long enough for me to reach the trellises. Of course, I could have timed some magnesium to burn farther down the fence, which would have registered on the heat sensor circuit as a violent increase in temperature above the highest nighttime setting and this would have created enough of a diversion for us to cut through the barbed wire where we were and for me to go in. But when they found the flare, it would only be a matter of seconds before they knew that it was a decoy and would come looking for us. This way was more trouble, but hopefully it wouldn't alert them at all.

Donning a pair of canvas gloves, I quickly filled the coat lining with the freezing dry ice that Milt had chipped into hand-sized pieces. As I stuffed them into the coat, Milt just as quickly taped the coat lining shut again with two-inch-wide masking tape. I checked the flashlight and heavy wire cutters and, with Milt acting as temporary butler, put on the heavy ice-padded coat. I walked slowly toward the fence, steaming with dry-ice vapor like some great lumbering ghost while Milt stayed behind well out of range of the heat sensors.

The barbed wire was tougher than I'd anticipated and the cutters were awkward to handle in the heavy coat, but finally there was a thick-sounding "clup" and in two minutes I had a hole big enough to get through. As I gingerly edged my way through, I heard the sharp snap of the shotgun's pump action and prayed that Milt wasn't operating on overproof. The wisp of moon hung suspended in a canopy of frost-lit stars and I could see the borders of the black holes within the dark sky. As I approached the trellises a hundred yards in from the barbed wire, I turned the flashlight on once and held it low.

They were there—three sensors, twenty feet apart, sitting staring quietly at me. I allowed myself a congratulatory grin, muttering softly, "Tough luck, fellas," and in the next few seconds found myself touching the nearest trellis. I walked slowly, feeling the weight of the ice coat, to the end of the fifty-yard row at the end of which there was a tractor roadway running through the meticulously straight-lined trellises that supported the forest of hops, spreading for miles into the dark hills beyond. I moved my fingers gingerly among the leaves until I felt a small protrusion, a piece of wire, or rather small tubing, coming out at right angles from the trellises. At the end of the piece of tubing, a couple of inches out from the trellis, another vertical T-shaped piece of tubing was attached. I shone the flashlight quickly through the maze of leaves and saw the chicken-wire-like supports, for the hops were all made up of hundreds of the three-inch T-shaped protrusions. I also noticed that here, fifty yards in, the leaves, unlike those at the edge of the farm, were speckled with brown spots. I shone the flashlight on the next trellis. It was the same. And on closer inspection I could see that the T-shaped protrusions formed six-foot-square webs which in turn were bolted to pylons with the hops growing over the squares. I slid my fingers silently down the edge of one of the squares until I felt the rough metallic edge of a patent number. With the ice steaming from the great coat, the cold preventing my body heat from escaping and exciting the high-level desert setting of the sensors, I backtracked, carefully spilling the aniseed oil in the dust. When I reached the end of the trellis line where I had originally started I felt the cool hops and the taut wire supports.

I was very cold by now and had difficulty using the cutters on the numbered piece of tubing. Being the edge of the square, the tubing was thicker. And I had to be careful not to bring down a whole section of trellis, which would alert them in the daylight that someone had been snooping. I picked up the cutters and began making my way back to the fence.

I was halfway there when I heard the first bark—followed by the whine of a jeep and the gabble of voices. Damn it! My ice trick had fooled the sensors, but there must have been infrared visual detectors or something hidden somewhere within the trellises beyond the sensors. The barking exploded into twice the volume. I fell, got up, and heard the Rottweiler coming for me—the panting like a frantic steam engine.

Suddenly the pounding paws stopped, a whine—the aniseed. It would have worked only for a second or two on a tracking dog, but this was an attack dog and he was confused for almost five seconds, scurrying madly in the aniseed-flavored dust. Then he saw me. Now the attack would come full bore. Movement, not scent, was his target. It was too close for Milt to fire—he'd just as easily get me. I shoved my left arm into the pocket of the big coat, took out two lumps of burning ice, stood perfectly still, then threw the ice high into the air against a trellis fifteen yards away. The Rottweiler went straight for the movement toward the steaming ice. I was safe until he reached the ice which was in about five seconds, then he turned and started straight for me.

Running, I pulled the chloroform out, ripped the tab, doused the coat and had it off, tossing it high in his path. He leaped, took the arm, shaking it violently. As I hit the wire he was still coming after me, though momentarily grogged by the rush of chloroform while pulling the coat to the ground. I dived through the fence. There was an orange flash, the roar of a twelve gauge, a long, torturous whine, and a cloud of loam shrouded me as I leaped into the back of the pickup. I was coughing and being thrown about the back like a puppet as Milt put his foot to the floor and screamed off, down then up the other side of the gulch in a cloud of dirt.

There were shouts and two more blasts. The shot peppered the truck's side like hail and I heard the hiss of air, but Milt was in top gear now on the summit. Another shot—light hail and we were out of range. My right hand was hurting, and, looking down, I saw I was still gripping the T-shaped piece of tubing even though the blood from a gravel scrape was trickling down my forefinger. At the turnoff to the main highway Milt stopped and I jumped into the cabin.

"Christ," he said, "I thought you'd bought it."

"So did I, mate. Why'd you fire, you silly bugger?" The Merry Olde flooded the tongue in times of near misses.

"I never shot. I'm not that stupid. They shot the dog. He was too damn close to you. They shot him by mistake."

I opened the glove box and gulped heartily at the bottle. There was about a teaspoonful left. It tasted surprisingly weak.

I held up the T-shaped piece of tubing. "That's the key, Milt," I said excitedly. "That's the bloody key!"

"To what?"

I was still catching my breath. "Well you see . . . even before the SPS . . . if anyone had been in the path of a beam—an experimental beam—they would have had to have been near a rectenna. An experimental-beam source need only be relatively small; its lateral swing, its arc, wouldn't be anywhere as long or as wide as an SPS arc coming from 22,000 miles away. It could be mounted on a truck. But even a small beam would have to be aimed at a receiving antenna—a rectenna. Back there, when I asked you how big the hop farm was, I was remembering what had been said at a White House meeting Dermit attended. He was complaining that a rectenna requires an area of a hundred square miles. At least ten miles by ten. But how would you hide a thing like that in the desert?"

"The farm . . ."

"Right! Right! But, dammit, you see the farm isn't just hiding a rectenna. It *is* the rectenna!" I rapped the T-shaped tubing hard against the dash in my excitement. "Every single trellis, mate. Every bloody trellis is part of the receiving mesh. And Will Orlet's place was too close." I checked the side-view mirror. No lights following. "I think," I said, "I think I know what's going on, Milt. Not just the farm but the whole stinking business."

Eight miles on I looked out, and in my jubilation at having beaten the sensors and infra-red I told Milt that the tire was still half full. Milt said that that meant it was half empty. But even without the spare it looked as if we might make it to the Chevron station ten miles farther on by one of the big berry-packing plants. It was ironic that just after this, the second puncture of the day, we saw another truck, this one loaded with empty fruit cases, which had jackknifed ahead of us. The driver, illuminated by a safety flare, was kicking the offending wheel, obviously having a one-way conversation with it, his rig more or less blocking the highway. It was obvious we couldn't help one another, the wheel sizes being too disparate, and we didn't have a spare anyway. Still, Milt poked his head out of the window. "Anything we can do?"

"No, thanks," said the driver as he protected his eyes from the glare of the flare. "Should have her fixed up in half an hour."

As Milt was talking, I took the opportunity to look at the small patent number on the T-shaped tubing I was still holding. U.S.–OZ321–14–53. I wrote it down on my left wrist with my ballpoint. When I got back to the motel, I'd ring Erica and check it out. She was the expert on rectennas.

"Out of the truck!"

No please, thank you, how-de-do—just the Pekingese nose of the snub .38.

"What the hell—?" I asked.

Milt bumped the muzzle against the bridge of my nose. "Get out of the truck." He opened the door so that I couldn't bash him with it. "Slowly," he said. "Over by the rig."

I could feel the sun's heat in the blacktop not yet dissipated by the approaching cold of the desert night. "I thought you were my friend," I said, and it wasn't meant sarcastically. "Instead you're just a drunk." I could see his face muscles tighten in the light of the flare.

"Sit down," he said. "Around the other side—away from the road." He swung the gun at me. "Now give me that."

"What?"

"Give it to me, Sturgess!"

"Whatever happened to 'Harry'?" I handed him the T-piece, and he tossed it to the rig driver who now reemerged from the shadows, climbed into the cab, sucking on a Coke while using the other hand to start up the big Mack to move it off the road. He turned the lights off so that now only the slit lights of the once loyal pickup remained, making it look strangely ominous, like some monster that had come with the night that had now fully descended upon the desert. I glanced at the stars. They gave me the illusion of freedom. "So?" I said. "They got to Charles E. Milt as well?" Now I understood why he'd reacted so unexpectedly when I'd praised his courage for picking up the torch when the doctor in Grand Coulee had been frightened off. "What happened?" I jabbed. "They promise to let you work on live people again?"

There was still no answer. He just stood there, the eyes cold, not at all alcoholic it struck me. Now I knew why the booze had tasted so weak, like cold tea with nothing more than a dash of rye. Just enough to make it smell boozy. That wasn't to say he wasn't an alcoholic, of course, but with all the driving we'd had to do and the attention he'd had to pay to the Hopsville incident, he'd cooled it for a while.

The thing I couldn't figure out at first was, why wait till the experimental farm? They could have nabbed me after I'd shown the initial interest, and at Will Orlet's farm. But then I realized that it wasn't till then, until I'd actually found the tubing, that Milt knew for sure what I'd discovered. I thanked

God I hadn't mentioned the patent number to him. Best to let them think that I didn't suspect who else was behind it. "You kill Dermit?" I asked. "Like the corpses, do you? Bit of a Sweeney Todd? Give you leave from Riverport, did they?"

"Who are *they*?"

He had me there. He wasn't going to be baited into making another mistake.

After a few seconds I could hear the low moan of an approaching car through the desert hills.

"I never killed Dermit," he said. "We never killed anybody."

"But you know who did?"

He didn't answer.

The police car wasn't flashing any lights when it pulled off in a cloud of salmon-pink dust that wafted over us like talcum and across the slitted lights like the smoke of a nearby caldron. The sheriff—the one I'd seen that morning—shut the door with that easy nonchalance that comes from having the upper hand.

"What's the name?" he said, stuffing the back of his crumpled shirt into his khaki pants, his belly hanging over the wide brown belt.

"Hobbes," I said. "Harry Hobbes."

"Sturgess," interjected Milt. "It's Harry Sturgess."

"All right," said the sheriff, thrusting his thumb toward the squad car, the pipe gripped firmly between his teeth. "You get yourself in the back there."

"You know who I am?" I said as officially as I could. "If you ring Washin—"

"Get in the back, fella."

"What's the charge?"

He reached into the front window and took out the billy club and strode toward me, all two hundred pounds. I got in back. Milt poked his head in. Now I found the residual smell of booze disgusting.

"Sorry about this, Harry."

"Tell me about it, *Chas*."

"It's for the best."

"So's Christmas."

"I just want you to know that personally . . ."

"Just shove off, Chas. If you don't mind."

They handcuffed and blindfolded me. Boozehead was sorry about that too, but it still didn't stop him from tying the knot so tightly that it throbbed against my temple like a hammer. I started to struggle violently against the darkness, the unknown, the numbing, terrifying panic of suffocation.

The needle was sharp, very cold, and it hurt. In a few minutes I could feel my heart pounding like a piston, but it was almost like being outside myself—in some vast night—watching clinically as the drug coursed through the blood, slowing the heart, making me sleepier by the second until I felt a smile begin to spread over me like a warm, gentle blanket.

CHAPTER 21

Roth wasn't dressed for the occasion—unless you consider polka-dot pajamas appropriate for receiving guests. The sight of his pudding belly made me wish I'd kept the blindfold on. But one thing I'll give him, he didn't procrastinate. "Mr. Sturgess, you've caused us a great deal of inconvenience. Now apparently you are committed to sticking your nose into areas where it does not belong. In my opinion you're very fortunate that someone didn't cut it off. I see we have to chat."

I was grinning.

"What's the matter with him?" snapped Roth.

"He got boisterous." It was my mate, Milt.

"What did you give him?"

"Fifty milligrams of Nembutal."

Roth shook his head disgustedly. "Who did you intend to put to sleep? Sturgess or the entire population of Riverport?"

"It's been a while since I've been allowed to work on live specimens," Milt said bitterly.

"Obviously." Roth sat down in a large wicker chair that was decidedly out of place in the Pacific Northwest. I expected natives to appear any minute with long, cool drinks, telling Bwana that his boat was ready to go "Upriver." I felt well enough even though I was hardly mentally alert, and in the mirror I looked pretty stupid, like a happy drunk.

"Bring some coffee will you, dear?" Roth called out to the kitchen. When I saw her, the Nembutal fled my veins and I leaped from the chair. The sheriff took one step and smacked me hard on the forehead.

Roth looked at Erica. "You were right, my dear. He did pursue it."

"It's not what you think," said Erica, looking at me with a mixture of concern and irritation.

"No?" I snapped. "What *do* I think?"

"You think," interrupted Roth, "that you are some poor victim."

"Aren't I?"

Roth sipped at the coffee. "True in a way. A test case if you like?"

"For what?"

"Our security."

"*Our?*"

Roth yawned. "In the morning, I think. We're all tired." He yawned again. "Who shot the Rottweiler?"

The sheriff was embarrassed. "Hartley. He's one of the new guards."

"Dock his pay," said Roth, stirring the coffee and tapping the spoon gently on the side of the pure white cup.

"He wasn't killed, Professor. He'll be all right. Just grazed in the hind leg."

"I will not tolerate that kind of fumbling. He was instructed merely to test the defenses. To make sure they were up to standard. Which clearly they are not. Sturgess was the first real test. This failure to"—Roth hesitated—"to take him . . . unharmed . . . and instead wounding a valuable dog is not acceptable. Is that clear?"

"It won't happen again, Professor."

"Dock his pay."

"Yes, sir."

"Excuse me," I said. "Am I on Mars?"

Roth roared with laughter, pointing the silver spoon at me. No longer the professor, he looked more like a jolly cook. The pudding gut wobbled like tickled jelly. "In the morning, Mr. Sturgess," he said happily. "In the morning."

As he rose to go and the sheriff lifted me from the chair before taking me to my "quarters," the thing I was angriest about was that Roth hadn't worn a bathrobe in front of Erica, as if she was used to it. And I told the sheriff so. "It's bloody disgusting," I said. Wyatt Earp said nothing until we got to the small room. It was furnished pleasantly enough, if you don't mind bars on the windows.

"Now you have a good rest," he said. "And if there's any trouble we don't want you falling, do we?"

The Nembutal was really making me dopey now. "What . . . what d'you mean?" I asked. "What you mean, falling?"

"I mean"—Wyatt smiled—"if there's any trouble I'll come and beat the shit out of you. Good night."

It was about five in the morning. All was quiet. The first thing I became aware of was a slight "clink," the second was the sweet, grassy smell of alfalfa on the night breeze. The second "clink" slid to a click and then a barely audible bump of the door closing. I didn't move my torso, partly because I still felt very drowsy and secondly because I didn't want whoever it was to see my right hand gripping the bed ready to give me support for the kick.

"Harry darling." My eyes caught the wisp of nightgown—pink with white lace.

"Erica bitch," I answered.

A long pause. "Harry, you don't understand."

I propped myself up on one elbow. I wanted to say that if one more person told me I didn't understand, I'd punch them out where he or she stood. But instead I smiled graciously. "Sure." I spoke softly, honoring her own cautious tone but also remembering Roth's lack of a bathrobe. "I understand, Erica. You're Roth's rectenna."

The slap sounded like a gunshot and my cheek was burning. I was glad.

"You filthy bastard . . ."

"Pray go on."

"I was going to tell you, you bastard, that if it wasn't for me you could have been . . . the CIA could have . . ."

"Your first name Mata, is it?"

"I wasn't just spying on you. Well, all right, I was—to start with—but then I got to like you."

"Pardon me while I break down. When's breakfast?"

"I found out you weren't from the other side. That you were genuinely concerned."

I wanted to ignore her but curiosity wouldn't countenance it. "What other side?"

For the first time she looked absolutely puzzled. "KGB, of course. We thought you were a mole. Advising the President against the SPS would have been the perfect cover."

"*What?*" I was about to proclaim that she and Roth and the whole inner circle of superclassified SPS administrators were stark raving mad when she knocked the wind out of me.

"Like Tier," she said. I recalled how Hoskins had also told me that Tier was KGB. I'd thought he was mad too.

"You see," she continued, "why we were so suspicious. You going to meet Tier in Vancouver and Tier so much against the SPS and NSA expansion—using his 'environmental' concern to cover his espionage and then you opposing the plan with the same kind of arguments."

"You were tailing me there."

"That's right."

"Who killed Tier? Hoskins told me it was the CIA. That Tier tried to run."

"Yes. Professor Roth explained that someone from the CIA had to—"

"What's the problem, miss?"

It was Wyatt Earp. He took the keys from her as one would a cookie from a child. I was surprised to see the Ph.D. give them up to the sheriff so readily.

"I was informing Mr. Sturgess that he's barking up the wrong tree."

Wyatt wasn't paid to think.

"But"—Erica hesitated—"it can wait till morning, I guess."

He let her out without a word. Roth would know about that breach of procedure the moment he woke up. Wyatt looked over at me, using the key as a range finder. "You have a good sleep now."

"You have a good run," I said. The face clouded.

"Too many Coors," I said. "You're carrying a bit too much of the old back yard."

His eyes narrowed with suspicion.

"The old lard," I explained. "Around the gut. Fat!"

He smiled happily and strode over. I could hear an early robin outside.

"Y'know," he said, "Professor Roth mostly works alone up here. Know what I mean?"

I said nothing.

"Well, I guess when he calls up Dr. Sarn to check on developments I reckon he dips the old wick. Hear she's a screamer. Y'know—'Gimme more' . . ."

I threw a punch. He sidestepped neatly for his weight and hit me in the stomach. I couldn't breathe, the pain exploding all through me. "You want to *fall* again?" he asked politely. He flicked my ear, making it sting like an acid burn. "You want to fall again, Mr. Hobbes? Well?"

I still couldn't speak. At the door he turned. "I guess they have to use a couple of pillows. But"—he shrugged—"maybe she goes down on him, eh?"

I was so furious I could have killed him, but I was still frantically trying to get my wind, wondering what she'd been about to tell me, knowing I'd have to wait till morning to find out. And visualizing what Earp had just told me.

On the way to the big log cabin with the EXPERIMENTAL FARM HEADQUARTERS sign on it, I saw a strange sight: Roth, in track suit, naked from the waist up and lathered in perspiration, was sitting cross-legged, yogi fashion, his eyes in the world of the trance. I looked at Wyatt. "Well live and learn—the jelly meditates."

The venerable professor looked like a Buddha, hands humbly cupped in somnolent contemplation of the universe. But the great white belly, fully distended and glistening with what smelled like coconut oil, undid the holy image. He actually seemed to be nodding off, what the Bali islanders call "awaying." Earp opened the cabin door, ordering me to have a nice day.

"And you do your three miles," I said, pointing my finger at his ram's horn buckle that was holding up his gut. "Just like Sloth over there."

While I waited inside the cabin, I got really scared. I knew what the little three-inch T-shaped tubing was. A dipole, one of millions that made up the long wire-webbed trellises. All right, the miles of green hops were nothing more than a verdant blanket, a cover for a hundred-square-mile rectenna—a receiving antenna for the SPS. But why the hop cover? I didn't know. All I knew was that Milt knew I'd had the dipole, which meant Roth knew. They all knew. So the problem was very simple—what would happen to me?

Showered and dressed, Roth was transformed. Gunmetal-gray suit with a drooping but authoritative maroon bow tie that all by itself was intimidating. The log cabin lodge, set in a clearing completely surrounded by the hop trellises, like a park bench in a hedge maze, was lavishly decorated in early American colonial but wasn't ostentatious.

The moment Roth smiled, offering me the most comfortable seat, I had a gut feeling that I was to be threatened rather than informed. It turned out to be a bit of both.

Roth stirred his Sanka. "Mr. Hobbes," he smiled. The others didn't get it. He thought the "in" joke would set me at ease and make me more receptive. It did. "Harry, you've created a very embarrassing situation for us."

I said nothing. Erica was in a loose blue blouse and white pants. She looked good in anything. Roth refilled the cup himself. There were only the three of us. Milt was smoking in the kitchen, downing orange juice, and whatever else was in it. Roth piled in the sugar.

"The problem, Harry—you mind if I use your Christian name?"

"Not at all." I looked at Erica. "A lot of people do."

"Good. The goal, Harry, that we are engaged in establishing with our Canadian and British colleagues, is the greatest alternative power source in history. Solar power—right?"

I nodded.

"There are certain requirements, however, that must be met. Security, for example. In the event of nuclear attack against this country."

"And Canada." I smiled.

"Of course. Of course."

"Well," he continued, feeding the coffee more sugar, "the situation is that we need to protect our receiving sites. Make them secure as possible. Solar energy could be the only source of power left after an attack."

"How about the hunter-killer satellites?" I said. "Rectennas aren't any good if there are no SPSes to send power."

Roth conceded my point, with one qualification. "If nuclear war were extended to space, it would be uncontrollable. Any nuclear explosion out there will affect New York and Moscow as the world spins. There would be a radiation rain all over the earth. No one benefits."

"SPSes don't have to be taken out by nuclear blasts, Professor."

"True, there could be such a thing as limited war in space. Nonnuclear. Conventional destruction of one satellite by another. We know this."

Roth sipped at the coffee. He knew his smokescreen about protecting rectenna sites had failed.

"Besides," I said, to rub it in, "don't try to tell me that the Russians can't photograph a hop field. A hundred square miles of metal supports and . . ." I stopped dead. He had me. He'd fed me the nuclear-attack yarn. I'd challenged it and in so doing revealed that I knew any so-called attempt to hide a rectenna site from the Russians was impossible and that therefore there must be another reason for hiding it beneath a cover of leaves.

Erica was looking at the floor as if the carpet would soak up her embarrassment. Milt, his glass empty for a change, was staring glumly at the empty kitchen sink. Roth reached into his pocket and extracted the dipole. "You're quite right, of course." His hand froze on the tubing. "They can photograph the field easily enough. Infra red would see through the leaf cover and show up the metallic mesh. That's true, but otherwise it just looks like any large irrigation farm on the Columbia."

My brain was racing. If he thought for a second that I knew the rectenna had long been operational and had been the cause of the unexplained deaths, the burned-out eyes, the sterility, and the cancers in the Riverport area months *before* the SPS was launched, I'd be letting on I knew more than was good for my health. I'd try to shift direction—concentrate on finding out the real reason for the elaborate cover. Make him believe that I thought the rectenna was just being built, in keeping with the President's original proposal, simply trellises that could be moved and re-erected in a hurry if need be. "Yes," I said, "the hops are a good idea—won't interfere too much with the microwave reception." I thought of my own report to the President against the SPS and, mustering all the enthusiasm I could, added, "I guess growing hops will stop the farmers from objecting to *us* using the land for a rectenna now that the SPS is official." I nodded sagely. "Yes, it's a damned good argument against charges of land despoilment."

Milt had poured himself another orange, but Roth didn't move.

"Don't insult me, Sturgess." He moved the coffee quickly. Some of it spilled. I started to answer but he cut me short. "You know the whole area is a rectenna, right?"

"A potential one. Yes," I lied.

"I *said* don't insult me. You know we've been using it. You penetrated our defenses. Beyond the perimeter you must have seen the spottiness of the leaves—the water molecules in them have absorbed some of the beam's energy." He picked up a stiff linen napkin and mopped the saucer. The stained napkin went limp. "The hops are meant to dissuade local interest from a distance, yes, but you know about Mr. Orlet, I understand." He glanced at Milt and sipped the syrupy coffee. "And others . . ."

I watched Erica. She was watching Roth, her mouth wide with surprise like a small child. "Others?" she asked. "What others?"

Roth's eyes followed a buzzing fly. His fat hands shot out with remarkable speed. The buzzing did not stop but continued somewhere behind the sofa in agonizing little bursts. "There've been some unfortunate accidents," he said. He tried to kill any possible alarm with the cool, matter-of-fact tone. "While you were working on improving rectenna design in Washington," he said to Erica, "we had some difficulty with the beam focus on the mobile SPS simulators—long before the SPS launch."

He turned to me as a pacifier. "No use sending the SPS up if we couldn't receive a wide beam at the rectenna here and convert it and feed it into the existing conventional grid system."

"You had some difficulty?" she said, alarm in her voice. "Such as?"

"Such as killing people," I interjected, remembering the photos. "Causing cancer, impotency . . . just little things like that."

Roth's eyes were cold. "That was quite unnecessary."

"Quite," I parleyed. "They would have preferred to be alive and well."

"I meant your tone, Mr. Sturgess. Your implication. They were accidents."

"Accidents!" I snapped, glowering at both of them. "Pardon me for asking, Professors It'll-never-happen-here, but what went wrong with the superduper DT button? Or didn't you have any on the mobile simulator?"

"The deactivating button was working fine—it could have saved them from being unduly exposed."

"Zapped!" I said.

"If you like."

"I don't like."

"The DT button could have prevented their *exposure* but

unfortunately the focusing mechanism—the transmitting cone —was slightly off."

"Off?"

I could hear the ticking of the big grandfather clock.

"And Tier found out?" I said.

"Yes." Roth was unequivocal and unapologetic. "Forgive me if I don't express any sorrow for his demise, Mr. Sturgess, but we know he was a KGB agent. He was trying to wreck the entire program. Pushing his arguments onto you about microwaves interfering with NSA listening activities. Unfortunately he uncovered our—teething troubles, the focusing mishap, before the SPS was launched. He could have ruined the entire program—doomed this country and the western hemisphere, deprived it of an alternative energy source for generations to come."

"So you killed him?"

"As I explained to Hoskins—he gave us no choice."

"Who?" I spat the words out. "Who did it?"

The sheriff's voice was the most unemotional I'd heard it. "I called him—he tried to run for it."

"Sure," I said. "In his hotel room?"

"I mean, he tried to draw first."

"Ah!" I nodded knowingly. "Like Billy the Kid?"

"Don't be a smartass, Sturgess. He was KGB and he blew it. He damned near blew you. We thought you were in on the same team."

"So I hear," I said sarcastically, looking over at Erica. "Then you sent garlic guts."

They looked at me, perplexed.

"The bellboy."

"No," answered the sheriff, "we didn't."

Roth coughed awkwardly. "That 'gentleman' surfaced from a subcontractor." He hesitated. "They were concerned about your reputation."

"What the hell—"

"Your reputation as an EPA investigator, before you joined the White House. And that, Mr. Sturgess, is the—how shall I say?—the most regrettable side. The ugly side, and quite frankly we are appealing to your appreciation of the national and, I might add, the international problems, to put it in perspective. You have every right to refuse of course. But—" He glanced at Erica. "Could we have some more coffee, dear?"

Germaine Greer would have had kittens. Erica didn't like it either, but she had enough sense to see it wasn't the time for a women's march.

Roth started the little sugar-spoon business again, unrepentantly piling in the calories but in reality buying time, marshaling his verbs for the least shocking effect. I was too impatient to wait.

"The beam-focusing gear," I said. "You were saying it was flawed."

He seemed almost relieved. The word "flawed," like his "difficulty," wasn't as harsh as "screwed up."

"Design problems?" I proffered to draw him out. "With the contractors?"

"Exactly. Tier told you, I expect?"

"No, but I knew he was on to something," I answered.

"Of course," he went on, with an eyebrow raised in concern. "These things happen in all programs. You'll remember the Thresher—the nuclear sub. The pipes froze I believe, the ballast tanks couldn't pump out water fast enough for them to rise. Poor beggars."

"Yes," I commented. "And Three Mile Island—and the Macphearson leak." I tried to make it sound nonaccusing.

Roth extended his hands in papal gratitude at my apparent reasonableness. "I told you Mr. Sturgess would understand," he said, looking at the other three then back to me. "Exactly what you were trying to explain to the White House staff I believe; that you were not against nuclear energy but bad design. You just can't dismantle a vital project because of a few design problems. You work them out." He was still watching me, smiling broadly but most of all gratefully. "You're a man of the world, Mr. Sturgess."

"But one that doesn't like coverups," I said, looking directly at him. I could still see the joker with the knife going for my throat. "Problems with legitimate contractors are one thing. Problems with thug contractors are another."

Roth's smile deserted him. It was right then that Erica saw the light. "He's right, Professor," she said. "If I'd known about others being hurt—being killed—I'd never have agreed to go along with smoothing it over." Her eyes were wet and shiny.

"Excuse me," I asked, "but how do you smooth over Will Orlet's impotency and his sterility and his wife's and the effect on their family?" I stared at her. I didn't doubt her, but I wanted to make absolutely sure. "You do know about all that, sweetie?" I said viciously. "You've come to terms with that one, have you?"

The bottom lip was quivering.

Roth glanced at his watch. "We'll arrange to completely pay off the mortgage on his farm—which, I might add, is very considerable. Plus there will be a substantial cash payment. By that I mean in excess of two million dollars. The same for the others who were inconvenienced."

"Inconvenienced?"

"There are other people in this world, Mr. Sturgess, who are impotent, who suffer sterility. They get nothing."

"They're not guinea pigs."

"It was . . . an accident."

"Lovely. What will you tell them? How will you explain it?"

"Temporary water pollution. Mercury dumping on the Canadian side. Since rectified."

"You believe they'll buy that?"

"Yes."

"Why?"

"The sums will be substantial, as I said."

The bastard. "The truth might be nice," I snorted, "—that you screwed up in the design of the transmission antenna—the focusing mechanism. Even if it is fixed now."

Roth exploded. Rising swiftly, he sent the coffee cup flying. "Use your head, man! The truth would merely mean monetary compensation anyway. And jeopardize the entire program. You'll kill far more people with smog alone if the SPS program doesn't go on. It's not kindergarten, Sturgess. It's not black and white. It's gray, my friend. Unsavory contractors—yes, I grant you"—his right hand chopped the air—"but allies of necessity—we cannot have delays—union trouble—that sort of thing. But that's now rectified and we're pressing on. They *will* get the job done. It's sad, tragic, that a handful of people have been killed. But so are test pilots. So are pedestrians. Write the Washington *Post* if you want. Go public! Risk the whole program, destroy our greatest chance in a century to extricate ourselves from the grip of this . . . this energy monster." The massive bulk loomed over me. "Are you that goddamn self-righteous, Sturgess? Eh? Well, man, are you?"

I could hear the kitchen tap dripping like a jungle drum.

He put his hand gently on my shoulder. The voice was soft and paternal, almost priestly. "You'll lose sleep, Harry. The handful of us who know will. We can't bring them back. So now you know. The photos were right. There have been accidents, but we've corrected it." The hand returned to the coffee cup. "And, by God, the one thing we can do is keep their children warm—which means nothing less than survival in the next century. We can keep this old world moving. That's worth something isn't it? That, I think, is worth a little insomnia?"

I sat there for a long time before I spoke and when I did it was tired and slow. "This all happened before the SPS went up?"

"Yes—except Orlet."

I didn't say a word about the old man, Thompson, whose corpse I'd seen only a day before.

"All before you had launched the SPS?"

"Yes."

I remembered Orlet and the air glow. "So what happened to Orlet second time around—three weeks ago?"

Roth sighed, and opened up his hands plaintively. "We thought the focus system was corrected from tests on the mobile unit, the SPS simulator, and so we went ahead and installed it on the SPS. But it acted up one more time when the SPS got up before we got it ironed out. It was only off point zero one five of a degree at the very most. Much less than the error with the simulator unit, actually." The bastard, trying to make it sound like nothing. I didn't have my calculator with me, but if five degrees, 22,300 miles out in orbit, meant an arc of 3,000 miles long, .015 meant about nine miles. "Probably metal stress on the antenna during the transfer from LEO to GEO," he added.

I thought of the others—the white-eyed dead. "Where was the mobile simulator—the beam source?"

"In the Okanagan, southeastern British Columbia. We moved it about occasionally—testing different conditions. It was dismantled once the SPS was up."

"Where'd you get the energy for it?"

"We milked the Pacific northwest grid." He grinned boyishly. "There were a few blackouts reported in the news."

"I'll bet." I smiled just as boyishly. I was trying for camaraderie. It was my only hope. It all seemed so civilized, our conversation, but the danger signal was beeping in my brain. "The beam from the SPS now. It's working well?" I asked suppliantly.

Erica handed me a coffee. "Beautifully." The eyes were a little drier.

I nodded. "What kind of efficiency are we getting?"

She was clearly and genuinely saddened by Orlet, but now the professional pride quickly surfaced. Still, there was something forced about it. "The efficiency coefficient is excellent," she said. "And the conversion rate is much better than we thought. Loss of Load probability is less than half a day a year and the waste heat at this rectenna is less than twelve percent."

"Pretty good," I said in my best congratulatory tone.

"It's phenomenal," confirmed Roth.

"It's quite an achievement," I commented, and it was.

"We're sorry about the dogs and so on," said Roth, brushing his hand apologetically in the air. "But we have to keep people out for their own safety."

"You mean we're receiving the SPS beam here? Right now?" I must have sounded alarmed.

"No," he laughed, his arm resting on my other shoulder. "We alternate with the Canadian rectenna. We're on tomorrow. It's a good exercise in the event that one of us breaks down for some reason. We can switch to the other and feed into the grid system. The delay would be minimal."

Roth, borrowing a tobacco pouch from the sheriff, began stuffing a bent stem briar, tapping in the sweet-smelling Cavendish with the end of the pearl-handled penknife. Everything he did had an air of professional ease about it. He didn't drop one strand of the tobacco, handed the pouch back to Wyatt, and waved a match hypnotically back and forth over the pipe. "These little troubles we've had with the program . . ." He sucked heavily and a gray-blue cloud wafted up.

"Yes," I said. "What about them?"

"The President knows." He said it as casually as if he were announcing lunch. But I was under full control now so I played it cool and simply shrugged unconcernedly. Roth blew the match out, stuck one hand in his pocket, and looked pensively out of the window onto the vast green hop fields. "We've discussed it in some detail. He agrees. It's regrettable —always get a few unsavory characters in such a huge program —but the stakes are just too high to go public, Harry." He flashed a thin smile. "Same way as FDR had us sinking ships before we actually declared war. Can't always wait for a public debate. As I say, regrettable but necessary for a new world of energy, for national security."

Milt brought in sandwiches. Roth struck another match. "It's a hell of a decision," he conceded.

I was almost starting to like him.

"It's the last job I'd want," he said. "The President's."

That I didn't believe, but I nodded. I nodded at everything because it was as clear as the proverbial crystal that Roth citing his "new world" and "national security" wasn't about to protect anyone who rocked the boat. The threat hadn't been made overt, of course. It didn't have to be. No contractors were mentioned, it was all merely alluded to: "unsavory characters" . . . "but the stakes are just too high . . ." etc. Roth knew I understood perfectly. He put his arm around me, his moist, predatory mouth opening like a giant gopher's. "Have a good trip home—and, Harry!"

"Yes?"

"I appreciate your concern. I really do."

When Wyatt drove me out from the cabin to the high chain entrance of Hopsville I was surprised to see the pickup ready and waiting for me to drive back to Riverport. Roth wanted to be as helpful as he could, to expedite my departure. Except for my bags at the motel, I had no reason to delay. Or so he thought. I was the most depressed I'd been for years, ever since Linda's death. Erica had used me—and for a good cause, she thought. Milt the same.

I was also depressed because while all the loaded fruit trucks were passing me on the highway a green Ford sedan stayed behind me. I couldn't see the occupants. All I knew for sure was that there were two shapes, and one, the driver, was wearing a bright yellow shirt. They stayed behind me even when I pulled up at the Chevron station near the isolated packing plant. The station was out of gas, which wasn't unusual these days, but I didn't want gas. I rang Ralph Stein at Langley. Thank God for real friends. I gave him the patent number of the T-shaped dipole. The answer came through via computer in seconds and he told it to me in two words: "Sudley Steel."

"Orders given to them for the SPS program?"

"Five point two billion dollars."

Now I knew for sure why Roth had let me drive away. Sudley Steel were the "unsavory characters." They had had a "chat" with Dermit and Dermit was dead. If the Sudley Steel gentlemen did anything to me . . . well, what you don't know about you can't help. Right?

A few miles on I noticed the Ford was still behind me. They must have pulled off and waited while I was phoning. I slowed down to let them pass. It struck me that Roth might never have met them after all. Not that it mattered. The point was that now they'd seen me drive out of Hopsville they knew that I knew too much for their own good.

Now I was sure that Art Lane, who didn't want the SPS,

had been killed by thugs from Sudley Steel—two of whose lads had also helped Dermit into the limousine that day on Pennsylvania Avenue. And Roth knew about the thug contractors. How much did he know about Dermit's murder—and Art Lane's "accident"? Just how far would he turn a blind eye? I was so wrought up that for a moment I even imagined he'd told Sudley Steel to leave an air pocket in the Macphearson wall—thereby halting nuclear construction entirely.

As I pulled into the Riverport Motel, I started to worry about something else—the old orchard laborer, Thompson, who was on ice in the morgue. He'd lived nowhere near Orlet's farm, nowhere near nine miles from Hopsville's rectenna, but thirty miles on the other side of Riverport. And he'd died *after* the SPS had been put up. If his death was beam-related it wasn't the effect of the dismantled experimental beam from the Canadian side—but the direct result of a beam error from the SPS. And because of the distance he'd lived from the rectenna it couldn't have simply been a .015-degree error. Which meant Roth had lied—which meant that the SPS beam could just as easily have been out twenty degrees or more—and accidentally hit every major city in the United States and half a dozen other countries as well. I was so deep in thought about this, about what I was going to do, about how to warn the President that this kind of change from the original figures could turn an unpalatable coverup of a few accidental victims into something much more ominous, that I didn't notice that the Ford had vanished. I did see one thing clearly, however, and that was why Milt's moods had been so mercurial—why he'd been friendly one minute at the morgue, then suspicious, then angry—all in the space of an hour—and why he'd shown me Thompson's eyes. Roth's government lads had gotten to him as they'd gotten to the doctor in Grand Coulee. But showing me Thompson's face was Milt's last act of defiance—telling me that the zapping was still going on—that the "error" hadn't been corrected. Poor drunk bastard; "deep down," as he'd said, he really had meant to help, before they got to him.

Where were the boys in the Ford?

When I entered the motel the proprietress gave me my Sears package. Insufficient postage. I owed her ten cents. "Gladly," I said, and gave her a dollar.

After I inserted the key in the lock, I tapped the door open and stood well back. There was no one there. I put the safety lock on the door, took the Smith & Wesson from the box, and had a long soak in the tub. I had to get to the President, to convince him that the transmission antenna wasn't corrected by any means. I heard the door rattle and lifted the .38, sitting motionless in the bath. It was only a draft.

Before I saw the President I'd have to have proof of what I thought was happening beyond the "unfortunate accident" Roth had told him about. The point was that if an old man had recently been zapped dead so far away from the rectenna, it meant that the beam's aiming mechanism that was supposed to have been corrected wasn't and that there might be a much higher "intensity" of power than we'd been told would ever be used by the SPS beam. So intense that even thirty miles from center you could die. But was I simply too tired to think straight? Was I really blowing everything out of proportion? There was one way to be sure. It was unsavory, but it would give me the answer. I'd have to go grave-digging and . . .

The tap on the door was quick and urgent. I wrapped the towel around me, cocked the hammer, and went to the off side of the door. "Who is it?"

"Message for you, Mr. Sturgess."

"I know," I said. "From Miss Erica Sarn. Right?"

"Yes."

"And you're the bellboy?" There was silence.

"No. We don't have bellboys. I'm sorry, I don't under—"

"Doesn't matter. Slide it under the door."

To my utter astonishment, a note appeared. It was from Erica Sarn. It read: "Meet me at Chelan Lodge, 7:30. Do not use your telephone." I looked at the map. Chelan Lodge was eleven miles to the north.

I read the note again and shook my head disbelievingly. I pulled the chair well away from the bed and tapping out a few drops of linseed oil I lubricated the waist holster. I rubbed and rubbed until it was so smooth that a good hiccup would throw out the .38.

CHAPTER 22

The road from Riverport to Chelan Lodge is perfect for ambush. There is a stretch close on fourteen miles strewn with car-sized boulders left over from the gravel-filled moraines of ancient glaciers that had inched down from the Canadian Okanagan to the north. In one section where the long black one-in-thirty grade road ran parallel to the sky-blue race of river, someone could see you coming three miles away. The boulders were scattered so close to the road that he wouldn't need a telescopic sight.

At first I hadn't believed it was Erica's note at all, and even now, driving toward Chelan, I still wasn't sure; but two things argued for its authenticity. First, why try something that had failed to get me in Vancouver, and secondly, why try to draw me out onto the Chelan road when they could have blown me off the road on the way in from Hopsville?

Why? I asked myself as I walked down the thorny hill to the parking lot, why did Erica Sarn want to see me?

Down by Chelan Lodge's deserted marina a lonely yellow neon told me that "Hertz Is Here."

The dark cedar of the lodge stood before the moon like a paper cut-out, and below it the long purple-black finger of the lake stretched westward, away from the desert and toward the black Cascades, which crouched like giant bears against the horizon.

"Were you followed?"

"I thought you'd be glad to see me," she said.

"Were you followed?"

"How would I know?"

"A Ford—British Columbia license HJC-648."

"I don't know," she snapped.

"You were careful enough about your note and my telephone, but you don't know if you were followed?"

We were talking fast and angrily.

"I was worried about *you*. If you can believe it? Not about me."

I studied her face as you would a portrait, the brown hair shifting to auburn in the soft light, the hazel eyes sparkling above the firm yet delicate skin of the neck that was taut with anxiety, and below, the quickening, hypnotic rise and fall of the dark green sweater sculpted to her body.

Finally I holstered the gun. The tension was ebbing from her too, but the usual fullness of her lips was still drawn in a tight red line. "You must believe me, Harry—I never knew anything about the others who were . . ."

"Killed!" I snarled. I still had enough bile in me for that.

The thin line broke and the lips began quivering.

"I'm sorry," I said. "I believe you."

She eased herself onto the edge of the bed. "What are you going to do?"

I walked over to the window and looked down on the sheen of lake. The toll ferry that ran the fifty-five miles to Stehekin looked dead at the water's edge. "What can I do? The President knows." Until I'd heard her out, I wasn't going to tell her about the old laborer. I'd rolled dice before, with someone called Milt, and he'd ended up sticking a gun up my nose.

"It's a company called Sudley Steel," she said, "that had the trouble with the antenna."

I said nothing but I was thinking—fast. Now the pieces were

sliding nearer together. Sudley Steel had screwed up at Macphearson with the air bubble, and Roth had got them off the hook—at his price—to build the SPS on the quiet. Well, he'd bummed out on that one. They'd made another error here. Or was it an error? Maybe it all went further back. Goddamn it—had the Macphearson "accident" been an accident? It *had* allowed Roth the perfect excuse for his superboosting of the SPS.

Come on, Sturgess, I remonstrated, who in his or her right mind would deliberately set up a nuclear accident so they could enlist support for an alternative energy source?

"Did you hear me?" she asked.

I answered without turning—acting almost uninterested. "Yes, I heard."

"They're the major contractors," she added.

I kept looking out the window, watching for any movement, and not letting on I already knew about Sudley Steel. Best I played it this way. Damn, she was beautiful. I wanted her and I wanted to believe she'd come to help, but for all I knew she could be as wired up for sound as Mike Wallace. An old Langley lesson—in any kind of building, assume you're on tape.

Her finger traced the winding pattern of the bedspread. "They would lose a lot if this gets out. I"—she hesitated—"I think Roth was warning you."

"About what?" I asked noncommitally.

"That if you went . . . public with this it wouldn't do any good."

"I know that," I said, piqued. "I just told you, 'What can I do?'" If she was wired, here was my chance for the big insurance coverage. "You think I'm nuts?" I spat it out. "I'm not risking my neck for any congressional grandstanders to look into Sudley Steel—or the SPS—then have them leave me out in the cold. Besides," I said sullenly, lowering my voice, "Roth is right."

If her startled look was an act it was ripe for an Academy Award nomination. "What do you mean, he's *right?*" she demanded, outraged.

I just wanted to have her, there on the bed, make love to her. Drive her right through the wall. "I mean," I said, "your boss is right. We lose a few people perfecting the beam focus but in the end we save thousands."

"But—" she began.

"Look," I cut in sharply. "Do you know what would happen if Con Ed blew it again in New York? Straight off a thousand people might die in hospitals before the auxiliaries could start up—*if* we had any oil left to start them up. I don't like it. I hate it. But Roth's right, dammit! We blow the whistle and the whole program is put back. Besides, with the President knowing, I'm not sure a whistle'd be heard, and if it was, it would be publicly denied by the White House. It's the best shade of gray we can hope for."

There was a long, sad, angry, disappointed silence from her. She was staring at me as if I was somebody else. Right then I was.

"I think," she said very quietly, "that's disgusting. You disgust me."

I shrugged. "So what are you going to do, Florence Nightingale? Carry the lamp?" I caught her hand, an inch from my face and held it. "Well—are you?"

"Let me go, you bastard!"

I did, and she hit me with the other hand.

"I don't know what I'm going to do," she said. "But it's not just that those people have been killed. I want to make sure that no more will be. Are you stupid enough to believe the experimental beam only moved point zero two degrees? And even if it did, beam center shouldn't kill people. Not unless they were in it for more than ten, twenty minutes."

I sneered appropriately. If I was going to test her, it might as well be an acid test. "C'mon, Erica, you're not telling me they were deliberately zapped? Used as guinea pigs?"

"No, I think it was an accident all right. But it's the power intensity. It would have to be much higher than the SPS beam was designed for. And they were killed *before* the SPS was launched."

"So?"

She looked at me as if I'd suddenly gone stupid. "I've not slept well," I said weakly. "I'm tired. So what are you getting at?"

"So I'd like to take a look at the SPS control center on the Canadian side."

If Erica Sarn was wired for sound, and Roth and Sudley Steel were listening to that little hypothesis, she'd just put herself in the electric chair.

"You telling me you haven't seen the SPS control center? Hell, you're in the program aren't you?"

She gave me one of her rare exasperated looks. "I told you in Washington, Roth deals with beam transmission. I only work with rectenna development. Besides, I'm not supreme commander—he is. I'm just one of hundreds of scientists all over the country. Only Roth knows the whole picture. But now I want to see that control center."

"Okay, but can we eat first?" I said. "I'm starving."

She was utterly amazed at my lightning change from Hyde to Jekyll. "But . . . but I thought—"

I gave her a crash explanation of my Langley-taught caution against being taped.

"You bastard, you never trusted me."

Before I could answer she raced on, smiling, forgiving. "I don't blame you." The smile vanished and she turned away. "Not after what I did for Roth. Meeting you in Washington for drinks and pumping you the way I did." She turned back and was coming closer. "But you see I believed—no—I *believe* in the program so much." She paused. "Tell me we're right to try poking around, Harry."

"We are. Better to clean house before it gets too dirty to clean. Ends don't justify the means. It's an old bedtime story."

"I'm glad." She kissed me. "I'm glad we're together."

"Where's Roth?"

"He's on his way to an international science conference in Finland. He'll be in Vancouver by now, meeting with Sudley Steel executives."

"Thugs, you mean?" I told her about the cockney accents and the jogging and the little torn photographs. How it was clear that Roth wasn't going to risk the SPS to put a few unsavory contractors out of business. Over dinner I told her about the old man, Thompson, who'd been killed in the last week—long *after* the SPS launch and weeks *after* the latest Orlet incident—*after* Roth had said the SPS had been fixed.

It spoiled her dessert because it meant that if the old man hadn't been zapped by the land-based experimental beam then he'd been zapped by the SPS with its control in southern British Columbia. And if *its* beam focus was even slightly off, if it hadn't been fixed after the Orlet incident, then all the horror of a fatal SPS arc was no longer a mere possibility. It was a dire probability. But even if an accident should happen, the arc wouldn't be instantly fatal unless, as Erica had just pointed out, the power was exceptionally high. It was to find that out that we really needed to know if the old man, Thompson, had been badly burned. I'd only seen his eyes. If we knew that any other part but the most vulnerable, the eyes, had been cooked, then we'd have a good idea of the amount of power being used. Without that we'd have no proof. I told Erica about my nocturnal plans for going to Lincoln South Cemetery the following night. I wanted to go then and there, but I'd have fallen asleep at the wheel.

After dinner the nervous exhaustion hit both of us and as we entered the room I slipped the chain across. We undressed each other like two sleepwalkers. The bed creaked. It would. It put her off. I opted for the carpeted floor but the air conditioner was a bit too cold. With two interruptions I thought we were headed for "Oh well—sorry, darling—next time, huh?" but no, we soon warmed up and I forgot Roth, Sudley Steel, and the world. The truth, of course, is that it rarely happens together the first time around, but fortune was with us and it was full of happiness and perfect timing.

I covered her with the bedspread and put the pillow beneath her head, then went to the little fridge and celebrated with a beer. Still tired but relaxed and happy I was mentally much more alert, and then it struck me like a cold blast from the conditioner just what Erica had said, even though she hadn't seen the chillingly logical conclusion of her own comment. If the old man had been zapped by a shift of the SPS beam when it had been *moving* it would have had to kill him in a few seconds. To do that the power would *have* to be enormously higher than even we'd imagined. There was no way I could sleep now.

I flicked on the TV—the weather was to remain sunny with the possibility of rain, and the latest ash cloud from Mount St. Helens was more or less stationary, but a light northerly moving down from the Arctic had now reached northeastern Washington. The ash would soon shift. Changes were definitely in the air. I felt cold.

It was 11:30 P.M. I rang Richmond. Only as a sleepy Mrs. Reardon answered did I remember the time difference. It was 2:30 A.M. there.

"Hello?" Her voice was raspy and bewildered.

"Is Sylvia there?" I asked.

"Oh—"

I felt my throat constrict. But it was all right—it was so early it obviously took her a few seconds to recall the safe response. "Sylvia's on vacation."

Thank God. I wanted to go home, but Jenny would only be truly safe when I was safe and I would only be safe when I knew . . .

"Erica." I shook her gently. "I'm going now. To the cemetery."

She grasped my arm strongly for someone in her somnolent state. "I'm coming with you," she protested groggily, stubbornly.

"No," I said.

My powers of persuasion were evidenced by her sitting next to me as we drove northward in the night for Lincoln County South. The Hertz people had done what I asked and the light tan Chevy Impala had been brought around to the back of the lodge. I was probably the first customer in a long while to have two rent-a-cars at the same time, but I was playing safe just in case the two gents in the Ford were still on the prowl watching us and the respective cars we'd used to drive to Lake Chelan.

"Won't you be missed?" I asked Erica. "I mean, won't they want to know where you are?"

"No. SPS people are on the move all the time, and I'm my own boss—after Roth." She put her arm around my neck. I swerved to avoid a ghostly sage bush tumbling straight for the headlights. "Anyway," she continued, "I did promise him in Washington I'd look after you."

To convey his suggestions she batted her eyelids. I didn't mistrust her anymore, but the idea of her being around Roth rankled me no end. It took me ten minutes to get up the courage, or the gall, to ask it, but I had to know. "Did he ever—I mean . . ."

"Oh, Harry, he's old enough to be my father."

"You know about some fathers."

"The answer's no," she said, punching my arm playfully, delighted at my jealousy and me absolutely delighted she was delighted.

"He should wear a bathrobe," I said pontifically. "He's a bloody exhibitionist."

"He cares a lot about the SPS, Harry," she said sincerely. "He really does. I admire him for that. I know you don't like him, but he's given it everything he's got."

"That's what I'm afraid of."

She frowned. "What do you mean?"

"I'm not sure," I said. "But we'll soon find out—I hope."

CHAPTER 23

In a city's daylight, cemeteries can be peaceful. At night they can be terrifying if you don't believe in the hereafter, and even if you do. There is something undeniably gruesome about the vision of taut, withered flesh yellowing on the bone, teeth nuzzled by armies of ants, and the fingernails and hair that seemingly keep growing long after burial as the skin contracts. That night I vowed that when my turn came it would be burial at sea. At least the fishes are quicker.

The light northerly wind had blown the ash clouds farther south so that when I opened the trunk beneath the brilliant disk of desert moon and glanced around I was immediately struck by the clarity of silhouettes, the sharp, dark hills of sage stretching away to the base of the monolithic mountains and the perfume of the pungent sage wafting down over us, mixed with a cool stream of air that was as cold as late autumn. A precursor of winter, I thought, as if warning that soon the gravestones might be snow-capped if the Arctic fronts so decreed.

The first sound of the shovel hitting the red-brown stony earth frightened the hell out of me. "My God!" said Erica. It resounded like steel on steel under the still, starry desert sky. The next time, I worked the shovel side to side, using my foot more, much as you do in a stubborn garden. After ten minutes I knew why the Indians hung their dead up on scaffoldings, away from wild beasts. It not only put the departed closer to the spirits, it also saved their relatives from a lot of hard work. I stopped to get my breath and heard a stone start to roll down, eventually striking the tire of the Chevy with a dull thump. Erica wanted to help, to spell me off. She said it would make her stop shivering. "No," I said. I heard a click. It was my back doing its little going out dance. I winced.

"Oh, don't be so macho," she said. "Let me help."

"I'm nearly there."

The hardest part was the last few inches, because I was like a hungry man trying to open a can of sardines with a blunt instrument. I had just enough energy to pry the lid open to peep inside but not enough to see clearly. An extra effort had to be made. I should have rested, but a certain macabre excitement got hold of me. The old man in this cheap coffin would hold the secret. I put the shovel under the lid. It wouldn't budge. I pushed the shovel's edge in harder—half afraid I'd go into the flesh. I'd expected an overwhelming stench from the effects of the desert heat but there was only a surprisingly faint odor of formaldehyde. The damn lid had been hammered on tightly. At least they hadn't skimped on nails. Nice of them. Sweating, I gave the shovel all my weight. I heard another click. It wasn't my back.

"Naughty!"

I turned. He gestured at the shovel. I dropped it. The night air was filled with garlic. It was the bellboy from Vancouver and the voice from the darkness of the Rockville riverside. The other one, yellow shirt, the driver of the Ford, had his hand on Erica's mouth, pushing her against the nearby boulder, while his mate pushed the shotgun against my throat. There was another click. Now both hammers were cocked. Yellow shirt had a revolver. It looked like a .22. Garlic, with the shotgun, was plainly the main hit man.

"Naughty," he said. "Robbing old men's graves. You see that, George? Poor old bloke having a good kip and Mr. Blurt-it's digging him up."

"It's disgustin'," said George, studiously searching Erica's handbag before flinging it down. "Bloody disgustin'."

Garlic poked the muzzle farther into my throat. The sweat on my chest was frigid.

"Well—?" he said.

I didn't know what I could say. You've only got one chance, as they used to tell us at Langley. You have to play for time. "We're interested in archaeology."

Even under the moon he looked stupid, like a little moon. "Archie who?"

"Archaeology." He thought long and hard. My confidence kept looking straight at him but not my contempt. "Do not infuriate or incite inferiority complex in captor"—DEFENSE IN THE FIELD: MANUAL DD-147.

"I fought I told you to shut your mouf?"

"But you just asked me—"

"Before! Before in Washingtun, eh? Mr. Roth told you too didn't 'e? But no, you got to play Dick Tracy."

Now I knew why garlic guts, who'd been so intent on killing me in Vancouver, hadn't followed up. Clearly, someone had decided to give me more rope so they could find out what I knew—what Tier knew. For whatever I knew someone else could stumble on unless it was fixed. Now I'd unwittingly shown them the gaps that had to be plugged. I was staring down the black eyes of twin barrels. Someone from Sudley Steel had decided it was time.

He eased my .38 out with his left hand, his eye catching its mint condition. "Very nice," he said. "Nice and clean."

His mate bent down and took off Erica's shoes, sliding his hands up her leg. He moved back, sitting down on a rock, half watching Erica and studying the shoes, running his fingers over them like a child with a toy he'd never seen before, as if trying to figure out how they worked. I couldn't see clearly what he was doing. I wish to God I had, but my eyes stared down at the shotgun. Garlic shoved it forward. This close it looked like two sewer pipes stuck in my larynx. "I'm sure that Professor Roth wouldn't approve of this."

"What Mr. Roth don't know won't 'urt 'im. 'Sides, we're looking after his interests, aren't we?"

"Really?"

"Yeah, we are."

I could see he was sweaty from the long quiet walk they'd had up to the cemetery. For some reason I kept wondering what size shot was in the cartridges. As if it would make any difference at point-blank range. My head would explode like a melon. Roth might be madder than hell, of course, at Sudley Steel's bungling, but he'd have to ride with it. They had each other over the barrel now. His career—their money.

"Well then, George," said Garlic. "Don't you think Sturgit here—"

"Stur*gess*," I said.

He pushed the now warming barrels hard under my chin. "Shut your mouf!" I decided Sturgit would do nicely.

"Let's 'ave a look then." He grinned, pointing to the partially opened coffin with my .38 before sticking it into his belt. I knew he wasn't really interested in having a look—most people wouldn't be.

The cold sweat now spread over me like an ice sheet. The old man's grave would hold another two. The sidekick, George, would just have to pat down hard with the shovel to compress the extra earth we'd displace. I had a vision of ants crawling over my teeth and saw Erica's body. And the rats. No, I'd rather put up a fight. At least go fiercely—raise some noise—a fighting chance. But I had to have the shovel. I kicked the handle to him. "Open it yourself."

The scatter-gun almost pushed my head back six inches. "Shit on you, Sturgit. Cheeky bastard. You hear that, George?" he said without turning his head. "You hear the cheeky bastard?" He moved the shotgun down over my heart. "Who was your servant last year, eh? You cheeky prick. You open it up, and if you don't hurry up I'll blow your ass off."

"Cheeky bastard!" echoed George.

"If you're not real quick," added Garlic, "I'll blow your nuts off."

There was a kind of stifled spitting noise. It was George,

laughing at his compatriot's high humor. "That's a good'un, Frank. That's a good'un."

I placed the lip of the shovel beneath the lid and looked over at Erica. "I hope you don't do that," I said. "If you did that I couldn't do any shoveling. I couldn't do anything, could I?" Erica was sitting still and gave no sign that she'd gotten the message. But even without the full moon I would have known that she'd gotten the signal. She never moved, but I felt her eyes on mine. "When I get to the last nail," I said, "what are you going to do? Blow my balls off then?"

"Get to work, Sturgit."

I kept easing up the lid, nail by nail. I took a rest and immediately felt Frank poking the shotgun into my ribs. I didn't feel cold now. I was hot. It wasn't just the work of prising up the stubborn lid, it was that poking of the twelve-gauge that enraged me. A born bully, I thought. A finger-stabber. I remembered a kid at school like that—the biggest kid. He would stand there poking you in the chest. "What you gonna do about it, Sturgess, eh . . . eh? Whatcha gonna do about it?"

Christ, I thought, sweating in anger. Here I am—fifty thousand a year plus expenses. I was used to shaking hands with ambassadors and now I was out in the wilderness, not only politically but literally. The goddamn wilderness, being poked by a bully. I remembered George Patton, forced to take cover under a table from a strafing Messerschmitt in the African campaign. Finally he jumped up from under the table, ran out into the street, and drew his pearl-handled six-shooters. "That's enough!" he'd yelled, and started shooting at the fighter. I reached the last nail and stood up.

"What you stopping for, eh?" Another poke.

"That's enough," I said quietly.

"What you mean?"

I exhaled tiredly and tapped the last nail with the shining edge of the shovel. "That, my friend, is a tempered K-8 four-inch nail. Can't budge that without splitting the wood. I need an ax."

"What's a K-8 nail?"

I tapped the nail head. "See the extra wide flange on the edge?" I was looking at Erica.

Garlic looked forward for a second to see the fictional K-8. It was no more than a second, but his head had gone forward and slightly to the left. And so had the shotgun. My left hand smacked the barrel away. I yelled, "Now!" I let him have it in the crotch with the shovel—the .38 flying up and out from his belt—and Erica elbowed George.

Garlic went down, pulling one trigger. There was a deafening roar, and an orange flash passed my head. My ears were ringing with an electronic scream. Ten feet away, Erica had missed George's crotch and hit him in the stomach instead, but he'd made the mistake of turning on her, punching her in the face. Only as she rolled down the hill was he raising his .22 toward her. Grabbing the shotgun, I fired. Another roar—reddish flame. More powder. More ringing.

George didn't scream. Not a word. At first. He just sat there, like a circus clown, absolutely stunned, looking at his trousers—or rather their remnants—as if he'd peed himself. There was bloody flesh like ground round on sticks, but they were still legs. He was lucky it had been number nine, double O buck. He could have been looking at mashed bone. I snatched up my .38 and helped him to his feet. Erica picked up the blood-splattered .22 as if it would bite her. I took it from her. I fairly bristled with hardware. Garlic was throwing up by the grave. He wouldn't be moving properly for days. I strolled over, took the rest of the cartridges from his pocket, and looked down with decided satisfaction.

He was groaning like a small child. "You bastard!" he said. "You bloody—"

"Oh, you'll live. A couple of bucks for a suspensory belt—any drugstore has them. They come in several sizes. Creep size should fit you nicely."

"I could bleed to deaf."

"Yes."

Erica, surprisingly calm, came over to me. "We can't leave them here," she said imploringly.

I knew we couldn't but I wasn't about to take them to any

emergency ward and get involved in answering gunshot-wound questions at the Lincoln South sheriff's office. "They'll tell Roth," I explained. "So we'll need a head start—humanity notwithstanding. We'll drop them on the outskirts of Lincoln. Let *them* answer the questions."

I reloaded the shotgun from the cartridges in Garlic's pocket and gave it to Erica, whom I stationed about six feet from them, in a clear patch, bereft of any stones they might try to use. "If they act up, just pull the triggers." She looked down at the gun in terror, as if it had suddenly been grafted onto her.

"It's double-barreled," I said. "You don't have to aim, at this distance, just pull."

I would have preferred to guard them myself, but it was a steep drive up the cemetery hill and Erica hadn't driven the Chevy before. Besides, they didn't look as if they'd be going anywhere in a hurry. George was sitting staring at his legs, while his mate, Frank, was rocking, cradling his pelvis, his voice giving off a steady deep grunting sound. I almost felt sorry for him. Almost, but not quite. I remembered Dermit and the photo with his folks. Erica whispered urgently so they couldn't hear. "I . . . I couldn't do it."

I put my arm around her, pulling her close. "I know," I said softly. "But they don't. I'll only be five minutes."

It was ten minutes before I got to the Chevy and had driven it up the steep, rocky hill to the edge of the cemetery where we could pile them into the back. This time I stationed Erica well away from the door in case one of them recovered enough to try and use it as a battering ram. Then I returned to the grave at the top of the hill.

I prised off the lid and swept the flashlight over him. The eyes and mouth were closed, for which I was grateful. There were no insects, the burial had been too recent. Actually, he looked as if he'd just nodded off. The face was a little red but nothing more than you'd expect in desert country. I started to undo the tie and the head lolled to one side, which surprised me, in view of the rigor mortis that normally sets in. My hand slipped in fright, landed on his stomach, and a low moan of air erupted. Trapped gas escaping. Its smell soured the air. Startled, I jumped back, dropping the flashlight and hearing my back click into place. A wisp of cloud suddenly bisected the moon, and the flashlight rolled to a clunking stop inside the coffin, its beam penciled on the white shirt.

My hands shaking, I undid the black tie and pulled open his shirt. The chest was pink and hairless. Nothing looked unusual. I undid the trouser belt and pulled them down. More pinkish-white skin. I gently touched his stomach. It felt soft but not flesh soft—rubbery soft. I poked the thigh. More rubber softness. I held the flashlight close and asking forgiveness scratched the surface of the chest with a sharp, flintlike stone by the grave. No embalming liquid. I pulled gently, then harder and the whole firm pink torso layer came away from the body. Rubber! I grabbed the flashlight, pushing it against the neck. So that's why the head had lolled so unexpectedly. It had been pinned—literally pinned into place. The head was human—the rest was a dummy, the kind of look-alike that medical and first-aid types practice on. It had all been made to pass the casual inspection of relatives as they filed by an open casket, but once the collar was undone and you looked farther down, you could see where the head had been sawn from the torso during the autopsy. I unpinned the head. It slid to the side, bumping the box. The base of the neck was brittle, not black from the microwave zapping as I would have expected it to be but crisp, crackly, like overdone chicken skin. From the neck down the old man had been literally cooked. Other than the eyes, the head, probably because of the angle or the bone structure, had not been so affected. He'd been hit by a power which the Congress of the United States had never authorized. Sudley Steel's equipment failure was one thing. This was another. It was no longer possibility—or probability. It was confirmed. We had a fatal arc.

I worked like a navvy refilling the grave and patting it down. I never let up. I was mad as hell. It wasn't until halfway down the hill that I got even madder and stopped dead in my tracks. The burial was a coverup in more ways than one. Chas. E. Milt knew, because he'd prepared the old man for burial, but did Roth know how much power had been used? Not just about the antenna accident but the power—the microwave density? And if the old man had been killed *after* the SPS had been put up, the power capability was in the SPS now.

As we drove the two goons to a drop-off place a half mile from Lincoln Hospital, Garlic mumbled something.

"What?" I asked absently. I was so preoccupied thinking about old Thompson's body, or what was left of it, and with the terrifying question it posed that I hadn't heard him properly.

"We're a big operation, Sturgit."

He had guts, I'll give him that, but then, he could afford to threaten us. We were the solid middle class who ate meat without ever thinking about the slaughterhouse. He knew I wouldn't kill them in cold blood.

"So?" I said. "You're a big operation?"

"We got lots of representatives on the road, see."

I looked at him in the rear-view mirror. The question in my mind, like some giant amoeba, was blotting out everything else. I answered him very slowly, robotlike. "I'm sure you have."

His voice was wafting in and out of my consciousness like an angry wasp. "You've blown it, Sturgit. Your eyes are too big for your belly."

Now it was really starting to annoy me—his voice, his bloody "representatives," and his stinking bloody breath. I stopped the car, walked around to the other side, unloaded the shotgun out of sight, walked back to the front seat, and poked the double barrels toward their heads.

"No! No!" screamed George. "Jesus, no! No!" I pulled the triggers. George stopped breathing, his eyes nearly popping out of his head. But Frank just grinned. He was tough, the bastard. And I knew he was right. There'd be more "representatives."

"What will they tell the police?" asked Erica, after we'd dropped them off.

"Assault. Roth hasn't only convinced the sheriff of Riverport he's on a supersecret government project. The law's in his pocket."

It was then Erica broke into tears, then sobs, clinging to me and starting to shake. "Oh, God!" she said. "What's happening? What's this all about?"

I knew we wouldn't know the answer to that one until we'd had a look at the SPS control center, set in a huge clearing in the hills of southern British Columbia. Someone besides Roth had to know what they were doing—Roth was head of it, but someone else had actually been working the machine.

It was 4:15 A.M. The moon was a high golden ball in the cold, star-filled desert night. I did my deep breathing exercises while we were driving. I had to think straight. It's too easy to force a connection when there is none. The fact that Milt knew about the old man didn't necessarily mean that Roth knew about the amount of power being used. Roth could be part of a Defense subgroup or something within the SPS administration. They could be using him as the big-name interference runner. He might only be the puppet, unknown to himself; the scientific front for any "accident" with the SPS. I had to force that possibility onto myself. The temptation to see him as the willing linchpin between government shenanigans and private contractors was too easy, because I didn't like him. And that's not professionalism.

I held Erica very close while she cried the tension out of her, reassuring her, telling her to go back to Washington, D.C. She said no, she'd stay. I was glad she wanted to be with me, but then I saw that where we were headed might be a hell of a lot more dangerous for her than the capital. But she insisted and I accepted. If somehow Roth *was* in on this, Washington wouldn't be any safer for her.

Driving northwest toward the border, we were sitting in silence, the fatigue gradually overtaking us, when Erica suddenly sat bolt upright. "My God—Roth said the President knew about the accident."

I nodded, my jaw clenching as we took a hairpin turn entering the foothills of the Cascades.

"Does that mean . . ." began Erica.

"Does it mean," I anticipated, "that the President knows about that much power being used intentionally?"

"Yes."

I said nothing.

"I can't believe it," she said.

"Or *won't* believe it?" I could feel the cold mountain air. The wind rushing past the window woke me up like a cold shower. "Either way we'll have to find out," I said.

"But surely the President—" She fell silent as I took another curve. It was 4:30 A.M., Saturday, September 27.

My eyes strained for a highway pay-phone sign.

I used the special White House number.

"That you, Hoskins?"

"Yes. Sturgess? Where are you?"

"Never mind. I must speak to the President. Immediately."

"What's the problem?"

I thought fast. If I could just get through to the President maybe . . . "Hoskins, this is presidential priority. I have to speak to him."

"On open line?"

"Look, I can go into the details later. But right now—"

"Why can't I pass it to him?"

"Sorry. I have to speak to him personally."

"What's it about? General area, I mean?"

"SPS."

"Uh-huh." He sounded too casual—as if he'd been practicing. "Well, I'm sure I could arrange for him to call back. Where are you?"

By now I knew the FBI's Phone Tap Computer would be halfway to zeroing in on the call zone and forty seconds away from having the specific number. "Hoskins, I *want* to speak to the President. Now!"

"Now look, Sturgess, old man—"

I hung up. "*Old man*"—if ever there was a play for time that was it.

So Roth had gotten to Hoskins—after receiving a call from

Sudley Steel's "representatives," no doubt. It wouldn't have been hard for him to put Hoskins against me. My stock was already rock bottom. But I was hoping that Hoskins had only recently been got at—that he had no close ties with Roth or whomever. If he had he could easily have stopped me from leaving Washington, D.C. Instead he'd let me have free reign —until now! Which meant that something had happened since I'd left—like a dead man's head rolling off—and Hoskins was being pressed, or rather being used, no doubt on grounds of "national security," to prevent the President from hearing from me. That meant that Hoskins didn't know just how far the experimental beam had gotten out of hand. And that idea, that the President might *not* know, was the first hopeful thing that had happened all night. What wasn't hopeful was that now I knew for certain we were being hunted. "Where are you?" "*Old man*"*!* We were on our own. We were on the run. And what we needed most of all next to sleep was hard evidence of what Roth was up to. It was no good even trying to contact the press or rather the few press contacts we had between us. Now that Roth had gotten to Hoskins he'd certainly use the "national security" blanket to smother any legitimate press inquiry. Also, managing editors need hard evidence too when they're going up against the government. Besides, I had a good hunch that if anyone went anywhere near the hop farm now, all they'd find was hops. For sure the SPS beam was now being received on the Canadian side by the rectenna in the Canadian Okanagan. Roth wasn't only a first-rate scientist—he was a first-rate tactician. He'd not only engineered a convenient "out" for the President by creating the SPS administration and rectenna on the Canadian side—in the event that Congress hadn't approved it—but he'd simultaneously arranged for the Canadian rectenna to be the backup if something had gone wrong, scientifically or politically.

When I nearly ran off the road around 6:00 A.M., I stopped for sleep. Erica wanted to drive, but she was as worn out as I was. Now I knew I'd been too hasty in depriving us of the night's sleep at Chelan. My sense of urgency had nearly caused us to wreck our only means of transport—not to say ourselves. That wouldn't help anyone, except Sudley Steel and Co. I pulled off behind a sage-covered bluff that hid us from view and we slept.

By 11:20 A.M., still tired, as much from nervous fatigue as anything else, we were ready to go—but the car wasn't. Murphy's Law, with a thoroughly perverse sense of timing, had descended upon the Chevy's V-8. Nothing spectacular, mind, just infuriating and, for us, very dangerous—a fan belt, no longer with us. Only Murphy knew where it had dropped off.

After I'd finished swearing, and swallowing, instead of chewing, half a granola bar for brunch, I cooled down long enough in the hot sun to remember that I could use Erica, or rather use her stockings. Anything else, rope, string, is no good, it'll just slip, but stockings will work at least for a few minutes at a time. I'd remembered that little trick from a group undergraduate camping trip in France—some of the coeds hadn't been particularly fussy about what us men had seen when the stockings came off. But right now I wasn't thinking of sex. With Erica around, that was a real measure of my predicament. Instead, I thought only of the damn delay. If the stockings held out for thirty miles, it would still be four hours at least to the lone garage at Lone Pine and back, even if we got a lift. And all that time Sudley Steel would be marshaling its forces.

I was wrong, it didn't take four hours to Lone Pine and back. It took *six*. The stockings gave out after just twenty miles, barely giving me enough time to pull the Chevy off and hide it again. While at the garage I thought of getting another rent-a-car. Sure, he could get us one—in two days' time. No thanks, I said. We got some Cokes and chocolate bars. He was a young guy, all by himself, alone in the forsaken garage in the middle of nowhere, kept alive solely on tractor repairs, it seemed. They were all around him. He would have loved to drive us back, but what could he do when he was alone? Well, then, could we take his pickup and one of us drive it back when we'd reached the car? Well, he'd like to, you understand, but these days . . . well, you understand . . . you see . . .

"Yeah, forget it!" I grumped.

By the time we'd hitched back it was close to six. We were dog tired, dusty, angry, sniping at each other, and wondering. Where was Sudley Steel?

We were heading westward now rather than directly north where we would be naturally expected to cross into Canada. Out of the dusk, Winthrop appeared. The small town nestled in the purple foothills was bright with color. Refurbished in the old Western style with fake saloon fronts and replicas of the days of "The Virginian," the town was the liveliest Saturday night rest stop for two hundred miles.

Before we booked into the Crystal Hotel in Winthrop, I drove back past "Dawson's Hardware—Fishing, Hunting and Camping Supplies" to the gas station and filled up, ready for an early start. Even here at the edge of the Cascade Mountains, in such a tiny township, the gas rationing was strictly enforced. It was my luck to be an odd number on an even day but I bribed the attendant. At first he was very offended; so was I. I didn't like doing it, but I had little choice. He got less offended as I increased the price. When I put the twenty down with my gas card, he became a lifelong friend.

It was my second mistake that day. We'd been forced into too fast a pace for the last twenty-four hours, and I'd already made one big slip—a small detail but a big mistake. I hadn't realized how our Sudley Steel friends had gotten onto me through the second Rent-A-Car at Chelan Lodge—the one I thought I'd been so crafty with by having it delivered at the rear. They hadn't known what car to follow other than by seeing me driving on the highway and parking at Chelan Lodge with Erica's car parked nearby. But they had gotten onto us—either through the lodge desk clerk or the Hertz people. The mistake was we'd used our real names for lack of any false identification. It didn't take a genius, just a little forethought. It would have been Frank, of course; George would never have caught on to it. Neither had Harry Sturgess until twenty-four hours later. I pleaded fatigue. We had to have sleep, which is why we had to stop in Winthrop. But the point was that it wasn't until we'd parked and eaten at the Crystal, and booked a room above for the night, that this first mistake hit me and soon made me realize my second blunder.

I was sitting on the edge of the hotel bed staring blankly at the wall. Damn it, I should have shot those two bastards dead at the cemetery. By now patriotic sheriffs would be crawling all over the counties looking for us. But how could they find us? I hadn't given them time to check out my call to Hoskins—to trace it back to the highway call box I'd used. Without such a check they wouldn't know if we'd headed east to Omak, then north to the border crossing at Osoyoos, or west, then north through Vancouver, or east to Spokane or southwest to Seattle. It was then—thinking about the phone—that I saw my blunder!

The gas station's credit-card receipts, including mine with the Chevy's license number on it, wouldn't be sent in till the end of the month—in two days' time. But that wouldn't necessarily protect us. Using Chelan, fifty-nine miles away, as their base, the Spokane FBI field office, by phoning the few stations which dotted the vast, sparsely populated counties, could do a number-plate check in a few hours and close the noose.

I couldn't sleep. Dog tired and not a wink, but we had to get out of Winthrop. The FBI wouldn't wait till morning and if they did a routine credit-card check, we were trapped. They could box in the place before we'd had breakfast. I got up and rang Storm Lake Resort, forty-seven miles northwest of us—the way I would not think a man would run—that is, farther west into the mountain-locked canyons and farther away from the greater number of escape routes to the east. The Storm Lake man wasn't happy—it was midnight. But yes, he had a cabin, number 3. He'd leave it open.

I explained to Erica what we'd have to do. Uncomplainingly she dragged herself down with me to the little main street. I took the screwdriver and pliers from the convertible's tool kit and waited until several cars pulled into the nose-first parking lot by the cafe-cum-hotel.

Finally a Chevy Impala pulled in, Washington State plates. An old couple got out. After they'd entered the cafe and Erica kept watch I switched their plates with ours. It was a lot less risky than stealing their car. It was nasty but necessary. The paint was an off-white, one of the popular cream tones of those days. Ours was a light tan but the police go first on the license number because people's perception of color is so poor. Any traffic cop will tell you that—a hundred convictions a day are lost because of it. Anyway, the main thing was that anyone looking for us would, on recognizing our number plate on the old folks' car, pull the old folks off the road, advancing on them cautiously, assuming we had donned elderly disguise. Of course, once they found they'd been fooled they'd go solely on the color of the car and a description of us. Anticipating that, I wanted to get into Dawson's hardware store. In a big city it would have been impossible, but the nice thing about small country towns is that everybody knows everybody else and who owns what. Usually two or three men own pretty well everything. They get that way by being willing to open up whenever there's a profit to be made. And this was no exception. Mr. D. opened the door himself. I bought twelve cans of Ditzco Alkyd Enamel—dark blue spray paint—as untannish, as unlike our Chevy, as you could get. The store had old souvenir frontier-day newspapers, and I bought twenty-five of them and four big rolls of masking tape. I dumped it all into the trunk of our Chevy, which was now parked several blocks away in a back alley, and prayed it would be fine tomorrow.

As I opened the door for Erica, I saw a rat, a huge, fat thing, scuffling noisily through some spilled garbage. Erica could feel me stiffen behind her. "What's wrong?"

"It's all right," I lied. I'd always feared those creatures. I hoped it wasn't an omen.

CHAPTER 24

From Winthrop along the sparkling olive ribbon of the Methow River to Mazama you pass from foothills to mountain. Fifty-one miles northwest, beyond Silver Star's nine thousand feet of granite peak and Washington Pass, you are in the cold country of the Cascades which have known more than two hundred inches of snow a year and where you wonder what could happen if you run out of gas, aware that you're traveling on no more than a thin scratch of road through some of the wildest mountainous country on earth, the warm cocoon of the car and its glow of gadgets small comfort in a vast moving sea of gorge and peak. It's then you realize how urban you are, just how much you depend on the gas pump and thermostat. At five thousand feet we could see the moon riding high above the distant crags of Mount Triumph and Mount Terror. For a moment I felt what it must have been like heading westward a hundred years ago. The isolation and grandeur were so awesome and powerful that we sat in silence as the huge black forests swept by.

Here the radio was stopped by the great amphitheaters of granite while the pencil-thin streaks of headlights only emphasized how pathetic and tentative man's invasion of nature can be, how short the distance from blacktop to the dark mouths of chasms roaring with wind and water in the blackness of a thousand years ago. It was so spooky that I was glad to have a car pass us by James Dam about five miles before Storm Lake. Fleeting company, but at least another soul had ventured forth and it wasn't a Ford.

Suddenly tracers of September snowflakes were streaming toward the windshield. Soon it was like clouds of dizzying confetti swirling through the headlight glow, momentarily putting me off balance, nearly causing me to veer into a safety rail. Erica moved closer, holding my arm. When we finally saw the string of white and yellow pin spots that mark Storm Lake, I could hear her exhale from sheer relief. But driving down off to the right of the highway along the top of the dam with its sheer drop on the left-hand side, I couldn't help wondering if I'd made the right move. Eventually they'd check Storm Lake, but since it lay in the most unlikely direction on Highway 20, I was betting their men would leave it till last. By then I'd have done what I wanted to do and we'd be gone.

Cabin Number Three had a weak forty-watt bulb outside, enough room for six hunters inside, and was damp and cold. It gave you the feeling it was always damp in the mountains, that it could never possibly be dry. At 2 A.M., opening a box of Rice Krispies the right way would have been formidable enough—lighting a twenty-year-old oil furnace was impossible. I leaned my head against the casing in sheer exhaustion and felt the damp seeping into my bones. I must have looked like an old man bent with arthritis. "Damn the energy crisis."

Erica was already undressed. "Come to bed, Harry." It was for warmth, not for love, and I finally fell asleep. Until I heard a bump outside. Waking in fright I thought I was still in Winthrop. Reaching for the .38 from the bedside table I saw the faint glow of my watch. Three-thirty. I stared, blurry-eyed, out into the big living-dining room, at the unfamiliar couches and chairs gathered around the old furnace. I couldn't see anything move. I lay very still.

There was another noise. A rattle! I glanced at the window; a dripping pine branch brushing the pane. Then a crash! Outside the door! I flung the covers back and dove toward the door, crouching beside it. Another crash! A light went on somewhere—the next cabin across the dirt track. I unbolted the door slowly, then flung it aside. Disgusted, the grizzly withdrew his head from the garbage can, knocking it over, grunted, and ambled away into the night.

I was at once relieved, then too depressed to get back to sleep. After explaining the ruckus to Erica I tucked her in, drawing a blanket around me, and boiled the water for tea. Now I was awake I sat in the darkness thinking morosely about the coming day. The steam kettle screamed. I jumped up, knocked the top off it, and searched the cupboard as quietly as possible. No tea. Decaffeinated coffee would have to do. I turned off the light and sat sipping the warm liquid like an Indian watching over the dead.

Slowly but surely, along with the dark mountains taking shape in the dim, cloud-shrouded light, another monstrous possibility crept out of the Storm darkness. The President might not know that the experiment had gotten way out of control but he might have known about the "experiment" *before* Roth. That is, he might have actually initiated it. Hoskins might have been under pressure merely to stop me from informing the President of the "accidents." The gray dawn was full of "mights" and "ifs." They made me more aware of how much I needed to see the control center in the Canadian Okanagan. You could speculate all you wanted in the rain forest miles away from where it was happening, but you could only know for sure if you were Johnny on the spot.

Erica was calling dreamily for me. The bed was deliciously soft, probably bad for your posture but marvelous for love. It was an old four-postered early Depression bed. Nothing fancy, just plain solid, and it didn't creak once. After, Erica kissed me softly and said we'd better fix the car. I agreed and promptly fell asleep till nine.

Warmth. Bacon and eggs sizzling, wafting deliciously around me. Hot coffee, toast and jam, or was it honey? Or was it a dream? It was Erica, hazel-eyed and bright—already been to the small store for the breakfast goodies where she'd dazzled the owner's seventeen-year-old grandson into explaining in great detail how to light yon furnace. Cholesterol in bed it was and let the arteries clog. Damn the scientists! Straightaway I remembered Roth. Damn him most of all.

Erica said she felt "Ugh!"—that her hair needed washing. It did look a bit stringy, but it was too early for frankness. "You look great," I said. "Absolutely, positively scrumptious. I could eat you I could. Without salt."

"You," she said, sitting beside me and kissing my forehead, "were not looking at my hair."

Marvelous what sleep will do. I pushed the empty polished plate away and slid my hand beneath her light knitted skirt. "We have to fix the car," she said.

"I wish to fix you."

She held me at bay. "The *car*."

"The car?"

"*L'automobile*."

"*Oui. L'auto*."

"Immediately."

"Right."

"Today!"

"Right!"

This time the bed creaked—a lot. At least it wasn't as loud as the bear.

By 11 A.M., which high in the mountains seemed like 7 A.M., the sun was one-all with the low stratus cloud, peering through here and there, gaining slightly so that the cloud had a constantly shifting, dappled look, at once half depressing, half bright. It was how I felt thinking of Roth, then Erica. I drove the car the fifty-odd yards to the store and asked the proprietor of the cabins whether there were any small roads nearby.

"Hunting?" he asked.

"No." He waited for an explanation. He got none. That was the idea. Nothing like noncommittal to arouse suspicion.

"Uh—well there's a timber truck runoff a few miles back. Used it when they were building the highway. Bit overgrown, weeds and all kinds o' rubbish."

"That'll do," I said. "Thanks."

"You stayin'?"

I started moving the paint cans from the trunk of the Chevy to the back seat. "Maybe."

Erica walked up from the cabin. A blue-jeaned younger version of the grandfather appeared from near the two gas pumps which stood forlornly by the mist-covered lake. The sun was losing on a technical knockout.

"Can I help you, miss?"

Erica, bending over the back seat, handed me the last of the paint cans. "No thank you," she said. She gave him a sweet smile. He'd have swum the five freezing miles to James Dam if she'd wanted.

"You on rationing?" I asked the kid.

"Hell, no," cut in the grandfather. "We got all the gas you'll need."

"Fill 'er up now?" asked Junior, still looking yearningly at Erica.

"Later," I said. "Before we leave." It was important that the kid see the car before we left. The thing I was worried about was whether he'd see it at all with Erica around.

"Don't excite him," I whispered.

"Oh, Harry," she smiled delightedly, "he's only a boy."

"Sure." I loved her and she knew it.

The timber-truck runoff was hard to find, overgrown by small alder and bracken but that suited my purpose perfectly—or I should say *our* purpose, for by now we were acting completely in concert. We had to have hard evidence and the only way to get it was to buy time for us to investigate further. While I taped the newspapers over the wheels and windshield, Erica covered the headlights and any chrome that showed.

We waited until a threatening cloud inched overhead. It looked as if it was enjoying the prospect of teasing us. The lake was still shrouded in heavy mist, otherwise I'd have tried to charter a small plane. We ate the sandwiches we'd brought and waited. Six thousand feet up, feeling better in daylight and free at last of the vast, open basaltic tableland to the east, I began to feel more secure than I had for weeks.

I knew these little mountain enclaves of a few cabins, boat ramp, and sad booms stretching across the skin of water, and steep ashen dams that interrupt the natural charge of mountain streams can be gloomy places, especially in winter when the rain clouds wrap around them in great gray sheets constantly dripping. But now, though mist still locked in the lake, the cloud had passed and it was as if a curtain had been drawn from the mountainside. The early morning blue had become a dozen shades of dazzling greens. Down by the highway we could see mauve flashes of late-blooming rhododendron and a great red spill of fireweed and variegated wildflowers scattered between the icy torrents, transforming the purple gorges and dense primeval forest of the night before into a country alive with sound. Somewhere in the distance I heard a rush of pheasant and chukar. Soon it was like high summer, the heat forcing its way through the thick, steaming overgrowth onto our backs as we moved out from the brightly mottled shade to the tall, sweet-smelling grass around the car.

Erica shook the paint cans and I began the spraying. For some mysterious reason the paint in one can ran more freely than the rest and so I had to wipe the trunk area and go over it again. I hoped that those extra ten minutes wouldn't catch up with us somewhere down the line. The longer we took, the greater the danger.

By 5:30 P.M. the car was dry. A wee bit sticky in spots but dry enough. We'd just pulled up by the two lonely pumps when young Romeo materialized again, as if risen from the lake.

"Filler 'er up, ma'am?"

"Yes," said Erica, her smile winning and seductive as ever. I don't think he noticed I was driving—or that the Chevy had turned from tan to blue—he was too busy helping Erica carry our meager grocery supply from the cabin to the car. But the old man noticed it. It bothered him so much that his brow looked like a plowed field. Some of the paint that hadn't dried was around the shaded edge of the gas cap and it marked his fingers as he closed it. It was killing him. He started to speak. "How come . . ."

"Pardon?" I said, just as friendly as could be.

"Three fifty," he said. "Tank was nearly full—you must have filled up at Winthrop."

"Well, with rationing you get it where you can."

"And that's a fact. Where you headed?"

Thank you, God.

I looked perplexed. "Sho-squamish. I think that's how you say it. South of here."

"Sno*homish*."

"*Homish*. That's it. Yeah. Snohomish. Know what the gas situation is there?"

"Around the 405? Heading for Seattle?"

"Yeah."

"Short, I hear," he said. "Better keep filling up wherever you can."

"Don't worry. I will." I went to give him the credit card, hesitated, and gave him cash instead.

Don't let anyone tell you country people are slow. They're used to picking up the slightest change in the weather—their livelihood can depend on it. And they watch people just as closely.

"Thanks," he said casually, pocketing the bill, but I'd bet my socks he'd memorized the number plate. Not that it mattered. The color change would be enough.

Erica was silent for a while. Then she muttered, "Hydraulic lines." She was looking back at the overflow pipes shooting out long, foaming jets at the base of the dam.

"How do you mean?"

"A beam set at low resonance frequency can be aimed at water molecules to drive off the water. That's how flesh"—she hesitated—"how meat is cooked—and why the hop leaves were spotted. But if the beam is set for high-resonance frequency it can attack the CH molecules, the hydrocarbons, anything made out of petrochemicals."

"That's half the world."

She nodded. "The beam will cook anything that's roughly the same consistency. For a start that means it would virtually cook millions of hydraulic hoses. Most people can't even begin to imagine what that means. Everything from aircraft landing gear to plastic in the kitchen—to every automobile it touches. Everything from planes to cars will be uncontrollable. And God knows how many millions will suffer from electrical systems failing; everything from TV and control tower circuits to traffic lights, from trains to pacemakers will go haywire."

I shook my head. No matter that the President had initiated SPS, he wouldn't risk that. It was unthinkable. We had to get inside the control station. "Look," I said, "there have to be at least three shifts of technicians in any one day. They must all know."

"Not necessarily. Not with capacitor banks."

"Explain."

"Well, remember when the SPS went up, the capacitor banks went up too. Like storage tanks their flow can be regulated, like an irrigation ditch. You can have a trickle or full flush." She pointed down at the fast-receding dam. "Like those overflow pipes. That's what makes such high levels possible. You simply store up and release the energy in short, powerful bursts rather than using a constant low-level release."

"So?"

"So only certain technicians, like foremen, shift supervisors such as they have at nuclear plants, would be authorized to utilize 'full flow.'"

I heaved the car away from the gravel shoulder. "Brilliant!" I said. "Abso-bloody-lutely brilliant. That would mean you could keep the organization relatively small?"

"A dozen operators at the most."

"Then we've got to find out who are the ones operating it."

"*If* we get there."

She was right, of course—Roth and his "allies of necessity" had everything to lose if we made it. The odds against us had been high from the start. Our only chance was to decrease them for just long enough.

We ditched the car a few miles farther down on a timber track that looked as if it had served a base camp during the construction of the highway through the Cascades. We hitched, Erica out front. Several cars passed us by, pretending we weren't there. It was a truck loaded with apples that pulled up.

"Car broke down at Storm Lake," I said. "Can you give us a lift to Interstate Five?"

"Where you headed?"

"North. Bellingham."

"I'm going to Seattle. I'll drop you off at Mount Vernon. All right?"

"Great."

Erica was amazed at the thirteen forward gears and four reverse gears on the big Mack. So was I, but I never let on. Instead I was thinking how, when they came after us—Roth's government men or Sudley Steel's "representatives"—the Storm Lake man would tell them about the car. There'd be an all-points bulletin out for a Chevrolet Impala . . . "no longer tan. Repeat. No longer tan but blue. Repeat blue. License number Washington State . . . Believed headed south for Seattle via Snohomish on Interstate Five."

That would buy us a day, maybe two days at least. I congratulated myself.

CHAPTER 25

I bought a copy of *Penthouse* from a small store. The owner leered knowingly at Erica.

"What on earth . . . ?" she began.

"Later," I said. "I'll explain later." I looked at my watch. We caught a Continental Trailways north as far as Bellingham, then hitched through the beautifully green and immaculate Dutch farming country around Lynden to Sumas on the U.S. side of the forty-ninth parallel, forty miles southwest of Vancouver.

The border between friends stretches for well over three thousand miles all the way from the Straits of Juan de Fuca in the West to the Gulf of Maine in the East. It is unlike any other border in the world. The Americans and Canadians intuitively know this and simply refer to it as "the line." And that's about all it is. There are customs officers, immigration officials, some polite, some rude, as in any country, and when your car passes through they know more about you than you think.

But for all that, the line is unlike any other border because it is so long it's virtually impossible to keep you out, even with the heat sensors they have in parts. Bears and other animals are always setting off false alarms. The result is that many hikers and canoeists, particularly clean-shaven ones, have passed unobstructed over the forty-ninth parallel with marijuana and worse in their backpacks. The biggest danger in British Columbia is a grizzly in spring or an avalanche in winter.

So we headed away from the official posts where they would have our description and crossed in the dense alder bush in the near darkness east of Sumas. The only man-made things in sight were light planes, a good percentage of them learner pilots, one of them circling around and around overhead as if he only knew one way to turn, and the odd glider that dotted the air above the great, rich green alluvial Fraser River valley.

In three hours we were in Vancouver, the farthest point west from our intended destination in the south-central part of the province—where the SPS control and alternate rectenna were situated. The Chevy was now hidden in the Cascades while our pursuers were madly dashing south, looking for it and us in it. Now that we had crossed the border on foot, we needed a vehicle. And then another one of those small but vital details that make life difficult, especially life on the run: we were both low on cash and our credit cards would leave a sure trail.

My ace in the hole was Jonas.

When we arrived I gave him *Penthouse*—and he saw Erica. His eyes brightened and the arthritis in the left leg all but disappeared.

At breakfast, eating one of Ida's special dishes, Jonas found it very difficult to concentrate on what I was saying. There is at once something pathetic and comic about a middle-aged man trying to play the younger lead. He gave the impression of drooling, though he wasn't. Erica handled it with class. There were three reasons. Firstly, she'd liked Ida straight off, secondly, we needed help, and thirdly, she knew that if she'd given Jonas the same smile as she'd given Romeo of the lake we'd have had an attempted rape right there in the gun shop. Despite his leering, Jonas was a true-blue friend and did go out and rent a car and two trail bikes for two weeks. I made sure he used cash, a fake ID and home address, and no credit cards

—so that if anyone took our license number they couldn't trace the car back to him. The car was a bottle-green Pontiac sedan, not at all like the tan, now blue, Chevy we'd left behind. Ida got me some new shirts, underwear, etc., and she and Erica went shopping together.

They didn't ask Erica and me any questions, just if we'd be back in Vancouver. I said, "Not for a while. Until it's over, Ide."

She'd been married too long to Jonas to ask, "Until what is over?" She didn't turn a hair, just told me to take good care of Erica. "She's a good girl."

"Yes," I said.

"Bright too."

"I know."

"So long as you know."

"I do."

"More power to you."

Jonas gave me his Chargex, he had a spare, and two hundred dollars.

"I'll send it back with the *Penthouse*," I said.

"What . . ." He was still gawking at Erica. "Oh, yeah, right. Good. Thanks, Harry."

We left at noon. The first stop was Hope. Appropriately named, I thought. Here the gray-green Fraser River shows you just how tough it is, swirling out of its canyon into the wide, curving bend of rapids and whirlpools which have ended many a life in seconds. Here again we met up with the spine of the Cascade Mountains. In the last couple of days from Storm we had come northwest for almost 200 miles to Vancouver, then swung northeast 100 miles to complete a huge semicircle. Now, after lunch in Hope, we would drive another 150 miles, past the great Hope rockslide, through Manning Provincial Park, on through the mountains, and down to Penticton in the dry scrub pine hills of the Okanagan country which marks the continuation into Canada of the Columbia River basin. This country was the thinner northern end of the pork-chop-shaped basaltic basin.

Over one hundred and twenty miles south of Penticton, through the Sonora-like desert country where the Okan*a*gan River becomes the Okan*o*gan, lay Riverport in the even drier hills of the Big Bend Coulee Country which we had fled just over forty-eight hours before.

At the best of times the Hope slide is an eerie place to pass through. In the early hours of the morning of January 9, 1965, six people were driving through the Nicolum Valley when half a mountain side slid down, at a hundred miles an hour, burying them in a hundred million tons of mud and rock. The odds of a mountain slipping on you started me thinking about the odds of being found by Roth's lads and Sudley Steel. At least, I told myself, Roth's government men might harbor some moral restraint in the methods used in tracking you down. But Sudley Steel was like the mountain—big and brutal. As Frank had delightedly told us, there were more like him, and they weren't the types to be inhibited by constitutional rights. I guess what depressed me most about driving through the slide area was that Hope has always marked the turning point for the traveler in British Columbia. From there it's either north or east and we were heading east. It was the moment of final commitment. Now there was no turning back. And if anyone by chance had picked up our trail they too would know that this was the point of no return. The beautiful, winding, graceful rivers in the Nicolum Valley helped calm the eye but not the mind. I scanned ahead and saw one of those highway signs that at once seem to me totally useless yet intimidating: BEWARE OF FALLING ROCKS.

"How the hell can you watch for falling rocks?" I snapped at Erica. "If you watched for falling rocks you'd go off the edge."

"It's only a warning," she said sensibly.

"I know. I know," I growled. "But what the hell can you do about it?"

"Nothing."

That was true too. But I wished she hadn't said it. Again I determined to get to the control center outside Penticton, track down the evidence we needed, vindicate ourselves, and go back to calm, warm, peaceful home. "What we need," I said, "is to find whoever was on duty during the accidents with Orlet and old Thompson—when the SPS moved during maximum power transmission. Or whoever sent the photo to Dermit. If they'll talk we've got our firsthand evidence. It'll be proof positive of how catastrophic that thing could be if someone touches the wrong button."

"I thought Milt sent all those photos."

"Photos—on the film, yes—but there was an earlier one Dermit showed me—no name of sender—it was of a Finn that had been killed near a big Soviet microwave site. He told me someone had sent it from Kelowna in the Okanagan."

"How do you know? You said no sender, no . . ."

"Postmark. Someone else who'd seen Dermit in the papers or on the tube. Friend Milt isn't the only person who watches TV."

"What makes you think he, or she, will talk? If we find them?"

"Conscience," I said.

"*Conscience?*" She looked across at me inquiringly. "I hate to be cynical, Harry," she said, "and I really do believe in the Boy Scouts, and I know you go to church occasionally, but what makes you think conscience—"

"Someone," I cut in, "someone sent that photo for a reason. Right?"

Erica thought for a moment. "A call for help?" She was looking at me again.

"For support troops. Yes."

"Good point," she said. "Very good point."

Just then I saw another highway sign: WATCH FOR FALLING ROCKS.

CHAPTER 26

The Ritz Motel wasn't ritzy, but along Highway 3A the NO VACANCY neons shone all about Penticton in the velvet twilight and we were lucky to get anything. As I pulled a hair and shut the door on it I noticed all the cabins were shabby with bright peeling red doors, giving the whole motel an air of impending demolition. But the Ritz, overlooking Skaha Lake and brown orchard-striped hill country, had a view that was unbeatable.

The coffee shop nearby, below the summit of the hill, was beatable however. The coffee was so weak I thought it was tea but the waitress was a young country lass and I didn't have the heart to complain. She had a wonderful earnestness about her, the braid-framed face bursting to please in what was obviously her first job.

I rang Richmond for the first time in forty-eight hours.

"Could I speak to Sylvia please?"

"Sylvia is on vacation."

Relieved, I began watching the young girl feverishly wiping the tables.

"Is she that pretty?" asked Erica, stifling a yawn from the

long trip through the mountains down into the dry, irrigated Okanagan.

"I was just thinking how simple everything is for her," I said, wondering now what would become of Jenny.

"It's all relative," replied Erica. "I bet she can't wait to be twenty."

"Guess so." I was still thinking of Jenny, of how dangerous my life had become. My early relief gave way to anxiety. The young waitress had that fatherless, only-child look about her. Just she and her mom, I thought. It probably wasn't that simple for her after all—more like a struggle. I could see Jenny plainly, and I determined once again to be very careful about what we were about to do. Getting evidence was one thing, getting killed was another. There might not be anyone on our tail—if my brilliant car paint plan had worked—but I imagined there'd be Rottweilers at least in the scrub pine hills that curtained the Canadian rectenna and the SPS ground control station, which had to be a minimum of fifty miles away from the rectenna, beyond the beam's edge.

They shouldn't be hard to find. Probably more big "orchards," I thought. Bound to be protected somehow as government experimental farms, common enough in such a heavily agricultural country. The trouble would be getting close enough. With Sudley Steel around, trespassers would not be prosecuted, they would be shot. No thanks. Still, we'd have to get near enough to see the cars of the personnel who worked inside.

As we walked back to the motel room it looked as if we'd have to take rain gear. The clouds were gathering for one of those interior storms where the cumulus swell and pile up all day, grow dark, and then let fly with a thunderous downpour. I hoped the roof of the motel room was watertight, as we'd be here a week at least.

Before I opened the door I bent down and looked for the hair. It was still there. So far, I thought, so good though I knew a really good professional could have come in and gone out and left it in exactly the same place. But for now I put my money on optimism. What I had to do first off was find the nearest high, long barbed-wire fence. Then we would need to use the two trail bikes. Even so, we'd have to be prepared for a long walk. The last thing we needed was for them to hear us a mile off.

CHAPTER 27

Brown bush and an occasional red-barked gum—thirty miles north of Penticton. And dust—a cloud of it moving north to south along a barbed-wire fence that was fifteen miles by ten, set upon a flat sagebrush plateau hidden from view by a perimeter of scrub pine. At first we thought the dust cloud coming across the access road a hundred yards to the right of us near the big wire gate was simply a wind scurry. The five by ten-foot sign by the gate read:

CANADIAN FORCES BASE
BASE DE FORCES CANADIENNES

It was more believable than "Government Research Station," I'll give them that. I grabbed Erica's arm, pulling her down. At the bottom of the dust cloud there were boots—army boots. Thirty or forty pairs, moving in unison like a platoon of fat bugs. Then the sound of muffled thumping. Paratroops. The cloud was coming toward us. Now and then, concentrating on the dust, I could glimpse a flak jacket: a khaki brown mottled with light chocolate brown with smears of green—perfect camouflage for the Okanagan. Above the concerted thudding of boots as they crossed the powder dirt road there was an ominous grunting, the whole platoon having the appearance of one huge animal moving fast, with grim determination. Soon the grunting became louder and louder. Then sounds like badly spaced firecrackers, boots breaking the tinder-dry twigs, and gaiters scraping sagebrush.

"Get down!" I whispered hoarsely. "Get . . ."

"I am," she said just as urgently. "They've found us."

Then we could see the sweating, red faces and camouflaged berets with the dulled combat badges. This control center *was* an armed camp. At about twenty yards a voice exploded the silence of the bush. "Right tarn!"

In deadly unison the black boots instantly swung westward, away from us, down closer to the fence. Then, almost upon the fence. "Left tarn—shut up, York!" and they were gone.

"My God, I thought it was all . . ." I slapped my thigh from pure excitement.

"What's so funny?" Erica had had a bad fright and amid the red flush of sunburn there were splotches of white.

"We can get closer," I said.

"How? I don't . . ."

"There can't be sensors. A crowd like that would trip every damn circuit within two miles."

"Why wouldn't they have sensors?"

"They probably did." I lifted the field glasses. "But I can't see any. The point is, even if they're there, hidden, they're not being used."

"I can't see any reason . . ."

"Because," I said, "I got in at Hopsville. That's why. I beat the sensors. With ice. Very tricky I am, you see."

"You didn't beat the infra-red cameras. I'll bet that platoon was on a videoscreen."

I wasn't excited anymore. "Damn! You're right. Okay, so we'll have to be careful. We'll keep under cover and use the binoculars. The cameras won't pick us up this far from the fence. Too much scrub."

It was fine in theory, but the trouble was I've no patience with heat. Talk about being hot—it must have been eighty degrees Fahrenheit in the shade and so humid that every time you moved your shirt peeled off your skin. And the flies were carpet bombing, a seething black mass constantly trying to penetrate our waving hands to crawl into eyes and mouth. It was a good place to train paratroopers all right. If they could survive this and run at the same time they deserved their bloody badges. Not a breath of breeze and the sun a white flare in a pale washed sky, beating down so hard that pretty soon my blood pressure started to rise just from the sheer irritation of it all. To make it worse, I discovered that Erica was one of those infuriating people who never perspire, or rather perspire just the tiniest bit, a few little spots on the forehead to show they're mortal. It wasn't summer, but for me it was like a steam bath, and in two hours, crouching in the same hideaway, waving off insects and having noted only three cars that stopped and went through the guard gate, all I could think of was drinking a tall, cold Singapore sling smothered with crushed ice, and sitting in a long, cool bath. By four-thirty nothing had changed, along with the weather, but it must have been a shift change for the eight-to-four crew because we took down three more license numbers in five minutes.

We walked back through the bush, watching for any more patrols. I think I would have surrendered for a Coke. We rode out on the trail bikes. Everything about them annoyed me: the noise, which you never hear in the commercials, the fumes, which you never smell in the commercials, and the bone-jarring, bumpy ride through the powdered dust. By the time we got back to the motel we were covered in it.

"You look like a clown," said Erica jokingly.

"Very funny," I said, marching into the room, heading straight for the fridge.

Half an hour later, after a silly, heat-induced argument about the proper way to make iced tea, ice first or tea, I began being half civilized again. "I'll call Jonas," I said, lowering myself into the old rocker by the phone. "He'll be able to get the addresses to fit the license plates. Then we can stake them out."

Erica nodded agreement, too tired to think. I dialed Lionel, the dry cleaner next to Jonas.

"How come you never perspire?" I asked Erica.

"I do."

"No you don't."

"Yes I do," she said. "You can't see where, that's all." She gave me a shy smile over the edge of the frosted glass.

I got through to Jonas, gave him the message, and hung up. I took a long, cold sip. "Can I see?"

"What?" she asked demurely.

"Where you perspire?"

"Will you behave yourself?"

"Of course not."

"Come on then."

Halfway through I slowed down to neutral.

"What's wrong?" she whispered.

"Nothing," I lied and returned to my happy work. I'd remembered I hadn't checked for the hair in the door. We'd been so eager to get back to cool off I'd just charged into the cabin. I wouldn't have thought any more about it but after we'd finished and I was gently scratching Erica's back, thinking it a hogwash thesis that sex is really another form of violence, how it was tender and loving for us, Erica murmured, "It was too easy."

"What? You want me to strap you to the bedpost or . . ."

"No. No. I mean today. Getting those number plates. That patrol swinging around, as if suddenly they'd been ordered away from us."

I thought about that and my scratching got slower and slower on her back. "You mean we shouldn't have been allowed that close?"

"Not if it was well guarded."

I slid my hand down her spine, gently kneading the small of her back. "You're not saying we were . . ."

"I don't know. But there were no dogs. Dogs would have smelled us a mile off in that heat."

Now my hand stopped rubbing altogether.

"More," she murmured. "The left side." My hand trailed over and under her thigh.

"My *back!*" she said.

"You're right," I said. "There were no dogs. Not a sign of them. So you do think we were allowed to get that close?"

"Maybe."

"Why?"

She sighed. It was a mixture of pleasure, exhaustion, and confusion. "I don't know. Maybe there's nothing wrong at the control center at all."

I got up, my left leg asleep from the crouching position, and hobbled as quickly as I could to the door. The hair had fallen. Of course the door had been opened by us. Or by someone else? I unscrewed the phone to look for a small harmonica. There was none. I checked the room. There were no bugs at all.

In ten minutes Jonas, having used his connections in the Motor Vehicle Branch, had fitted names and addresses to the three number plates I'd given him. It would cost me another *Penthouse*. Already I felt tired as I contemplated going out again at 10 P.M. to our scrub hideaway in time for the change-over to the four-to-midnight shift. We'd have to be quick and get the numbers from the cars as they stopped briefly under the guard gate light before moving off into the dark bush of the control center. There were four controllers for each watch. In all we got eleven number plates, one car being used by two of the controllers—probably neighbors.

At first I was surprised at the length of their watches. Eight hours is a long time staring at electronic gear, even if it was, as Erica said, fully automated, with the beam focus guided by computer tape, with simple two digit numbers indicating beam location instead of the more laborious latitude and longitude printouts of older radar systems. Eight hours is too long a time, I thought, because one slip and, well, I'd seen what one slip could do when I'd peered into the grave at Lincoln South a few nights before. But then, the next day I had Erica do some more snooping around Dixie's Cup, the coffee shop frequented by some of the controllers. She discovered that the shifts weren't really eight hours after all. Apparently they split up into two hours on and two hours off. This meant only two controllers were on duty, one senior and junior, the other two relaxing in what we gathered were luxurious leisure facilities. So while they technically put in a forty-hour week they really worked only twenty hours. The shift teams changed over every six months.

The question was, who was it? Twelve names may not seem like many, but we couldn't go around to twelve different addresses. We'd only been here three days, but by now I knew the old painted-car trick must be wearing pretty thin and the security people here would be on special alert—unless Erica was right and we'd been allowed to go near the fence.

We were resting our weary bones from staking out the three shifts, and I was making another long, cool drink, not worrying about patrols, sensors, or dogs for a change, when it came to me how to figure out who the contact was. It was prompted by my having spent so much time staring at my wristwatch every five minutes during the long stakeouts—that, together with the fact that I couldn't shake the memory of old Thompson's eyes or those of the dead Finn. I didn't say anything to Erica because if I was right, it would be the same information the "representatives" were after and if things went wrong and they thought she knew . . . well, that was half the reason I didn't tell her. In any event, what she didn't know she couldn't tell them.

I took the photo out of my suitcase and studied it for a long time—the bright, new-looking wristwatch on the Finn. It had struck me, I remembered, when Dermit first showed me the photo and told me to keep it. The watch on the old man had been touched up—and read 12:45. But 12:45 in the midnight to 8:00 A.M. shift or the 8:00 A.M. to 4:00 P.M. shift? Whoever had taken the trouble to tell me it was 12:45 would also be telling me what shift they had been on when they'd sent the photo to Dermit. I cast my mind back to the coffee-shop meeting, trying to recall what else had struck me about the photo—if anything. I peered at it again. The open lunch bucket at his side! The 8:00 A.M. to 4:00 P.M. shift. With that discovery, my list dropped from twelve to four—the four who were on duty during that watch. Two women, ages thirty-seven and twenty-six, and two men, forty-one and fifty-nine.

The fifty-nine-year-old immediately went to the bottom of the list. He was old enough to have seen a year or two of action in World War II—just six years until retirement. Why should he protest, risk his pension and evening strolls in Victoria, even if he *knew* about the superhigh energy being pulsed at certain times? Besides, they'd be more likely to have trained a younger person as a better long-term investment. Next I eliminated the forty-one-year-old man. Married with three kids. Erica had rung up to inquire about buying his house. He was on a second mortgage. Again, job security and financial responsibility spoke against it—unless he was very brave, and they don't come by the dozen.

I settled on the two women. One, the twenty-six-year-old, was married. The older one wasn't. I went for the younger. I'd seen her changing shifts. Not pretty, teeth a little too far apart, full figure, possibly pregnant.

I told the owner of Dixie's Cup that I represented a new diaper company. "We've just selected Penticton and environs as a test-market area." Could she possibly tell me of anyone around who was recently married and who was thinking of starting a family, someone my company could approach with two months' free supply of diapers? The name of the twenty-six-year-old, Brenda Pret, née Rolston, was on the list.

That'll be her, I concluded confidently—pregnant and knows enough about microwaves to be worried. Right, but how would I approach her with it?

Before we left the motel early the next morning I very carefully pulled another hair from my scalp and put it in the door a few inches above the sill as I closed it. If I stayed around here long enough, I'd go bald.

I couldn't very well order Erica to stay alone in the cabin, but driving down through the brown hills toward the town I tried to think of a gentle way of explaining why I wanted to go the next part alone. I told her that as far as we knew, none of the controllers had ever met her. But if by chance the person I was seeing remembered seeing her somewhere, as Roth's assistant on the widely broadcast TV launch, for example, we might not get to first base. I parked the car, six blocks from the address I had in mind.

"Won't you at least tell me where you're going? I should know just in case . . ."

"I don't want to tell you."

She glared. "You mean you won't tell me?"

"Look, close the door, you'll get cold."

"It's scorching hot, Harry!"

I shrugged.

"Thanks for the vote of confidence."

"Look, you . . . don't understand," I began, "it's—"

"If they get to me, I can't tell. Right?"

I shifted uneasily. She was right, it was going to be another Indian summer scorcher.

"Well, what if they get you?" she snapped. "It's better we both know."

I shook my head. "Let's do it my way. I don't want you to get hurt and if—" I went to touch her.

She withdrew and looked out the other side of the car. "You're a bastard, Harry Sturgess."

I fingered the chrome around the window, squinting awkwardly in the bright sun. "This is hard ball. It's not just for us, sweetheart. If we don't find out . . ."

"Have you got a Kleenex?"

I gave her one.

"I'll wait here," she said quietly.

I kissed the top of her head and closed the door softly.

"Yes?" she asked suspiciously, the eye hidden behind the peephole. A peephole! And I thought the Okanagan was still a territory of the trustful.

"I'm from Dermit Insurance," I said. "You wanted your household goods assessed?" The peephole closed.

An elderly gent hobbled by down the apartment building hallway, lifting his stick in greeting. I nodded, glanced quickly but carefully at the stick. It *was* a stick and the man was old.

I moved closer to the door, listening for the sound of a telephone being dialed. If she'd gone to her bedroom and rung I wouldn't hear it but just possibly I might hear her voice. Instead, the door chain clanked before she opened it to a slit. Now I could see both eyes stilled with fright. The Okanagan had lost its innocence. A legacy no doubt from the arrival of large barbed-wire fences.

"I never rang for any insurance."

"Oh!" I thumbed through my notebook. "This is the address isn't it?" I held up the photo Dermit had received. The Finn staring—mouth gaping in suspended terror. He'd never even had time to close his lips. The eyes completely white, like a zombie.

Her face drained of color. "I . . . I . . ." I could see she was about six months pregnant.

"We'd like to help," I said quickly, urgently. "We've come a long way to help." I looked back at the hallway so she could see my caution. "We're especially worried," I began. "We're especially worried about the children, the unborn, what will happen to them if they're not insured."

The chain was off the hook and I was in. She wasn't friendly. She was scared—but intelligent enough to know that if I hadn't been there to help I wouldn't have been knocking on her apartment door asking to come in, that if I'd been part of Roth's security force I'd take her at work where there was no danger of any fuss and where, incidentally, it would have made the most impact on her fellow workers and any other potential leak. Still, she wasn't committing herself. She pushed back a wisp of short blond hair. By contrast the eyes were dark and worried. I didn't say anything about the glistening carving knife she was holding in her other hand, tapping it nervously against the faded blue jeans.

"I never asked for any household insurance but maybe . . . maybe I should have it reassessed. There's some new clause now, isn't there?" she said nervously.

"Yes," I answered, recalling my own policy in Rockville. "The Extended Theft—Full Value clause. Surprising, the number of people who don't know they're only insured for the original purchase price of goods lost or stolen. Inflation can wipe you out. You need protection."

The apartment told me a lot about Brenda Pret. Immaculately, almost obsessively, neat but not in keeping with the casualness of the red and blue plaid shirt hanging comfortably over the faded Levi's. I glanced around—thick beige Custom Weave carpet; big, sensuous leather sofa; a polished teak coffee table with a glass inset of a verse from Kahlil Gibran—the "lift your glass of wine" bit. And on the polished dining room table, which was no doubt another antique donated by neat and wealthy parents, there was a striking bronze marble statue of a man and woman melting into one long orgasmic embrace. That didn't come from Mom. Above the Marantz stereo there was an oil painting of a nude Indian boy with spear, gazing out over a spring-flowered desert. It was all an odd mixture of Old World propriety and stateliness and New World luxuriousness and liberation. Most striking of all was the absence of any living, breathing man, only the statue and the boy in the oil.

"Your husband? Is he . . ."

"Gone." She'd been ready for it.

"Where?"

She blushed, then lifted her head sharply, defensively, as if I was going to make an issue of it.

"We're separated."

I nearly said, "Good," but what I meant was that now I could relax without wondering about a second unknown. I was sorry, but if the husband was out of the picture, so much the better. The odds were high enough already; we could do without marital complications.

"I'm sorry," she said, her hand darting to her forehead as if suddenly remembering her manners. "Would you like some coffee?"

"I'd love some."

While the kettle gurgled I looked around for the usual family photos. None. The child she was carrying would be the first. She smiled awkwardly a couple of times. I complimented her on the interior decor. She ignored the comment—it must have been hubby's choice. As the water bubbled furiously, I worked out that it had been just about six months ago that Dermit had received the photo, about the time she would've suspected she was pregnant. If she'd been that convinced about microwaves causing birth defects, why hadn't she left?

"Sugar?" she asked.

I doled in two heaping teaspoonfuls. She still hadn't committed herself. I looked up at the oil painting, giving it the old connoisseur treatment. She'd have to be pushed a little. "You insured that painting?"

"No," she said guardedly, obviously puzzled by my question. "It's quite valuable, I've been told. Should I—I mean, what do you think it's worth?"

"Nothing," I said.

She was genuinely shocked.

"Nothing," I repeated, getting up and looking more intently at the Indian boy.

"Nothing?"

"Not if he's fried to a frazzle."

She went decidedly pale.

"By microwaves," I added. I was looking right at her. "Not if the SPS is misused." I glanced at the kitchen recess. I was surprised to see a microwave oven. "You use this?"

"My husband—he wanted one. He said . . ."

I nodded.

"How . . ." The lip was going out of control. "How did you . . . why did you come to see me?"

I took up the coffee and used the spoon slowly. "Process of elimination."

She sat down, wound up tightly as a spring. Then I showed her the photos from Dermit's microfilm, the special White House number, and credentials, inviting her to ring the President. Had she taken me up on it and rung Hoskins, it would have all been over—for me, her, and Erica. But as with most people, the very offer of such grand evidence was enough.

She poured it all out. The energy was pulsed, she explained, whenever they got the word from Roth. It was all part of a NORAD scheme, she said.

"Several years ago, in 1979, July 12, to be exact, a Canadian general gave up what they called a 'key planning post' at NORAD headquarters in Colorado Springs because he said that NORAD's defenses were so dated that the Russians could slip ten bombers through Canada at night and there'd be nothing we could do because all available funds were being spent on improving protection from missiles rather than bombers. It wasn't classified information—I read about it in the Vancouver *Sun*.

"How about Pine Tree?" I asked.

"Oh, it wasn't just the fighter interceptor guidance system he was worried about but the step before that. The actual Distant Early Warning system that wasn't up to snuff. The DEW Line."

"So?"

"So Roth told us that a 'swing SPS'—under perfect cover of being an energy provider—could double as an early warning station."

"Okay. But why such highly *pulsed* energy? Early warning only needs regular power. Low level and steady."

She visibly relaxed at my recognition of the weak point in Roth's argument. Her secret was being shared.

"Exactly," she said. "That's what I wondered about. Why the high-pulsed energy? Pretty soon we knew that the SPS wasn't just an energy source doubling up as an early warning scanner."

I stared down at the coffee, waiting. She walked toward the window, her hands folded. She seemed suddenly calm now. The dam had burst.

"Pretty soon," she continued, "we knew it had a third purpose. We knew that it was a killer ray." She turned slowly to face me. "And not just for Russian bombers. Not when that antenna moved. That was an accident during a high-pulse transmission. But when I worked out how far that beam could have moved, I knew what we were doing."

I put two more spoonfuls of sugar into my coffee. "What were we doing?" I asked slowly, trying to contain my tension.

She was gazing at the long green lines of orchards on the hills across the lake. "Ironically that was the easiest part. The SPS admin had sent us crates of material on setting up MW rectennas, etc. One of the papers was on the complex at Koitsanlahti."

"And the photo of the Finn?"

"In the report—along with several other shots. I took a photo of a photo, that's all. And sent it to Dermit."

I tried a curve ball. "And sent it from here—Penticton?"

She turned around, puzzled. "No. I sent it from Kelowna. It's a little . . ."

"I know . . . so what *were* we doing?"

She came back from the window and sat down next to me. Her pale face was washed by the early morning sun. "We're developing a weapon that isn't just part of an updated NORAD defense plan—it is part of a retaliatory attack plan against Russia. The computer-fed tape issued from Washington by Dr. Roth will give top-secret two-digit numbers from the bomber index—"

"Targets for an SPS arc?"

"Yes, or we could hit them independently, one by one if we liked—like flashing a flashlight on and off instead of sweeping it in one movement. The perfect attack plan because a Russian hunter-killer satellite won't come near the SPS because of its 'peaceful' use—a simple U.S. energy station. We'll have the numbers on tape as soon as the beam's perfected. Then a word from Washington and we just push the button. The tape goes into BAC."

"BAC?"

"Beam Aiming Computer. We just press the button. The tape goes in, and it's done!"

I felt my ears roaring like a river in flood and two things rushed through my brain. Of course, letting the operators know the general plan, or what they thought was the general plan, was a very smart move. For a start, the beam might have to be aimed by semi-automatic manual-assisted control in the unlikely event of computer foulup, so they'd have to know the general idea. Besides, why would they object? What could possibly be immoral about a NORAD plan for counterattack? Patriotism was the potion. Why would anyone squeal about the deadly pulses if they thought it was in the interest of national security—of international security for that matter—and told so by the head of the whole SPS program? It was foolproof—it was bloody brilliant—because of one detail. Roth would issue the orientation of beam focus by computer tape. That is, targets would be designated by bomber index numbers, the operators not having access to the highly classified bomber index.

The second thing that hit me, the thing Brenda hadn't seen, was that the Russians must be able to detect such high pulses of energy coming from space—from *international* space. Why hadn't they objected? Instead, Sutherland had received congratulations for implementing the alternate energy source "for all mankind." And the hops? Soviet spy satellites must clearly show the vast Hopsville rectenna receiving the massive punches of energy. Yet they'd said nothing. *Not a word.* It could only mean that the eminent Dr. Roth was producing a weapon all right—with Soviet acquiescence. Why? Was he *their* man? Was the smarmy, brilliant, spotted bow-tie sonofabitch *their* man? Was he perfecting a weapon—not for NORAD but for the KGB?

It was so simple. It was brilliant! With one computer instruction, a target designated by a two-digit number, he could have his innocent operators shift the beam on any city in the United States. In seconds. An electronic Trojan horse. Unless—

"Jesus Christ!" I said.

My head was already pounding from this when the killer blow fell—quite matter-of-factly, as if she was merely adding a footnote. "Don't worry," she announced calmly. "The focusing mechanism will be perfected in five days. But I'm still worried about the environmental . . ."

"*Perfected!*"

"Well it's better than the SPS swinging off course through faulty equipment I suppose. That's what I was worried about. That's why I sent the photo to Dermit in the first place. But if it's for NORAD and it has to swing I'm glad Roth is at least going to perfect it."

"Jesus Christ! Five days!"

"But what . . ." she began.

I didn't let her finish. "Listen!" I said, clutching her arm. She was scared.

"I . . . I don't . . ." she began again.

"No, listen. Listen. Can you get me the series of two-digit numbers on the punch tape—designated target numbers? When the very first tape comes in?"

"Yes . . . but we won't know what the numbers are for. I mean the actual targets—place names. That's very highly classified. It's . . ."

"Never mind that. If you give me the digits and I can get them to Washington—to the President—and he sees where they're situated and . . ."

"In Russia," she said.

"Yes," I lied. "Then he'll see that the SPS is being used as a weapon. He never authorized that."

She started to object.

"I can promise you. He never authorized that. Never! Not that kind of power."

"But the NORAD plan. I don't . . ."

"No. No. Listen, Brenda! It's Roth's idea. It's *his* weapon, *not* the President's."

"I'm sorry, but I still don't understand why . . ."

"Never mind for now. You said Roth will perfect the beam focus in five days?"

"Yes. He's just about synthesized the deflection coefficient and—"

"Can you get me those numbers?"

She thought hard. "Maybe . . . I don't . . . it's dangerous."

"Will you do it?"

She was biting her lip and unconsciously touching her stomach.

"Will you do it?"

"Yes."

I squeezed her hand. "Good girl."

I was in overdrive. Now I'd made contact I had to move fast back to Washington, D.C. Erica and I would leave the minute I got the numbers. One thing was for sure, Brenda and I shouldn't risk meeting again. So I'd use the old middle-man ploy—old but reliable. I gave Brenda Jonas' number in Vancouver, which she was to ring from a public phone booth in case her line was being tapped. I arranged a safety code with her, which I would pass on to Jonas, not only to protect them from knowing each other's identity but to protect them from capture if, as I felt certain, the line to Jonas' gun shop was also tapped. I went over the code once more with her.

"Ring as soon as you get those digits."

"I will."

"One more thing . . ."

"Yes?"

"After you give Jonas the digits . . . if you can get them . . . give me five days. If you don't hear from me it'll mean . . . if you don't hear from me then you'd better start sending your photos again. But, Brenda . . ."

"Yes?"

"Play it carefully—very carefully."

I gave her Ralph Stein's address at the CIA. At this moment, the adrenalin screaming through me, I wasn't even 100 percent sure of Ralph. I couldn't be 100 percent sure of anyone except Brenda. Other than me she was the only one who could get out the vital info that would tip off someone in D.C. to the full implications of what was going on—that Roth was perfecting a massive, pre-emptive strike capability *against* the United States in the United States. A surprise attack that could be launched from within.

I rang Lionel and gave him a message to have Jonas ring me back from a public phone. When he called, I explained to him that, first off, I wanted him to stay in his shop for the next forty-eight hours. He agreed. I raced on. "Someone calling herself Elizabeth might ring and say she wants to speak to Barney. You say he's out. 'Can I take a message?' The message she'll leave will be for Barney to ring Elizabeth at the following number. She'll give you a number. I'll ring you later today to see if she's called. You give me the number she gave you. Got all that? Even if your line's tapped at the gun shop, they won't know what the numbers mean."

"Coded?" I could sense the old excitement in Jonas' voice.

"Yes, coded."

"Okay—rerun. Woman, Elizabeth, calls me at gun shop—asks for Barney. I say, 'He's not here. I'll take a message.' She gives me a number. I give it to you when you call Barney. Right?"

"Right. Or if anything happens to me, I'll have Erica ring you. But, Jonas—"

"Yes?"

"Can you muffle the phone? I don't want her to recognize your voice."

I heard a soft, crumpling sound—probably Kleenex. His tone was heavy, deeper now—quite unrecognizable. "How's that?" he asked.

"Perfect, Barney. You're a pal." I paused. "Have to play this one close to the chest. Less she knows, the safer she'll be. All she's got is a telephone number. She doesn't know it's you."

"I understand. But why don't you arrange to have me called through Lionel? You said yourself the gun shop could be tapped. Save all the cover story."

"No. We have to be able to contact you any time—night or day. What if Lionel's closed?"

"Got it."

"Tell Ida not to answer the phone."

"Not to worry. You just send me *Penthouse*."

"I will."

I felt a right bastard, but it was a race against time. I had to cover all the angles I could think of. I reran it like a film in my brain. If Erica knew and they caught her as well as me and forced her to reveal Brenda's name or even a phone number through which she could be traced, it would be all over. They'd have sealed the leak for good. This way, the only phone number Erica could reveal was Jonas' and he didn't have a clue that Elizabeth was Brenda Pret.

Christ! I thought, running down the alleyways and jumping into the car next to Erica. We've got five days!

"Five days and Roth will have that beam fully operational."

"On whom?"

"On us—the United States—Canada—anywhere he damn well pleases."

We sped up to the motel. "I'll check out," said Erica in a voice drawn tight by my news.

I was out of the car in a second flat and ran toward the cabin to pick up our bags and get out of Penticton. As Erica headed for the motel office, I inserted the key, looked down, saw the hair was still in place, and wrenched open the door. In two seconds I was inside.

CHAPTER 28

It was because I'd been looking down at the door's sill for the hair that I hadn't seen him straight off.

He was sitting there holding a copy of *Playboy* upside down, studying the centerfold with what was meant to be impenetrable concentration. His cool was calculated to frighten me. It did. The door clicked, and from behind a big hand deftly relieved me of the Smith & Wesson. The efficient paw belonged to an old friend—Wyatt Earp—in clean pressed khaki. Wordlessly, Earp forced me down on the kitchenette stool, dropped the gun into the khaki windbreaker, stepped back a pace, and clasped his hands choirboy-like on his protruding gut.

The man with the *Playboy* was tall, about six feet, but much slighter than Wyatt and wore a brown tie and jacket. Next to him, in the rocker a few feet to his left, sat a small, pudgy, dark-haired man in a denim suit. The man in the brown jacket was obviously the boss. He turned the nude right side up. "You've been very naughty, Harry. Hasn't he, Roger?"

Roger was the little dark one in the rocker. His stomach was growling and he was reading a gaudily-colored horror comic. "Yeah, Mr. B."

I had the impulse to laugh—"Mr. B.!"—but I could see it

wouldn't go down well. What people, especially the comfy savings class who have never met thugs like this, never understand is that they love acting like second rate movie types. For the most part they're not very bright, and their imitation of cheap screen hoods is the closest they ever get to originality, to feeling their individuality. They're pathetic really—and very dangerous.

B. slowly rolled up the *Playboy*, the thin, pale lips smiling gently, and patted me on the head with the magazine. "Not really your line of country, is it, Harry?"

I'd never seen him before. He waved the magazine in the general direction of the South Pole. "I mean, thumping heads, shooting friends in the legs, and whatnot? The law here tells me you've been going absolutely berserk!" He said "the law" with ill-concealed contempt. "Poor old Georgie's legs. They say he'll be on crutches for months."

He paused to pour himself a drink. He was side-on to me now and his right profile was no better than the left, lean, tanned, and ugly with a long nose that flared slightly at the end, making him look like some kind of carrion bird I couldn't remember the name of. He plopped another ice cube in and stirred slowly. "Should have finished what you started," he said, forcing a hard little smile. The accent was English but not cockney, more middle class and a little pretentious.

"Should have thought with your background you'd be the more academic type of adviser. You know, 'The Effect of Pepper on American Culture.' Important stuff like that." he sneered.

"The Effect of SALT is more my line," I said.

"Oh. Oh, well done! Roger, did you hear that? That was quick."

Roger coughed into the horror comic. "Comedian is it? That's what we got, guv?"

"Yes," said B. "We have."

"Not healfy 'round here, Harry," said Roger. Another cockney.

Sudley Steel did have more where he came from. B. sipped

his gin and tonic, looking over with obvious impatience at Roger reading the comic book. "Do put Revelations down, Roger. I need your undivided attention."

"Right, guv." It was the way he closed the comic—immediately—not even the trace of a second glance. It didn't look "healfy" at all. Desperately, I remembered Clemenceau: "*L'audace! L'audace! Toujours l'audace!*"

"Look, Mr. B.," I said, glancing authoritatively at my watch. "Whoever the hell you are—I'll give you thirty—no, I'll be generous," I was almost shouting so that Erica might have warning, "I'll give you sixty seconds to get out of here. You've bitten off a piece of the U.S. government." I glanced angrily at the county sheriff. "The *federal* government. A little piece, I grant you, but still U.S. government property," I went on. "And if you eat it, you'll get very nasty indigestion. So be a good chap and shove off! Now. Right now!" Erica should have heard that.

Little Roger went purple, the laughter rolling around his rolypoly face and gut, threatening to pop his eyes out. "Gawd—he's got—Cor . . . 'e's a bloody corker that one, guv. He'll give me a bloody 'eart attack 'e will. A bloody coronary."

Mr. B. stifled an errant yawn. The paws behind me were still clasped, awaiting instructions, but there was something in Earp's silence that plainly said he'd rather not be here. Mr. B. yawned again. "You see what you're doing, Harry? You could kill one of my best associates. You really must contain yourself. We all like our bit of fun, U.S. government or otherwise, but Roger could burst a blood vessel or something."

I figured that Erica must surely have checked out by now and be heading toward the cabin. "Listen, *you*," I shouted with some difficulty, pointing at B.

Roger heaved himself out of the chair, lumbered across, and smacked me right off the stool. "Shut your face!" he said and ambled back to the rocker. My nose was tingling, numb, and there was the metallic taste of blood in my mouth. I expected the sheriff to be grinning with satisfaction. This should make his day. But, strangely enough, I got the impression that he didn't like the present company any more than I did. Roth's phrase, "necessary allies," floated back. But what I had to remember was that neither of them liked *me* at all.

"You know," began B., peering at the two others. "I think" —he tapped his forehead knowingly—"I think he's shouting because he wants to warn his crumpet. Yes, that's it."

"Now," said Roger, pushing himself back and forth, "that's a laugh, guv."

"It is," said B., "that it is."

Like me, Earp didn't know what they meant. He was simply rent-a-muscle, or what was left under all the cholesterol. Unemotional muscle, backup sent by Roth. A show of solidarity in plugging the leak.

I wanted to avoid giving them the satisfaction but curiosity won out. "What's a laugh?"

"Will I tell him, Mr. B.?"

"Why not?" said B., adding a dash of tonic to his gin.

Roger's jolly face was puffing with enjoyment. "You really fink you fooled us, eh? I mean that switching license plates business and painted car bullshit. Eh?"

I said nothing, but suddenly there was a cold surge in my bowels.

"The old man at . . ." continued Roger.

"Storm Lake," said B., sipping very slowly and watching me with ill-concealed delight.

"Yeah," said Roger. "Storm Lake. That old codger telling us about you painting the car and then you turning off at Mount Vernon—heading north instead of south to Seattle where you told him so he'd tell us. You really fink you'd fool us, eh? Harry Sturgess, big-time operator." He threw the comic book at me. He'd stopped laughing. "You bloody twit."

"You see," said B. smugly, "we thought that seeing as you were so inquisitive and had been given some kind of information from . . ." B. snapped his fingers impatiently to capture what was on the tip of his birdlike tongue.

"Dermit," said Roger. "Dinky Dermit."

"Yes, Dermit," continued B. "We thought, well"—he spread his hands beneficently—"we thought why not let the intrepid Harry Sturgess find out who our weak link is?" He slapped both arm rests, glancing condescendingly at the sheriff. "Seeing as how our *colleagues* couldn't find out . . ." He turned back to me. "We suspected a controller—trouble was, which one? But now we know. Mrs. Pret." He examined his fingernails in the shaft of bright sunlight. "Pretty young thing."

"Was," added Roger malevolently.

"What?" asked B.

"She was pretty." Roger had a sick grin plastered on his sallow face.

"No, no, no," admonished B., diligently flicking lint from his lapel. "No, we'll let her be for the moment. Don't want to alarm the poor lass. Besides, when we tell him who it is, Mr. Roth'll want to keep an eye on her—see if she has 'cohorts' at Control." He smiled gratuitously at the sheriff. "Think you could handle that, Yank?"

The Sudley Steel lads obviously relished the irony of the law being forced, by Roth, to help them. My brain was racing. So one of them must have followed me to Brenda's apartment and then hightailed it back to the motel. But how had they managed to find us—to follow our trail—after I'd taken so much trouble to . . .

"And of course," said B., "we know of your little visit to your friend in Vancouver."

Jesus!

"Could have picked you up there but we thought, why alert you? Why spoil your little holiday in the sunny Okanogan—let you do the nosing around for us." He stifled a yawn—pretentious bastard. "You did very well, Harry."

Erica, the bitch! No wonder she wasn't here. No wonder the sheriff was. Dirty, rotten little bitch! Where the hell had she made the calls? From the restrooms anywhere along the way? From Winthrop to Storm to Hope—and Vancouver. Her shopping trip with Ida—she'd had a hundred chances. Son of a—no wonder she'd suggested checking out from the motel. Very convenient. Of course I should have seen it from the beginning, but I'm no better than anyone else—anyone that's been lonely. I'd let my loneliness be filled by a pretty face.

How sloppy could you get? She'd worked it to the full. Chief assistant to Roth, so she knew I'd be on guard at first. Hence the cold reception to my initial advances on board the plane; and after that the "too busy tonight" routine in Washington, D.C. All to convince me she wasn't trying to work her feminine charm on behalf of Roth. And telling me jokingly how she'd promised Roth to "look after" me. I'd laughed. Bloody stupid fool! Hook, line, and sinker!

I was in a blind rage. What an actress! Roth's watchdog. His bitch. His insurance after Hopsville that he wouldn't lose track of me. And her *surprise* at our getting so close to the control center—"As if we'd been allowed to get close," she'd said. That was another brilliant bit of bloody camouflage that was—for if ever I'd suspected her, that would be the perfect cover—for her to cast doubt on the ease with which we got close enough to get the number plates from what was supposedly a highly guarded camp. And "no dogs," she'd pointed out. *She'd* pointed out. Cunning, beautiful bitch. All this flashed through my brain in seconds. I could see the great vulture face of B. and his little jolly friend guffawing at me. And suddenly I was humiliated as well as enraged—as if I'd been undressed in public—as if they'd known what I now suspected—that even her last gasps of passion had been acted. The anger drained out of me, driven by the sheer weight of humiliation.

"Yeah," said Roger. "You should have shot George before he got to the shoes."

I stared at him uncomprehendingly. "Before George . . . what the hell . . . ?"

There was a knock on the door.

"In!" shouted B., and Erica came in, florid, half-stumbling, being shoved by what looked like a wrestler. Eastern European by the looks of it; broad, muscular face and barrel chest.

It was like being in the middle of a nightmare or just getting off one of those spinning swings at a fairground where you've completely lost your balance and any sense of direction. You've no idea where you're going—you just want to throw up. If Erica had betrayed me . . . but then why would they bring her in? Unless . . . ? It didn't make any sense.

Roger shook his head contemptuously at me. B. merely smiled. Roger lurched out of the chair and, bending down like a store clerk, put his left hand up high on Erica's leg. The sheriff moved forward a pace. He was hardly the chivalrous type, but he knew Roth wouldn't go for this particular grope. Erica stiffened, but the wrestler held her tightly.

"Left or right, guv?" Roger asked.

B. shook his head. "No idea. Take both of them off. I'm curious."

"I'll bet five bucks on the left," added Roger.

"You're on," answered B.

While the wrestler applied more pressure, holding her back, Roger again ran his hand high up Erica's leg before he lowered it and pulled off both her shoes. Standing up, grunting hard from the effort, his stomach growling noisily again, he turned the shoes over. He studied them for a second then looked somewhat despondently at B. "You win. Right shoe."

I stared at the shoe and now I knew and my darling Erica knew why George of the dimwit brain had outsmarted us—part of the price we pay for the modern world. When it was first invented in the mid-seventies, the microchip had meant that a computer that once had required a warehouse to contain it, literally a warehouse, could now be fitted into the trunk of a car. As an offshoot, the microchip beeper was less than half an inch in diameter, no bigger, much smaller in fact, than a thumbtack pushed into the arch of the shoe. Not into the sole or into the heel, where Erica would have noticed it walking, but in the hidden angle between sole and heel. The one thing that they knew she'd be wearing all the time. The one thing that never left her. The purse would have done, but it could be lost, left in the car or in a cafe, or she might have, unlikely as it is for a woman, cleaned it out once a week. But not the shoes.

I had to give it to the bastards. They'd had a constant beep from us all the way. I realized that the car that had passed us that night in the Cascades had probably been one of the trailing vehicles. But how did they follow us across the line? Where there were no roads? Then I understood the presence of the aircraft circling around and around our heads. This would have been the trickiest part, tracking the beeper in the bush, where a car couldn't follow us, until we were once again on a highway, hitchhiking for Vancouver.

My head must have dropped. I couldn't look Erica in the face. Not only trapped, outwitted, but deeply ashamed that I'd doubted her. Not simply that I'd doubted her but had done it so quickly—so willingly. That would take a lot of making up.

All my anger exploded at B. "B. for bastard is it?"

Roger got up, but B. motioned him back with forced good nature.

"No, no—not here, Roger. I think it'd be better in the country, don't you?"

Roger got the point. "Yeah. Yeah, Mr. B., you're right." He looked at Erica, flipping his jeans pocket open and shut. "In the country is right. I like picnics."

B. pointed at the wrestler while fishing in his jacket for keys. "Go get the car."

"Mr. B.?" It was Roger.

"What?"

"Let's take some Colonel Ernie's. We 'aven't had any nosh for bloody hours."

"Excellent suggestion," said B., slapping his hands together. "Yes, let's all have a nosh up in the country, shall we?" He looked up, as if any of us really had a choice. He handed the wrestler a twenty-dollar bill along with the car keys, all the time looking around, still smiling. "Who's for Colonel Ernie?"

He was insane.

"Could I use the bathroom?" asked Erica, still stunned from the grope.

"No," he said. He gazed blankly at her for several seconds. "Check her handbag."

"Already did, Mr. Bell." It was the first time the sheriff had spoken.

"Then do it again," insisted B. Earp looked defiantly at B.

The Englishman's voice was shrill. "Do it again, you dolt!"

"Satisfied?" said Earp, spilling the contents on the bed. "Only the usual things."

Roger rifled through them quickly, stopped, and looked up at Roth's man while slowly extracting the long hatpin.

"Usual, eh? That's a bloody shiv, mate."

"Ladies often have hatpins."

"Yeah—forty years ago!"

B.'s jaw was clenched as tightly as a steel trap, his hand trembling.

Erica spoke quietly. "I have to go."

He grabbed her backside. She stumbled backward. "Then go!" he snarled, lunging at her breasts. My fist came up—blocked in midair, Roger pointing the gun at my left eye.

"Then go!" shouted B. again, whipping Erica's face left, then right, pushing her across the room. She half fell, half stumbled toward the bathroom door. Excited by the violence, Roger was moving in toward her as well.

"Just watch her," said B., straightening his tie in an effort to appear nonchalant after his mad sadistic outburst.

"I will, guv." Roger leered, "I'll just watch her." He chuckled, his face puffing again with enjoyment. The bathroom door closed.

"Real class," I said, looking at Bell. "Yes sir, Sudley Steel knows how to pick them. You've got real class you have. Chase little girls too, do you?"

He whirled so fast I didn't have time to move. The breath exploded from me and I went down, knocking over the stool, crashing into the coffee table. His shaking finger shot out toward my face. All the cool had gone.

"It's a gorge for you, Yank. A nice high gorge. I want to see you falling." Now the pale lips were only inches from me, like strips of albino hide. "Your head'll crack like an eggshell, Sturgess. I want to see that."

"Keep your hands off me, you filthy little creep!" It was Erica's voice coming from the bathroom. Earp strode over to the bathroom door to investigate.

What a crew, I thought. Sudley Steel must have scoured the gutters of London for this pair.

"Roger!" called B.

"Yeah?" came the hollow voice from the bathroom.

"Hurry it up in—!"

There was a sudden rush of water and what sounded like a moan from inside. The sheriff was wrenching at the handle. It was locked from inside. There was a low, scrabbling sound in the bathroom like a giant crab whose legs kept sliding on the linoleum. I guessed what had happened—Erica had lured Puff Face into false security and felled him with a good strong knee to the crotch. I had to act—fast.

"Break it in!" B. yelled at Earp. "Open the friggin' door!" he kept on, waving a black 9 mm about in the air. Earp stood back from the door. I could still hear the slight scrabbling noise and the odd moan from inside as the felled Roger struggled to stand. Earp lowered his shoulder and rammed the door. I went for the stool with my right hand but the warm steel of Bell's automatic was pressing on my temple—shaking. The toilet door opened. Instinctively, Bell turned toward it. I dropped. Erica fired Roger's gun. The shot went wild—past Earp. I shoved Bell's hand away, holding it above me in a vise grip, bashing it against the wall. Shoving, grunting out of the bathroom, Earp and Roger were locked together—Roger, already half crippled, getting the worst of it. Desperate, I kept bashing Bell's hand against the wall. Suddenly the gun dropped with a thud behind him. He scrambled for it. I turned, saw Erica, opened my hands. She tossed over Roger's gun. I fired twice. Bell sat still, crumpled in the corner. Another shot. The sheriff's jacket exploded. I saw Roger pulling again at my .38 in the jacket pocket. The jacket bucked. The sheriff was dead.

Erica screamed a warning. Puff Face, knowing he hadn't time to retrieve the sheriff's gun from beneath the body, or my .38 from the bloodied mess of jacket, was charging, half holding his crotch where Erica had fixed him. He bashed her aside, coming straight for my heart. I saw the glint of the hatpin, fired point-blank, and saw an implosion of red bone and some gray stuff like mashed sardines.

While we waited for the wrestler to return I poured Erica a whiskey. The motel operator was already hammering on the door, small chips of red paint dropping to the floor.

"Just a moment." The banging on the door was reaching a crescendo.

"I'm calling the police, Mr. Herne!" Herne was the fake name Erica had given her when she signed in. "If you don't . . ." she continued.

I wrenched open the door and dragged her in. She started to scream but I had my hand over her mouth. "Be quiet!"

When she saw Bell, crumpled, staring at her, she gasped so hard I could feel my fingers being vacuumed against her teeth. Her eyes seemed to swell to twice their normal size as if about to pop. I tore out the phone cord, took her to the bathroom, tied her kneeling to the toilet pipe, and gagged her with toilet paper, using Bell's tie to keep it in place. "Sorry about this," I said ineffectually. "Be quiet and you'll be all right."

The details, I told myself. Get the details right. So you've had a near miss, so you misjudged Erica—all right, but stay calm. Think it out, Harry. Think it out. The shock hadn't hit Erica yet—she was too outraged by Puff Face's sick glee as he'd watched her in the bathroom.

The Penticton police were ten miles distant, but there could be Mountie highway patrols only minutes away. I sat still for several seconds as Erica collected our bags. I took the tiny magnetic beeper from Puff Face's pocket and whispered to Erica so the proprietress couldn't hear. "I'll stop at the next curve out of sight of the motel and you double back. Take your hair down over your shoulders or something, put on your sunglasses, and drive their car ten miles south. Pull off at Okanagan Falls."

I was thinking of Brenda Pret. These goons had only just found out her name when I made contact with her less than an hour before. So they hadn't told Roth yet. What was it that Bell had said before Erica had appeared? Something about "When we tell him who it is, Mr. Roth'll want to keep an eye on her," etc.

I glanced around at the three bodies with a definitely un-Christian but deep satisfaction. Now they *couldn't* tell anyone. But after hearing what had happened to them, Roth would want me quickly, to try to get the name of the leak. As Bell had said, they suspected one of the operators in the control center. The only problem had been, which one? With Roth and his friends hot on the trail I just prayed Brenda Pret would be able to get the two-digit numbers in time. Five days. "Listen," I said to Erica, "if anything should happen to me." I waited, expecting some expression of concern. She was probably too wound up. "If anything should happen to me before the next five days are up, I want you to make a call." I gave her Jonas' number.

"Who's this?"

"Don't worry about that. Just remember when you ring and it answers, ask for Barney. The person at the other end will say Barney's not there, but he'll give you his number. Got it?"

"What does the number . . ."

I saw the car, an off-white Mercedes, pulling up outside. I opened the door wide enough for the wrestler to see the .38 poking above his Family Bucket. "Get in!" I said. I took out a drumstick and waved him toward the kitchenette. Still grasping his dinner for five, he stepped over Bell, then Puff Face, and his mouth fell open, agape at the slaughter. "Hey . . . hey listen," he began imploringly. "Hey, look, mister, I don't know anything about what's going down here . . . I'm just . . ."

"I know," I growled. "Just a working lad. Did you know you were working for the KGB?"

"Hey? Hey, I'm not a Commie. No, sir, I . . ."

"Shut up. Sit down and stay still."

Never any rope when you need some, but I had three men's belts that weren't being used. Kleenex did for the gag and a torn towel strip to hold it and, the sweat blurring my vision, I finished it off by wetting several towel strips, laying him down, and tying him to the S-pipe beneath the sink. He'd need two Boy Scouts to undo him in a hurry. I took the keys from his pocket and motioned Erica out of the room, quietly shutting the door on a clump of Kleenex rather than having it click, so the motel owner couldn't hear, couldn't be sure whether we were still there or had gone. Every second counted. Fortunately most of the guests were out, only an old couple a few doors down poking their heads inquiringly out into the sunlight. "Were those gunshots?" the old man asked.

"Get inside!" I commanded. "And stay there! Police."

The heads disappeared. The old people would no doubt be peering at us from behind the flimsy curtain, taking a note of the license plate, color, and so on.

Inside the Pontiac, as the engine roared to life, I gave Erica the keys to the Mercedes as she raced on with her questions. "What do I ask for when I ring this Barney?"

"You don't. You ask for Barney. The person at the other end will say Barney's not there but they can give you Barney's number. Write the number down. Memorize it, then burn the paper."

Erica's eyes were the most beautiful I'd ever seen them, sparkling, alive and determined. "Write it down. Memorize. Burn. Right?"

"You got it."

"The target numbers?" she asked.

"Yes and no."

"What does *that* mean—apart from the fact that you still don't . . ."

"It means I'm not telling you."

She was silent for a few seconds.

"Look," I began, "if you get caught . . ."

"You told me before."

I didn't answer. It was hard ball all right, but the stakes were too high to do it any other way. She didn't remonstrate. She was tough when she had to be and now she had to be.

She took out the tortoise shell barrette and let the sunlit hair cascade over her shoulders. "But giving me the numbers like that won't fool anyone if they've got the line tapped. I mean, just pushing the target numbers together to make a fake telephone number?"

"I know," I said. "Don't worry, our contact won't be giving me the actual numbers."

"Then how . . . oh, all right, I'll shut up."

I stopped the Pontiac around the next bend out of sight but

not far from the Ritz Motel. Erica changed into another dress, ran the comb through her hair, put on sunglasses, reapplied her makeup, and looked like a different person. Like most women, she was prettier with her hair down.

"Ten miles south?"

I nodded. She kissed me. I pulled off the shoulder and put my foot down. At the next gas station about three or four miles farther up the highway heading north—the direction opposite to Erica's destination—I screamed in and brought the car to a rubber-burning stop. The usually slow-paced country attendant rushed out. "What the hell—?"

"Fill her up!" I snapped. "And make it fast." It only took two gallons. "Well how about checking the oil?" I said unpleasantly. "If it won't burden you."

He did it very slowly.

"Don't hurry," I said. "Don't bust a gut or anything."

As he sullenly wiped the dip stick I took the microchip out of my pocket. There was a hoody-looking biker also heading north, now pulling in and dismounting a Suzuki 700 about ten yards from the office. German iron cross, second class, and a tattoo reading "Mother." He stalked menacingly over to the office, bashed the Coke machine, and only then put in his coins. He bashed it again. I walked in and took the men's room key. It only took me a fraction of a second to slip the beeper under the bike's gas tank as I casually strolled by. He was still thumping the Coke machine.

I gave the attendant, who I was glad to see was looking quite hostile by now, a five-dollar bill and made a big production out of checking the change just to make sure he'd remember me. He said nothing but glared darkly. I roared off in a cloud of dust just to make sure he'd remember. What hadn't worked at Storm Lake, because of the microchip Erica had unknowingly been carrying, should work now. In any case, I prayed that at least my ruse would hold them for a half hour.

Three miles on I made a fast U-turn and doubled back at a nice legal fifty miles an hour to meet Erica. By now the motel owner and the wrestler would probably have been freed, since the old folks, hearing them kicking or something, would have called the police. And the old couple had seen Erica and me drive off in our car—in the green Pontiac sedan—not the cream Mercedes which she, in her new look, would now have picked up, driving south to wait for me.

The sixteen-mile drive back down 3A, 97 to Okanagan Falls was uneventful. Erica had pulled off the highway by the tourist park. A good move, blending in with the summer visitors. It took a few minutes to make a number-plate swap for added insurance and then south, heading for the border, twenty-five miles away at Osoyoos. It was only then, away from the heat of the moment, that I was struck full force by the carnage I'd left behind. I'd better be right because the moment they found Bell and company all the stops would be out. They'd know that because Bell had shown himself, we must have contacted the leak. They would double surveillance on all the operators, of course, and come all out for us. Roth already had Sudley Steel riding left flank for him, but with three corpses littering the Ritz Motel, one of them his own man, he'd quickly have the B.C. police and the Mounties riding the right flank on a legitimate murder hunt. There was no point trying to sneak across the border now. It was simply a race against the focusing beam being perfected—a race against Roth's Sudley Steel army getting us and shooting us "in self defense!" Once across the border, we'd only have three things to worry about: the Washington Patrol, the FBI, and the counterespionage section of the CIA. So we needed three things: speed, daring, and George Patton's Third Army. The Third Army was long gone, but we might still muster speed and daring.

The Osoyoos crossing came into view. We had been gone from the motel thirty-five minutes. It all depended on how long the old people had taken to report us, how long the police had taken to check the gas station, and how long the motel lady had taken to give a reasonable description of us. Surely, I thought, even with all the computers, etc., they couldn't have contacted the border crossing yet with a description of the Mercedes. Surely human reticence and my carefully faked escape route north would mean that the Osoyoos border crossing wouldn't yet be alerted for an off-white Mercedes heading south—back into the open Riverport country from whence we'd come.

As the Customs officer approached I turned off the engine and took off my sunglasses to convince him we were at once respectful and in no particular hurry.

I was polite, not overly friendly, but with that neutral, half-subservient tone you reserve for border bureaucrats. My free hand felt the .38 in the door pocket, hidden by a map of Washington State.

"Where you folks from?"

"Vancouver."

"Citizenship?"

"Both Canadians."

"Uh-huh. Carrying any alcoholic beverages, cigarettes, plants, or fruit of any kind?"

"No." Erica flashed a quick smile at him.

"How long you down for?"

"Oh, two to three days. Going to drive through the Cascades Highway. Hear it's quite a ride?"

"Have a good stay."

"Thanks."

My left hand came off the .38 and I eased the Mercedes forward. Erica was looking ahead at the long brown sagebrush hills stretching to the distance beneath the pale, blue-washed sky. "The immigration official is on the phone," she said quietly. The engine revved a little as the automatic gear moved into the higher slot. She was watching him in the rear-view mirror. "He's running out to the Customs official."

I put my foot to the floor, heard a faint "Hey—!" a hundred yards back, and two sharp cracks. One of them hit the trunk. Suddenly there was a spurt of sponge rubber and leather debris pelting the backs of our heads as the bullet ended its journey, ricocheting madly in the springs of the back seat. The engine was howling now, the speedometer needle on seventy, and climbing. The breeze had become a roaring wind.

"Where to now?" shouted Erica. "We've got every kind of police after us."

"Where would you suggest?" I called out. I answered for her. "Storm Lake."

"Are you mad?" It was a statement, not a question.

"*L'audace!*" I shouted. "*L'audace!* Last place they'd think of looking. And we need a plane. Car's no good now. Just pray the lake's clear of mist. We'll ring in a light float charter Cessna. Take it to Spokane. Regular airlines will be alerted."

"So will the charters," countered Erica.

"They're more discreet."

"More bribable?"

"Exactly. From Spokane we can fly to Chicago."

"Minor detail," she said. "Our Chargex cover is blown."

I slid the .38 into my shoulder holster and patted it. "I carry American Express."

"That's hijacking."

"Homicide is the worst you can go. Roth already has us on that. It's Washington, D.C., any way we can. Or we're finished."

"What makes you think we'll reach Storm? It's a hundred miles from here."

I didn't answer. I was trying to work it all out.

"You think the old people at the motel saw you drive south in this car?"

"Maybe," she said. "But they wouldn't have recognized me. Besides, we changed the plates."

"Well the plates won't matter now," I said. "They'll be looking for an off-white Mercedes." The needle quivered at ninety-seven, then jumped to a hundred and three miles per hour. Neither of us spoke for at least five minutes. Now and then I could see Erica glancing from the speedometer to the rear-view mirror, back to the speedometer and ahead at the long, black road. She turned on the radio. We were in the foothills now and the speaker flooded with static. Past Twisp and screaming around the corners toward Winthrop. The hills were hot and steamy, but the breeze was cooling. Erica was actually perspiring.

"Car!" she said. "Up ahead! State Patrol!"

"Probably recognize us," I said.

"Or get us for speeding."

Quickly but gingerly pumping the brake in a long dip between two rises, out of sight of the oncoming police car, I brought the Mercedes to a shuddering, sliding stop in a cloud of dust that rose like smoke from the graveled shoulder. "Get out!" I said. "Look as if you're examining the engine." I ran across the road into the tall fescue grass on the other side. I was hidden for barely ten seconds when the highway patrol car flashed past, its rear lights glowing on, off, like two red eyes, as it slowed, reversed, and finally stopped adjacent to the Mercedes.

There were two of them.

"Need some help, ma'am?" the driver called. The other was leaning forward, his elbow out the window on my side, either to get a better look at Erica or to pull the twelve-gauge automatic from its floor cradle. I couldn't take the chance. I stepped out quickly, pressing the .38 against his temple. "Nobody move!" I pulled the hammer back to make sure they got it absolutely right. They did. "Hands behind your head. Now!"

Their obedience gave me an unbelievable sense of power. I reached in, took the gun from the officer on my side and tossed it back over my shoulder into the jungle of grass and weeds. Erica opened the door and removed the shotgun. They didn't say a word. While Erica covered them with the twelve-gauge, I switched off the police radio just in case they had it open for transmission. Then I took the gun from the other patrolman's holster.

"Out!" I said.

They wanted their pensions, and unhesitatingly spread-eagled against the side of the car. I heard another car coming in the distance. I checked them for hidden weapons. There were none. I stood in front of them, my arms folded, the .38 cradled against my chest, its barrel ready to fire at either one. "Right," I said. "Arms down and casual. Lean on the car. Quickly. We're just chatting—understand?" Erica went behind the patrol car with the shotgun. When the oncoming car passed us it looked as if we were having a pleasant chat with the law.

No use taking the patrol car. When it didn't report in they'd be looking for it anyway, but more important, if we took their car and their HQ radioed them for a routine location check, I couldn't be sure that the cops wouldn't risk a fake call-in. They were sure to have a call sign for being held captive. We tied their hands behind them, then their feet and sat them in the back of the Mercedes. In our haste, it didn't occur to us that we should have put them in the Mercedes before tying their feet. Now they had to hop several yards to the car, like two kangaroos.

"What do you call that?" I asked Erica.

She was puzzled and tense, holding the shotgun. "What?"

"The cop hop!"

Erica placed the twelve-gauge between the bucket seats while I drove. It was no use telling them we weren't guilty of murder, or telling them about the beam. One word about the killer beam and they would be convinced we were crazy. The problem was, what to do with them?

"I'm not going to kill you," I added. I guess I expected them to thank me. They simply squinted in the glare of the noonday sun. I pulled the visor down, not that it would help much. "When did you get a description of us?" I asked, glancing at them in the rear-view mirror. Silence. They hadn't done a course in hostage-taking, that's for damn sure. If they'd been taken like this by a crazy, nothing would have put them in quicker jeopardy than silence. Glimpsing them in the mirror again I realized how young they were. It occurred to me that their silence might be nothing more than sheer fright at being suddenly transported from a common everyday patrol in one of the quietest parts of the country into this nightmarish situation. I knew the feeling.

"You know who I am?" I asked.

"I don't think you're John Dillinger," said the older of the two. The other one laughed but it was thin, frightened.

Silence.

I grimaced at the cloudless sky. Trust my luck for it to be clear over the mountains. It would be good flying weather for us, but it would also have been good enough for their CB radio to have picked up the police-band description of us that had probably been flashed from Osoyoos to Spokane, then across the desert to the Cascades. I tried our radio again. Nothing but static. But I was betting you could get Radio Peking on their cruiser's radio. How else could they have known who we were? Unless—it made me sick to think of it again but perhaps they *had* pulled up to offer Erica help as they would have anyone else. Of course now that I was someone who jumped out of fescue grass and stuck .38s against people's heads they'd sure as hell want to find out who I was. In any case my problem was the same. How to get rid of them at Storm Lake. They were right, I wasn't John Dillinger. He'd have just dumped them over the wall of the dam—down to the hard polished rock hundreds of feet below.

I slowed down before the James Lake turnoff, onto an old dirt road that wound over two long, steep hills, heading into the mountain country. Erica glanced over at me, wondering what I was up to. I drove on for about twenty minutes or about ten miles in. The road was thinning now, overgrown from nonuse, pock-marked with potholes, and crisscrossed with a green profusion of weed-filled runoff channels. The trees either side were pressing in, arching over us like giant flying buttresses of some vast Gothic cathedral. I stopped the car, turned around, untied their feet and leveled the .38 at them. "Out!"

I didn't mean to frighten them. It must have been my preoccupied look, my abruptness or something, but their eyes met in alarm. The older one smiled weakly at me, almost imploringly.

"Oh, hell!" I barked. "I'm not going to kill you."

I told Erica to untie their hands. "Take off your clothes," I commanded. "Down to your underwear."

Erica discreetly went to the other side of the car. I tossed their uniforms, together with their ID, into the car. "Take off your shoes." And that was the way I left them. Unarmed and shoeless. Seldom has western man been left so utterly helpless in the wilderness. Ten miles without shoes. Even if they were joggers, which I doubted from their hash-brown bellies, it would be hours before they would negotiate the ten miles of steep, gravel-strewn mountain road in bare feet. And when they got to the highway it was a hundred to one they'd get anyone to stop for them. I was starting to feel safe. When we got to Storm Lake, I drew the Mercedes up by the store and saw that the old man was in serving two customers with bait from the long freezer he had by the door. The lake sparkled beneath the cloudless turquoise sky but it was becoming overcast in the east, whence we'd come. The question was, how fast was it moving toward us?

When the two customers had left I walked in, flicked the STORE CLOSED sign on the door, waved the .38 at him, and took him out back to the office. And to my shame, I enjoyed doing it. Although I'd wanted him to report me before, I took a perverse delight in letting him think I'd come back to even the score. Maybe I was so tired of being hunted I didn't mind getting a little of my own back. It wasn't fair, but it was satisfying. That damn gun really does give you a sense of power.

"Look here, mister, I don't want . . ."

I already had the air charter number for him. "Ring me in a plane."

He didn't seem nearly as tough as he had the first time I'd seen him. Perhaps it had been the overcast weather that had made everything seem more forbidding. Now the old, callused fingers trembled violently as he dialed, which made me thoroughly ashamed. "Where . . . where to?" he asked unevenly, his voice on the verge of cracking with fright.

"Spokane. You'll be coming with us, so no tip-offs."

"I—I don't know what you mean."

"Yes you do. Remember you're coming with us."

Someone at the other end must have asked if he was all right. He hesitated. I shoved the .38 into the overalls.

"Fine. Yeah. Damn lumbago's acting up again."

When he hung up I stared at him. "What's with the lumbago bit?"

"Eh? Listen, that was no tip-off. I just thought that in case they . . . honest—I—I've had lumbago for years. You can ask . . . I mean . . ."

"All right. What did they say?"

"They'll ring back in five or ten minutes. They won't hold on, on long distance." I must have appeared unconvinced.

"On the level. It costs too much on long distance. It's busy in early fall. A peak period. They'll have to check their bookings. They'll ring back in five or ten minutes."

"They'd better."

"They will. I promise."

"Where will it land?"

"Just below James Dam. Too narrow here—too much debris. Up there there's a nice two-mile stretch."

"You have a boat ready to go?"

"Yes."

I nodded and as we sat there I took in the office. It was like a museum of fifty years ago. We sat in silence for a few minutes.

"What's the fishing like?"

"Eh—sorry, I didn't . . ."

"What's the fishing like?"

"Good. Fishing's good."

"What kind?"

"Dolly—Dolly Varden mainly."

"Where's your grandson?"

"Out. Gone to Newhalem."

There was one of those plain-faced clocks with the twin bell arrangement sitting on top. "That must be old?"

"Eh—yeah."

"Wedding present?"

He was absolutely stymied. "Yeah! How'd you know that?"

I shrugged. "It's old."

"Still works."

"So I see." He picked it up. His old, stubby hands began trembling again. Then his whole frame started to shake, or rather convulse. He tried to put the clock down but dropped it. His arms covered his face. He was weeping. "God, I wish Emma were here. God—I—"

It completely discombobulated me. Can't stand men crying. I've done it myself but can't stand it in others. I never know what to do. For me it's like seeing the end of the world. In a close friend, an arm around the shoulder and something useless like "It'll all work out" will do, but what do you do with a stranger? I didn't know. Who the hell was Emma? I ran out to the car. I could hear the faint hum of a plane approaching, but it was still hidden by the mountains. "Erica!"

"Yes?"

"The old man's . . . I—see what you can do, will you?"

With me leading we both ran back toward the office. I froze in my tracks and pushed Erica in among the rows of canned goods, away from any line of fire.

"Crafty old bugger!" I crouched and made for the side of the door, stood up, lifted the .38 high and pulled back the hammer. The sobbing had stopped. Inside I heard a soft click. Of course, that's where he'd keep the scatter-gun, squirrel gun or whatever it was. At this range he'd take my head clean off. The only way was to act now. Go in low and fast. I dived toward the floor, my left shoulder leading.

He was sitting there calmly smoking a cigarette. He wiped his oily sleeve across his weepy eyes and put the old cigarette lighter down. It had been the lighter that had clicked.

The phone rang. A Cessna would be here in an hour. So the plane I'd heard a few moments before wasn't ours and soon its noise disappeared to the west.

I yanked the phone cord out—and cut it in half—just to be sure.

The motorboat trip up Storm Lake between Needle and Emerald mountains was beautiful. It was the most peaceful thing I'd done in weeks. The old man sat silently at the tiller as we watched two deer fawns slowly eating young grass by the placid lakeside.

CHAPTER 29

Sheer and precipitous, the huge slab of the dam wall thrust up before us. High above it a lone bird dotted the sky. Atop the massive gray wall from the bunkerlike concrete block that was the control tower, the green flag was up, fluttering in the breeze to show that the overflow gates were closed—safe for a float plane landing. Dead ahead of us, not a hundred yards away, the giant overflow pipes, each twelve feet in diameter, stared out from the bottom of the dam like a row of wide, dark-mouthed monsters. Closer now, the wall was an algae-streaked cliff towering into the pale wash of sky.

The yellow single-prop Cessna circled twice, checking for any obstacles in the lake. I waved. The canary-colored wing dipped in recognition, then went wider for the approach. By now we were next to the small float jetty that jutted out from the green and rocky shoreline where here and there you could see a vein of black rock four or five feet above us marking the border between high and low flow marks. Two white cabbage butterflies flitted about a spill of pale green watercress, while an underwater spring bubbled happily nearby, breaking the reflection of sky and cloud that heralded a change in weather.

I was watching the Cessna, its power now below stalling as it touched the still lake water, its floats cutting the water like a knife on blue frosting. Then I heard the tremendous roaring. I swung around toward the dam wall. "What the hell—?" The green flag was still flying but now its mouths were open, vomiting great thundering jets of white water, surging for the high-water mark, instantly sending shock waves into the lake.

"Head for shore!" I yelled, jumping onto the jetty and helping Erica and the old man from the boat as it rocked violently, bashing the pylons. Suddenly the high-water streak vanished from the rocky shore and in its place—racing white foam. From the forest edge we stood helplessly, waving frantically and shouting at the control tower. The green flag dropped and the red was hoisted.

"You stupid bastards!" the old man cried out. "You stupid sons of bitches!"

It would take at least ten minutes to close the pipes—an hour for the man-made sea to subside.

"Oh my God!" It was Erica. The pilot was gunning the engine for takeoff, the sound barely audible over the deafening roar of the water jets, each throwing boiling white arcs, over a hundred feet in length. He'd decided to run for it—to get away before the oncoming flood capsized him. The waves, which had been only six inches high moments before were now already two feet in height. It was through these that he had to turn in order to face away from the dam for his run. Two thirds of the way through the U-turn he slowed the engine, now plainly fearing that with the waves hitting him beam on he'd flip with the power at full throttle. He completed the turn, slowly increasing his taxiing away from the dam wall, gunning the engine again, readying for takeoff. From the bank barely a hundred yards to the left of him we could see his face clearly, and the hands frantically working the joy stick, trying to get the nose straight before giving the Cessna a final surge of power.

Curious, but, though I'd never seen the man before, in those few seconds I knew him. He'd come to help us, had waved good-bye to someone, perhaps a Jenny, an Erica, and said he'd return soon; the daily reassurance given to those we love. Even from this distance I could see the terror in his eyes.

Finally the nose was facing directly away from the deafening crescendo of the wall and through it all the engine screaming to escape. The Cessna shuddered forward in the man-made surf. Agonizingly, it built up speed, bouncing forward like an awkward tub, but then, catching a wave like a body surfer it miraculously increased its speed, the wave pushing him forward, the engine screaming louder and louder. The nose lifted slightly. We were cheering him on when the wave collapsed, the nose suddenly dipped, the following wave sloshing ineffectually over the floats. He gunned the engine a little more, bouncing crazily over the waves in a zigzagging pattern. The nose lifted again—this time higher than before. We gave a shout of encouragement, as if he could hear us. Then the right wing dipped in the surf, catching a three-foot wave. The plane was taking off, but at such an angle, pivoted by the right wing tip, there was no way he could clear the oncoming trees. The nose lifted almost vertically, the engine stalled, and the Cessna fell belly first into the sides of tall pines. The explosion threw orange-red sheets of fuel over the water where the current quickly carried them downstream.

The pilot's body, headless, was hanging limply like a rag doll from the branches of a scorched pine. I said nothing to Erica, but farther down, off from the main torrent in a quiet eddy on the far shore, the frothy crimson-moated head was bumping gently among the rocks.

The old man sat down on a nearby boulder. He tried to speak but nothing came out. I thought the roaring of the overflow pipes had deafened me because they didn't seem so loud anymore, but then I saw that they were being closed, the jets now decreasing in diameter from twelve feet to nine, then six, and gradually to three and soon only spurting fifty feet into the lake.

"Get in the boat." I spoke softly. Erica's arm rose like a child's, pointing helplessly across at the scattered burning metal that minutes before had been a plane.

"Into the boat!" I said. "Quickly." She was in tears.

"I've never seen the dam . . ." began the old man. "I've never seen . . ."

It was too choppy to be safe, but we had no time to lose.

"Into the boat!" I said. "Come on!"

I was worried about two planes: the one that had just crashed and the one I'd heard earlier. Things had gotten out of hand. The Cessna pilot probably wasn't supposed to try to take off immediately but simply to ditch his airplane, or sit still and ride it out. Either way would have prevented us from leaving. The incident had me fearing the worst, namely that Roth knew where we were, that the two highway patrolmen had confounded my efforts after all, had been lucky, had flagged down the cruiser that would have gone looking for them when they failed to make their call in and then had directed the first plane to spot us and instruct the dam control.

Heading back, none of us spoke. The old man clearly thought it had been a terrible accident. It had been terrible all right. But it would be explained away as "pilot error," no matter what the old man said about the flag foulup. There wasn't a thing I could prove, not a thing, but if Roth wasn't behind it I'd eat my .38. Erica wasn't fooled either. As we approached the dock and tied up, she asked quietly, "Why didn't they wait?"

"Wait for what?"

"For us? For us to get aboard?"

"Because," I said, stepping off onto the Storm Lake float, surprised at how cramped and shaky my legs were. "Because then they wouldn't know who the leak is. No use killing us before they find out. They want to catch us first. That was just to cut off our exit."

The old man was wobbly. Paying no attention to us he looked as if he didn't know where he was.

"Don't worry about notifying anyone," I said to him. "The people on top of the dam saw what happened. They'll look after it. The government, I mean."

He stared blankly at me. "But . . . they . . . the flag . . . ?"

"Yes, I know," I said. "But they'll look after it, pops. You just rest a while. You feel okay?"

"No."

A big, silver-gray Lincoln stood arrogantly by the gas pump. The driver's wave was more like a command. "Hey, how about some gas here, fella?"

He was a short, stocky man with sunglasses, a tight-fitting navy blue shirt opened three buttons from the top, revealing a bunch of gorillalike hair and a gold medallion on a chain with PEACE emblazoned on it. The big, wide belt around his red-check trousers was barely visible, hidden by an enormous paunch. The white shoes completed the wheeler-dealer look. A dizzy-looking brunette peered somnolently at us through the smoky-tinted windows of the Lincoln. From inside I could hear the screech of a disco assault.

"Can't wait all day!" said Blue Shirt. It reminded me of my act at the gas station near Penticton, but mine had been an act for a good purpose—to give us time—to send them looking for us in the wrong direction for as long as possible. This clown wasn't acting. It looked like his usual modus operandi. "Hey," he called out, "move a little ass, eh?" He shook his head knowingly at the brunette. She smiled and lit up a long, slim cigarillo.

I was tired, hot, angry, and we were running against the clock.

If Roth knew where we were, then we were really up against it.

And while his troops were scouring the Northwest for us, he'd be working like hell to perfect the beam.

"Come on, come on, come on!" called Blue Shirt. "Move ass!" He clapped his hands. "Let's go! Let's fill this baby!"

I walked over to him, glanced at the number plate, and said, "You're odd."

"What the hell—?"

"You're odd," I said. "Your license number. It's odd. This is an even day."

"Are you kidding?" he sneered. "Don't hand me that crap, fella. Gas isn't rationed like that out here in the goddamn boondocks." He patted the Lincoln. "This baby's thirsty. I've been waiting here a whole goddamn—"

I wiped the sweat from my forehead, pulled out the .38 and stuck it into his lunch. "Shove off!"

He was gone in fifteen seconds, swallowed up in a cloud of dust.

Erica drove the Mercedes up to the pump and we filled it.

"How's the old boy?" I asked wearily.

"I don't know. He's very shaky."

"We'll ring a doctor in Winthrop."

"Winthrop? They'll have both ends of the highway blocked. West to east. East to west."

"I know," I said. "I know."

"How are we going to get out then?"

"Damn it!" I smacked the steering wheel in sheer frustration. "I don't want to kill anyone. I'm trying to save people. Trying to save them from that mad bastard. Did I shoot those two cops? No. I took off their shoes. Their shoes! You think they'll take our shoes off?"

"Yes," she said.

I stopped ranting for a minute. "*What?*"

"When we're dead," she said gloomily.

I stopped beating up the upholstery. "When they find out who the leak is."

"If they do."

I nodded, my fatigue enveloping me like a heavy blanket.

"We'll have to run for the desert. Too many police west of here on the main Pacific Highway—besides, west is farther away from Washington, D.C."

"I never thought of that before," she said.

"Of what?"

"Of how they'd hold off killing us until they found out who the leak is."

"No?"

"But they . . ." she began, "they'll try to get it out of us."

I was sure she was thinking of Puff Face with her in the toilet. I put my arm around her, holding her close. "Which is why I won't tell you the name until we've reached safety." Well, it was part of the reason. "I don't want you hurt."

A gust of wind buffeted the car. She squeezed my arm. "I love you."

"I love you too."

There is lightning as they say and then there is lightning. It was the first kind which crackled overhead. Not very close and not very threatening except that when Erica tried relieving the tension by switching on the radio all we got was a rush of static which only further jangled our nerves. In fact, though we didn't know it then, it was all that electricity in the air fouling up radio transmissions that was giving us an edge.

At Winthrop, just before five, I rang Mrs. R.

Her voice was breathless—she'd been running to the phone. "Yes?" she gasped.

"Could I speak to Sylvia please?"

"I'm sorry—Sylvia's on vacation."

Thank God.

I called Jonas. We went through the previously arranged routine. The number was 281-7794. God bless Brenda!

I memorized it, forcing it into the lethargic brain for permanent filing. I had to admit I felt ambivalent about Brenda getting the code numbers so quickly. I mean, I was happy to have them but if Roth had selected targets he must now have perfected the means of striking them. God help us.

Back in the car Erica watched my preoccupied slump behind the wheel.

"What's the matter?" she asked. "You look worried."

"I just made the call to Barney."

She sat up excitedly. "You've got the numbers! That's wonderful. Now we can . . ."

"I'm worried that his line might have been tapped." I still didn't mention that Barney was Jonas. "The numbers aren't any use to them without knowing the conversion code I've worked out with the leak, but that wouldn't stop them picking up Barney. If they get him, I'll feel . . ."

The lightning receded but still made a horrible mess on the radio of what I guessed was a brave attempt at a country and western tune.

She turned it off and ran her long, soft fingers over my aching neck. It felt great.

"You're taking too much on yourself. You had to do it." She paused. "Won't you let me share it? Why don't you tell me the number and conversion formula? If—if anything does happen, Harry, one of us might have a chance."

She had a point, the same one she'd made twice before. I heaved the car away from the shoulder, and several rocks that were strewn over the road. "No!" I said.

"I want to help, Harry." She looked at me imploringly, as earnestly as a hurt child excluded from a family effort.

"I know, honey, but I won't risk you anymore."

She still looked hurt. "You think I'd talk?"

I had trouble watching the road through my bloodshot eyes. Soon we would have to rest. "I'm thinking of what they might do to you if you find out." I gripped the wheel with both hands. "I'm not risking you anymore. That's it! Okay?"

Then I saw the sign: WATCH FOR FALLING ROCKS.

"A bit bloody late!" I grunted.

"What?" Erica looked up. She'd been deep in thought.

"On the road."

There was a landslide, or more properly speaking, a mudslide half a mile ahead at the foot of a concave fifty-degree cliff face that looked designed by nature to funnel any miscellaneous debris down onto the road and into the deep canyon below. I braked the Mercedes, gnashed the gear into reverse, and let the V-8 howl back up the hill we'd just descended.

"What's wrong?" asked Erica, not having dared to interrupt my concentration during the sudden reversal.

"It's too—too nicely timed," I said.

"It's a mudslide."

"Well, natural or not, it'd make us sitting ducks."

"What can we do?"

I heard the tires crunching on the gravel as we came to a slow stop. Three hundred feet below, the normally peaceful Methow River was streaked with rapids. "Time to hitch a ride."

"But it's starting to rain."

"No other way. If we sit here we could be picked up. If we go onto the slide they could be waiting. We can't take the chance." I grabbed the overnight bags. "C'mon. Let's go!"

The trek through the bush off the road was easier than I'd expected with the undergrowth having been burned off in a flash fire that stopped short of becoming a tree destroyer. The result was a soft carpet of needles to walk on. I went ahead and reconnoitered but didn't see anybody near the slide, until I crossed the summit of the concave hill. A work crew from an orange Washington State Highways truck was standing around, gawking at the slide as if they'd never seen one before, probably discussing the easiest way to fill in the eight-hour shift.

We came down on the highway a half hour later and waited for traffic to start appearing from the direction of the slide, traffic that would tell us the debris had been cleared. I rested, despite the rain's steady downpour, for I knew that if the slide had been a putup job, we'd outsmarted them. All they'd have found by now was the deserted Mercedes.

The rain eased for a few minutes, enough to see a lone biker stream by in a cloud of spray. Ironically, it wasn't until the rain stopped pouring, when we didn't need shelter, that a truck appeared on the far horizon, rumbling eastward like a huge, overladen bug, its big tires singing happily on the wet asphalt.

As we waved him down and I heard the air pressure hissing out of the tubes and the gears shifting down, a lone sunbeam sliced through the dark green trees. The Kenmore was carrying apples to Chicago and had plenty of room for us in the front; it had one of those big cabins with a curtained sleeping bunk behind the driver. The sense of power and security you have in a high truck cabin is remarkable when you're not used to it. You don't look out in front at the road, you look *down* on it and with the big, blunt snout of the truck protruding in front you have the feeling that you're unassailable. The truck driver, not surprisingly, was curious as to where we'd come from.

"Car broke down," I explained succinctly.

"Bad place," he said, double clutching her into a higher gear as we reached the steep grade of a long hill before surging on over the summit. He pulled a small, striped hand towel that was hanging over the curtain that separated us from the sleeping compartment and handed it to Erica to wipe her hair. The towel was smudged here and there with oil stains and Erica politely declined. "Thanks all the same," she said, "but it's too late now. My hair's ruined, I'm afraid."

After what we'd just been through in the last few hours she was afraid her hair was ruined! It sounded so absurd that we both started to laugh, spurring one another on, stopping, gagging for propriety, then spluttering and bursting out again uncontrollably. To his credit the driver grinned indulgently, not taking offense even though he didn't understand. We'd been putting the brakes on so hard and so often in the last little while that now the lungs and chest were relaxing, unchoking in sheer, unmitigated relief.

Coming out of the mountains the driver's CB crackled to life: would Lou tell Big Joe that Ellen had the hots for him—watch out for Smokey on Interstate 90, east of Spokane, and a report of early snow to the east of us in western Idaho.

Another long hill loomed ahead. The driver dropped gears and something cold rested on my cheek. It was a Hi-Vel .22. The arm that held it came out from a slit in the curtain. Another pair of hands came out and took hold of Erica's left arm. I jerked around and got poked in the eye for my trouble.

"Watch the road!" the voice said.

I swung around at the driver. The gun slapped my right cheek. "Watch the road!"

A gasp exploded to the right of me as Erica struggled. She gave a sudden, violent thrust, but it was no use. I could see the syringe, exhausted of fluid, slowly withdrawing from her arm. I looked murderously at the driver. There could have been a sheet of solid thick glass between us. Without even casting a sideways glance, he casually switched CB stations and then I heard behind me, "Roll up your sleeve."

I did nothing. My mind was an absolute blank.

"So give it to him in the neck!"

The long, cold needle slipped into the vein and I could hear a kind of crunching noise as the plunger went down. There was an icy feeling that flowed all over me, then a warm flood. I wanted more than anything to turn my head, to see Erica.

"Thorough . . ." I began, ". . . thorough bastard, Roth—" I remembered smiling, first feeling extraordinarily happy, then very scared, but I couldn't fight it. "Thorough . . ." I began, trying to focus the driver. "Always has backup . . . Roth al-ways . . ."

The driver ignored me completely. He leaned forward and filtered out a rush of CB static. I was vaguely aware of someone taking my watch. Heavy raindrops began splattering the windshield. The storm hadn't ended, it had merely shifted.

CHAPTER 30

The next twelve hours—or was it eight, or twenty-four? or was it days?—was like an interminable preparation for surgery. Instructions were given above, under, and all around me, snatches of brief, terse conversation making no sense, alternately bothering me and sliding over me, at once awful and threatening like a starved rat coming straight for me, all smell and fury, then tranquil, silent fish flitting by. Erica was nowhere in sight. I was shunted, flown, carried, wheeled, and sometimes jostled from day to night, from night to day and back to night. Light bulbs were golden orbs of incredible beauty, rubber tubes shoved down my nose into my throat were snakes, and I was sure I was screaming inside but somehow the noise couldn't get out, then again the soft, cold slide of steel in my veins.

Then calm—for a while—but never complete sleep, more like constantly turning, trying to get out of one of those terrible dreams that you know you are dreaming but can't muster the strength to break free of. The only things that were absolutely definite were the smells. The smoky upholstery of what seemed to be a small airplane seat. I remember glimpsing apples, vast pine forests, then fish again, not the unpleasant odor of defrosting fish or decaying fish but the fresh sea smell of fish, the smell or rather feeling of pure ocean, of kelp and surf and ozone. Then for six, twelve hours?—the suffocating, nose-stuffing oppressiveness of marine diesel and again the smell of cigarette smoke, but not the regular cigarette smell, not the one I was used to. This smell was the pungent odor of Turkish tobacco. And always the fleeting noises—the deep, steady thump of a ship's engine, as I was rocking. And then the long, low drone of an aircraft, not the small one now but a big jet. A glimpse of ice-cream-white icebergs on the bluest sea I had ever seen. Then dizziness and nausea and finally stillness.

Ear-ringing stillness and a completely foreign smell, like stewing cabbage, overwhelming all other smells. Above the stillness, a black-brown stone, glistening with moisture. And then in the silence, a little squeal—not imagined but real. A huge rat, running up my stomach, staring at me, its whiskers twitching either side of the pus-colored teeth.

I jerked upright, and the rat skittered to the far side of the room. At least I thought it was a room, until my vision cleared. My head was thumping with a tremendous headache and an eyeache that was at once pulling my eyeballs and spreading down my neck into the shoulders like red-hot iron. The pain was so severe I couldn't lift my head; the muscles in my neck were taut as stretched cables. Massaging my temples, I felt my palm scrape against the side of my face. I hadn't shaved in days. When I finally did manage to lift my head I saw dimly that the door had a peephole in it, dead center, and the window, a foot square, high above me, was barred. The lone light bulb, reflected weakly in the wet stone ceiling, was encased in a fine wire mesh and the body of a dead moth lay scattered through it like torn rice paper.

I eased myself off the solid wooden slab. The mattress was nothing more than a six-by-three sack, half filled with straw. The blanket was a rough wool, thick, and stinking of old sweat. The small pillow was covered with brown calico, not dirty but unbleached—a wide dark-red stripe down one side. It was the only bright color in the dark seven-by-seven stone cell.

Besides a black wooden stool there was a slatted, chocolate-colored wooden bucket squatting in the corner covered by a light wicker lid, the wicker rotting with the dampness and the foul contents of the bucket. The lid might keep flies out but it did nothing for the smell that had permeated the wood from long use. A roll of abrasive grayish toilet paper sat forlornly on the wicker top. I vaguely remembered having used the bucket but the memory was fuzzy and as dismal as my surroundings.

With considerable effort, I dragged the wooden cot over to the far wall beneath the window and stood up on the bed. I had to pause and rest for a few moments against the damp stone wall, my head throbbed so badly. I gripped the ice-cold bars and put my forehead gratefully against them, sighing with the slight relief. When I opened my eyes, I could see nothing but white. An endless expanse of snow.

"Merry Christmas," I murmured, and pressed my head against the bars once more. It was only then that I realized my watch was gone, along with everything that had been in my pockets—a pen, wallet, some loose change. Even the balls of used Kleenex had been taken.

There was absolute stillness, except for the continual pounding in my head, and all about there was the pervasive smell of cabbage. Right then I didn't know where I was, what had happened to Erica, but right then I didn't care. All I wanted was water and a fistful of aspirins.

I got the water a half hour later, together with some soup. The door opened, and a giant of about six foot six entered. A smaller man, in the same khaki-green uniform, came in and put the rectangular soup dish down and a blue chipped enamel jug of water with an equally battered but clean cup. He also put a lump of blackish bread on the small wooden stool by the bed. The soup was the smell I'd been whiffing for the last hour or so. I asked for an aspirin. The big guard looked at me impassively while the other man went out and pushed a trolley on past my cell. The thing I noticed most of all about the tall guard, apart from him not speaking English, was the red, cardboard-stiff epaulets and the flat cap. Its peak wouldn't have risen at all had it not been on his head. The aircraft sounds, the marine engine, the glimpse of icebergs came back to me. "Russia?" I asked. "East Germany—Deutschland?"

"McDonald's?" I yelled after him. There was urgency in my voice and a pain in my head I couldn't believe.

On the dank, brown walls there was a scrabble of international graffiti. The dominant language was German, which I recognized as such but couldn't understand; one scrawl in French, "Vive la liberté," and several more in what appeared to be East European languages—Slavic. Only one in English: "Totalitarianism is doomed."

Where was Erica? Was Jenny all right? I said the Lord's Prayer, aloud, to give me the feeling that someone cared. It didn't help.

For eight, maybe twelve, hours I sat, snatching fits of nervous sleep, and trudging, or rather hobbling, one leg being particularly sore, around the seven-foot-square cell. Next meal was the same sweaty, sock-smelling cabbage soup, the black bread which tasted much better the second time around, and water that, thank God, was ice cold and clear. I held the pitcher hard against my forehead and eyes. The shock of cold, even in the cold cell, helped subdue the pain for a second or so. I took note of how they entered, the guard first, Sancho Panza with his gruel second.

I told the tall, silent one in sign language that I was suffering from a headache. Did he have any pills? No answer—the long, bony face, especially the eyes, as impassive as stone. He shut the door without a word and followed the trolley.

"And thank *you* very much!" I shouted. My head vibrated with pain. I prayed that soon the effects of the drug they'd pumped me full of for the journey would wear off. They did, just when Stoneface brought me two aspirin. Still, there was enough pain left for them and more, and I thanked him. I noted that the imprint on the pills was in German.

When I woke it was dark, but without my watch I had no idea of the time.

Morning came—the second or third day? My head was still aching, but it was bearable enough for my curiosity to drive me to the high window again. Still white.

The toilet bucket had been emptied only once, and despite the cold the stench was making me feel pretty low and lonely. There's nothing like realizing your utter dependence on others for the basic necessities, food and garbage disposal, to undermine your morale. When your sense of self-sufficiency starts to falter, your resolve starts to melt, even though you know what they're trying to do. Your head tells you what's happening. The rational man appeals to your training, but for all your training your gut is empty with fear. I've seen Mr. Average with a few too many drinks spend a night in a drunk tank. When they take your shoelaces, your belt, your tie, and your dentures, anything you might use to slash your wrists with, and you discover that the simple act of turning off the light has been denied you, then an hour becomes a day and the conviction that the world outside not only doesn't know what's happening to you but doesn't care grows, not slowly but with startling rapidity. In its early stages it's like losing your job—only ten times worse. Forty-eight hours of this and Mr. Average, with his confidence, made in the United States or anywhere else for that matter, is reduced to someone who is ready to sign a confession just to get out, just to be free. I wasn't Mr. Average—at least I'd been trained not to be. I knew how to hold out a little longer, but my gut was cold. And then, as if they knew the time was right, they came for me and, pushing me, ordered me down the corridor. I counted the other cells—ten in all—five either side which, allowing for wall thickness, meant the building was about fifty feet long and thirty feet wide.

The office, approximately fifteen feet square, at the end of the corridor, was shabby but clean—its high off-white walls and chocolate linoleum poorly lit by one bulb. A card calendar told me it was 5-OE-OKTIABRIA. Three days ago in Washington was a world away.

A huge, dark-stained cedar desk stood bullyingly in front of a large, lead-paned bay window that faced east, toward a bleary eastern sun. To the right of the window there was a dull painting in tired reds and browns—Lenin, fist raised, addressing the proletariat. A small globe sat forlornly on a pedestal to the left of the solid-backed wooden chair. Despite its gloomy air, the office, in contrast to the grimy cells a few yards away, had the look and smell of an old but efficient hospital. With two "in" and "out" trays and a blotter placed dead center, the desk was immaculately organized, and sitting there was an immaculately dressed Russian officer. Smiling.

He indicated a chair. Stoneface pushed me toward it. I started to speak. Immaculate held his finger to his lips. I obeyed. Before I knew it I'd lost the first round. He quietly sipped coffee from a small blue and white china cup which looked, with its delicate pattern, markedly out of place in the austerely oppressive room. Stoneface cleared his throat several times. Through the window I could see distant black rectangles in the whiteness—three barracks about a mile to the north. Near them were some kind of armored personnel carriers, three of them, too, which looked as if they had half tracks in the rear and big skis in front.

It was several minutes later that they brought Erica in. Her left eye was black. She looked wan and brave and held her head high. A reassuring smile for me. I smiled at her, my rage thumping my temples.

Immaculate got up, came over to her and, looking straight at me, grabbed her breast. She tried to shrink from him and the chair gave a rough, retching sound. But the guard behind her steadied it.

I rushed over, thrusting my hand between her and him, accidentally brushing Erica's blackened eye with my sleeve. Immaculate took a step back.

"You bastard!" I yelled. "You—you bastard!"

He had me dragged back to my chair, letting me rave for a minute or two longer while Stoneface silently, tightly tied my hands, and then he returned to his desk, taking files from a drawer, ignoring me as if I was just something in a cage. I was wild. It wasn't the obscenity of his act that enraged me—for the most part it had been curiously asexual—it was the sheer bullying, the sheer pleasure he'd taken in exhibiting his power. It mightn't have been so bad if Erica had screamed or yelled at him but she was so shocked, so humiliated, that all she could do was look down at the floor like a molested child. I felt outraged and helpless. Finally I subsided. I made one final attempt to get out of the chair. My breath exploded from me and I sat still, exhausted. "You . . . you bloody—" I began but couldn't finish.

"We have not much time," he said in only slightly broken English. "We need information quickly."

"I'll bet you're good to your kids," I said, packing in as much venom as I could muster. "You types always are."

His head dropped, not in consternation but in dire warning. The eyes darted toward Erica and back in my direction. I got the message. He wouldn't take any more from me. "You want pain? I will give it. But I do not want to."

"Not half," I said.

He bent forward over the desk, supported on his fingers arched like talons.

"I will touch her again? Yes?"

I shut up.

"Good! Now I offer us all a pleasantness. You tell me informer's name and—"

"And you'll release us?" I asked facetiously.

He laughed casually, incredulously. "Of course not, Mr. Sturgess. You will be sent to labor camp."

"Exchange?" I pressed.

"Out of the question. If we exchange you, you will tell all. The potent—" He tried again. "The potentiality of our beam will be compromised. *Da?*"

"Then what have you to offer?" I asked brazenly, and a little courageously, I thought.

He sat on the edge of the desk. "Life, Mr. Sturgess. That is what I offer you."

Before I could answer he rose. "We heard you praying."

I said nothing.

He put his hands behind his back and looked out at the endless snow. "So, what to do, as you Americans say?" He turned back from the window. He looked at Erica but spoke to me. "I do not want your life. You do not tell me in one hour we touch *Doctor* Sarn. Pliers to start. Then ends—" He hesitated, snapping his fingers impatiently. "Ends . . ." Then he remembered. "Butts, yes? Ends of cigarettes. Correct usage!"

The decision I would have to make was stark. There was no room for negotiation, no possibility of compromise. Like the SPS decision itself, it would either be yes or no. He was no sadist. He hadn't mauled Erica for kicks; he'd simply wanted to show me he was in a hurry.

I could feel the ropes cutting into my wrists, and my back aching from being unable to move on the chair. He walked between Erica and me, lifting his head toward the clock.

He grabbed my hair and pulled my head back against the chair. "I will kill her, Sturgess, if you do not give me information. You know this."

I said nothing.

He banged my head hard against the chair again—then suddenly forward. "You know that?"

I couldn't speak. It was her life against thousands. My chin forced onto my chest, I was staring down at the hard polished floor, my face grotesquely distorted in the image of his boots.

They untied me and threw me back into the dripping cell.

From a torturous room to a torturous hour. Immaculate knew his job. He'd carefully orchestrated the little scene in his office so as to terrify us. He knew that we knew precisely what he was doing, but he was so sure of his weapon that he was sure it would work—that while alone I might hold out during what I knew were the final, critical hours of beam development, I might not hold out against the torture of someone so close to me. He knew the question that was hammering away at me—the private versus the public—save one and doom thousands. Save thousands you don't know and doom one you know—and love. He didn't know my answer to that. No one ever does.

I could smell perfume. Perhaps it had come from Erica. Perhaps I was imagining it. Lord knows I wanted her with me. She was closer to me than the public could ever be. The problem was, who was the public? Mrs. Gort? A whining cab driver? Muggers? I didn't know them. I knew Erica. I'd made love to Erica. I'd told Erica I loved her and I did.

I loved Jenny too, but in Jenny's case I could make a deal, even though I knew they wouldn't release me. If I did what they wanted—if I told them the name of the leak then maybe, as part of the deal, I could make arrangements for her to live in England away from the high-priority targets of the beam in the United States. But a voice told me that this wasn't solving the problem, it was only moving it. In any case, I could only look after Jenny if they let me live. And they'd only let me live if I gave them the name of Brenda Pret. But if I gave them her name, they'd remain unchallenged. They would win.

Out of this maze of conflicting thoughts one clear thing emerged unencumbered by a legion of "what ifs?" and that was that if I didn't give Immaculate the name of the leak he would surely kill Erica. That was certain. Or so I thought until, despite my self-disgust, a nagging suspicion slid into the corner of my cell like an unwanted whore. Erica had kept pressing me to tell her who the leak was. She'd argued, very reasonably, that in the event we were split she might stand a chance of getting through. I'd replied that if she was caught I didn't want her in the position I was now in—of possessing a secret that force might expose. But I recalled how insistent she'd been. Immaculate hadn't struck her either—he'd simply grabbed her. Bad enough but not exactly harmful physically. Maybe the beeper on the car had been a cover—maybe Erica had—. But then she had a black eye . . .

I pressed the palms of my hands against my eyes, cursing myself for even thinking that Erica had been a plant from that very first night, in the northwestern United States, when she'd shown up at my motel. But it made sense. Double insurance for Roth. Let Sturgess think he'd been turned loose from that hop farm in Washington—then have a beautiful woman turn up, eagerly on his side. And all the time she's Roth's lookout. Very neat. I'd had the same suspicions before—with the thugs in the motel. But then, I'd been wrong about Erica, or I thought I had.

"God damn you!" I shouted. Listening to the cell microphones they would no doubt think I was cursing them. I shivered in the early morning cold. At the last moment, when they put her in front of me, I would buckle, I would tell them everything. Then an idea hit me, almost like a physical blow, so strong was my excitement.

I couldn't tell him right off. An early capitulation would reek of insincerity. I had to be prepared for some pain. Or rather I had to be prepared for Erica's pain. I decided to play decadent American—apprehensive at the first sign of torture and quickly terrified once they started in.

As it turned out, I didn't have to act at all. Decadent American came very naturally. Had someone else but Immaculate been watching me, someone who respected me or someone I liked, I might have held out longer. You always do when it's someone you want to impress. Alone, you've no grandstand at all, just your own conscience. At best conscience nods approvingly—it seldom applauds. It expects. Still, I determined to go a reasonable distance, to steel myself, to make it as convincing as I could.

This time I could hear the boots echoing like gunshots. They were coming not from his office but from the other end of the building. I could smell perfume again.

It was a different room—a room with a view.

Almost bare and very cold it afforded a much wider vista of the countryside. The snow, much lighter now, still stretched far to the east where the sun was a fibrous blur above the nimbostratus that hung like a great morbid sheet unfolding by the minute from the grayer horizon. Before the guard had tied my hands and left, before Immaculate, in a long khaki greatcoat, "invited" me to sit down, I did see a long garage stretching below, about fifty yards east of the building. One of its sliding doors was open, revealing what looked like a canvas-covered troop truck of some kind, though at this distance it was hard to tell. Once in the chair, below the level of the window, all I could see beyond the telephone on the small table, a tape recorder, and Immaculate's red epaulet to the right of me, was a metal-gray sky and a white blob that was the summit of the nearest hill.

From the next room I could hear a short scuffle as they readied her. I became aware of a high-pitched ticking. It was Immaculate's watch. I became aware too of a small electric fire huddled in a far corner of the room ineffectual against the chill. Goose bumps peppered my skin and I clenched my teeth in an effort to stop shivering.

I held out during her first scream. By the second I had difficulty focusing on the naked light bulb. There is an awful difference between a woman screaming from fear, and her screaming in pain. And Erica was brave. She wouldn't give out a sound unless they were . . .

Like a recording in my brain I could hear the CIA instructors—now long ago and far away—telling us, matter of factly, "Some strip women prisoners and start with the breasts. Nakedness humiliates, lessens resistance straight off. The breasts first, not just because they are sensitive but because the psychological value women place on them is enormous. As you know."

The third scream was more like a gasp, the sudden intake of air so explosive, so utterly unexpected, that it had reached the vocal cords, causing a sickening, choking sound, barely audible but more terrible for that.

I stared at a spot of fly dirt on the wall. Soon that was all I could see. I let the fly dirt expand to become the world. The spot began to change, its roundness blurring into an unstable ellipse.

The next screams were so loud, so piercing, they stabbed my eardrums like needles. Even Immaculate glanced toward the other room. The fly dirt was completely losing its shape—breaking up. "I don't know what to do," I said, grimacing subserviently like a lost child.

He drew a knife from his pocket and walked behind me. Suddenly my hands were free. "Tell me the name."

I began massaging my wrists to restore the flow of blood. "I don't know what to do," I repeated, in a whimpering voice. "You won't believe me. You can't believe me."

I saw him click on the recorder and heard the soft purr of the tape.

"I will believe you," he said, "—if it is truth."

"No," I said. "It will seem too fantastic."

"Tell me."

I shook my head unwillingly.

"Would you like to see her? Soon it will be too far or . . . how do you say . . . too much. A vegetable. After—they never fix the mind. They try but—" His hands spread into the gesture of helplessness. He seemed genuinely sorry—and determined.

"Do you have double agents?" I asked very quietly, almost inaudibly.

"Repeat?"

"Do you have double agents?" I knew the answer but I had to hear it from him. There was a thud in the other room. My head rose slowly, heavily as a rock, weighed down by the pain I was feeling for Erica. "Stop it," I murmured. "Please stop hurting her."

His eyes never left mine but his right hand pressed the desk buzzer three times. "Go on." The noise ceased.

"Do you have double agents?"

"Soon we start on the face."

"The leak is VIP."

There was a flicker of surprise but nothing more. "Go on."

I made a cathedral with my fingers and watched the spire falling and rising. "Well, I've been thinking all night. If I tell you the truth, you'll hurt her even more. You'll think I'm lying and take it out on her."

"You do not know what I will do. Tell me!"

"You'll think I'm making it up, playing for time." I looked straight at him. "I would think I was playing for time if I were you."

"Tell me," he repeated, his hand sliding toward the buzzer.

"It's your boss."

He didn't answer for several seconds. "Who is that? I do not mean Kremlin. Who?"

I hesitated. His finger was hovering over the buzzer. "Who?"

"Roth." Before he could say anything I began talking

quickly. "He's CIA. You think you've got control of the beam?" I sneered. "Roth is *our* man."

His eyes narrowed, looking beyond me at some indefinable middle distance.

"It's simple," I said, slumping back into the chair, not having to feign exhaustion because I was exhausted. "We knew you'd want to get in on it, the hottest weapon yet developed. Its peacetime uses are the perfect cover. So Roth came over to us. It's that simple."

Immaculate was still staring beyond at the snow.

"There are precedents," I said with all the condescension I could muster. "It's done all the time, you know. It's that American decadence you people are always talking about. He has a choice of polka-dot bow ties, the good wines, the Cadillacs, the women, the expense accounts and American Express. It's tough on Soviet realism." I saw his red epaulets moving behind me. "Of course," I added, "you won't believe it but what can I say? I mean, what can I do? I can't prove it."

The red epaulets came back into view.

"But he has had you followed?" proffered Immaculate, the first time I'd seen him even slightly uneasy.

"Naturally, to make it look good. And I got away."

Immaculate was very worried now. He was behind me, but the epaulets coming in and out of view gave him away. He was pacing. The bastard was really on coals. I was rolling dangerous dice already, so I figured why not go for the six? *L'audace, l'audace, l'audace.* Hit him while he was off balance. I rolled up my sleeve. "You do have pentathol in the Urals?" I asked. "Or some other truth drug," I added. "Whatever you've got. I'm willing."

He looked down at me suspiciously, but at the same time was confronted by the simple, stark, undeniable fact that the world of Intelligence is full of double agents.

I decided a quick shot of nonchalance was called for, as if now I'd told the truth we could all afford to relax. "Where are we anyway?" I asked, straining to look above the window.

Still thinking, his eyes slowly followed my gaze into the middle distance, but then suddenly flashed back at me as if wrenched out of a dream. "What?"

"I said, where are we?" He was back at the window, pondering the endless snow. "The Sahara," he answered.

"Very funny," I countered. I was happy at his irritation. It showed I'd driven a wedge into his plan of interrogation. I didn't know how long it would last but now he was on the defensive. I started making cathedrals again with my fingers.

"You are lying . . ." he began in a tone of pure venom.

"Why would I?" I snapped with equal ferocity. "You've shown what you can do—against helpless women."

He stared at the window a long time, turned, and pressed the buzzer.

"You bastard!" I yelled. "You . . ."

"She is being taken back to the cell," he said evenly. "Relax yourself—until tomorrow."

"Until tomorrow?"

He was still staring at the snow. "Dr. Roth is flying in."

I sat very still, trying to look unconcerned. As he picked up the telephone I couldn't see the dial face so I watched his hand to try to get the sequence and tried to remember the number of digits. It didn't help. I was far too flustered to remember what number it was, even assuming it went from zero to nine. All I could think of was Roth flying in.

"From where?" I said disbelievingly, trying to sound brave. "From the United States in a day?"

He looked perplexed. "Yes, if that is where he was—San Francisco via London. It is easy. It is done often. But he is coming from Helsinki. *Da?*"

Oh, Christ! I remembered Erica telling me about the Finnish conference. It reminded me too of the photo young Dermit had shown me—a dead Finn, the eyes cooked white.

Immaculate spoke quickly in Russian, put the phone down, and turned smugly, looking much more confident than he had a few seconds ago. "I have arranged for another visitor," he said happily.

I was silent.

"Lie detector," he said. "Tomorrow."

"Fine," I shrugged nonchalantly. "Then we'll know."

"*Da*."

I was feeling weak from the cold and their soup diet. One of the instructors at the farm had taught me that if ever I felt I was about to black out I should wriggle my toes to boost the flagging circulation. My toes were working overtime. I had just under twenty-four hours until Roth and the lie detector arrived.

CHAPTER 31

Back in the cell I could smell stale cabbage and again the odor of what seemed like a cheap perfume. Now, I told myself, my senses were starting to play tricks on me, as if Immaculate's little games weren't enough. My God, was I cracking up?

It was only then, when I was nervously making another cathedral with my fingers, that I felt the powder—two of my fingers being almost devoid of any friction between them, one slipping off the other as if there was a spot of grease between them. It wasn't really grease, it was powder, a greasy bluish-black powder which, in the dim light of the forty-watt bulb, looked almost purple. I sniffed it, wondering where it had come from. It smelled just like talcum powder, like dyed talcum powder.

The perfume smell!

So I wasn't imagining things. But where had it come from? There was nothing like it in the whole cell. What had I touched recently that had given my finger the purplish stain? It smeared as I wiped it off on the rough toilet paper. Then I saw a small patch of it on my sleeve. I thought for a moment then realized my fingers must have picked it up from the sleeve while I'd been massaging my rope-worn wrists. And the smell had been wafting up now and then from the cuff. But where the hell had my cuff . . .

"Oh no," I moaned. "Dear God don't it . . ."

The door burst open. I leaped up from the bunk. Smash! The guard knocked me back against the rough, cold wall. I lifted my hand to fend off the next blow and stumbled.

"*Ahsadee!*" snapped Immaculate and Stoneface lifted me like a sack of onions and plopped me onto the stool, standing behind me, pulling my arms back. A red-hot pain seared through my right shoulder. Immaculate walked over, lifted my chin, and punched me in the mouth. I heard a crunch and then felt a rapidly spreading numbness. My mouth was warm and tasted very metallic. This time he grabbed my hair, shoving my head back toward the guard's stomach. "You are going to need dental repair," he said. "Some drilling—no anesthetic."

"Who needs it?" I mumbled through the broken teeth. I never even saw the stomach punch coming. All I knew was being thrown back, the vise-like pain of contraction and the feeling I was going to die as the air exploded from my solar plexus. "Oh, God—"

"*God? God?*" sneered Immaculate. "You are talking to the thin air, Mr. Sturgess." There was silence except for the steady drip! drip! drip! from the cell roof. When I got my breath, I spoke again. "Well, at . . ."

"What?" He was pulling my hair again. "What?" he yelled.

"At least . . ." I continued, "this is like Coke." I felt the tension in his grip slacken, only slightly, but enough to tell me that he didn't know what I meant. I didn't intend to keep him in doubt. I didn't want to lose any more wind.

"It's the real thing," I joked weakly, but he obviously hadn't had a course on American commercials—only on KGB-style interrogation.

"What do you mean?" he snapped, his eyes strangely cool for such a violent encounter. "The real thing? What is that?"

"I mean this little workout is real. It isn't faked." I sneered, "Like Sarn's! The fake black eye!" I kicked at the ball of scrunched-up toilet paper I'd used to wipe the makeup powder from my fingers and cuff. "The makeup job." I could feel the warm blood dribbling down my chin. I hesitated, alarmed by the looseness of the front teeth. "Nice try," I said, with mock admiration. "You nearly took me the full distance."

He was a very intelligent man, which is why I was surprised, almost disappointed from a professional point of view, when he tried to deny it. Of course I supposed he would have to; what was the point of threatening me with hurting her if I thought—if she were one of them?

"I know it will not convince you," he said, letting my head drop and lighting up an evil-smelling Sobranie. "I know you will think I am—how do you say—*conopting*? No . . . concocting is the word. I know you will think I am concocting when I tell you the only reason we have Miss Sarn look so—the eye—is that Dr. Roth does not like his property damaged. *Da*?"

I feigned shock. "Property? Uncle Karl would crap in his grave!"

He reddened and I stiffened for another body blow. His fist clenched. He was doubly angry I guessed because his own use of "property," however indirectly, supported my story of how some Soviet bloc agents, especially moles who spend so long in western capitals, finally succumb to the seductions and temptations of "property" which is precisely what I'd told him about Roth.

"She is not our agent," he said emphatically. "But as I cannot harm her until he is here, what else could I do but use the —how do you call it—makeup job?"

I didn't reply. He ignored the petty noncooperation. In fact I was thinking of how Wyatt Earp had also been protective of her.

"My 'makeup job' on her was simply to save time, to get you to talk. But now, now you have discovered the black powder, I have to wait. For Roth. So, for the time being, I fail to convince you I will hurt her. No matter. You will change your mind when Roth sees my way is only way to make you people talk. Meanwhile . . ."

A phone rang shrilly. Immaculate stopped, listened, and strode from the cell, leaving the guard to watch over me.

Now I knew two things. One, that he must have been

watching me, possibly on camera, the moment I'd discovered the powder and two, that from the speed with which he'd entered the cell, he was desperate to know who the informer was. So desperate, so pressured by the clock that he'd pressed ahead before Roth and the lie detector were due to arrive. The moment he knew I hadn't fallen for the black-eye trick, he'd decided to give me a taste of Basic Brutal 101—prerequisite course for investigators not filling their quota. That was to help me change my mind before the detector and Roth arrived. Now, if he couldn't wait till morning, only hours away, it could only mean one thing: They were going to use the beam. An awesome demonstration for the Kremlin's bosses of what they could do—in seconds—anywhere in the world.

Brenda Pret's voice came back to me like an icy ghost. "We just press the button . . . the tape goes in, and it's done!"

Oh, I didn't think for a moment they'd hit a city directly, because even though the general public wouldn't know what caused it, such a disaster would receive enormous attention and soon, with no immediately visible explanation available, the subsequent army of news investigators might stumble on Roth's hidden weapon. No, it would be something much more subtle but just as devastating—the beam heating the atmosphere like a long, invisible flame heating metal, exciting the particles till they glowed. High resonance frequency . . . a quick zapping of forest-shrouded suburbia; massive fires in California perhaps, that could be blamed on anything from arson to leaking gas mains. Ample demonstration for Moscow that Roth had expanded well beyond zapping American employees in the U. S. Embassy in 1968. Ample demonstration of the huge power and pinpoint accuracy at his disposal, at Moscow's disposal, for a pre-emptive *invisible* strike against the U.S. from *within* the United States anytime they wanted.

Immaculate returned from the phone and stood menacingly for several moments, staring at me as if I were an insect and he an exterminator.

"Meanwhile," he continued as if he'd never left the cell, "you should know what we are capable of, Mr. Sturgess."

"I know what you types are capable of," I mumbled. More blood ran down my mouth.

"No," he said evenly, as if he were addressing a child or a very old man, almost with genuine concern. "No, most prisoners think they can imagine it. They try to imagine—to prepare themselves. To steel themselves. But the pain is always a thousand times worse—once we begin with instruments."

There was a long silence, and I could hear the steady drip of the water-polished ceiling. He looked around the cell as if seeing it for the very first time. "You wish to change your story? About Dr. Roth?"

"No," I said, just as emphatically, "I don't want to change my story. Because it's true."

He threw his head back at the guard. "*Padaydee!*"

They marched out. What he didn't know was how worried I was. Once the lie detector was strapped on and the needle swung far right, Roth would give the word and Immaculate would love it—all his anxiety would go into his work. On me. And what he said about *Dr.* Sarn? Could he be telling the truth? Had he really set her up? Or was she really . . . ?

"So where's the camera?" I called out after him. "If you say you set everything . . ."

"No cameras," he said disdainfully, without looking back.

All right, so they'd been watching me through the peephole. I'd plug the damned thing.

"The screams?" I called out.

"On tape."

He stopped. The metallic ring of his footsteps echoed off the long stone corridor as he strode back, wrenched open the door, and came to within two inches of my face. I cringed inwardly but forced myself not to show it.

"You believe that?" he asked slowly.

I said nothing.

"You will see tomorrow. When Roth sees we have not moved you by his method, he will give up his 'property.' She will scream. He will not risk failure for piece of—you see how it will be?" He smiled malevolently.

"Not if he is a double agent."

He looked at me long and hard. "I do not believe you."

Was Immaculate telling the truth? Had he really held off torturing her because he was afraid of cutting up a woman he believed was Roth's "property"?—just as Wyatt Earp had protected her at the motel? Or was she one of theirs? Had she been a plant all along? Were the false bruise, the taped screams merely her latest *performance*? But at the motel she'd thrown me the gun to shoot a man—one of theirs. Then again, if she was a pro that wouldn't have bothered her if she'd wanted to convince me. Besides, the thug I'd shot was from Sudley Steel, not from the KGB.

The pain in my shoulder moved up into my head and even the sickly pale yellow light was becoming unbearable. Still stretched across the mesh about the bulb was the black corpse of the moth that, like me, had once been free.

CHAPTER 32

The bar-sliced moon was waning now and platoons of clouds were moving in ominously from the south. I took it as an omen. "Get out!" my inner voice shouted. "Get out!" My brain was racing. Or was it panic? I could try being the sick prisoner as a means of getting free of the cell. But they were sure to be well on guard for that one, and if I flubbed it, everything would be lost. No, I would have only one chance. *L'audace!*

I examined the cell again. A wooden bed, a wooden stool, a wooden bucket, a rotting wicker lid, and a wooden handle. Not a single piece of loose metal to fashion into any kind of tool. No one was going to dig their way out of this hole—even if they had the time—which I didn't. But it got me thinking about the problem.

The moon's glow was being curtained off by the minute as the platoons of clouds now passed into company strength. Soon the battalions would be here, together with Roth. The rat scurried again, but I tried not to think about it. I tried to think of Erica Sarn instead. We had to get out before Roth came. I'd have to take her with me. What if she wasn't an agent? I'd be leaving her to die. Besides, as long as they had her and as long as I wasn't sure of her, just as Immaculate wasn't sure of Roth, they'd have leverage on me. The rat scurried again around the toilet bucket. I tried to evict the burning little eyes from my mind but I couldn't and the vision of the teeth tearing into *my* eyes spurred me on.

To keep my courage up I hummed "When Johnny Comes Marching Home." It was also good for the microphones to pick up, adding to the illusion I'd worked so hard to create, that I'd really been telling the truth about Roth and so had nothing to fear. If the illusion held, they would be just that much less suspicious when they came around with the morning soup. And that much less suspicion might swing the seesaw in my favor.

First thing I did was to make a wad of toilet paper and plug the peephole.

Taking its lid off, I moved the toilet bucket toward the bottom of the bed so that I was sitting to its left on the bed. My body blocked any view of it from the doorway but not so much as anyone would immediately notice it had been moved. Lifting its wooden handle up, I checked that the two wooden lugs which fitted into the holes in the top of the bucket were firmly attached to the bucket. Then I took a strip of toilet paper and wiped it along the cell wall. It was sodden after only a foot or so. I divided it into two lumps, squeezed them out to the point of plasticity, then pressed, molded, and jammed them tightly in the space between the sides of the bucket and the handle so that now the once loose handle stood straight up, immediately to my right, ready for a quick, easy grab with my left hand. Taking the thin wool blanket from the bed and using my teeth to serrate its hemmed edge I tore off a strip that was about eight inches across and as long as the blanket itself—about six feet.

I tore this strip into half a dozen smaller strips—each about an inch wide—and using the rest of the blanket, I wiped the damp stones beneath my feet. The last thing I needed was to slip. Speed and force would be everything. The guard I called Stoneface would come in first and, as was his habit, move slightly to the right, followed by Sancho Panza hobbling in to empty the doings and, with the same unsanitary maulers, plonk down my cabbage soup. I was shivering enough from the cold already, but I took off my shirt and, by pushing the ends of the sleeves and collar into cracks, tacked it high up above the bed, just below the window which was directly opposite the door. I then placed the strips of blanket on the sack mattress and covered them with the remainder of the blanket, taking care to put the torn edge toward the wall out of sight. Finally I sat on the bed, leaned forward in a tired-looking morning slouch, folded my arms across one another so that my left hand was holding the bucket handle, and did several dry runs in slow motion. The left hand would have to go out, then up, otherwise there'd be an ungodly mess.

As the mauve light of dawn silhouetted the three stark bars of my prison window I heard the hollow ring of boots coming down the corridor toward me. Then the intermittent jingling of keys that hung from Stoneface's hip. My heart started to pound and the adrenalin rushed through me. Suddenly, I could smell everything with an exactitude I'd never known, my excrement smelling peculiarly foreign and repulsive while the occasional waft of cabbage smell became a thick cloud. It was as if the approaching danger, step by routine step, had turned on all the sensory nerves. Even in the dim light every brick in the cell, every word of graffiti, stood out with a surprising and alarming clarity.

The keys rattled. A pause. More rattling. A Russian word whose tone said, "Hurry up!"

My muscles froze but I forced myself to look relaxed, staring at the floor in front of me. More rattling. The same word again, and another, then the heavy door swung open. The guard stepped in and moved sharply right—impassive as ever—and the old man shuffled by him toward the stool and mess gear.

It was just a flicker as Stoneface's eyes momentarily lifted in surprise at the shirt pinned high on the wall opposite him. As I rose, my left hand jerked out and up, the bucket shooting across my lap, the right hand pushing.

The putrid mass hit him full on. Instinctively his hands flew to his face. I kicked him in the testicles. He crumpled. I wrenched the bucket back, swung it hard over and down, smashing him on the head.

"*Nyet! Nyet!*" It was the old man cowering in the corner. Stoneface slid, a khaki heap, moaning and writhing on the slicked stone, his hands alternately moving from his face to his groin. The old man hadn't moved, frozen in terror. I'd planned to have to bolt after him as he began a shuffling escape down the corridor but he was transfixed. In a totally absurd stunned gesture of surrender he held up my soup in supplication. I indicated the stool and he sat down without a word. I turned to Stoneface. He was barely conscious—still moving like some long, manure-covered carcass, squirming in his soiled uniform. I gagged and tied him with the long strips of torn blanket, making sure that he didn't tense up to gain slack before I tugged at the final knot. I took out his pistol, a Makarov 9 mm, grabbed the keys, and relieved both of them of the heavy serge jackets.

Next I tied the old man then stuck the muzzle into his chest. "Sarn?" I said. "What cell?"

He stared at me like a dumb beast about to be slaughtered. I jangled the keys. "Sarn?" His eyes bulged. I held up the keys. He pointed to the seventh one on the ring.

"Sarn?" I repeated. "*Da?*"

"*Da!*" he answered, nodding eagerly toward the left. "Sarn, *da!* Sarn!" I returned the gag, sat him on the bed, and ran, half crouching, down the corridor.

I was ready for her "cell"—probably hot and cold running water and stereo with earphones. It was different from mine all right, a slightly smaller cell because of a recess that bulged in from the outer wall, and much filthier. I could smell rats and saw two of them scurrying under the bed. She was pale and thunderstruck to see me.

"Come on!" I half shouted, half whispered, shoving one of the jackets at her.

"But . . ."

"Come on!" I dragged, pulled her toward the door.

"What are we . . ."

"We're escaping. What the hell do you think?" I snapped.

"Now shut up!" I whispered hoarsely. "And follow me." I hesitated, let her arm drop from my hand and glared at her. "If you want to?"

"Of course. Harry I never . . ."

Beautiful, I thought, they'd arranged everything nicely, including her cell, just in case I knew where they'd put her. They know that a prisoner can smell someone who's been living in a clean room. That would've given her away, if she was one of them. But—maybe she was as much a prisoner as I was. It was the old, nagging, bloody question. But right now I had to put it into "pending." I couldn't find anything out until I got away from here. I looked at her suspiciously, pityingly. "If you cross me—"

She looked at the gun. "Harry—" She couldn't speak. I thought I saw a tear. Maybe I wanted to see a tear. Maybe she was making sure I saw a tear.

It had been barely a minute since I'd got out of my cell. Now, with Erica beside me, I headed toward the end of the dimly lit corridor, away from the office and where Immaculate was, waiting for Roth's imminent arrival.

I opened the door slowly and looked down the deserted stairwell. The unpainted concrete steps and railings were of surprisingly modern design, unlike the Transylvanian corridor and cells we'd just vacated. The concrete bounced sound much more than the cobblestones of the cell block, and when I eased the door open farther its creak seemed to fill the cavernous gray exit well. It was loud enough, I thought, to bring Immaculate out, but just then it was smothered by another noise much louder and more sustained—the roaring of what sounded like a small convoy thumping and coughing to a stop outside on the narrow, snow-plowed driveway. The door had swung shut behind us when Erica pulled me back from the top step.

"Where can we go?" she whispered, alarmed. "It's nothing but snow all the way to the horizon. We might as well be at the Pole."

"Look," I grunted, "outside there's little chance. But here there's *none*. Here I'm dead!"

There was silence outside as the small convoy ground to a halt. Then voices. She hesitated.

"You want to stay?" I snapped.

"No, but I mean what can you do . . . What can . . ."

"*We*, lady." I swung the muzzle at her. "You're not staying to blow the whistle on me. You're coming with me. Now move!" I shoved her so hard in front of me that she almost fell down the stairs, barely stopping herself, gripping the top stanchion while her body swung down farther, bumping against the rail.

The bottom door swung open.

Silhouetted against the rectangle of snow was an unmistakable figure—complete with bow tie.

"Freeze!" I yelled. The door slammed shut. He was gone. I hit the bottom step in three seconds, wrenched open the door. Snow, and the puffing of an obese scientist way out of condition, struggling awkwardly through the snow a few yards ahead of me, the black coat waving, trying to call out to the group of three khaki-coated men who were working the noisy chain pulleys on the garage door fifty yards away. Roth veered left, exposing me to their line of fire. One of them heard him, reached into his down jacket, and yelled at the others. I kept going for Roth. Their first shot whined past me, then a staccato as a submachine gun began its stutter, kicking up puffs of white around me. Roth's frantic breathing was like a train going uphill. I was gaining on him. The bullets were starting a small symphony overhead. For a second I could hear my old rugby coach at LSE—"The knees! The knees!" I dived. He fell into the snow, arms spread like a fallen angel.

The khaki figures stopped firing—they might hit Roth by mistake. They were running toward us. Out of breath I slid—pushing the Makarov's muzzle through the snow until it rested behind Roth's right ear. The ear was pink like a baby's. "Call 'em off, Roth. Off!—or you get it!" I jabbed the muzzle in hard. Kneeling, I jerked his head back with my left hand. The black-sleeved arm rose like an injured wing. He could hardly talk from exhaustion. I jammed the muzzle hard on his neck.

"St-stop!" he gasped. Then much louder, "Stop! Stop!"

The three figures froze. I stabbed the gun out toward them. They looked at each other, then the one on the far left dropped his gun and put up his hands. "*Nyet,*" I called, motioning to him to throw the gun farther. He understood, picked it up, and tossed it a good fifteen feet. It disappeared in the snow. The others followed suit. I'd have to watch that left-wing bastard—he was the leader. Stop him and you'd stop the rest. I thanked God for my luck; with the snow stuffing the barrel of my Makarov it was fifty-fifty that if I'd fired I would have breached it—the snow-ice in the barrel causing it to split, exploding back in my face.

Pulling Roth to his feet, I walked toward the three men, stopped and glanced at the submachine gun, a Shpagina, that had belonged to the man in the middle. The barrel was clear and I picked it up, stuffing the Makarov in my khaki jacket. In the distance, well over a mile away, I could just make out one or two figures moving out of the barracks, obviously wondering what was going on.

I heard crunching behind me. I swung around, jerking Roth with me.

Erica started to say something. Twenty yards behind her the door burst open again and Immaculate appeared. I saw his legs go apart and his hands move together for the crouch shot.

"Down!" I yelled to Erica, pushing Roth away to my left. She dropped and I squeezed the trigger.

The Shpagina coughed violently. Immaculate shuddered against the wall amid the flying chips of stone and fell, two long streaks of blood, one shorter than the other, going down with him. Without hesitation, as Erica ran for his gun, I swung 180 degrees to the far left figure. Just as I'd guessed, he was going for one of the two revolvers that had been dropped. I fired again, the snow flicking up about him like confetti. He screamed, crouching and grabbing his legs like a diver during a one and a half somersault. The other two froze en route to the remaining gun and one of them started babbling hysterically—begging for mercy.

"Harry!" It was a scream—Erica's. I whirled. A black blur.

Charging me like a rabid bear, Roth, florid-faced, lunged

wildly at my throat with his cigar knife. I stepped to the right, tripping—his blade ripping open my left cheek. The machine gun, pushed by my fall, was packed in snow. I kicked Roth back, his belly taking the blow like a bag of jelly, but still winded. Erica fired. Two shots. From my prone position I saw one of the two remaining drivers sprawled in the snow. So Immaculate had been right. Erica wasn't one of them—she'd just warned me about Roth—and shot the driver who was going to shoot me. If she was one of them she wouldn't have . . . Unless she was the consummate professional, ends justifying *all* the means, the end being to find out the code numbers, the conversion codes, and the contact. But right now I needed all the help I could get.

Running toward the remaining driver, I took his truck keys, instructing Erica to do the same with the other. By now I could see at least twenty men emptying out of the distant hut like black ants from a black hive against the pure white snow and could hear the spitting and rumbling of three half-tracks starting up, their front skis already jerking forward. I snatched up the machine gun, waving it at the remaining driver.

"Go!" I yelled. He understood perfectly and immediately started running for the cell block a hundred yards to the left. Roth, on his knees in the snow, shouted after him, "Stingray . . . immediately! Stingray . . ."

My mistake, of course. I shouldn't have let him go but Roth was all we could handle with those half-tracks coming much faster than I'd anticipated.

As Erica covered Roth, I madly worked the pulley chains on the garage doors. "You take one of the three-ton trucks. I'll take the four-wheel-drive—the jeep. Go ahead of me and stop when you hear three horn blasts." Suddenly, a remaining doubt assailed me and I changed my mind. "No, you drive behind me. When I blast the horn three times, you stop and join me. Got it?" That way I figured she couldn't take off in front of me. So long as she stayed behind I had the initiative, just in case.

The roar of the approaching half-tracks was reaching a crescendo, rolling unimpeded across the vast snow field. Taking turns covering Roth, Erica hurriedly sorted through the keys, started up the khaki three-ton truck, and I revved up the canvas-canopied four-wheel-drive, its loaded jerry cans of gas vibrating noisily in the back. I quickly tied up Roth's hands and feet, tied a tether rope from behind him to the roll bar, and sat him on the floor of the army jeep. Then I grabbed a fire ax attached to the jeep's tool box and ran over to Erica's truck. It surprised me that all the vehicles were West German—MANs. Apparently Soviet realism didn't exclude importing quality. I took careful aim with the ax and whacked the truck's gas tank horizontally. A gash about a half inch wide and six inches long appeared, and the gas started running out. I hit the tank again. It wasn't neat, but now the gash in the tank's side was a dog leg of about a foot long.

"What are you doing?" asked Erica.

I could hear the pursuing troop carriers, not more than a half mile away. "Drive in an S-shape, make sure you go as close to the sides of the road as you can—but for God's sake, don't get stuck!"

"But what are you doing? I don't—"

"Just follow me." I jumped aboard the jeep, knocking a pair of field binoculars off the seat onto the floor, gunned the engine, and took off. I switched on the welcome blast of heat. Canvas-covered jeeps were necessary, of course, if you were to mount machine guns, but right now I wished we were covered by metal. It would have been a lot warmer.

"What the hell was that?" I said to Roth.

He merely smiled up from the floor of the jeep, his big frame bumping against the door as we bumped over the corrugated ice sheet that was the road out.

"What the hell was that?" I repeated, moving my boot menacingly toward him. "Stingray immediately? What did that mean?"

He sneered contemptuously at the boot. He knew I wouldn't kick him.

"We'll get you, Sturgess. The odds are too great. We haven't played all our cards yet. You're a small potato, Sturgess. Who's behind you, eh?"

"Who's on the floor?" I retorted.

"You're gone, Sturgess. Look at the snow. It's the last you'll ever see."

"Who's on the floor?"

"Oh, for now you're on top," he shouted over the engine's whine. "For how long? I'll tell you, Sturgess. Half an hour. Look at them." He jerked his head toward the back of the jeep. "There are too many, Sturgess. Sometime you'll have to sleep. Kill me and you've got no protection. Run with me—run with me where? Where are you running, Sturgess? No matter, they'll wear you down. They'll wear you down, Sturgess. We've got all the cards."

On the floor or not, he had a point. Despite myself I glanced anxiously at the rear-view mirror. Erica was weaving in the S-shape from shoulder to shoulder, spilling the gas in a steady wide stream, the wind splashing it onto the narrow, icy road. In another minute there'd be no more gas left in the top half of the tank. Farther back but closing fast, the three khaki half-tracks were taking a bend in a flurry of plowed ice. I grabbed an old cleaning rag that had been stuffed into the jeep's side pocket.

"Have you noticed," Roth shouted, "have you noticed the little birthmark?"

I was still glancing back at the half-tracks. These weren't the old World War II types. They were definitely gaining. They wouldn't see the gas leaking because it was almost gone—but they were definitely gaining.

"Just below her left breast," he taunted. "I always found it fascinating. I guess everyone did."

I wanted to smash his face with my boot. Instead I gripped the wheel harder.

"She's like Grand Central Station," he laughed. "Everyone's been through, Sturgess."

The bastard, he was trying to unnerve me, put me off balance, and he was doing a bloody good job. Maybe he'd read it in her file—maybe, and maybe—how the hell did he know that? Why would he do this if she was really one of them? Unless he too was trying to convince me she wasn't with them. The stream of gas was almost to a trickle from Erica's truck. It had spilled over about a half mile of road from side to side in an invisible weaving snake pattern. I began pumping the brakes and honked three times. I reached her truck as she got down from the cabin. I took the rag, stuffed it in the three-tonner's by now half-empty gas tank and lit it. She half ran, half slid back with me to the jeep. We'd barely moved off when we heard the loud "crump" of the tank exploding, then a more subdued "woof"—the flames racing back in a widening orange river.

We were two hundred yards ahead, with the half-tracks still gaining, when the first one, its steering skis vibrating violently, its guns spitting fire at our tires, swerved to avoid the burning wall. It jackknifed savagely, nose-dived to a sudden halt, its skis broadside on swinging it viciously sideways, burying it in the snowbank, its tracks furiously propelling it farther into the deep drift. The second half-track plowed into the first and the narrow road was blocked. Without a change in beat the remaining half-track swung off the road into the snow field in a wide arc but here it was eaten up by the drifts, losing half its momentum in the soft powder.

There were a few cracks like distant whips as some of the soldiers spilled out, knelt, and kept firing at our tires, but we were away. Roth was subdued. Erica leaned back in nervous exhaustion on the rear seat of the jeep. I looked down at the big SPS chief. "You were saying?" I said, smiling victoriously.

I shouldn't have been so presumptuous because we were in for two shocks. One led directly to the other.

It was half an hour later, when we had just topped a hill, that I saw the tip of the olive-green sign, barely visible, peeking above a snowdrift. I stopped the jeep and was about to get out, when I asked Erica to go instead. I still wasn't 100 percent sure about her and I wanted control of the jeep.

She brushed away the snow from the top of the sign and stood there, shivering. And stunned. She stared back at the truck, as if asking for help, then turned to the sign and dug quickly, looking strangely like a dog retrieving a bone. When she returned her face was blank with shock. "It says Highway 8."

"So?" I said. "You can read Russian. Congratulations. Where are we?"

"No—" she began, the chill on her face making her eyes water. Watching her, Roth was wearing his Mark I inscrutable mask.

"It's in English," she said quietly. "It says U. S. Highway 8, Idaho—" she shouted. "Harry, we're in Idaho!"

Not only had the screams been on tape and the sounds of the boats, aircraft, etc. I'd heard when I'd been drugged, but even the location had been faked for the purpose—and the graffiti, the stinking cabbage soup, everything. I'd never been out of the United States. It had been the old *Ipcress File* deception trick—with variations.

I sat on the snow, dumbfounded. Soon the snow seemed different, somehow cleaner, revitalizing, better. "We're home," I said quietly. I could hardly speak. "We're home."

Roth smiled malevolently. Only later did it dawn on me why. Right there and then all I knew was they'd failed in their big gamble against me.

"What's Stingray?" I yelled at Roth above the scream of the overdrive, moving my right boot toward him. He closed his eyes, as if it was time for his midday nap. The sheer human panic of a fat man running in the snow of a few hours ago had disappeared and in its place was the old cool arrogance. My God, he actually seemed to be nodding off—like the afternoon I'd seen him in Hopsville. Was he "awaying" or was he simply convinced beyond the shadow of a doubt that he would win, that what he'd told me was true, that he hadn't yet played all his cards?

My eyes darted toward the rear-view mirror. Erica was gazing up at the canvas canopy. "Stingray?" I asked her. "Have you ever heard of that?"

"No. What is it?"

"I don't know. But I wish to God I did."

From the pale wash of the sun and the highway number I

knew we must be heading west. West again. Would I never see the end of that damned sage desert? I thought of Jenny. Well, there were no call boxes out here. I'd have to wait.

As we stopped atop a snow-spotted crest on the Idaho-Washington border to fill up with gas from one of the jerry cans, Erica breathed in deeply. She was trying to catch some of the warmer air of the desert which, in dramatic contrast to the snow-blanketed hills we'd left behind, stretched out before us in a shimmering rust red blur.

"So far so good!" she said.

I looked out at the distant blur. "So far so lucky."

CHAPTER 33

The thin black ribbon of road stretched before us, disappearing like a pencil mark in the darkening desert. The folds of gullies cast long shadows over the landscape, and to the north the big bend of the river curved in a shining black crescent. In less than two hours on the lonely highway we had passed from white to brown. The premature snowfall in Idaho had kept all but the foolhardy away and not a car was in sight. The sky was split in two, fore and aft, as sharply divided as a muddy river from the clean blue sea into which it flows. Behind us, to the east over Idaho where the snow still lay, the sky was magical, a turquoise sea all the way to the horizon, that beautiful blue-green expanse that soothes like some great calm of God. But before us and above, heading eastward into the calm, was a vast, bruised canopy descending upon us as a plains storm continued to build. Soon, I told Erica as we sped through the El Greco light for Spokane, we would learn what lightning was all about.

Dotted here and there beneath the increasingly darkening sky I could see cattle grazing behind the millions of sagebrushes that resembled giant pebbles cast about the austere countryside.

Already I could hear a roll of thunder. Unlike that which I'd heard in the mountains a week—it seemed like a decade—ago, this was deeper, more persistent, like the rumble of an advancing army, of massed cavalry collecting itself beneath the flashing sabers of lightning, menacing at the trot before the charge.

It was Erica who saw it first, a salmon-pink patch high above to the north, forty miles or so away, throbbing rhythmically, deep in the heart of the purple sky.

It disappeared.

Then it reappeared farther west, still pink, still throbbing rhythmically, expanding, contracting, expanding—still advancing in our direction.

Erica's hand clasped the roll bar like a claw in spasm. "My God! Oh, my God!"

I kicked Roth. I remembered what young Orlet had seen. "Air glow red?" I asked.

Roth looked as if he was in a dream. His eyes were wide open, staring beyond to the calm sky of the east.

Erica spoke. "It must be. It's high above the clouds. We're only seeing its reflection thrown down by the meosphere."

"Meo—deo—what the hell's that?"

"The layer fifty miles up. The glow's coming from there, thrown down onto the top side of those storm clouds." Her other hand clasped the bar in panic. "That's what he meant, Harry. They're going all out. They're using the beam. On us!"

So this was Stingray! Roth was "awaying," trying to psychically remove himself from the present, the jeep. From the danger. Soviet realism couldn't handle this. The patch was moving more quickly now. I pushed my foot down as far as it would go, and in seconds the jeep was howling up past eighty. I glanced at the patch. It was now thirty miles off and closing. A flash of frost blue lightning, rolls of thunder overhead. As if on cue the patch changed from salmon pink to a light rose red. "Holy Father—!"

The sagebrush was a constant blur—the road ahead, already wet from isolated showers, came rushing into the windshield like slivers of broken mirrors. The air glow was pulsating faster now, rose red to blood red—fifteen miles and closing. Ten miles and closing. It was passing over a herd of grazing cattle and suddenly, almost inconceivably, they seemed to disappear. I braked, snatching up the binoculars. They were dropping, simply toppling over dead like cast-iron toys, blackened beyond all recognition. A mile or so on, we could smell their death, the sweet succulence of burning flesh—cooked beef—mixing with the strange clean smell of storm. All around there were charred hulks that moments before had been living, breathing creatures. Suddenly, black rain—flocks of dead birds. The sagebrushes burst into flame. Simultaneously—a thousand burning bushes. But this wasn't the hand of God, this was the hand of Roth.

"You stupid bloody bastard, Sturgess!" I yelled, opening the door and dropping to the roadside. Of course it made sense—it wasn't just now and then that they used it. It was standard equipment—on all their vehicles. Sliding underneath the jeep I glanced at the tar-colored clouds and the throbbing patch deep within coming closer and closer. A quarter-mile wide, the blotch, now only seven miles directly north, had turned the color of arterial blood.

Frantically I searched the chassis area. Nothing! Erica was out and she was bending down, shouting at me. "What are you—"

"Where is it, Roth?" The glazed look fell off him a bit but that was all.

"Open the tool trunk!" I shouted at Erica.

"What?"

"The tool trunk, God damn it!"

By the time I'd slid out from under the jeep and was examining the trunk the patch was about ten miles to the north, having swung slightly west after the last lightning flash. But now it was back on course—moving inexorably toward us.

"Where is it, Roth?" I grabbed him by the throat. No answer. I dropped him back hard onto the floor, rummaged through the tool trunk. Nothing. Damn it! It had to be somewhere easy to get on and off. I ran my hand around the inside rim of the spare tire. Nothing! I thrust my fingers down into the recess of the spare tire clamp and there it was—the size of a matchbox. I guess what little lightning there had been had run some interference with it for a while, but now they'd picked us up—as quickly as the two highway policemen had picked up our car near Storm Lake—as quickly as the spotter plane that had flown over the dam a half hour before the Cessna crashed and the Cascades storm had started, temporarily ruining their surveillance.

Of course I should have thought of it after they'd used it once already, on Erica's shoe—once bitten, twice shy. But who the hell had had the time? It was the last thing I'd have thought of during the escape. But I could see it made good sense. If you were going to use the beam then you'd better know exactly where your own outfit—where your own vehicles—were at all times. And I'd thought I'd been very smart using *their* car, the Mercedes, in the run from Penticton to Storm. Now I knew how they'd managed to be just a step behind all the time. I tossed it angrily yet triumphantly to the side of the road. "Nice try, Sloth."

We hopped back into the jeep and drove on another three miles, stopped, and looked back. The road was so straight, we could still see the place where I'd thrown the beeper away toward a bunch of sagebrush and a stubbly wood of stunted pine that had survived the desert by virtue of a nearby artesian spring. The blood-red blotch passed over the area, stopped, moved off in short, quick, nervous tangents, and returned in rapid circular motions over the site that hid the beeper. The arterial red became dark cherry red, throbbing violently like an aneurism about to burst. Suddenly, more sagebrush erupted in flames, the tops of several pines exploded in unison, belching fire and smoke like spiked cannons, then burned fiercely down the trunks while the black tar road nearby buckled and twisted as violently as a dying python. The pulsed power was enormous—a city killer.

A tremendous crack!—the sky splitting open with forks of frost-blue lightning. Then the thunder. Transfixed with fear and a kind of horrific fascination we watched the air glow red. Erica clasped my arm.

"Thank God I thought of it," I said, partly in self-congratulation but mainly from sheer relief. "I knew," I continued, "that it couldn't be a satellite photo they were using to track us because of the overcast. So it had to be . . ."

"It's coming toward us!"

"What? But I—" I grabbed the binoculars. It was moving slowly, I'd say about half its former speed, but Erica was right. It was still coming.

"But I got rid of the goddamn beeper. You saw me—"

Quickly I began emptying the pockets of the khaki down jacket I'd taken from Stoneface. Erica started searching her pockets—then threw the jacket to the ground. I rifled my pockets a second time, my shoes, anything that might have conceivably concealed a microchip beeper. I began frisking Roth. Sonofabitch, I'd never have the time to . . . I saw the blotch speeding up like a bloodhound suddenly regaining the scent. "In the jeep!" I yelled.

In ten seconds I was up to sixty miles per hour, then eighty. "What is it, Roth? What's going on?" I gave him a boot to the kidney. "What is it, you bastard?"

Ninety miles per hour, going for a hundred. My brain was no longer tired. It too was in overdrive. How the hell could—. "Wait a minute!" I said aloud. "It can't penetrate metal. No matter how strong microwaves are they can't penetrate metal, can they?"

"No," answered Erica.

I was jubilant. Then I was shattered—Erica tapped the roof. "This isn't metal," she said.

"Damn! Damn them!" I yelled childishly, pounding at the canvas sides that wouldn't protect us at all from the high-powered megahertz. "But how the hell can they still be tracking us? I mean—"

"Radar screen," Erica blurted excitedly. "The beeper let them find us up to now, but now it's the jeep. Don't you see? They've got the body of the jeep on the radar screen. They're bouncing a radar signal off the car. It's sniffing us out just ahead of the microwave beam. Heavy traffic might have saved us. I mean without a beeper they wouldn't know what vehicle it was on the radar screen. But out here we're the only moving metal in sight. They've got a fix on us. They're coming after the jeep!"

"Beautiful! Beautiful! Any ideas, Dr. Sarn?" The speedometer was now pushing ninety-three and screaming. The patch was homing fast, like an animal frenzied by the new-found scent.

A multiple crackling, like stock whips, as long fingers of lightning skittered over the range toward a clump of scant pine. The air glow slowed, stopped, and retraced its path, momentarily confused. God bless lightning! It would play hell with the radar tracking, at least for a few seconds at a time. They weren't smart enough yet to outdo a thunderbolt. But it would only temporarily confuse the radar, and, like rain, it wouldn't alter the pursuing beam, only scatter it at the edges over a wide area. There'd still be enough power density in the center to fry whole cities. And us.

"Tell me the contact," said Erica. "And the target numbers."

"What?"

"For God's sake!" pressed Erica. "We've got to get clear of the jeep and we'll stand a better chance if we split. Tell me the numbers!"

"But how in hell . . ."

"Stop the jeep!"

I did.

"Take off everything metallic you have on you." She was undoing her bra. "The slightest metal object—a buckle, a strap. The radar beam'll pick it up," she said. "Rings, small change, wallet metal clips . . . anything that will register. It'll pick up a quarter, never mind a jeep."

The air glow was onto the scent again. Seven miles to the west and now moving swiftly, unflinching, like a shark oblivious to all but point of attack. I threw away everything I could, finally discarding the metal-buckled belt that had shown up on every airport metal detector I'd been through. Erica was beautiful, even in her disarray. She had thrown away the bra to be rid of the metal clips. We then took away whatever metal Roth was carrying. No way we could be rid of all metal but hopefully enough to stop . . .

"Tell me the contact," she asked again. "We'd better split just in case one of us gets—"

"Pret," I said. "Brenda Pret. Numbers are eight one—seven seven—nine four. That's Fahrenheit temperature. Convert to Celsius—the nearest decimal place. Ten to one it's the code for three U.S. cities."

"You know which ones they are?"

The blotch was five miles away and closing.

"No. You need the bomber index to know that. Ralph Stein, CIA. Tell him it's 'Forty-Love. Match point.' He'll take it to the President—I hope."

"You hope." It was Roth, out of his trance and sneering.

"If we fool them with the jeep," I told Erica, releasing the hand brake while the engine was still roaring in neutral, and stooping to lift a boulder to put on the accelerator, "if we fool them, meet me on that ridge." I indicated some lone pines high on a rocky escarpment. "Otherwise you'll have to make it to Washington and . . ."

I stopped. I felt cold all over. My God, if I'd been suckered by that beam—if Erica and Roth had suckered me into prematurely revealing the contact, who could testify and unravel Roth's plan? Had I blown the lot—had I jeopardized NORAD's defense, the DEW Line and a decent woman called Brenda Pret? If I had she'd be dead within the hour and the Soviets would have the biggest pre-emptive strike capability of the century, *intact*. Is that why Roth had so suddenly come back to earth—his "awaying" arrested upon hearing the contact's name? He'd been willing to die, the bastard, to stop me getting through. But now he knew what cards I was holding, now he'd learned who the contact was, he wanted back in the game. If he could break free he could recoup everything. He could have his bloody scheme intact and run it after all. It was enough to revive anyone.

The beam was almost overhead—a giant red sore, pulsating

in the purpled sky. Another flash of lightning, more thunder, and the patch moved away—a thousand yards to the west—then started back in our direction. Now I could hear the strangest clicking noise, a crackling, all around me. It was the audible range of the beam's high frequency, the sound which years ago they'd thought was impossible to hear and hired psychiatrists to explain away.

If I'd had any doubts about Roth waking up, the Shpagina removed them, its barrel dead level with my eyes as I straightened up from putting down the boulder on the accelerator. The engine was screaming. Uninvited, while Erica was putting her now buttonless jacket back on, Roth had taken it on himself to get out of the jeep. His feet were still bound and his hands were tied but resting the stock on his end of the seat he could still point the machine gun in our general direction. He had little room for maneuver, but he had the gun.

"Come around here," he ordered Erica, "and untie me." He was still tied securely to the roll bar behind him, but it hadn't been short enough to stop him reaching the Shpagina.

"Untie me," he shouted again above the screaming engine, "or I'll blow his head off!"

I nodded for Erica to do as he said.

At five hundred yards the air glow was zeroing in.

Frantically he motioned at the boulder. "Get rid of that!"

"Don't worry," I said. "I wasn't going to leave you with the jeep . . . I was . . ."

"Hurry, damn you!"

Three hundred yards.

Erica bent down, working fast on the rope about his ankles.

"Be careful," I warned him, but I was looking straight at Erica, my heart thumping like a jackhammer. "Don't knock it into gear. You'd be off before you could count to three."

"Get rid of that rock!" He poked the muzzle, bullying, sneeringly toward me. "You lose, America." He jabbed me with the gun again. "Now move that rock." The beam was two hundred yards away.

"Sure," I said. I reached down from my side of the jeep opposite him toward the boulder on the accelerator. Now I would know if she was one of them. She had to choose. It was him or me. The fierce frying sound of the beam's edge was dancing all around us. Erica was behind him. I saw her left hand moving toward the gearshift. I took a deep breath, pretending to lift the rock. "One . . . two . . ." Erica's hand darted from behind Roth, shoved the gearshift to Drive, and in the second the automatic took to engage, we both pulled back, just in time to see a blur of canvas pass us as the jeep shot away.

Roth fell and fired, still tethered to the roll bar. There was splintering of windshield, the shredding of the canopy, long ribbons of shot-torn canvas flapping madly, and the most ungodly noise I've ever heard as the jeep, gaining speed by the second, roared off the highway, creating a high dust trail like a wild stallion charging across the rocky sagebrush range, dragging and banging Roth like a man caught in the stirrup.

Suddenly, the air glow darted at right angles following the jeep, increasing in speed with it. A quarter mile from us, the jeep zigzagged crazily up a ridge, turned down, then around, its driver's door swinging wildly like a broken wing, tore up an escarpment in frenzied haste, dragging Roth behind, still screaming . . . an orange scarf of flame erupting silently from the canvas roof, burning fiercely as the bulldog beam locked onto its moving metal target. Then a veritable river of flame as the jeep hurtled forward, its upholstery now ablaze. Then a crashing jolt, a somersault, Roth thrown high in the air, still tethered, a loud crump as the gas tank caught. Finally, a roaring vermilion explosion, the jeep and Roth disintegrating in a rolling ball of flame against the thick, bruised sky.

We waited.

Like a vulture, the air glow hovered for a second longer over the wreckage, as if to make sure, then vanished as swiftly as it had come—like a light switched off in the night, its target stilled and burning, dead on some distant radar screen.

The sky flashed with lightning and soon the rain came down in torrents, cool and refreshing. Too breathless to speak but strong enough, glad enough, to hold each other, we slowly made our way to the highway. Now, having rid ourselves of metal, having disappeared from the radar screen, we too, as far as Roth's outfit was concerned, had officially ceased to exist.

Surely we would make it home.

We did.

CHAPTER 34

Wednesday, October 8

As soon as I got to the White House, I rang Mrs. R. from my office. No answer. They must be out again.

Using my Fahrenheit/Celsius scale, the coordinates 81-77-94, which Brenda Pret had given me came out as 27-25-34. We gave them to Ralph Stein. I watched the printout, cross-referenced through the Soviet "bomber index":

> PI [Positive Identification]—Def. STIUS [Definite Soviet Targets in U.S.]
>
> 27 Washington, D.C.
> 25 Trident Base—Bangor, Washington State
> 34 SAC HQ—Offutt Air Force Base, Nebraska.

Once these PIs had been conveyed direct to the President, everything looked roses—except for my filing cabinet. Hoskins apologized, somewhat sheepishly, for the slight disorganization. While I'd been away a month before, Roth, citing "national security," had requested that several of his people be allowed to search my office. Hoskins had agreed.

"What was taken?" I inquired.

"Your SPS notes I expect."

"You expect. Didn't you see?"

"No reason to supervise them," he said. "After all we had no idea that Roth was . . ."

"All right," I sighed. "But maybe I can borrow someone to help me clean it up."

"You'll get whatever you need."

I looked up. That was more like it.

Now Erica and I were alone with the President and an increasingly embarrassed Doug Hoskins, who was confronted with the indisputable fact that as chief domestic affairs adviser, he'd backed the wrong horse. Believing Roth, he'd temporarily, and nearly fatally, shut us out of access to the President on a matter vital to national security. I didn't press it. He was no enemy agent, otherwise, I reminded myself again, I'd never have been able to leave Washington in the first place. No, old Doug, like so many others, had seen Roth too many times on television. And like those others he'd merely fallen for the image Roth had worked so hard to create. So why should I be cocky? I did expect thanks, however.

After I'd told the President how the CIA and the FBI would find Brenda Pret a willing witness who would open the way to exposing Roth's pre-emptive strike plan against the United States, I was ready, and so was Erica, to graciously receive presidential congratulations, the nation's unspoken thanks, and the satisfaction of seeing some action. That is, of seeing the CIA and the FBI springing into action, publicly exposing the Soviet espionage and dismantling the dangerous pulse capability of the beam.

We got the congratulations—but nothing about anyone springing into action.

I was stunned into silence, then got enough air to speak. "But aren't you going to expose the Soviets!" I spluttered. "This is every bit as dangerous as the Cuban missiles!"

The President fidgeted awkwardly with his letter opener, looking outside at the rose bushes. But the roses were long gone. Snow was heavy on the thorn.

"I've talked it over with Langley." He fidgeted some more with the opener. "We've been discussing the larger implications."

There was another, shorter silence as I refused comment. I had no intention of making this easy.

"You see, Sturgess"—he smiled at Erica—"and Dr. Sarn. We're terribly grateful for what you've done." He picked up the list of people he'd agreed to compensate, from Jonas to the lady with the badly mauled motel. "Words can't express how grateful we are to you—and to Mrs. Pret. But of course the Soviets don't know. As far as they know, Roth is dead and so are you. They had a good thing going and now it's finished—kaput!" He grinned.

"You're not going to let them be?" It was Erica. "The people who helped Roth."

"No!—no. Of course not. They'll be picked up in time along with those Sudley Steel thugs. But quietly. Until then we think it's best you and Miss Sarn take a well-deserved rest." He flashed a campaign smile. True, we needed a rest. How we needed a rest! But I wasn't smiling—nor was Erica.

"Doug has arranged it," said the President.

"What about the beam?" Erica shot out. Hoskins was suddenly fascinated by the design of the oval floor rug. He couldn't take his eyes off it.

"The fatal arc?" I pressed. "The arc that nearly killed us and could wipe out whole cities. That could decimate London, Washington, Paris?" I shouted. Then I saw what they were up to. "Oh *no!* My God, you can't . . ."

"You're out of line, mister." He said it quietly but very firmly, then moved behind the globe on his desk. He tapped it lightly with his finger and Australia turned golden in the sunlight. North America passed into shadow. "You want to play black and white, Harry. You think I'm a cynical man." He glanced at Erica. "Well, I'm not, but I have to live in a world of gray. I don't have the luxury of black and white." Roth had talked of gray too. The President spun the globe a little faster, watching it become a blur as he spoke. "You think with the CIA or the KGB we can live in a world of black and white?" There was no answer, because we knew he was right. It was gray—God help us all.

He exhaled heavily, tiredly, as if suddenly the whole weight of his office was bearing down on him. "We have to play the lesser of evils."

He had a point. I was still angry at what they had decided upon but he had a point. It was heavy with undertones of motherhood, apple pie, and the Statue of Liberty, but the President did have a point. He was looking at us both. "Like it or not, and believe me I *don't* like it, it comes down to a balance of power. A balance of terror. What other choice do I have? To dismantle the SPS capability is to forsake too much. Besides, if we dismantled it, the Soviets would build it anyhow, once they'd caught up in SPS technology. They just wanted to use ours for the interim."

"A nasty interim," I said.

"Very."

I suddenly felt like a country priest having prematurely judged the Pope. I still didn't like it, but I couldn't help mellowing. Damn it—I could see his point. Erica's eyes told me the same thing, and she nodded, however unhappily, in agreement with the President.

"Thanks to you two," he continued, "we've discovered that in developing the fatal arc capability of the SPS, Roth has unwittingly given the United States a decisive edge over the entire Soviet attack and defense missile system."

The President's phone was frantically blinking. "Yes? One second . . ." He put his hand over the mouthpiece, addressing us in a semi-apologetic tone. "Classified NIA report on Africa. You'll have to excuse me." He flashed a smile and shook hands. Hoskins opened the door for us.

"Harry, Erica!"

"Mr. President?"

"You've given us the high ground. Thank you."

High ground—high space.

Walking out toward the east gate, we didn't speak until we were passing the snow-draped Jacqueline Kennedy garden.

"Of course the Russians will catch up," I said. "Eventually—even without Roth."

"Yes," Erica sighed tiredly. "But not for now. And that's

what it's all about." She stopped just before we got to the East Gate awning. She turned to me, her hair catching the golden sheen of the winter sun. "Now you and I catch up."

I took her hand and squeezed it. The East Gate guard apologized but explained that he couldn't let me use the phone for a private call. I rang instead from the foyer of the Washington Hotel. Mrs. R. answered.

"Could I speak to Sylvia please?"

"I'm sorry"—there was silence—"Sylvia is ill."

Someone was tugging at my sleeve. "What's wrong? Harry! My God, what's wrong?"

CHAPTER 35

Mrs. Reardon was unrecognizable—her face wet with Richmond rain and crumpled with terror. "It happened"—she sobbed—"just before you rang."

Sweet Jesus—why hadn't I thought? My office phone! Roth must have had it bugged ever since Hoskins had let his "people" into my office.

"How many of them?" My voice was trembling, fighting for control.

"One," she said.

"English?"

"I—" She turned to Mrs. Leern, the apartment owner.

"Yes," the old lady agreed. "Like Eliza."

"Like who?"

"You know, Eliza Doolittle—*My Fair Lady.*"

"Cockney?"

"Yes, I think—"

Sweet Jesus, help me!

"Did you ring the police?" I asked.

"No . . . he said . . . if we did . . ." She couldn't go on.

"All right—all right." I turned to Erica. "Ring Hoskins. Now we're in the clear have him call in the FBI—anybody he can get. And get Ralph Stein—CIA."

"But, Harry, if you do that, won't they—"

"Do as I say!" I held her, lowered my voice. "The odds are worse if you don't call the police in a kidnap. Okay? I'll try to do something before—"

Mrs. Reardon was butting in. "He said they'd . . ." She couldn't finish.

"It's all right," I said. "We won't take any risks, Mrs. R."

It was a lie. There is no risk-free kidnap recovery. "What did they want?" I pressed.

"He . . . he didn't say. He said he'd ring."

But I knew what he wanted—what *they* wanted. Revenge and money. I was back in Washington, D.C., and they knew the game was over for Sudley Steel—which meant the game was over for them. They wouldn't be paid. No bonuses for screwups. Jenny was in lieu of. My daughter for cash. It was about as subtle as those bastards would ever get. Sought now for the murders of Dermit and Art Lane, they had nothing to lose. I rang Ralph Stein myself and asked him to bring a .38.

Three FBI men arrived, followed shortly after by Ralph Stein, carrying what looked like a thick leather tool kit.

The senior of the three FBI men immediately took charge. He introduced himself quickly, "Lawson," shook hands, unfolded a Polaroid, asked for a picture of Jenny, and instructed me exactly what to say.

"Are you sure they'll contact me straight off?" I asked. "Why not someone—"

"They know your voice, Mr. Sturgess. They won't trust anyone else. Not on the first call—not for the first four hours. Later on they'll negotiate with an intermediary—perhaps. But not on the first call. That's the pattern."

"What are you going to—"

"Leave it to us, Mr. Sturgess."

He propped Mrs. R.'s photo of Jenny against a vase in the living room and adjusted the camera. "I know how tough it is, Mr. Sturgess," he added, stepping back from the photo, lifting the Polaroid to his eye. The flash bulb popped, scaring Mrs. R.

witless. "But believe me," he carried on, "it's better you do what we tell you. That way—"

"It's my child."

The camera whirred, slowly extruding a flat gray picture of Jenny.

"I know that, Mr. Sturgess." He was watching the photo. "But if you let emotions run the show, you're in trouble. Believe me." He held up the photo, frowned at the overexposure, and dropped it into the wastebasket. I turned away.

I heard the camera whine again. This time he was satisfied and made another five for immediate distribution.

The call came an hour later. At three-fifteen.

"Sturgit?"

"Is Jenny—is my daughter all right?"

"She's great."

I looked anxiously at Lawson. He nodded encouragingly.

"What are your terms?" My voice was tight with the strain.

"To the point. Very good. All right now, listen. No boys in blue. A million dollars. Unmarked, nonsequential, and in a bloody hurry. Got it?"

"Where?"

"We'll ring you, sweetheart." A click.

The bastards. I turned to Ralph. He shook his head and put his portable phone back in the bag. "Sorry." He turned to Lawson. "Too short to trace. They know their business."

We had the cash by six-fifteen.

It was already dark—the moon was shining. Even in the bright light the SPS twinkled silver in the clear, cold night, a star in black velvet.

He called again at seven o'clock. "A red airline bag. Union Station—the information desk. Turn right as you go in; 11 P.M. Any cops, and cars, anyone else but you, and she's gone. Got it, Sturgit?"

"Yes. But—" Lawson's arm was on my shoulder. He held a finger to his lips. I put down the phone.

There was concern among the FBI. Union Station was a damned silly place. Too public, they said. A stakeout would be easy.

"A stakeout," I snapped. "What for? If only one of them comes—the other one keeps Jenny. What good's a stakeout?"

Lawson said something to Erica. She told me I should eat. I ignored her, but she brought me coffee and an aspirin. One FBI man said they could use rifles with infra-red scopes.

"No," I interjected. "This isn't some agent swapover. This is my kid. Everybody got that?"

There was silence. I was starting to feel like an outsider, uninvited and in the way.

"What do you think?" I asked Ralph.

Lawson took my elbow and steered me to a chair. "If there are two, not one, it'll be a strict money-for-hostage situation, Mr. Sturgess. It's all their way. One takes the money. One stays with the—with Jenny. They pull back, count the money at leisure, then they might let her go."

"You think so?" I pressed. "They'll let her go?"

He nodded but only slightly. "Well, if it's the cockneys you mentioned—there's no point in them . . ."

"Killing her." I said it for him.

"They've no interest in killing her as a possible witness have they? You know them already."

I knew them all right. I should have shot the bastards. My head was thumping like a drum.

"Those bastards would do it for payback," I said. "They'd do it for vengeance—after this." I waved at the sky—at the SPS. Lawson didn't know what I meant. He looked at the ceiling, nodded as if he understood, and rejoined his two agents. I didn't catch all of it, but it seemed no one had any good ideas. We all knew that if "he" or "they" saw any agents, they'd be gone and then they might kill Jenny. Erica sat by me. I tried desperately not to see Jenny's face—the down-soft cheeks—the eyes. Soon I had to remind myself, for a few seconds at least, to look at it objectively as I had when I'd escaped from the cell. But I couldn't—it was impossible. She was my child. I sipped the coffee Erica had given me. It was bitter. The FBI men were huddled over a sketch one of them had drawn of Union Station. My fingers shook as I took a sugar cube, dumped it, and watched the coffee eat it away. "Honey," I said.

"Yes?"

"Ask Mrs. Leern for some needles and thread. Red."

I turned to Stein. "Ralph?"

"Yes, Harry?"

Lawson was talking and one of the agents was nodding. The other wasn't so sure. I waved Ralph over. I forced myself to speak as slowly as raw nerves will allow. I told him what I wanted and I told him that it had to be no bigger than a dime.

He bit his lip. He looked over to where Lawson was huddling above the sketch.

"Never mind them," I said. "It's my kid, Ralph. And Sudley Steel doesn't fit their pattern." I couldn't tell he didn't like it. "Look," I said as forcefully as I could. "To them I'm just another kidnap victim's father. But I've had a bit of field experience myself, right?"

He took the point and relented. "All right."

He patted my shoulder, "I'll get it. We've got 'em small as a pea. Smaller."

Only when he'd gone did I tell Lawson my plan. He surprised me.

"Smart! I like that, Mr. Sturgess."

"I hope to God it'll work," said one of the others.

I prayed and prayed it *would* work. At least it put me back in the action—a chance to do something instead of waiting around feeling utterly helpless. I went to the bathroom and loaded the .38 with hollow point. If I got the chance I wanted it to hit them and spread as big as a dinner plate. They deserved nothing less. When I returned, one of the three-man FBI team was reconsidering whether I should be allowed to play any part after all, mumbling about Bureau policy—keeping the family out, etc., etc. Maybe Lawson was just humoring me.

At 10 P.M., another call. Lawson lifted the phone and handed it to me by way of reminding me he was still in charge.

The Union Station meet was off. "Just in case you'd planned a party, Sturgit."

"What can I do?" I said. "You're calling the shots."

"That's right, Sturgit."

It would be Rockville, he said. "The road by the river." A small picnic area 4.7 miles exactly from the turnoff on Highway 190. "Leave the bag by the trash can. There's only one—green."

"When?"

"Now!"

"When will you return Jen— when . . ."

"I'll call. First the money."

"I mightn't be here," I said quickly, "when you call. There's a meeting with the President. If I don't show, people will start asking questions. My housekeeper and Miss Sarn'll be here. They'll take any . . ."

Lawson was waving frantically for me to stop. But I knew what I was doing.

"All right, all right, but you bring the money. Understand?"

"Don't worry, I will. I don't want—"

He hung up—probably fearing a trace.

There was no meeting with the President, but now I could move without my absence from the phone's arousing Garlic's suspicion. And now he'd asked *me* to bring the money, the FBI couldn't keep me corralled. I was free to move. I respected the FBI but I knew Sudley Steel's "pattern" better than anyone.

"They'll use the river," said one of the FBI men. "We'll bring in a surveillance van."

I agreed they'd probably use the water, but I asked the FBI not to be anywhere near *me*—or near the bag drop. I said two cars on the other side of the river, in Virginia, on Route 193, would be all right, but that the van should be at least a mile from the site. And the closest they should allow a chopper—blacked out—was five miles up the highway. There were enough choppers in the Washington area not to arouse suspicion. Besides, if the Washington sky was cleared of police choppers—or choppers, period—he'd be suspicious because to do that would have meant alerting the police—which he'd warned me not to do.

The sound of crickets. Unnerving. And the darkness, heavy with the promise of rain. A long side road between Potomac and Seneca. I watched the odometer. At 4.7 miles exactly, I stopped the car, got out, walked across to the left-hand side of the road—facing the river bank—my finger rubbing nervously on the spot in the bag's handle where, using Mrs. L.'s red thread, I'd stitched in the tiny transistor. I couldn't feel it. Good. I put the bag down by the trash can, returned to the car, and drove back to 190, where Ralph and Lawson and his men were waiting—about a mile, as the crow flies, from where I'd left the money.

I jumped out of the car and ran over to the Dodge van that was pulled off in a breakdown zone, squatting like a huge copper bug in the darkness.

"Have you got it?" I asked anxiously.

Ralph, his earphones sticking out like growths in the dim light, calmly pointed to the oscilloscope. The tiny green dot moved along the horizontal axis, then suddenly hiccupped. "A hundred percent," he said quietly. "He's picked up the bag. He's moving." The green dot kept jumping—unhurried and steady. "He's using the river to get away." Ralph's voice was unemotional, like a surgeon's. "I'll need a chopper to maintain the track." Lawson called in the helicopter.

"Let me go with him," I said.

He hesitated.

"Damn it! I've got to have something to do. Your team's coordinating everything from here anyway. Up there I'm out of your hair."

"All right," he said. "But remember we call the shots, Mr. Sturgess."

"Understood."

Ralph's monotone cut in. "He'll be across in Virginia—in about ten minutes."

The chopper had Ralph and me above the river in five. Ralph was busy with the direction finder and giving the pilot instructions through his mike. I couldn't see any boats along the moonlit reach, and the banks of the Potomac were pitch black. "Nothing," I called out.

Ralph was watching the green hiccups. He spoke in his mike to the pilot. The chopper swerved hard left and down. My stomach fell. The hiccups went crazy. His eyes still glued to the tiny screen, Ralph pointed westward. "Anything?"

I glanced upstream. I still couldn't see any boat, but on the Virginia side there was a short, stubby jetty jutting out like a black finger from a jungle. I showed Ralph. He nodded affirmatively. "There must be a road." The hiccups skipped. He spoke to the chopper pilot again. "Hard right this time—away from the jetty. Now it's going down river."

I followed the moonlit river eastward. I couldn't see any boat in that direction either. But glancing back, westward, I spotted a black dot on the silver sheen about a hundred yards out from the D.C. side—from the direction we'd come—heading over toward the Virginia shore. But at this angle, it was hard to tell. "There's something up there," I pointed.

Ralph ignored me. "It's going down river."

It didn't make sense. Someone was crossing upstream—across the river, but the cold, objective oscilloscope was calmly telling us it was downstream. "You're sure it's working okay?"

"Positive."

I sat motionless as we headed down and circled, the noise of the blades so loud it was no longer noticeable. Think, I commanded, think like that bastard Garlic. He'd used a beeper and he— "Upstream!" I shouted. "He's going across upstream."

Ralph calmly tapped the oscilloscope's screen. "It's downstream."

"He's dumped the bag," I said. "He figured we'd use a chip. He's using our transmitter as a feint."

"I don't know," said Ralph, looking faithfully at the scope.

"I do!" I insisted. "Swing upstream. He's headed for Highway 193, the Virginia side. Beyond that jetty we saw."

"You're taking a risk!" yelled Ralph—nearly deafening the pilot.

"Well, where's the goddamn boat downstream, Ralph? If the beeper's going downstream, it's on something, right?"

"Yes, but . . ."

"It's on an empty bag. He's ditched the goddamn bag. Head for 193."

Ralph shot me a worried glance. "Lawson won't like it."

"For God's sake, Ralph. It's my kid!"

He tapped the pilot's shoulder, shouting, "Head for 193."

Hard right again and down toward the bright ribbon of 193. The pilot radioed to the two cars stationed on the Virginia side, then turned to me. "Too many power lines," he said. It would have to be a ladder descent.

"Sturgess—Lawson here. Listen, I don't want—"

I went out first—the cold wrenching my breath away. The FBI car that moved in to pick us up on 193 had two agents in it. The one sitting in the passenger seat turned around to face me in the back seat. "Mr. Lawson called in. Says to tell you that we're handling things this side, Mr. Sturgess."

"Right!"

The agents glanced at each other. Another two, in the second car, were parked on the other side of the highway facing us. It would depend which way the creep went. My hunch was east toward some built-up area like Alexandria.

It was a red MG. It turned right into the fast lane but still safely within the speed limit—cool bastard. We followed, two cars behind. The transmitting pulse was killing me. Like a heartbeat, its hip-hip-hip—green ghosts in the darkness—was a frenetic reminder that Jenny's life was on the line.

"Only one driver," said the FBI calmly.

"What now?" asked Ralph, not taking his eyes off the trace for a second.

"We follow," said the FBI. Which meant we had no option.

Dark, and spitting rain. A shabby house—brownstone, two-level on the outskirts of Alexandria. A stone's throw from the capital. A fire hydrant was dripping and the street cleaner was overdue. We kept going down the street; a smart black Ford might look out of place in this neighborhood. We turned the corner and inched up toward the next street where we could watch the exit from the brownstone without anyone in it seeing us. The agent on the passenger side checked his button mike and pocket transmitter unit and got out at the corner.

"Take off your tie," I told him. "You look like a broker." He threw the tie in and ambled back in the direction from which we'd come, walking up one leg of the L formed by the two streets—heading toward the house.

Nothing for seven minutes, then a crackle from the radio receiver. "Taxi arriving . . . Virginia plates. Front door of house opening." His voice was quiet and measured. "Male Caucasian—not the one from the MG. This one's on crutches."

"Damn!" I said. "George."

"What?" asked the other agent in the front seat.

"George," I said. "His mate. They're splitting up."

"Watch for the girl," he instructed his colleague.

"No girl," the other reported.

The taxi took off, carrying George. Already the FBI was radioing the license number and description into the D.C. computer. The car's receiver crackled. It was Lawson's voice. "Tail suspect. Do not apprehend until instructed. Repeat—do not apprehend until instructed." We sat.

Ten more minutes. A call came back from Interstate Patrol. The taxi was on Interstate 95, heading, it seemed, for the turnpike by Glenn Dale.

"Baltimore probably," said Ralph.

The agent shrugged. "Or New York. One leaves from Dulles—Crutches leaves from JFK."

Another five minutes. A couple of youngsters roared past us on motorcycles—one of them yelling an obscenity at the Ford. Four more minutes—I was sweating despite the night air. The rain eased off, then stopped.

"Do we go in?" It was Ralph.

The agent shook his head slowly. "Not till Lawson knows what the other car's doing. Most acute stage. They've counted the money—split up. This one's got the girl too close. A wrong move now and it's over."

"You think he's on to us?" pressed Ralph anxiously.

"Don't know. Don't think so."

"Well, for God's sake don't pick up George," I commanded.

"Why?" asked Ralph. "The guy in the house wouldn't know."

Ralph had been too long at a desk.

"They could have arranged a call-in," I explained. "If George doesn't call in, Garlic knows something's wrong."

"That's right," said the FBI.

"What's with the garlic?" asked Ralph.

"It's a long story."

We waited. Seven minutes. I was starting to get the cold diarrhea feeling—what if the sonofabitch had access to the house next door? They weren't connected but maybe some basement suite—a tunnel—unlikely, but . . .

"Door opening," the radio spluttered. "Male Caucasian. He's looking around. It's our man . . . door closing."

Jesus Christ.

"Door opening again . . . a girl. It's her."

"Have you got cover?" It was Lawson.

"Affirmative. He's looking around . . . holding the girl. Heading for the MG."

"Can you rush?"

"No chance. Has a coat on his arm—holding the girl's neck."

"Firearm under the coat?"

"It's my guess."

"Don't rush!" I interjected. "He'll have a piece all right."

" . . . Entering MG. Both entering on the driver's side."

Silence.

"What's he doing?" Lawson again.

"Leaning over on the girl's side . . . hard to say . . . I think . . . he's sitting down. They're moving off."

Our driver answered his colleague, "We'll come around, when he's clear."

"He's turned the corner. Looks like he's heading for 395."

"We're coming."

Lawson's voice crackled from across the river. "Act as necessary." That meant it was up to us.

We slowed down. The agent slipped into the car. "I think he was tying her legs and hands around the passenger seat."

A report came in from the second FBI car coming in to rendezvous on 395—George was still traveling.

"He hasn't stopped for a call?" asked the agent we'd just picked up.

"No," grunted the driver. "Sloppy."

"They're confident," said the other agent. "Since they ditched the beeper."

"Good," I said. Confidence on their part was our only chance. "There's the MG."

The agent who'd rejoined us was putting his tie back on. "Relax, Mr. Sturgess. We'll take it from here."

"No you won't," I growled. "You need my help. I know these jokers. You don't."

"Listen, Mr. Sturgess—"

"No—you listen! You wouldn't have gotten this far without me. You'd still be down river!"

Ralph squirmed.

The MG slowed. We fell back.

"All right," said the agent challengingly. "How would you handle it, then?"

"They're not going to call Mrs. Reardon to make the swap," I said as calmly as my anxiety would allow. "Put yourself in his position. He has Jenny. We know who he is. He's an open target. And he wants revenge."

The agent nodded. His voice was soft and chilling. "I agree. That's always the bottom line, Mr. Sturgess. He's got false papers, makeup probably. Into Canada—Mexico—reasonably good disguise and our immigration people would never get him. Your daughter would be like a neon sign."

"So we have to stop him now."

"That's my reading."

I had no choice.

"Next traffic light," I instructed. "He's in the inside, fast lane, so go into the middle lane but fall back—behind his right rear." I drew the .38. "I'll slip out our right passenger side—the farthest door away from him. Get your second car up behind him."

"He might see you open the door. Unlikely—but it's a possibility."

"Behind him," suggested Ralph. "Why don't *we* slip behind him?"

"No," I said, "he could see me in the rear-view. He's nervous." I was thinking hard. I could attack him side on, but I could hit Jenny. "Radio the other car to get behind him. When they're in position, we wait for the first red light. This is how we do it—"

The MG speeded up. We didn't bolt after him but increased our speed gradually until, once again, we were just behind him to the right, in the middle lane. The second car, a Buick Century, was in position directly behind the MG, but the next three lights were green. On the second light we moved up—not quite abreast of him. I was slumped low in the seat so there was no way he could see me. I was deep breathing—pushing the air into my abdomen, letting half the air escape then holding the rest.

"Some kind of bag—like a lunch box. On the dash," said the FBI casually. "Ten to one that's his piece. So watch the bag."

"Where is it? Exactly?" I pressed.

"On his right—to the right of the steering wheel. Halfway to your daughter."

"Okay. Thanks."

"Light coming up. Still green—about to go amber."

I opened the door quietly, pushing it out about a foot.

"Light is amber," said the FBI. "We're right beside him."

We stopped gently. "Pump your brakes three times when I cross our front. Got it?"

"Yes. Light is red."

I slipped out, just letting the door touch against the hinge, crouched, ran forward, stopped, hidden by the front right fender, waiting, watching our rear brake lights—waiting for them to glow three times as a signal to the Buick behind the MG. There they went—one, two, three. A horn blast—from the Buick. I swung in front of our grid. A glimpse of Garlic watching the Buick in the rear-view—startled by the horn. I straightened in front of the MG, swung left, froze, held my breath . . .

"Daddy—Daddy!"

His eyes darted from the rear-view mirror to the front, his hand striking for the bag.

I fired. The windshield went milky, and the car screamed toward me. I jumped aside, grabbed at the door handle as it roared past. Missed! I was spun around. A screech of tires—and Ralph Stein's face flashing past, the FBI car streaking ahead curving in front of the MG. A tremendous thump—a hissing like a steam engine expiring—twenty yards down the highway, and stillness, pierced by the banshee howling of the MG's horn. The FBI Ford had successfully blocked; the MG hitting it broadside, pivoting and pushing its passenger side, Jenny's side, hard against the Ford's trunk.

I was up—limping—running through the darkness. An FBI man yanked the driver's door open. I stuck the gun in. He was slumped on the wheel. I tore the keys out, wrenched him back, off the horn, reached over and tried to scoop up Jenny. She was crying and still tied, her door buckled in by the impact. Ironically it was being tied up that had saved her from being thrown about the car interior.

A few minutes later I'd untied her. As I hugged her past the steering wheel, Garlic's body slumped sideways toward the passenger side. His face was no more—a burst cantaloupe—parts of it dripping from the rag hood where the hollow point had ended its lightning journey.

The traffic signal had turned to GO and cast an eerie green glow on the sugary fragments of glass laying scattered beneath the gouged headlights of the dead MG. Motorists looked, but no one stopped. The FBI had rung for an ambulance, and the wail of its siren could be heard somewhere far off in the night.

George of the dimwit brain was tried alone, in Garlic's absence, for Dermit's murder, and convicted. That was good to hear, but it wasn't the best news. That had come when they picked him up in New York, at the central Port Authority, waiting for a nice, relaxing cruise to South America. When they arrested him he said he didn't "do nuthin'." Well, he's doing it now in Leavenworth—twenty years of it and no parole for that lad. He got all due process and demanded his one telephone call. Panicking, he rang a Washington number for help. It was Roth's. Apparently George was quite irate when told the number was "no longer in service."

Jenny still has nightmares about it and I had to take her to a child psychiatrist a few times. Of course she'll never forget it but it shouldn't be a debilitating scar, he said, providing she got enough parental love. That she has.

During Erica's and my "catching up" holiday in a cabin on a cold October Chesapeake Bay, we studiously avoided newspapers and television newscasts, but it seems impossible to escape entirely and we did get a news break during an old "Mary Tyler Moore Show"—the one where Chuckles the Clown dies—telling us that a spy ring involving "industrial secrets" had been broken jointly in the United States and Canada, and so Sudley Steel was finished. It was during the same show that I asked Erica to marry me. She said, "Yes. But what will Jenny say?"

Jenny, like me, thought it was a great idea.

After we, including Mrs. R., had moved back to the house in Rockville, and Erica had gone back to work on the Solar Energy Commission and I had started again at the White House, I was shocked to find a brand-new air conditioner in my office. They told me that Mrs. Gort had ordered it.

"I could kiss you," I told her gratefully.

"Please don't!" she sniped.

There's no place like home.

A few weeks later someone told me that part of the now properly regulated SPS power is being fed into a grid substation outside Washington. I must confess it gives me a kick every now and then on those cold winter nights to think that part of that awesome power is heating our electric blanket.

Slater, Ian

Air glow red

$13.95

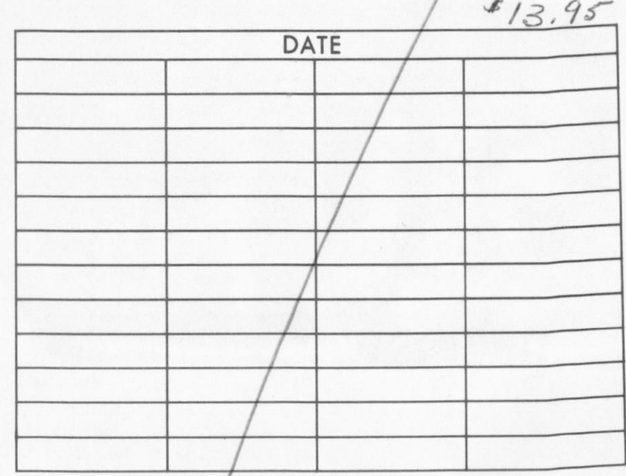

DATE